GROWING UP

RETRO NOSTALGIA AND HUMOR
OF THE
1940'S & 1950'S

BY

SKIP WALLACH

Michael
Please enjoy this trip back to
The Golden Age of Innocence
and
Thank you for many years of friendship
Much love to you pal,
Skip

First Edition
ISBN: 978-0-9728989-1-1
Library of Congress Control Number: 2009907562

HighSight Publishing
5102 East Cheery Lynn Road
Phoenix, Arizona 85018-6627

E-mail: HighSight@cox.net
Web site: www.HighSightPublishing.com

Printed and bound in the United States of America

Front Cover Photograph: Photo illustration from the M. Meredith "Millie" Hill Collection of Orpheum Theatre and John Eberson Movie Palaces Material, Special Collections and University Archives, Wichita State University Archives.

Coloration and Transformative Adaptation of the Front Cover Photograph (with permission from Wichita State University Archives), Front Cover Design, Back Cover Collage and HighSight Logo by Tracy Neale Wallach: © 2009 George C. Wallach. All rights reserved.

Kilroy Art on Page 11 by Carole S. Wallach:
© 2009 George C. Wallach. All rights reserved.

Cover Layout, Back Cover Design and Interior Design by Jill Ronsley, Sun Editing & Book Design, www.suneditwrite.com.
Fonts: Kabel, Adobe Caslon Pro

Front Cover Photo: Gratefully acknowledged is the advice and assistance of Dr. Lorraine Madway, Curator of Special Collections and University Archivist, Wichita State University Libraries.

DISCLAIMER

Although this book was suggested by historical events, it is a work of fiction, except for historically-known facts. Persons, organizations and occurrences (collectively and individually "p.o.o.") depicted in it are fictitious and/or dramatized (which makes them fictitious). Any similarity of fictitious p.o.o. to actual p.o.o. is coincidental and unintentional. Any real p.o.o. depicted have been fictionalized and dramatized.

"... if it was so, it might be;
and if it were so, it would be;
but as it isn't; it ain't."
Tweedledee

—*Alice Through the Looking-Glass* by Lewis Carroll

So, if you think it's you and you're not happy about it,
it ain't you and it ain't true.

This Book Is Dedicated To

Lyoris "Cyclone" Malone

Billy "The Drummer" Nelson

And my Uncle Sam

God Bless My Uncle Sam
He was really somebody

All completed their studies here
And have gone back "home."

Preface

You'll Be a Lot Happier if You Read This Before You Start the Book

Life is like a piano.
What you get out of it depends on how you play it.
Tom Lehrer

Inspired by true events.

Even though this story is inspired by actual historical events in and surrounding my life, it's not an autobiography and the names of almost all the characters are fictional, including mine. It's a novel because I've embellished almost all the vignettes of "Chip's" life. The foundation for these tales are, in the main, a combination of things which happened to me, or to my friends, or which I heard about happening to others, but could have happened to me or to you for that matter. In short, it's been fictionalized and dramatized except for certain important figures in my life and the references to publicly known facts such as the Second World War, music of the times and old radio and television shows.

TIME MAP.

In a series of short, funny and easy reading chapters, it's a journey from pre-school through high school, college fraternities and the army—basically Chip's life as a child growing up during World War II followed by his experiences in high school and college, the latter both in the 1950's during that Golden Age of nostalgia, innocence and joy, topped off by some humorous vignettes of his early '60's service in a peacetime army.

FUNNY, EASY READ AND WIDE AGE-RANGE APPEAL.

This novel is an "easy" read and will appeal to any reader who's lived before, during or after the period that includes Chip's growing-up sojourn. That clearly includes "Baby Boomers," younger adults, and teenagers. The initial-draft "test readers" (all of whom I thank profusely) of my generation and the Baby Boomer generation said they were flooded with so many of their own happy, cherished and funny memories called up by these stories that they were laughing out loud while reading and they were very glad I wrote this book.

These stories will also appeal to younger adults and to teenagers as an excellent and fun primer for experiencing the feel of those times as compared to today, as well as the values that influenced their parents and grandparents. As conclusive proof (perhaps of a nature that could influence Chip), not only did my thirty-something niece read it twice, my early-teenage granddaughter loved it, exclaiming, "It's soooooooooo interesting." Soooooo, at the risk of sounding like a politician—even though all of you are different, there's something for everyone in here—trust me.

YOUR MEMORIES.

Chip's journey is purposefully somewhat vague concerning exact locations and exact times. The intent is to leave the field more fluid for activating your personal memories, no matter what your age, of the times, places, people, things and amusing events you haven't thought about recently in relation to your siblings, parents, childhood friends, the struggle for identity, first dates, learning responsibilities, cars, high school, music, radio and television, all finished off by some of the goofy things that can happen in a peacetime army.

Universal Forces.

A word about the "Universal Forces" theme that runs gently through Chip's life. Most people I know feel on some level that there's an intelligent governing cause, an unseen spiritual force, watching out for them and helping to guide their lives in subtle ways. It's personal to each of us and different for each of us depending on how our view of the experience of living and being is arranged, usually shaped in large measure either through our religion or through other spiritual beliefs. For a great many in any category, I think it's safe to say their higher power is normally referred to as God, and they feel they are loved, protected and guided by God as well as spiritual forces in some form working under God's auspices. As you'll see, that's pretty much the way Chip feels. The results of that influence become more noticeable as Chip moves through life.

Thus, in consideration of the wide variation in terminology different people may use to describe these guiding forces in their lives, such as God, higher power, archangels, angels, guardian angels, saints, heavenly beings, guides, higher self and departed loved ones, to name a few, I've felt comfortable using the term Universal Forces in this novel. My sincere apologies to Dr. Jonathan Parker, whose quote is found preceding Chapter One, if Chip's conception of Universal Forces isn't foursquare with his intention (like I said, everyone's is different). If that's the case, I have no doubt he will forgive me. It's all good.

Of course, it's Chip telling the story the way he remembers it and, grammatically, he floats in and out of the past and present tense from time to time. Please bear with him, it's the way he recalls those events because often when he thinks about things "back in the day," he's still right there. The same thing happens to me. Every time I look in a mirror, I see a 17-year-old boy.

In all events, one thing I've learned is that life is truly what you choose to make of it, no matter what the circumstance, and I've been blessed with wonderful family, friends and acquaintances along the way. I'm grateful for each one of them.

* * * *

KILROY
WAS
HERE

Growing Up

Universal Forces ... arrange events for your benefit ... always.

Jonathan Parker, Ph. D.

Even though it may not be apparent at the time.

SW

1

Feelings

It's great to Arrive, but the trip's most always most of the fun.

Malcolm Forbes

I'M SITTING STRAIGIIT UP IN thc middlc of thc night staring into the open closet a couple feet off the end of the bed. I know there's nothing in there that can get me. Whatever that is lives under the bed and I'm on the top bunk so it won't pull me under if my arm hangs. My sister is six and has decided it's simply a ruse to get the top bunk. Hey, three-something-year-olds don't scheme, do they?

I'm awake from a sound sleep because I have a feeling I came here from someplace else, but I can't remember where or how I got here and into this family. I don't question why I'm feeling like this. I'm just kind of amazed. Oh well. I fall asleep again.

I wake up again. I think I feel something else. I might have picked Shirley for my sister somehow! What could I have been thinking?

"What're you doing?"

"Sitting up."

"Go back to sleep. You're squeaking the bed."

"Is there anybody under yours right now?"

"Go—back—to—sleep."

"Not sleepy."

"I'm telling Mommy."

My sister is not only brilliant, but incredibly smart. I sense there's no way she's going to wake my mother in the middle of the night to tell her I'm just sitting up in bed, and she doesn't tell fibs to get what she wants. Misdirection maybe, nondisclosure maybe, but no overt fibs.

"I can't get this off."

"What?"

"This." I flop on my back and hang my right arm down as far as I can. I know it's safe. That thing can't reach this high from under her bed.

"If I help you, will you go back to sleep and leave me alone?"

"Yes."

"Come down here then."

"You took the ladder."

"Putting it back'll make too much noise. Just come over the end of the bed. Stand on my footboard and let yourself down. If you fall, I'll catch you."

I should've known. I bang into the closet door during my hurtle to the hardwood floor. My sister stands there looking down at me in the glow of the nightlight. Shortly thereafter, Mommy silently appears.

"Kids, it's 3:30 in the morning."

As if I could tell time.

"He's bothering me."

That's not a fib. I always bother her.

"Chip, what're you doing? Where's the ladder?"

At this point, I decide my best course is to start crying.

It works. Mommy picks me up, asks me if I have to go wee-wee, tries to get an informative answer out of Shirley about the ladder, gives up, replaces it, tucks us both in and shuffles sleepily back to her bedroom in those well-worn, baby-blue, terrycloth, open-toed slippers.

"See, why don't you just be quiet?"

I start whimpering again.

"Okay, okay. Go to sleep."

"I can't."

"Alright. Be quiet coming down and I'll get it off."

"It" is a giant flexible torture thimble with rubber spikes sticking out of it. My mother ties it over my right thumb every night with thread wound around the bottom, firmly. It's pretty effective because I don't suck my thumb while it's on there, and it never occurs to me to suck my left thumb.

Jointly crouched by the nightlight, Shirley's been working on it for a couple of minutes.

I jerk my hand back, "Wait."

I'm sure I hear the faint strains of the Star Spangled Banner outside somewhere. I snap to attention and start saluting. I know she's rolling her eyes. It isn't clear to me why she finds me annoying, really.

Finally the threads start unraveling and off it pops. With the ethereal feelings concerning my origins forgotten, I scramble up the ladder with thumb in mouth and, fulfilling my sister's wishes, I'm instantaneously asleep.

* * * *

2

Dragging

Love builds bridges where there are none.

R.H. Delaney

BEFORE I WENT TO KINDERGARTEN, my life was simple and, in its essentials, perfect. So long as I followed a few basic mom-rules connected with normal living, everything was taken care of for me—my meals, housecleaning, attention when I wanted to be cuddled or thought I was hurt, a warm bed, playing with Lincoln Logs, Tinker Toys, an elementary Erector Set, and it goes on and on. Most importantly, I could play as much as I wanted and self-direct my activities based on whatever whim I had at the moment, like running after the Good Humor Man's truck tinkling its bell down the street so I could get a chocolate-covered ice cream bar on a stick.

I would unclench my sweaty little fist and the smiling man in the white hat and coat would pick the beat-up buffalo nickel out of my palm and hand me a chilly pleasure. I'd blow into the little white paper sack to free it from the bar and dig in, losing all contact with the world around me. I didn't know or care that the Good Humor Company had the first patent for putting chocolate-coated ice cream on a stick, taking its cue for the idea from the lollipop. I just wanted to gobble up the ice cream without any of the chocolate coating falling somewhere other than in my mouth, and without the melting ice cream running down the stick and all over my hand in the process. Upon licking the last of that marvelous confection off the flat wooden stick, I was always hoping I'd discover a star on it so that the next time the Good Humor Man came, I'd get a free ice cream bar—which could have a star on it too, of course.

My utopia was soon to change. My mother told me about kindergarten. She made it sound like a lot of fun and taught me the song, "We're all in our places with bright shining faces," and said I'd get to take a peanut butter and jelly sandwich to school every day. I liked peanut butter and jelly, but I'd heard the older kids in the neighborhood talking about school and they didn't think it was that much fun. My next-door neighbor and constant playmate, Bobby, was looking forward to it, but I didn't want to go.

When the appointed day arrived, I was being spiffed up to travel a block and four houses to Lincoln Elementary and I was not happy. With a firm hold on my arm, Mommy dragged my complaining, uncooperative little body up the block to school. She showed me all the nifty playground equipment in the kindergarten play yard, monkey bars, swings, sandboxes, teeter-totters and a platform merry-go-round that could be pushed by the riders, all of them really-fun things that would get that kindergarten sued out of existence these days. It didn't help.

As we entered the kindergarten room, a tad late due to my recalcitrance, I saw all other kids sitting on their little mats, and that sparked a last-ditch effort. I threw myself on my back, screaming that I didn't want to go. It wasn't an effective move. My mother reached down with a vise-grip on my ankle and began dragging me, yelling and flailing on my back, up the waxed wooden floor to the front of the class.

While I was lying there, sounding off at the top of my lungs, leg in the air in my mother's hand, the kindest, happiest, most quintessential-grandmotherly face I'd ever seen appeared and looked down at me—smiling. Mrs. Morgan had me. Before I knew it, I was cheerfully on my little mat listening to a story, not realizing Mommy had left the building. I don't have a photo of Mrs. Morgan. I don't need one. She's the teacher every young child has ever loved.

* * * *

3

Peeking

Yes, Virginia, there is a Santa Claus.

Francis P. Church

Toward the end of December during my initial semester in kindergarten, I had my first truly serious reality check. I'm tempted to call it my second, but when my parents got divorced a couple of years earlier when I wasn't quite three, I was too young to consciously process it. Divorce didn't happen much then, and if I'd ever heard the word, it was as meaningless to me as a lot of other big words I'd heard. So far as I knew, we'd simply moved to a different state and we didn't see Daddy as much anymore because his work was back where we'd moved from.

My reality check would revolve around the fact that we had a much smaller house. It had a narrow, enclosed, ten-foot hallway connecting the front and back bedrooms, our only two bedrooms. The hall was punctuated in the middle, on one side by the door to the bathroom, our only bathroom, and on the other side by a door to the relatively small living room, essentially the only room in our house not dedicated to the necessities of living.

In the wall next to that door was a furnace register that distributed heat between the hall and the living room (and into the bathroom or a bedroom if its door to the hall was open). The heater below the register, which produced the only heat in the house, was a clanking, iron, natural-gas beast down in the crawl space under the house, probably compact for its day. Demonstrating the laws of physics, the heat simply rose up to escape through the decorative holes in the two 15 inch cast-iron grills rising from the floor on either side of the wall. This description may be laborious, but it's important in relation to the horror about to come.

It was Christmas Eve and I was in the top bunk, as usual, desperately trying to stay awake so I could hear the sleigh bells and reindeer when Santa landed, probably in the front yard since we didn't have a fireplace and, consequently, no chimney. I didn't know anyone with a fireplace. Everyone in our subdivision just had a clanking furnace. I'd opened our bedroom door a little so I'd be sure to hear the "Ho, ho, ho," in the living room after Mommy let Santa in through the front door like she said. I must have dozed because at some point my eyes flew open when I heard rustling around in the living room. I wasn't sure if I'd heard the sleigh land or not, but I think I had heard the skittering hooves.

Despite Mommy's firm admonition not to get out of bed even if I did hear Santa, I lost it. I had to see him. With five-year-old stealth, I silently crept down the ladder, accidentally waking my sister, and crawled on my hands and knees the four feet across the cold floor toward the door to the hall. All our floors were cold because they were hardwood and we couldn't afford wall-to-wall carpet to cover them up. (Today people are ripping the carpet off to restore those beautiful hardwood floors.) The kitchen floor was covered with linoleum and was even colder, but of no importance to me at the moment because I wasn't crawling on it toward Santa.

"Don't do it," Shirley whispered.

"I've *got* to see him." I was so excited at this prospect it seemed I was floating inside a Christmas glow-bubble filled with golden flecks.

"Mommy said not to do it."

Ignoring her, I crept slowly and silently toward the furnace grill. I just had to stick my head forward a few more inches and I'd *see* him through the grill holes, putting the presents under the tree in the living room. This was going to be so great I could barely bring myself to look. It'd be the next best thing to seeing baby Jesus in the manger.

I looked.

Stunned, I crawled slowly back to bed, ignoring Shirley's inquiries.

In the morning, our mother stood at our bedroom door and told us to come out. Shirley rushed past her, but I confronted Mommy.

"I saw you last night."

"I don't understand, honey."

"I saw you putting the presents under the tree, not Santa."

Her eyes flickered, "Well … I was just helping Santa. He has a lot of children to visit on Christmas Eve."

I went into the living room. "I didn't see Santa at all and *all* of these look like the same presents you put out. Where are the ones he brought?"

She didn't skip a beat this time, "Well, these *are* the ones he brought. Santa dropped them off and asked me to arrange them under the tree. He came back later and checked to see if he liked the way I did it. You must have fallen asleep."

Somewhere inside, I felt I was being had, but Shirley was ripping her presents open with abandon and Mommy told me that two of the big ones were for me. So … what the heck, I'd be doubly careful to catch him next time. I'd already missed spotting the Easter Bunny this year anyway.

* * * *

4

Mr. Chips

He listens to his trainer real good.
He just doesn't listen to me. I still can't get him to do nothing.

Evander Holyfield

THE LAST PRESENT WE GOT that Christmas was brought over from Mrs. Brunghanel's across the street. She said it had been chewing on her fingers all night. It was a beautiful Irish setter puppy who ran all over and was as happy as he could be. We'd had a dog before, a mongrel mix like everyone I knew had, but more cocker spaniel than anything. It yapped all the time and ultimately bit me, leaving the scars of four puncture marks on my wrist for a long time after that. It was a nasty little dog and it was a happy day when my mother gave it away.

But this red dog was different. Unusual for our neighborhood, it had a pedigree, a fact of no moment to our family, but I overheard my mother telling Mrs. Brunghanel she thought it was really cute and was surprised to see it offered for such a reasonable price. It was so happy, you could do anything to it and it just made it happier. I liked it right away. We didn't feel the long name on the pedigree suited him at all, so we all agreed on the name "Prince."

Prince was a sweet dog too. He dug out a shallow, cool place in the back yard to lay in. As he grew he kept making it a little deeper, which happened almost every day because that's how fast he grew. In self-defense, my mother made it into a rock garden. That precipitated the neighbors on the block giving us a number of those little green turtles about an inch or two across that their kids would come home with or receive as gifts, some with decorations painted on their shells (there oughta be a law). They gave them to us to put in the rock garden because they didn't know what else to do with them.

Mommy converted the rock garden into a turtle environment the best she knew how and the turtles seemed to do well in there, but they would get out and walk all over the back yard in their spare time. Since I was a little too small to push the mower, Mr. Brunghanel would come across the street to mow the lawn and that created a big problem for the little turtles, but not a problem for Prince who had made friends with them. He knew he had to get out of the way when Mr. Brunghanel started pushing the mower, and as soon as he saw it coming out, Prince made sure his pals were okay too. He'd run around the yard, pick each one up in his mouth in turn and take it over to the rock garden, keeping them all herded in there with his nose until the lawn was done and the mower put away.

You could almost stand there and watch Prince grow. He ate and ate and got bigger and bigger, fast. He'd eat anything and he absolutely loved milk. When the milkman's truck stopped and he came clinking up with his metal 8-pack carrier filled with those thick glass milk bottles, Prince would get very, very happy at the sound. The milkman had to stop putting the bottles in the little compartment for them built into the outside wall of our "service porch," a small laundry-tub, gas water-heater utility room at the end of the kitchen, because Prince developed a remarkable proficiency for getting the compartment's inside door open to retrieve a full bottle of milk, followed by spearing the cardboard top with one of his huge canines and pulling it off. Then, if through some miracle the bottle was still upright, he'd knock it over, doing an excellent job of lapping every molecule of milk off the linoleum floor in approximately 20 noisy seconds.

We ultimately realized he had an unusual genetic condition, a malady for us, not him. He grew, perfectly proportioned, to the size of a Great Dane. I'm not kidding. Prince turned into one huge, handsome, mahogany-red dog—and my mother acquired him for such a reasonable price too.

When he really wanted, he could clear our six-foot backyard fence with one brief touch toward the top. He loved to run free with that beautiful, long, wavy-haired tail streaming behind and his ears flying up like wings. He was at his happiest then. He wasn't trying to get away; he just loved to run and always stopped after about half an hour of Shirley and I running after him yelling at the top of our lungs for him to come back. We'd tried to put him on a leash for "walks," but our joint death grip on that leather tether just got us dragged on our stomachs, body surfing across every lawn in the neighborhood while he bolted full speed down the block.

Finally, it was clear to all of us he'd outgrown our little house and yard. Besides, he cost more to feed than the three of us put together, not to mention the milk bill. We loved him, and vice versa, but he wasn't happy being cooped up most of the time. The Universe was concerned about Prince too, of course, because shortly after that my mother was listening to a well-known movie actor and radio-show host, Art Baker, on his radio program, *People Are Funny* (later to become the popular TV show of the same name hosted by Art Linkletter, while Art Baker hosted the popular *You Asked For It* on TV during the same period), and he said he had a wonderful ranch up in the mountains and wished he had a big beautiful dog up there to match it. She immediately wrote him a letter and told him about Prince. To our surprise, he called and wanted to come see the mountainous Irish setter.

At the appointed day and time, Shirley and I were staring out the front window, waiting. A chauffeur driven Cadillac about a hundred feet long pulled to the curb in front of the house.

"Mommy, he's here!"

The chauffeur, in a proper chauffeur's uniform, moved quickly around to the back of the car and opened the door. Dressed in a finely tailored suit, out stepped a tall, dignified gentleman with a shock of snow white hair who strode purposefully to the front door. It was just like in the movies. Prince was waiting with us and sensed how excited we were. When the doorbell rang, he got very excited and we grabbed his collar. Mommy opened the door, the introductions were made, Mr. Baker got down on one knee, we let go of the collar, Prince promptly knocked him on his back licking his face. Mortified, we pulled the giant, red, wavy mass off him, but Mr. Baker was laughing.

In his famous sonorous voice, "Wonderful, wonderful. What a beautiful, magnificent animal. May I take him today? I'll keep you apprised of everything I do with him." He chatted with my mother for a while more and it was apparent he was a very nice person who loved animals. Again he asked to take Prince immediately. Never having considered that the Moment of Truth would actually arrive, Shirley and I were speechless, but my mother, gracious and collected as always, "Certainly, but please remember to let us know, often, how Prince is doing."

"I promise, and I promise to bring him back to see you too."

We collected all of his toys and dog dishes and took Prince out to the Cadillac. The three of us hugged our big dog's head goodbye. Prince, clueless and happy no matter what he did, pranced around and licked our faces all over. Then the giant red dog commandeered the back of the huge vehicle and his new master got into the front with the chauffeur as they drove off.

Shirley and I were frozen with realization.

"Kids, this is what we talked about and all agreed on. Prince is going to be very happy running anywhere he wants on his new ranch. We've done the right thing for him."

I imagined Prince loping across the meadows with his mouth open, tongue hanging out, ears flying and his long red tail streaming behind. He was backlit by the setting sun, just like in the movies, and I felt okay.

About three months later, we got a call from Mr. Baker. He'd changed Prince's name to "Mr. Chips" and sent him to obedience school. He wanted to bring him down to show us his new manners, certain we wouldn't recognize him as the same dog. Again at the appointed day and time, the long Cadillac pulled to the curb. Shirley and I were pasted against the front window, watching. The chauffeur opened the back door and there was Art Baker with Prince, er Mr. Chips, the latter seated on the floor like a ramrod with head at the alert. Prince's, er, Mr. Chips' master got out of the car and Pr ... Mr. Chips didn't move a muscle until Mr. Baker made a slight motion with his hand. Then Mr. Chips quietly exited the vehicle, came around his master's back and sat at his left hand.

He was almost unrecognizable as Prince. His wavy coat had been so perfectly shampooed and groomed that it was absolutely gleaming in the sunlight. Had he come along first, Lassie not only would have been dwarfed, she wouldn't have had a chance. Mr. Baker smiled at us watching through the window and, beaming, he had Mr. Chips do a series of perfect maneuvers, using only subtle hand signals. When they finished, Mr. Chips again calmly returned and heeled, sitting at his master's hand. Then, with that beautiful red creature rising and flawlessly maintaining the heel position on his master's left, they proceeded smoothly to the front door.

As they got there, all three of us opened the front door, my mom pushed the screen door open and I heard the word "Prince" shoot out of my mouth. Mr. Chips instantaneously transmuted into Prince, knocking all three of us down as he charged into the house, running in circles at full speed around our small living room yelping, barking, banging into us and yelping some more. Art Baker was beside himself commanding "heel," "sit," "down," all to no avail. Once a two hundred pound dog standing around three feet at the shoulder gets that excited, the safest thing to do is join his club, which the three of us did, but Mr. Baker was helpless with disbelief.

Prince wasn't just running in circles around the living room. He was running in circles *over* everything in the living room. That included tables, chairs, lamps, knickknacks and us. In the process, he smashed two lamps, some ceramic figurines and cut his foot slightly on something so there were also dots of blood on all the furniture and cushions.

Art Baker was mortified. As he'd been so proud of Mr. Chips obedience training and was now so disappointed, I was sort of hoping he'd give Prince back, but he said he'd pay to have everything fixed and he was really sorry because Mr. Chips had been absolutely perfect until that moment and loved running outdoors at the ranch so much that he'd thought running indoors was out of his system, particularly with his obedience training. He said he was going to have him attend more training and then he'd bring him back again and we'd see how he progressed.

He did write us letters from time to time about how Pri . . ., darn, Mr. Chips was doing, but he never risked bringing him back.

So, we contented ourselves with cats after that. We had a lot of great cats, some mongrels and some purebreds. Our first mongrel was a huge long-haired yellow tabby we called Bootsie because of the white "boots" on his feet. He was a great cat who ruled the neighborhood and loved us as much as we loved him. Later, after Bootsie went to that Great Cat Tree In The Sky, our first purebred was a Siamese my mother named Ming Toy. I think that's a Chinese name, but our Siamese Ming Toy didn't seem offended, even when the other kids said, "Hey, is that one of those Chinese cats?"

Ming Toy was the smartest cat we ever had, Siamese or otherwise. My mom would say "Give me a kiss," and Ming would jump up in her lap, put both "arms" around her neck and hug her cheek. When Ming wanted to go outside to do her business, she figured out that if she stood on her hind legs and pushed against the screen door with her paws, watching us push I guess, her weight would force it open and she'd jump outside. The problem was that the weak spring on the door never shut it completely and it would always loosely stay open about an inch.

In any event, we all went out one night and Ming was left inside. We came back later than we expected and started rushing around looking for her to let her out. We found her sitting on the toilet doing her business. We should have waited to see if she knew how to flush. Anyway, from that, Shirley and I decided she was smart enough to learn to turn around and push the screen door shut when she went out. We only had to show her a few times and she started doing it. Ming Toy is my nominee for the Cat Hall of Fame.

Then there was Willy. We got Willy shortly before I started high school after Ming Toy went to visit the Great Cat Tree. Willy was a three-quarter Siamese. He had blue eyes and all the Siamese coloring and markings except a pink nose with white fur on it and four white stockings on his feet. He was a fun and affectionate little cat. He disappeared for a couple of weeks during my junior year in high school and my mother and I were very worried. Then he just showed up one day, but one of his eyes was hurt and it was obvious he needed medical attention.

I took him to a veterinarian who examined him and said he'd have to put him to sleep.

"Why?"

"Because his eye needs to be removed and he won't be able to function right with only one eye left. He'll always be bumping into things and won't be able to judge distance right when he jumps. He'll miss and hurt himself. It just won't be a good situation."

"People seem to be okay with one eye and they don't kill them."

"Look, it's not fair to the cat. He has to be put to sleep."

Since Willy wasn't able to make his opinion known, I decided to impose my view of fairness. Willy and I left. I found a veterinarian who was sympathetic to Willy and my thoughts on the matter. Willy became a one-eyed cat, looking like he was winking all the time. Without exaggeration, Willy was quicker and more agile after that than before. He lived a long and happy life, traveling with me from coast to coast.

Without wondering what the Universal Forces had in mind for me, I know they were looking out for Willy's benefit.

5

Rail Royalty

A private railroad car is not an acquired taste.
One takes to it immediately.

Eleanor Robson Belmont

ASIDE FROM SENDING US PRESENTS every few months, we would see my dad several times a year. He lived the next state over. He'd either visit us or, after I reached seven or eight and Shirley was ten or eleven, we'd ride the train to visit him. Once we got on the train, we didn't need an escort. My father was on emergency night duty at the railroad's hospital and just about every porter, conductor, brakeman and engineer on the run between the two states had contact with him at one time or another. They all knew and liked him very much. We would board in the late afternoon for the overnight trip and from the moment we were turned over to their care, we were treated like prince and princess with our own private compartment and the run of the train.

"Well here comes Master Chip and Miss Shirley. I heard you were going to be on our train today. It's sure nice to see you. Come on up." And they'd grab us by the arm and swing us up to the car, with our luggage to follow.

I thought this was normal and it was great. I had strict orders to obey my sister, but it wasn't necessary. I loved everything about the train, the conductor yelling "Bort!" as he looked at his watch on a long chain and waved his lantern, the blast of sound as the vestibule door opened between the cars running at full speed, standing in between the cars listening to the pounding clickety-clack of the wheels over the seams in the track in the same never-ending rhythm, and standing on the observation deck at the end of the last car waving to everyone and listening to the Doppler sound of the crossing bells rise and fade. There was always something new to look at whizzing by, and the best thing was a train going at full speed in the opposite direction on the very next track. Wowee! Not only that, in the dining car, we could have anything we wanted! And they always brought us special desserts! I loved the train.

At night, the porter would make up the berths in our compartment. The bottom seats would disappear and turn into a bed, and a top berth would just pull out of the wall! I loved the ones that were arranged so I could lie on one elbow and look out the window all night, well, at least until I fell asleep. My goal would be to stay awake the entire night so I wouldn't miss anything, but then I always woke up in the morning when the porter knocked on our door.

Before I fell asleep, I loved it when the train stopped at a siding in the middle of nowhere so the giant steam engine could take on water or let another train go by. Most of the time the hobos and bums would be close to the tracks cooking or warming themselves by their fires and I'd turn on the reading light at my berth, shine my flashlight at them and wave. Whether hobo or bum, they'd always wave back and smile. I personally didn't know the difference between a bum and a hobo, but it seemed like neither had homes. Anyway, I think the cooks on the train gave them the extra food because I would see the men run from their fires toward the dining car and then run back with cardboard boxes and paper sacks in their hands that made the others very happy.

Another nifty thing about those trains, they not only had refrigerated air conditioning, but *personal* air conditioning. I could draw the curtains around my berth so it was really a small private space with a window to the outside and *directable* air conditioning nozzles on the inside. They were about two inches in diameter and I could turn them up to full blast and point them right at me all night long if I wanted. Since I'd never experienced air conditioning except on the train, that's what I did the first time I rode it.

I didn't do it after that. I fell asleep with it blowing on my face and neck all night from about ten inches away. In the morning my head was tipped at a forty-five degree angle and I couldn't turn it. It took about three days to go away and my dad carefully explained how it had happened. Shirley lobbied for my being forbidden to ever turn the air conditioning on again, but my father was quite certain it was a self-limiting experience.

* * * *

6

Safe at Home

Peace is not only better than war, but infinitely more arduous.

George Bernard Shaw

OUR SUBDIVISION WAS NEW WITH small but well-kept houses on fifty-foot wide lots, twenty four young families on our block, twelve on each side of the street, so there were lots of us to form several age groups, but most were around my age. One day in the summer before I started kindergarten, all of us had just finished playing kickball on my front lawn and were having a spirited discussion about what we wanted to do next. We all got along well and had a lot of fun, but that particular day, one of my peers, little Jerry, whose voice was so high he was endearingly called "Bat Boy" by his older sisters, went a little rabid. He hit me while we were standing on my front porch, an outrageous violation of "my house—my rules," and definitely not on the "ok" list.

Actually, I'd always thought he was a little strange, and it wasn't because he communicated best with flying rodents. His blond hair was eternally-perfectly combed and never got mussed up, no matter what we did—very weird. It seems he discovered Wildroot Cream-Oil about ten years before I did. Anyway, he hit me high on my chest by my shoulder. I'm not sure why he hit me. We were having a disagreement about something, but I don't believe I made a smart-ass comment to him. I hadn't learned to do that yet. Well ... while we were having that serious discussion, I *had* idly reached into my pocket, found a pair of those big red wax lips in there among a lot of other things, pulled them out, popped them on without batting an eye and just stared at him. That might have set him off. I said he was a little weird. I wasn't hurt, just surprised. No one had ever hit me intentionally before. I don't think any of us had hit one another on purpose before. The other kids were like statues, waiting in shock to see what I would do. So I ran a couple of steps into the house and told Mommy.

"You go right back out there and punch him in the nose as hard as you can."

Stepping back out on the porch, I sort of knew that "punch" meant to make a fist. So I did, looked at it and it seemed right. Then I focused on his nose and swung as hard as I could.

I can still see his hands flying up to his face. Mommy hadn't told me what I was supposed to do next, particularly if he started hitting back, but the Universe saved me. He ran crying the full six-house distance to his home. He never bothered me again.

That pre-kindergarten encounter with little Jerry was essentially the extent of the violence known to the kids in our neighborhood, at least up to the start of World War II (WWII or the Second World War) during my first semester in kindergarten. The day after Pearl Harbor, which happened to be the day before my fifth birthday, I can remember my mother and some friends pressed around the radio in the living room. At that moment they were part of the largest radio audience in history, listening as President Franklin Delano Roosevelt told us that December 7, 1941, was "a date which will live in infamy ... we will not only defend ourselves to the uttermost, but will make it very certain that this form of treachery shall never again endanger us." Then he said something that ended in the most amazing phrase, at least in some circles these days, "With confidence in our armed forces—with the unbounding determination of our people—we will gain the inevitable triumph—so help us God."

Four days after Pearl Harbor, the other two Axis powers, Germany and Italy, declared war on the United States, and for the duration of the war, which lasted over three and a half years for us and had started earlier for those across the oceans, we learned the basic principles of community service and supporting our country on the "home front" by saving every drop of kitchen grease and every scrap of steel, iron, aluminum, tin, paper, and rubber we could and then contributing it to the war effort through scrap drives of every kind, not to mention learning the practical aspects of planning and math while utilizing our war ration stamps and tokens for shoes, meat, sugar, butter, coffee (for mom), and a variety of other foods. But not for gasoline, oil and tires—because we didn't have a car during the war.

However, mom had friends who did have cars. Every once in awhile they had some gasoline left over from their week's ration and we were lucky enough to go on outings with them from time to time. The wartime speed limit to conserve gas was 35 miles per hour to go anywhere, and it seemed to take forever to get somewhere on those trips, but we got to go there in a car. Mom would laugh, saying she could measure how long the trip took by counting the number of times we asked, "Are we there yet?" But once there, the length of the trip was instantaneously forgotten.

I remember mom's friends talking about how they had to have the car's tires inspected every three months and if they weren't wearing down, they would lose their gas ration stamps in order to prevent a variety of abuses such as hoarding gas or selling the stamps on the "black market."

When we stopped for gas, self-service being virtually unknown in those days, the attendant pumping it, checking the oil and cleaning the windshield (all a long-standing and customary part of the service then) was often female instead of the usual male, because the "boys" were "overseas" doing the fighting.

Women played an important role in WWII and it wasn't limited to those women who had taken over civilian jobs previously done by men presently in the military. By the end of the war, over three hundred fifty thousand women served in uniform, both at home and overseas, in the Army Nurse Corps, Navy Nurse Corps, Marine Corps Women's Reserve (MCWR), Navy WAVES (Women Accepted for Volunteer Emergency Service), Coast Guard SPARS (*Semper Paratus*—always ready), Army WAC (Women's Army Corps, originally WAAC—Women's Army Auxiliary Corps), and WASP (Women Airforce Service Pilots). The latter were actually the first women military pilots but not officially recognized as military members and veterans of WWII until the late 1970's, despite the fact that they ferried military fighters and bombers to and between military installations, flight tested planes, towed targets in live-fire anti aircraft gun training, trained male pilots and at least thirty eight women lost their lives in connection with those endeavors.

While, *theoretically*, women in military service were there to free a male for combat and did not serve in combat roles, women served on islands in the Pacific including Guadalcanal, Saipan and Guam, and in North Africa and Europe, on hospital ships, in air evacuations, landed on the beaches at Normandy, and also served at the battle of Anzio. Over eighty Army and Navy nurses spent several years as prisoners of war. More than two hundred military nurses lost their lives in the line of duty, and military women were awarded Silver Stars, Bronze Stars, Purple Hearts and other medals and commendations as a result of their heroic service during the Second World War.

Non-military women personnel assisted in equally important ways at home and overseas. For instance, with the Salvation Army, American Red Cross, USO entertainment, YMCA administration, the U.S. Public Health Service and its Cadet Nurse Corps, the American Legion Auxiliary, and of course, all the "Rosie the

Riveters" made visually famous by the fictionalized drawings published on the Westinghouse Corporation poster "We Can Do It" by J. Howard Miller and on the Saturday Evening Post magazine cover by Norman Rockwell, plus the myriad photos of women at work in the aircraft factories, shipyards, munitions factories, manufacturing operations, offices and other industries that supported the war effort.

The assistance of all those at home who waited and prayed was equally important—mothers, wives, fathers, husbands, children, sisters, brothers, grandmothers, grandfathers, other family members, fiancées and fiancés, sweethearts and multitudes of friends. Families with an immediate family member in the armed forces had a rectangular Service Flag (we called it a service banner) with a red border around a white field and a blue star in it for each person serving. It was usually about a foot long and hung vertically in the front window, often by a gold cord with tassels on each end. The saddest days in the neighborhood were the ones when a blue star would change to gold. Then the curtains behind that banner would be drawn for a long time and many neighbors would come and go offering deep condolences to the family. No mother wanted to become a "Gold Star Mother."

Back in my childhood life which was sheltered and kept safe by the courage and bravery of those in the military and others serving in the war effort, having the proper war ration stamps didn't guarantee you could find the item, and we learned to make do with what we had, as did every one else in the country. Folks developed a lot of inventive recipes, depending on what was available, in order to "Do with less so they'll have enough," as one of the ubiquitous printed war posters said. As a result, canned Spam, the un-rationed "Miracle Meat" made from pigs, was consumed in large quantities both at home and by the troops, as well as soup made from oxtail, an inexpensive food source in those days and now one of the most expensive items on a restaurant menu.

Of course, it was really from "retired" draft-animal oxen in those days and now it's somewhat of a delicacy from beef cattle.

Following the "make-do" maxim, we had what mom loosely referred to as "Scrapple" one day a week. Traditional Scrapple, centuries old, was usually ground-up pork parts, cornmeal and buckwheat flour. However, our Scrapple consisted of dumping every single edible leftover scrap (animal, fish, fowl, vegetable or anything else that was on our plates—which could include lettuce, bread, birthday cake, Jell-O, you get the idea) from the other six days into our hand-cranked food grinder, and then packing the springy, pulpified result into a pan and baking or slicing and frying it for dinner. It was always kind of beige with flecks of stuff in it. It didn't look great, but it tasted pretty good and was different each week. I never calculated if it ever reached almost 100% leftover Scrapple because part of it each week was always leftover Scrapple from the prior week and ground up again along with the new ingredients. As you might expect, we also had a plentiful diet of Kraft macaroni and cheese. I don't eat that delicacy much now, but I kind of miss my mom's Scrapple.

We mostly did without butter, substituting oleomargarine which was rationed too, but easier to come by. When it first came out, it was like a chunk of hard white lard we tossed in a bowl, breaking a little packet of reddish-colored liquid over it and laboriously trying to mix it in for about twenty minutes so the tasteless result would at least look something like butter. I was the one who had to mix it and my suggestion to use it without the coloring fell on deaf ears. In retrospect, it was really a matter of being a boring task rather than the effort, because cultivating and planting our Victory Garden in the back yard was a lot more work and took a lot longer, but that common patriotic vegetable-growing endeavor around the country was a lot more fun and I willingly embraced it.

Like almost everyone else, our mother acquired S&H Green Stamps as premiums for purchases from a wide variety of retailers including grocery and department stores. They were so popular that approximately three times more Green Stamps were issued by the Sperry and Hutchinson Company than postage stamps issued by the U.S. Post Office. Shirley and I were highly experienced at pasting them into S&H Green Stamp Books which we traded for merchandise from the S&H Catalog.

We didn't even try to save enough Green Stamps to get a washing machine because the necessary amount was astronomical. So, Mommy scrubbed the wash by hand with a corrugated metal wash board in a wooden frame (seen mostly in Zydeco bands these days) which she put in the wash-tub sink in our tiny service porch off the end of the kitchen (we'd call it a "laundry room" now). But, she did have a hand-crank, double-roller wringer that clamped to the side of the sink and squeezed the rinse water out of the clothes.

Sometimes she'd let me feed the clothes between the rollers with one hand while I cranked the handle with the other, but that task usually fell to Shirley who was older and not so likely to transform her hand into a pancake, since the only "safety-stop" was to have enough presence of mind to stop cranking before you cranked your own hand through. I don't know how we kept injury free since there weren't any decals telling us to be careful of the obvious, nor companion lawsuits for the benefit of the terminally stupid.

After that, Mommy would get her bowl of wooden clothespins and hang the wash on the clothesline in the back yard to completely dry. We were too short to do that. Those sun-dried clothes had a sweet, fresh smell that just can't be duplicated in a modern gas/electric dryer these days no matter how many little sheets of scent you toss in. When they were dry, she'd set up her rickety wooden ironing board, and since steam irons weren't very affordable, reliable or popular, she'd warm up the electric iron and press it down on the wrinkly clothes after first sprinkling them with a little water from a soda-pop bottle she'd forced the cap back onto, having first punched some holes in it with a hammer and nail. She bought the iron at Montgomery Ward (we called it "Monkey Wards") and it was a pretty decent one. It had a non-rusting alloy base plate and a Bakelite handle that stayed pretty cool. She still had to be careful though, because it didn't have an automatic shutoff.

To help finance the country's defense, we consistently saved our pennies so we could buy ten-cent war-bond stamps at school to paste in our war-stamp Victory Book, aided by our S&H Green Stamp licking and pasting experience. Comparatively, a first class postage stamp was three cents, so our goal of eventually accumulating enough ten-cent war-bond stamps to buy a $25 war bond was hefty indeed. The proper name was Ten-Cent Defense Stamp; it was red with a picture of a Revolutionary War Minuteman on it. The book held 187 of them ($18.70). We took the full book, plus a nickel, to the post office in order to purchase a $25 Defense Savings Bond, legally a Series E War Bond.

It seemed like a good deal, but we had to hold it for 10 years (2.9% interest compounded semiannually—a meaningless financial factoid to us) in order to get the twenty-five bucks from the United States Treasury at the end—a much longer period than we were able to comprehend. Because saving enough money to buy a bond was quite an undertaking for grammar school kids, our Victory Book was a joint effort between Shirley and me and took quite a while. I have no idea what happened to the bond. Maybe Shirley has it in her retirement account.

Of course, Shirley and I weren't the only ones interested in war bonds. Many movie stars and other celebrities constantly participated in successfully spearheading war-bond sales drives all over the country. Other movie stars and celebrities of appropriate age and abilities placed their careers completely on hold and joined the armed services, culminating in individual awards, among others, of Purple Hearts, Bronze Stars, Silver Stars, Distinguished Service Crosses, and the Congressional Medal of Honor.

Saving pennies for bonds materially reduced the volume of our penny candy purchases. We loved to go to the little neighborhood store not far from our grammar school and see if we could guess which chocolate was going to have a pink center. They all looked the same, but we could pick any one we wanted out of the big bowl. I don't know how we survived because there weren't any sneeze shields, tongs or plastic gloves—we just paid our penny, picked one from the bowl and bit into it on the spot to see what the center was before we ate it. The pink center (shown to the proprietor prior to complete consumption) was good for a free chocolate which could be good for *another* free one, just like the free stick from the Good Humor Man. As we all know, "Get one free" is a timeless incentive that works in all decades and at all ages.

For our penny we could also have purchased a Tootsie Roll, Bazooka bubble gum or a jaw breaker—and some of those big round candies were hard enough to do it too. I loved the ones that changed colors as you wore them down through the layers. We could also get two orange marshmallow peanuts or a wax Coke-shaped bottle with brown sugar water inside, or almost limitless types of other penny candies. For a few more copperheads (or the gray zinc-coated steel pennies in 1943), you could get a pack of candy cigarettes in a package that mimicked the genuine article. Of course, those were the days when a carton of real cigarettes was a thoughtful Christmas present and doctors recommended various brands in advertisements.

Even though I wasn't able to process how long a ten year bond-maturity date was, I did acquire an understanding of the scale of WWII while I was still in kindergarten. Shirley and I were in the back yard when a B-17 bomber flew over. Shirley told me its tail was higher than our garage door. So, I stood next to the garage door and looked up at the top of it. It was a long way up. I was amazed that an airplane could really be that tall. They all looked so small up in the sky.

In any event, since America's daily existence then didn't include watching television or surfing the internet on computers, we developed our imaginations and amused ourselves, often with the participation of the entire family. Among other things, we read books, played card games, board games, and listened to the radio together (more on that later), not to mention that we always ate breakfast and supper together, at least that's what we called the evening meal; however, on Sundays or if we had guests over on any day, we always had dinner, not supper. Go figure.

While that was a usual and voluntary part of our life, passing the time together was an absolute necessity during nighttime "blackouts" announced by the wailing of huge air raid warning sirens strategically placed all over the city. If those sirens sounded at night, no light could be visible outside the house until the all-clear siren blast was heard, so the enemy could not key in on the city lights in case of a real attack. If any light did peek through a crack in the window covering during a blackout, the neighborhood Civil Defense Air Raid Warden would be tapping on your door with his flashlight.

Even though we lived on the Pacific Coast, at the beginning of the war many people in our area thought the authorities were being over-cautious concerning the possibility of an enemy air raid attack. After all, the United States wasn't England just across the channel from the enemy. There were big oceans buffering us from the evil axis enemies, and while the Japanese may have snuck, just once, as far across the Pacific Ocean as the U.S. Territory of Hawaii (not to become a state until approximately eighteen years later in 1959), they certainly wouldn't be able to sneak that far a second time, and *certainly* not as far as the shores of the United States.

That viewpoint began to waver a short time after Pearl Harbor when reports began to surface that German U-Boats (undersea boats, that is, submarines) were sinking unarmed American merchant ships by torpedo in the Atlantic Ocean two or three hundred miles off the East Coast. By the way, by the end of the war, the civilian U.S. Merchant Marine (which becomes auxiliary to the Navy in wartime) ultimately numbered about 240,000 strong serving their country. Over 1500 ships were sunk or lost and approximately 9,500 mariners lost their lives as a result of transporting supplies and troops vital to the war effort overseas.

Mariners are reputed to have suffered a higher ratio of casualties to the size of their force in WWII than either the Marines, Army, Navy or Coast Guard. (The Air Force was part of the Army and not then a separate branch of the service.)

Next, a little over two months after the attack on Pearl Harbor (which most Americans had never heard of until that fateful day), a Japanese submarine surfaced one night in the Pacific Ocean about a *mile* off America's populated West Coast and lobbed approximately twenty five shells into some oil fields not far up the coast from us. Truly disturbing things like that usually weren't immediately known to younger kids, particularly to me in kindergarten or to Shirley in third grade because, in an effort to keep us from soaking up the really scary stuff, adults didn't talk about such matters in front of us. Thus, Shirley and I were oblivious of the fact that our homeland had been shelled by the enemy a few miles from our house.

However, in spite of efforts not to panic us, less than forty eight hours after that shell-lobbing, I was panicked, and abruptly concluded that any and all precautions were appropriate, when I was awakened in the wee hours of the morning by the sound of tigers growling and banging around outside my bedroom. I gingerly crept to the window, lifted a slat in the venetian blinds and peered into the dark outside. My kindergarten mind confirmed that I'd indeed heard tigers, and these were *magic* tigers! The flew and spit fire! I could see them chasing each other around in the sky.

I ran to Mommy's bedroom. The venetian blinds were raised and she was looking intently out the window. I declared those were magic tigers in the sky. She calmly said they were nothing to worry about since they were way up in the sky and I should just go back to sleep because they would lose their magic and disappear by morning, but she kept looking out the window while she was talking. The tigers were still flying around up there spitting fire at each other and there must have been some tigers spitting fire up from the ground too. I was oddly relieved to know that apparently all magic tigers couldn't fly.

The really peculiar thing was that there was another animal a *whole* lot bigger than the tigers up there. There were big lights from the ground shining up at it and it was flying really, really slowly across the sky. Neither the fire from the tigers in the sky nor from the tigers on the ground could hurt it. It was like it had more magic than they did and it just didn't care about them. That was interesting, but it certainly didn't diminish my fear of the magic tigers at that point, so Mommy let me sleep in her bed the remainder of the night. That was good because with her close, I knew nothing could hurt me.

Shirley slept through the whole thing and the next day told me there were no such things as tigers in the sky, magic or otherwise, and they certainly could not spit fire. After that, my mother continued to act like it meant absolutely nothing whenever I asked her about it.

A few months later, I realized from the Saturday matinee picture shows about war (we mostly call them movies now) that the growling of my magic fighting tigers were the engines and machine guns of dog-fighting aircraft (the propeller driven kind—no jet fighters then), the fire was their tracer bullets, and the banging and fire from the ground were anti-aircraft gun emplacements firing tracers and flak shells, the latter exploding in the air.

The real Flying Tigers involved in WWII were, of course, not the fighter planes on the West Coast that night. That now-legendary group of volunteer American airmen were flying their Curtiss P-40 fighters, with the famous shark teeth painted on the front, on combat missions for the Chinese over Burma at that time to assist in China's defense against the Japanese. Their combat missions started shortly after Pearl Harbor and ended approximately seven months later when the organization was replaced by a United States Army Air Force unit into which some of the volunteer Flying Tigers transitioned.

In any event, years later in connection with my "magic-tiger night," I learned that the U.S. government had acted in the same "it-was-really-nothing" way as my mother when the public asked about it, even though the event was startling headline news in the area papers the next morning, including the Los Angeles Times. Curiously, apparently no planes were shot down, nor bombs dropped, nor the planes even identified, even though the L.A. Times initially stated in the headlines they were Japanese. The government said there were no planes at all, it was all a mistake, only the anti-aircraft "ack-ack" guns along the coast and around the cities fired due to a false report of enemy planes and no U.S military planes had taken off in response.

But, contrary to the government's pronouncements, hundreds of thousands of people awake and awakened that night had seen a lot of things as the events moved down the coast through the air. The descriptions included a number of unidentified aircraft, fighter planes dog-fighting, including our fighter planes, and, locked in the beams of the searchlights, one very large unidentified craft that received direct hits from both fighter planes and the anti-aircraft guns with no effect on it whatsoever. One witness said there were several much smaller reddish craft initially accompanying it and very rapidly zigzagging around the larger one when it first appeared. The latter was variously described as orange, glowing, lozenge-shaped and enormous. Many saw it remain stationary at some points and/or move very slowly across the sky, too slow for any airplane they were familiar with, being visible for about half an hour while it was being fired upon.

There never was a clear explanation by the government authorities, who themselves seemed somewhat confused, and they continually maintained it was a non-event except for the mistaken firing of the anti-aircraft guns. Not only that, it was apparently not all that much of a news story around the country. Of course, at that time there were no digital cameras, no camcorders, no television, no camera-phones and no internet to graphically blast events all over the world either live or within minutes after their occurrence, and the media cooperated with the government in "sanitizing" reporting much more in those days than it has since. For instance, it was almost two years into the war before the American public saw any published pictures in the national media (Life magazine) of

American soldiers lying dead in battle. Reputedly, those pictures were held in a file in the Pentagon building (newly completed in January 1941) until President Roosevelt gave the okay.

By the way, if you're wondering, the famous events of the "flying saucer" sighting at Mt. Rainier in Washington, and the reported crash of a flying saucer at Roswell, New Mexico, both of which exponentially raised the public's awareness of the possibility of other-worldly flying craft and also resulted in the "flying saucer" label for them (followed later by the broader "UFO" label), didn't occur until more than five years after "The Battle of L.A." described above. Thus, even though there is a well known (in some circles) photograph from my "tiger night" taken by an L.A. Times reporter and published in the Times that shows a large circular object locked in the crisscross of searchlight beams with ack-ack shells bursting next to it, the general public really had no word for that "unidentified plane" early in the war. I did. It was a magic elephant that had upset the magic tigers.

Everyone in our area paid even more attention to Civil Defense after that, which included the advice of the federal Office of Civilian Defense (OCD), originally headed by New York Mayor Fiorello LaGuardia (who also read the Sunday comics to children over the radio during a New York newspaper delivery strike). The OCD printed Civil Defense pamphlets concerning air raid precautions, air raid warning sirens, air raid shelters, blackouts, poison gas protection, bombs, first aid and other subjects related to a possible enemy attack. It also encouraged civilians to volunteer for all the tasks related to the foregoing, and over ten million citizens nationwide volunteered for the Civil Defense Corps (CDC), including civilian pilots who volunteered for the Civil Air Patrol that patrolled the coasts and prepared for search and rescue.

Other volunteers acted as, among other things, civilian air-raid wardens, firefighters, first-aid specialists, decontamination specialists, and stationary aircraft spotters for whom large towers were built all over the country, manned by spotters who watched the skies twenty four hours a day. In areas without towers, it wasn't uncommon to see a Boy Scout peering for enemy planes from the highest point he could reach.

Some of the instructions in the Civil Defense pamphlets were inventive, even heroic. For instance, if a fire bomb should fall in the open, a citizen should "... hold a sandbag in front of your face, run up and place it squarely on the bomb, then dash away quickly." If there were a poison gas attack, the clarion gas warning would be, "A percussion sound—Bells, drums, hand rattles, etc." Then one should go to the gas-tight room that had been prepared in the home, although I didn't know anyone who had one. According to the pamphlets, it would be a room with a nine-foot ceiling (at least two feet taller than any ceiling in our little house) that allowed twenty square feet of floor space for each person in the room. Such a room would provide enough air for ten hours according to the CDC. In order to keep the room air tight, one should tape-up all the doors and windows.

The pamphlets didn't say what kind of tape, but it well could have been the olive-drab color tape the soldiers called "duck" tape which was invented by Johnson & Johnson to seal ammunition cases against water, and subsequently used by soldiers for every repair conceivable. The room-taping instructions might sound familiar to those who, over sixty years later, were given much the same instructions in relation to possible terrorist attacks by the modern counterpart of WWII's Office of Civilian Defense, today's Department of Homeland Security which has specifically recommended "duct" tape for that purpose. It's the modern version of the WWII duck tape with the color having evolved to silver-gray after the war because it was commonly used for air conditioning ducts. So today it's called "duct tape" as well as "Duck ® Tape," the latter having since become the registered trademark of one enterprising manufacturing company.

Air raid sirens, blackouts, saving scraps of things and "making do" soon became commonplace and automatic parts of life. There never was another tiger-in-the-sky experience for us, and our mix of neighborhood kids soon forgot about it, but our games all through WWII often mirrored the subject that consumed the attention of the nation. Woe the Fuller Brush Man trudging from door to door with his case full of samples if he wandered into our line of fire while the boys played soldier and the girls played nurse in many mock battles with our toy cap pistols (and we knew where to get the really loud rolls of caps too) or rifles that fired a cork on a string, becoming either wounded and receiving instantaneously effective nursing attention, or dying, particularly if playing one of the enemy at the moment, and miraculously resurrecting ourselves each time the game was over. Not like real war, not at all.

Playing outside produced only fun for us, not the doomsday child-risks perceived from many quarters to be inherent in playing out in the neighborhood now. To be fair, at that time there were many pairs of mothers' eyes constantly glancing out the windows to see we were safe. Of course, these days if kids played some of the games we did, the proper-parenting police would most likely complain to child protective services so that fragile psyches could be saved from the mental scars of that play experience, and their lives wouldn't be irreparably ruined.

In addition to our war games, we'd engage in games of Cops and Robbers or Cowboys and Indians (the kids who had bows and arrows with rubber suction-cup tips got those roles) and that didn't seem to hurt us either, although we didn't know any Indians to query concerning how they might feel about their portrayal. Not that we would have known to ask, since most of us were pretty much clueless about social issues at that age and time (continuing well into high school in many instances).

That included no knowledge whatsoever of the significant contributions of over 44,000 Native Americans who earned decorations including Purple Hearts, Air medals, Distinguished Flying

Crosses, Bronze Stars, Silver Stars, Distinguished Service Crosses and Congressional Medals of Honor on all fronts in the war effort. Their many battlefield accomplishments encompassed the U.S. Marine combat role of Navajos in the Pacific in the battles of Guadalcanal, Iwo Jima, Okinawa, Tarawa and Saipan, serving as military radio/telephone "Code Talkers." Speaking in their native language, it was a code the Japanese never broke, saving an untold number of American soldiers' lives.

Since our Cowboys and Indians or Cops and Robbers game scenarios were male-only adventures (we didn't know anything about Bonnie and Clyde), the girls usually played jacks, hopscotch or jump-rope, including "Double-Dutch" with two ropes going in opposite directions like an eggbeater and the jumper(s) reciting a rhyme as the ropes turned faster and faster. Thus, the girls were at least spared potential emotional scars that could result from imaginary law-enforcement and wild-west escapades, even though they were exposed to the possible psychological artifacts of playing a nurse in the war games.

It is possible, though, that the Women's Liberation Movement could have been accelerated by a decade or more if the neighborhood had played games that involved the girls working in aircraft factories and other formerly all-male jobs, but our neighborhood didn't (nor any other neighborhood I knew of), and playing Rosie the Riveter didn't happen, notwithstanding that it seemed a revolutionary discovery during WWII that women could do those and other things outside society's pre-war professional stereotypes for them of, primarily, secretaries, school teachers, librarians, or nurses.

The boys, however, did borrow the girl's hopscotch chalk from time to time to draw the ubiquitous WWII fence-peeking figure of two hands grasping the top of a fence with just a bald head, eyes and nose looking over it, accompanied by the phrase, "Kilroy Was Here," which came to symbolize World War II. While its origins aren't known to a certainty, and there are several stories, perhaps the most tenable is that a WWII Massachusetts shipyard construction inspector named James Kilroy would scribble the words "Kilroy was here" in yellow crayon on the parts of ships he inspected. This phrase then became attached to the likeness of a popular British graffiti cartoon figure named "Chad" who looked quite similar to the one described above. That's complicated by a similar looking Australian WWII graffiti cartoon figure named "Foo," reputed to have made his original appearance scribbled on the sides of railroad cars in the First World War. So, perhaps the little bald fence-peeker developed from Foo, to Chad, to Kilroy, the latter by far the most popular, spreading all over the world by the end of WWII, including the sidewalks of our neighborhood.

Every mother had a different method of calling her children in from neighborhood play, different-patterned whistle toots or very inventive vocal calls, and heaven forbid if you missed the call and she had to come down the street to get you. Often at dusk until the mothers called the kids to come in from wherever we were in the neighborhood, we played traditional games like kick ball or kick-the-can and hide-and-seek. It wasn't until I became an adult that I learned "Olly, olly, oxen free" was actually, "All the, all the, outs in free."

We played dodge ball too, at home and in school, and kids of both sexes were actually hit with the ball which, if anyone recalls, is how they got knocked out of the game and the single winner determined. It seems the competition made each of us more resilient—and none of us were psychologically bruised from it either. Today, I understand we'd be basket cases, and not just from contact with the ball, "Oh, my goodness, you mean *everyone's* not the winner?" Next they'll be cancelling Pop Warner football, Little League baseball, soccer and other sports leagues everywhere, ultimately filtering up to the Super Bowl and the World Series.

Thinking of things that can *really* mess with your mind, or your body anyway, in the year following the end of WWII on a Saturday in the late summer just before fifth grade started, we decided to go up to the schoolyard and play baseball on the softball diamond because it had a backstop and the bases were painted on the asphalt playground (they'd get sued at the first scrape these days, wouldn't they), and we had enough neighborhood kids outside at that moment to have two teams, including a few girls who didn't buy into the idea they should only play softball.

Our meager equipment consisted of just enough baseball gloves for one side, all fielders' mitts, two bats and one very hard scuffed-up baseball with frayed stitching around the leather cover. The other team was up first and, even though he'd never done it, Bobby wanted to pitch because his dad was related to the great Cleveland Indians pitcher, Bob Feller. Since I'd never played catcher, I wanted that particular position and, oddly I thought, none of the other kids were interested in it. I squatted down in my best catcher approximation. Bobby wound up and let fly his best approximation of an overhand fastball. The batter took a backswing smacking me right in the forehead just as the ball caromed off home plate hitting me squarely in the family particulars.

Writhing on the asphalt for an eternity plus ten or fifteen minutes, and clearly knowing where I hurt the worst, I agonizingly assessed the relative risks of the sport and decided to try playing *second base* in the future. It certainly wasn't apparent at the time, but it was part of an extended plan arranged by the Universal Forces.

* * * *

7

The Sweet Science

Float like a butterfly, sting like a bee.

Muhammad Ali

My dad lived in an adjoining state, visited us several times a year and was always sending toys, games and sports equipment. Not too long after the end of World War II, when I was around ten or eleven or so, he sent me a complete football uniform—shoulder pads, knee pads, thigh pads, hip pads, helmet, cleats, the works. After the first time I played with it on, the other kids wouldn't let me wear any of it again, not one piece of it. They had high-top tennis shoes, t-shirts, blue jeans or corduroy trousers. With my stuff, I was an armored truck.

In that same box, he'd sent two pairs of boxing gloves, which retroactively transformed my pre-kindergarten nose-punching encounter with Bat-Boy Jerry into the harbinger of my subsequent neighborhood boxing career. We set up neighborhood boxing matches on my front lawn after school. Because my only experience had been hitting Jerry in the nose, I didn't know anything about boxing, but most everyone else knew even less.

The neighborhood war games we'd played during World War II were all make-believe for us, but boxing was much closer to reality since the goal was to actually make contact with and punch out your opponent. We rapidly learned that if you were wimpy about it, you'd be the one punched out. Of course, you could refuse to participate, but then everyone dumped on you mercilessly, so peer pressure triumphed over pain.

At least after the matches were over, the mother of my next-door pal, Bobby, would come out with a big pitcher of nice cold, naturally sweetened Kool-Aid. While saccharine had become popular in the sugar shortages of the First and Second World Wars, mostly in the form of little quarter grain white tablets that sort of fizzed when dropped into coffee or tea, artificial sweetening was not ubiquitous as it is today, and even though sugar was still rationed in the couple of years after WWII, Bobby's mother always put enough real sugar in that ice cold Kool-Aid to make it taste really, really good to a hot, sweaty kid.

For good measure she'd bring out a couple of metal ice trays (no twist-plastic ones then) from the "ice box." They were actually refrigerators, but the nickname of their predecessors that were cooled with big blocks of ice was the name that stuck for quite awhile before it slipped away and "fridge" came into use, a generic shortening of General Motor's "Frigidaire." She'd pull up the metal lever that moved all the aluminum partitions separating the cubes and as they crackled loose, they'd squeak—the sound that meant "really cold." Then she'd pop a couple in each person's glass to make that sweet, refreshing liquid even colder. Mmmmmm.

A number of years later, after artificial sweeteners became a common sugar substitute and an inherent part of products in the 1960's, no matter how much ice you put in the glass, things tasted, well ... artificial. And for the record ... the *real* sugar did not rot the teeth out of any kid I knew.

In any event, our pugilistic rules didn't include weight classification. Instead, it was just a loose assessment concerning whether the smaller boxer would have any kind of chance in the match—an assessment made by the spectators, not the boxer. Comparatively, I wasn't very big in relation to my peers because my birthday was early in December, the cut-off month, which meant I was invariably one of the youngest, smallest kids in my class. My mother had the option to hold me out until the next year and then I would've been one of the older and bigger kids, but the Universe decided not to arrange my lessons that way.

Fortunately, the Universal Forces had given me something to compensate with. I was smart, very fast and had a naturally hard punch. The smart part helped a lot. I figured out quickly that in order to win, it was good to hit and not be hit, and when boxing against kids half-again my size, that was the only way I could survive.

Head gear, protective cup? Come on, get serious. They didn't use them in *real* amateur boxing then, and those were also the days when tackle football players just wore goofy leather helmets with almost no padding and no facemask. Our boxing matches eventually covered a span of years on into high school, and if at some point you got braces to straighten your teeth, like I did, the protective procedure was to be doubly careful, to include requesting that your opponent not hit you in the mouth. Whenever someone actually did get hurt during a match, he either declared the other guy the winner as he slowly collapsed, or he did everything in his power to retaliate.

My most memorable match was with Bobby after we reached high school. He had just hit me in the stomach and I was bent over gasping for air because it didn't feel so good. He made the error of leaning forward looking for another place to hit me. With my last retaliatory gasp I unloaded an uppercut, a punch initially disguised by my contorted form, and he never saw it. The ones you don't see coming are the worst.

Just like I remember Jerry's hands coming up to his face, Bobby's head snapped back, hair flying and stuff coming out of his nose. As it was my final Herculean effort and I was staggering away looking for a place to throw up, I don't remember him hitting the ground, but someone came over and told me they'd counted him out. After that, I came to the conclusion that trying to hurt my friends wasn't such a good idea, particularly friends like Bobby who'd been my neighbor since before we started kindergarten and the first person I'd met in the neighborhood. We had dinner a few years ago and he retold that incident. I claimed I didn't remember it. He's still bigger than I am and I wasn't looking for a rematch. That match with Bobby was my last *voluntary* boxing contest.

* * * *

8

Listening and Watching

If it weren't for Philo T. Farnsworth, inventor of television, we'd still be eating frozen radio dinners.

Johnny Carson

THE WAR FORMALLY ENDED SEPTEMBER 2, 1945, in front of General Douglas MacArthur by the signing of the Instrument of Surrender by the Japanese on the deck of the battleship Missouri (President Harry Truman's home state) anchored in Tokyo Bay. Home television had commercially started in the country shortly before the war, but production of television equipment for home use was banned during the war; thus, the industry was still in its consumer infancy at the war's end. In the fall of 1944, the nation's premier weekly photojournalism magazine, Life, had a feature article, "Television, the Next Great Development in Radio …," and the manufacturers and networks began to push hard immediately after the end of the war.

Through the next five years, affordable home television ramped up and ultimately exploded on the marketplace. It was very exciting, not only because we were originally a generation of "Radio Babies," but because we acquired (with some help from my grandparents) one of the first television sets on the block sometime in 1947, making me one of the most popular kids in the neighborhood. The abbreviation "TV" wasn't in use until a year or two later.

During that five-year period after the war, the number of television sets in American households went from fewer than 7,000 to 10.5 million and continued to grow, and grow, and grow. In those early years, owning a television set also meant a large television aerial that looked sort of like a down-sized five foot aluminum goal post fastened horizontally to the top of at least a five foot steel mast-pole bolted to the top of your house—a sign of being on the cutting edge of progress.

There was no option for the portable indoor "rabbit ears" antenna to sit on top of the set since they weren't generally available until just after the mid-1950's, but the roof-top antenna was imbued with a prestige factor, so no one thought they were unsightly in the beginning. After the novelty wore off in a few years, the sea of aluminum rooftop sentries pointing to the heavens were considered unconscionably ugly and now, of course, they're all but extinct in this country.

Our television set consisted of a very heavy gargantuan cabinet (an approximately three-foot wooden cube), little tiny screen, maybe seven inches (some were as small as three inches), and a huge liquid-filled magnifying glass hanging in front of it from a pole-like attachment. When we turned it on, the electronics made a big "klung" and a buzz. After the five minutes it took to warm up, we would watch the preliminary test pattern for hours through the magnifying glass, which increased the size of the picture to about twelve inches—if you were in just the right position.

TV was unreliable enough in those days that the test pattern for repairmen was continually broadcast each afternoon before the programming started in the evening. It was the head of an Indian Chief with headdress (long before anyone heard the term Native American) plus a bunch of circles, lines and numbers. The set had twelve channels, 2 through 13, on a round dial about two inches in diameter that mechanically clunked through the channels one at a time by simply turning it pretty hard. If you were on a low number and wanted a high numbered channel, you clunk, clunk, clunked all the way until you reached it. That doesn't mean there was broadcasting on each channel. There wasn't. At first there were only about three channels with something on them part time in the evening, at least for our part of the country. Some cities had only one or two.

Anyway, while I didn't like getting pounded on very much with those boxing gloves my dad sent, I loved the Sweet Science, particularly watching professionals trying to punch each other out. So, when television finally arrived for the masses, including us, I watched every match I could when TV started showing them in our area. By the time I was in high school, boxing was a well-known sport on TV, most of which was live as there was no videotape, and of course no digital technology, although some TV programs were "kinescoped" for rebroadcast, a technique of pointing a specialized movie camera at and filming a TV monitor, which resulted in an even worse quality picture.

Long before Sylvester Stallone made the "Rocky" movies, I can still remember the live rematch between Heavyweight Champion Rocky Marciano (the only heavyweight champ to retire undefeated at the end of his entire professional career) and Jersey Joe Walcott on the NBC *Gillette Cavalcade of Sports Friday Night Fights*, broadcast coast-to-coast which was a big deal in those days. At the opening of the Gillette programs, the bell would sound and the announcer (who was not Don Dunphy, the "Voice of Boxing," as many boxing fans of my generation now believe—he only did *Cavalcade* on the radio for NBC) would bellow in town-crier fashion, "Friday Night Fights are on the air!" Then, because it was black and white TV, often a black and white cartoon parrot would start playing the guitar and a male voice would start singing a jingle urging everyone, or at least men, to look sharp, feel sharp and be sharp with Gillette's Blue Blades. For reasons known only to the parrot, it would switch to the upright string bass and the commercial would end.

The Blue Blades were blades with a razor edge on each side—double-edged, "20 blades, 40 shaving edges." That was before safety razors and they forgot to add to the commercial, "Stick 'em in the razor and slice yourself, neat and easy." Styptic "pencils" were a medical staple in every shaving kit, but the sting of dabbing them on a razor cut was more painful than the injury, so most razor wielders chose to stick tiny pieces of toilet paper on the cuts for awhile until they stopped bleeding.

When the bell rang for the first round of that Marciano-Walcott rematch, a fifteen-round marathon, the standard length of a championship fight in those days, I was in the kitchen rushing to amass all my potato chips (there was only one flavor—potato chip) and a soda pop (my beverage of choice while watching television boxing was a nice cold bottle of Royal Crown Cola). I managed to get everything in my arms at once, juggled it the five steps into the living room toward the end of the first round and started settling in front of the TV. Just as I looked down to make sure I didn't spill anything, Rocky knocked Jersey Joe out. All I heard was the roar of the crowd and all I saw when I jerked my head up was Walcott flat on his back with his feet in the air. No instant replay or TiVo ® DVR then and I waited over 30 years for Classic Fights on cable TV in order to see how it happened.

A couple of years before that fight, while Rocky was still a contender and not yet champ, he fought then-former Heavyweight Champion Joe Louis, the great "Brown Bomber," who had then been retired as champ for a couple of years, following a fifteen year career that included defending his title successfully for close to twelve years and all twenty five times it was challenged (a record that stands today).

Joe is thought by many to be both the hardest puncher (in his prime) ever to don a pair of boxing gloves, as well as the greatest heavyweight champion of all time (with sincere apologies to Muhammad Ali). Without dispute, he has been America's greatest boxing hero ever since his legendary *second* fight with the German fighter, Max Schmeling. In their first fight at Yankee Stadium before Louis became the champ, Schmeling knocked Louis out in the 12th round. At that point in his young career, it was Louis' first and only professional defeat.

Joe was determined never to let that happen again, and during the subsequent two-year run-up to his second fight with Schmeling, Joe became the World Heavyweight Champion (there was only one in those days, not several as generated by the alphabet-soup hype of various sanctioning organizations these days). During that same period of time, Adolf Hitler's power in then Nazi-party dominated Germany was reaching the apex of its jackbooted insanity as he persecuted Jews while setting the European stage for the Second World War. Thus, as a result of the first fight, Hitler was arrogantly holding a reluctant Max Schmeling out as a symbol of the Nazi's so-called "Aryan master race" who would crush Joe Louis in the second match, conveniently overlooking that two months after the first fight, the phenomenal African-American track star, Jesse Owens, "The Buckeye Bullet," won four gold medals at the Berlin Olympics (with Hitler refusing to shake his hand), and also that Max Schmeling's American promoter was Jewish.

The second fight with Schmeling was also at the home of the Yankees and being broadcast on radio all over the world in four languages, including German. Joe stepped into the ring at a packed Yankee Stadium knowing all of America was counting on him, including President Roosevelt who met with him personally about the fight. Louis knocked Schmeling out in just over two minutes of the 1st round. When Schmeling went to the canvas for the third time in the round, his corner threw a white towel into the ring and surrendered. The referee didn't bother to count. However, Germany didn't get to listen to that part. Hitler had ordered the broadcast cut off at the first sign Schmeling was in trouble.

But, as is perhaps too often the case with "retired" boxers, Joe had been trying to make a comeback thirteen years later at the point he fought the much younger Rocky Marciano. A sad Rocky not only knocked out America's hero, he knocked his boyhood boxing idol through the ropes and out of the ring in the process. It was only the second time in his career the Brown Bomber had ever been knocked out. A generation of fight fans knew in their hearts that was Joe's last fight. For them, it was the night the music died.

Some years later, when Joe finally went back "home," Army Sergeant Joseph Louis Barrow was buried in Arlington National Cemetery. A pall bearer at his funeral was a gentleman who had become his good friend after WWII, a friend who had helped hide Jewish children from the Nazis in Berlin, who had steadfastly refused to join the Nazi party, and who had refused to accept an award from Hitler—Max Schmeling.

There were other very popular contact sports on TV too. One of my favorites was *Roller Derby*, with teams that were composed of men and women who alternated time periods skating against their own sex. The fans sat very close to the banked wooden track about 100 feet long and 50 feet wide. It was surrounded by low guard rails that were only marginally successful in keeping the skaters, on quad-skates (no inline skates in those days), from being knocked into the crowd during the roller free-for-all. Each team tried to block and knock down opposing players in order to get past them and score points. This spawned smack-down, drag-out hockey-like brawls that accelerated the spectacle to one of the most popular on television with idolized male and female stars on every team, none of whom missed a punching opportunity. My favorite teams were the New York Chiefs, Jersey Jolters, Brooklyn Red Devils and the San Francisco Bay Bombers.

Speaking of smack-downs, while that term didn't come into use until much later, professional wrestling is the contact sport that's most often credited with truly popularizing television at the beginning of its Golden Age. An usher at my church also ushered at the weekly pro-wrestling matches downtown and he'd get me in to see them from time to time. I got to see my favorite TV wrestling stars in person. I thought it was terrific even though it was light years removed from the angry, killer-like, human-growth-hormone spectacle it is today. By comparison, it was gentlemanly then. It even seemed like they were actually wrestling. My favorites were the bleached-blond Gorgeous George, the athletic, bare-footed, high-flying Antonio "Argentine" Rocca, and the "legit" Lou Thesz.

Rocca was a heavyweight at six feet and 225 pounds, kind of puny by today's supplement-standards. He transitioned from soccer in Argentina, a mysterious and unknown sport in America, and delighted audiences by jumping up and slapping his opponents in the face with both his bare feet simultaneously and then taking them down in his "pretzel hold," or by disorienting them with the "airplane spin" while holding them face-up on their backs across his shoulders and then forcing them to submit by pulling down on their extremities from that position in the "Argentine backbreaker."

Lou Thesz, another 225 pounder, was legitimately gifted as a pure wrestler and won almost every heavyweight wrestling title he ever competed for. He's generally regarded as the last undisputed pro-wrestling heavyweight champion of the twentieth century and was highly respected as a true gentleman, even after downing an opponent with his "flying head scissors."

Gorgeous George, at 5'9" and 210 pounds, was the wrestler everyone loved to hate. As wrestler George Wagner with short, dark hair, he couldn't get noticed in a women's locker room. So, he effected an effeminate manner, grew his hair long, bleached it platinum, curled and set it with gold bobby pins he'd ultimately give to the ladies in the audience, drove a purple Cadillac, originated the grand, lengthy, music-accompanied ring-entrance we see so much of today in wrestling and boxing, entered on a red carpet strewn with rose petals while wearing long, flowing, sequined and fur-trimmed robes, infuriated his opponents and the referee by having his valet spray his corner and them with perfume-laced "disinfectant," blatantly cheated in his matches, and made disparaging comments to the audience. Thus, he was extremely popular and set the original and revolutionary gold standard for gaudy showmanship. They say he sold as many television sets in TV's Golden Age as "Uncle Miltie"—Mr. Television, Milton Berle.

But, I've time-warped. Before families had TV, we Radio Babies loved our radio shows, a number of which either started from or later became comic books. Some also became films and, a few years later, moved into television when it became available. But when it was *only* listening, we routinely referred to them as radio "shows" because in our imaginations, we could see everything that was happening.

For example, in shows like *Let's Pretend* sponsored by Cream of Wheat, "It's so good to eat," where the "Pretenders" traveled a different way each week to many adventures, my personal favorite was getting there on the flying magic carpet. Also, *Smilin' Ed's Buster Brown Gang*, "Plunk your magic twanger, Froggy, (boing)," and then my favorite character, Froggy the Gremlin, would greet us in his froggy voice, "Hiya kids, hiya, hiya," followed by Buster Brown, (bark, bark—a dog, not Buster), "That's my dog Tige, he lives in a shoe, I'm Buster Brown, look for me in there too," (bark). Then, since there were no websites then, the announcer told the kids to have their mothers look in the "classified section" of the local phone book for the nearest Buster Brown shoe store. Of course, the classified or business section of the phone book has generically been called the "yellow pages" for decades now because it's been printed on yellow paper to distinguish it from the residential phone numbers printed on white paper.

As a little kid, my mother wouldn't let me listen to *Gang Busters*, the original true-crime radio show with a twenty-one year run reenacting real Federal Bureau of Investigation case histories approved by long-time F.B.I. Director, J. Edgar Hoover. They were narrated by chiefs of law enforcement agencies from around the country, and during the show, real alerts were broadcast for criminals wanted in the United States by the police. It was the Godfather of all the subsequent real crime shows including

Dragnet, Texas Rangers and the current widely-viewed television program, John Walsh's *America's Most Wanted.*

So, cut off from *Gang Busters* at a tender age, my radio fare, and my favorite local radio show, was *Uncle Whoa-Bill.* On the air on your birthday, he'd tell you where to look for your present. I was stunned when I heard him say my name and he told me to look in the broom closet in the service porch. Incredibly, it was there! That almost made up for the failure to catch Santa Claus at Christmas the year before. Both experiences involved a kindly deception. In the case of Uncle Whoa-Bill, mothers would surreptitiously write to him with the info in advance, a non-prosecutable non-disclosure kept among Bill and the moms.

We had cowboys on the radio too. *Tom Mix* (Tony the Wonder Horse) and the Straight Shooter Club. The *Cisco Kid* riding Diablo, "The famous Robin Hood of the Old West," with Cisco yelling, "This way Pancho, vamanos!" and Pancho followed with his horse, Loco. Of course, the legendary *Lone Ranger* with his gorgeous white stallion, Silver, "Hi ho, Silver, awaaaay," and his faithful companion, Tonto, riding Scout, "Gittum-up, Scout!" "Return with us now to those thrilling days of yesteryear ... The Lone Ranger Rides Again!" followed by the final charge of Rosinni's "William Tell Overture." Cowboys were *in* the air also. *Sky King* was a cowboy pilot and the uncle of Penny and Clipper. They flew around the Flying Crown Ranch in Songbird, capturing criminals, spies and rescuing lost hikers. The program announcer was a young Mike Wallace who ultimately became an extremely well-known news journalist for CBS.

Of course, there was *Roy Rogers,* the "King of the Cowboys," with his beautiful Palomino, Trigger, "Good bye, good luck and may the good Lord take a likin' to ya," sponsored by Goodyear Tires, which was weird for a guy who rode a horse. Roy was a charter member of the Sons of the Pioneers that had hits such as "Cool Water" and "Tumbling Tumbleweeds." His third wife was *Dale Evans* and he was her fourth husband but, singing their duet "Happy Trails," their marriage lasted more than 50 years until "death do us part."

Dale Evans with her horse, Buttermilk, became the "Queen of the West" and the most popular female Western-movie star of all time. Of course, we shouldn't forget Roy's semi-toothless movie sidekick, Gabby Hayes.

With apologies to Roy, there was also *Gene Autry*, "America's Favorite Cowboy," and his horse, the white-star faced Champion. In his early days he was originally Oklahoma's Yodeling Cowboy before becoming the Singing Cowboy who crooned "Back in the Saddle Again" each week at his Melody Ranch, sponsored by Wrigley's Doublemint Chewing Gum. Among many other achievements, Gene wrote "Here Comes Santa Claus," popularized "Rudolph the Red Nosed Reindeer," owned radio and television stations and ultimately owned Major League Baseball's California Angels.

Captain Marvel, the alter ego of Billy Batson, wasn't on the radio, but *Superman*, the alter-ego of that mild-mannered reporter, Clark Kent, was on the airwaves fighting for "Truth, Justice and the American Way." We all know by now that Superman was, "Faster than a speeding bullet ... Able to leap tall buildings with a single bound! Look! Up in the sky ...." The Man of Steel's radio programs included a number of episodes with *Batman and Robin*, but interestingly enough, Batman never did have his own radio show. Then there was the non-building-leaping *Jack Armstrong*, "The All-American Boy," the crime-fighting student from Hudson High who ate "Wheaties, the Breakfast of Champions."

One of my all-time favorites was *Captain Midnight* (Big-Ben-like-clock bongs and the roar of an airplane's engines through the sky), "Caaaaaaaptaaain Miiidniiiiiiiiight!" He flew around busting crime in his twin engine plane, sponsored by Chocolate Flavored Ovaltine. I was a member of his Secret Squadron (formerly the Flight Patrol when it was sponsored by the Skelly Oil Company) and loved the premiums that came with that privilege, like the Mystery Dial Code-o-graph with its turnable dial that would decipher the scrambled letters of secret messages given on the radio, and the Whirlwind Whistling Ring that had a siren in the crown I could blow and summon help from the other Squadron members, plus my favorite, the Mystic Eye Detector Ring with a mirror in the crown so I could hold it up to my eye and see anyone attempting a dastardly deed by sneaking up behind me. I went outside and blew into my siren ring once, but no Squadron members showed. I guess Bobby wasn't home that day.

Then, *Challenge of the Yukon* (later to become *Sergeant Preston of the Yukon*) with the dog-sledding Sergeant Preston of the Royal Canadian Mounted Police and his trusty dog, Yukon King, "On King, on you huskies," sponsored by Quaker Puffed Wheat and Puffed Rice. And, the man who had "the mysterious power to cloud men's minds," *The Shadow*, played at one time by a young Orson Welles, "Who knows what evil lurks in the hearts of men? The Shadow knows!" (followed by a sinister chuckle). He intimidated criminals and solved crimes with the help of his love-interest, Margot Lane, played for awhile by the wonderful actress, Agnes Moorehead.

Also announced by Mike Wallace for a period, *The Green Hornet*, with his faithful sidekick, Kato. The Green Hornet was the fictional grand nephew of the Lone Ranger, and the Hornet theme was Korsakov's "Flight of the Bumblebee" blended with a hornet buzz created by that eerily-weird, electronic musical instrument, the Theremin. Then, from the Far East foreign-intrigue comic strip originally created by Milton Caniff, there was *Terry and the Pirates* with Terry's nemesis, that not-so-nice Asian femme fatale, the Dragon Lady, perhaps the greatest female villain of the comics and radio, voiced in one of her iterations by Agnes Moorehead again, and sponsored by Quaker, "Here comes Quaker with a bang-bang," and Quaker Puffed Rice Sparkies, "The rice shot from guns."

Later, coming simultaneously on radio and the then-relatively-new television, was *Space Patrol*, "Spaaaaaace Paaaaatrol" with Commander Buzz Corey and his sidekick, Cadet Happy, "Smokin' rockets, Buzz!"—sponsored by Wheat Chex and Rice Chex.

As a Space Patroller, I wondered what it would be like to have a Spacophone and an Atomolight.

In the evenings and on weekends, my mother, along with Shirley and me, listened to programs that included *Fibber McGee and Molly*, sponsored by Johnson's Wax, with their closet of avalanching contents that Fibber would open every week against Molly's admonition not to do it, and their cast of characters including the pompously-likeable neighbor, Throckmorton P. Gildersleeve (Harold Peary) who ultimately spun off into his own show.

We also loved *Jack Benny*, "Well … frankly …," violin playing (poorly), vain, stingy and perennially 39 years old, with the laughs coming at his expense, and his chauffeur Rochester (Eddie Anderson), his friend Mary Livingstone (her stage name and Benny's real-life wife), the somewhat rotund Don Wilson announcing, and the following folks who all spun off from Benny's show into their own shows, young Irish singer Dennis Day, comic voice-virtuoso Mel Blanc (the "Man of a Thousand Voices" including the recalcitrant motor in Benny's car, and well known for the voices of Bugs Bunny, Porky Pig, Daffy Duck and Tweety Bird in cartoons), and hipster bandleader-singer Phil Harris ("Oh, you dawg!") who spun into a show with his blonde, singing, movie-star wife, Alice Faye.

If you liked Jack Benny, you also liked Benny's good friend, but comedically his long-time feuding rival, *Fred Allen*, with his topical, satiric humor, doing the show with his real-life wife, Portland, who played his wife on the show (a la George Burns & Gracie Allen and the younger Ozzie & Harriet Nelson), with the most popular feature being Allen's Alley which, during his sojourn down that narrow thoroughfare, included characters such as the blowhard Senator Claghorn, Mrs. Nussbaum and Titus Moody ("Howdy, bub").

The banjo-eyed comedian whose radio popularity hit even before Benny, Allen, Bob Hope and Bing Crosby, to name a few, was *Eddie Cantor*, "We want Cantor! We want Cantor!" who popularized the tune, "Makin' Whoopee!" His show made stars out of Jimmy Durante, the great Schnozzola with his trademark song, "Inka Dinka Doo," as well as ventriloquist Edgar Bergen (father of actress Candice Bergen) with Charlie McCarthy on his knee (just think of it, a ventriloquist on the radio).

Each week at the end of his show, Eddie sang his sign-off line "I love to spend each Sunday with you." Of course, while Eddie had popularized "Makin' Whoopee," he didn't sing it quite like Michelle Pfeiffer did a number of years later in her Oscar nominated, Golden Globe winning, sultry, top-of-the-piano, room-paralyzing, film rendition of it in *The Fabulous Baker Boys* (1989). In his hey-day, Eddie Cantor was the top-rated radio personality in America and essentially the second most recognizable person in the country after then-President Franklin Delano Roosevelt whose mobility was severely affected by infantile paralysis.

Infantile Paralysis was the early synonym for polio, the dreaded crippling childhood disease of more than the first half of the twentieth century, but not necessarily confined to children. Doctors believed it was the virus that was the cause of FDR's legs becoming paralyzed when he was 39, eleven years before he was elected president. Eddie Cantor was instrumental in raising research and treatment funds for the National Foundation for Infantile Paralysis which President Roosevelt helped found. Eddie urged his listeners to send their spare dimes to the White House. Children and adults sent them by the millions and Eddie coined the fundraising phrase "March of Dimes," which ultimately became the organization's name. In April 1945, Roosevelt died during his fourth term in office, a little over four months before the end of World War II. His likeness was placed on the U.S. dime in early 1946.

In the late 1950's, seventeen years after the Foundation's beginning, it was announced that the revolutionary polio vaccine discovered by Dr. Jonas Salk through research substantially funded by the Foundation would become publicly available. Within two years polio cases dropped 85-90%. Several years later Albert Sabin's vaccine that could be taken orally, instead of injected, was also licensed, and between the two vaccines, the once-dreaded paralyzing disease was eliminated in the United States and has been in other countries that also have continuing vaccination programs.

We also looked forward to the *Lux Radio Theatre* once a week, sponsored by Lux Soap, with famed director Cecil B. DeMille as the original host of its lavish radio productions of Hollywood movies. The films' movie stars played the parts, live and with a full orchestra, for example, Frank Capra's *It's a Wonderful Life* with Jimmy Stewart and Donna Reed. And, there was *One Man's Family*, radio's longest-running serial soap opera (but not sponsored by soap), or as they would have put it, the longest-running radio novel. Of course, *Guiding Light* was the longest-running continuous "soap" when you add TV, but it was on radio a shorter period of time than One Man's Family. Speaking of soap, our small kitchen utilized a lot of glasses and dish towels that came in boxes of soap powder, probably one or more of Rinso, Oxydol, Lux or Duz.

We got a big kick out of what was, essentially, radio's first family situation comedy, *The Life of Riley* starring William Bendix, "What a revoltin' development this is!" It dealt with the daily comedy of the life of aircraft-factory worker Chester A. Riley's family and their neighbors, all growing up in a wartime and postwar America. It set the stage for and was soon followed by *The Adventures of Ozzie and Harriet*, along with their sons David and Ricky, the real-life names of the quintessential all-American family. Those great old radio shows and stars are legion, including *Duffy's Tavern*, Jack Carson, Bob Hope, George Burns and Gracie Allen, Art Linkletter's *People are Funny*, Red Skelton, Kate Smith, Groucho Marx, Bing Crosby and many, many others. Just like the kid's shows, many of those shows or their stars migrated to television in its nascent years.

Some shows or stars, kids, puppets or otherwise, were first known on television instead of radio. They included the incredibly popular, *The Howdy Doody Show* ("It's Howdy Doody Time") started in 1947. Its characters included Buffalo Bob, Chief

Thunderthud (who originated "Kowabonga!") and was Chief of the Ooragnak Tribe (Kangaroo spelled backward), Clarabell the Clown played by Bob Keeshan who ultimately became Captain Kangaroo (Ooragnak spelled backward) on his own show, Princess Summerfall Winterspring and, of course, the next All-American Boy (radio's Jack Armstrong being the first), the red-headed, freckle-faced, perpetually-smiling marionette, Howdy Doody, one of the several inhabitants of Doodyville, which also included Double Doody. Parental complaints of violence on the show centered around Clarabell the Clown who did pratfalls and often brandished or fired a weapon, the seltzer bottle. Lordy, the Complaint Brigade was in full swing then too.

Additionally, there was the very popular TV show that included two puppets and one person in the middle, *Kukla, Fran & Ollie*. Other mostly-non-puppet shows were *Kraft Television Theatre*, *Meet the Press*, *The Ed Sullivan Show* (originally *Toast of the Town*), the incredibly popular comedian Milton Berle (*Texaco Star Theater*), "The Great One"—Jackie Gleason (*The Honeymooners*), Arthur Godfrey, *Omnibus* hosted by Alistair Cooke, *Today* with Dave Garroway and his theme song, "Sentimental Journey" (the first network early morning show), the *Hallmark Hall of Fame*, and the terrific *I Love Lucy* with Lucille Ball and Desi Arnaz, filmed in front of a live audience for later broadcast.

Also, the incredibly popular *Queen for a Day* with host Jack Bailey and the audience applause meter which determined which down-trodden, misfortunate, pathos-evoking contestant would win, a timeless theme even today. Then *Gunsmoke* and *Bonanza* and the list seems endless, but two highly recognizable "individuals" on early television were Betty Furness who did commercials for Westinghouse for over eleven years, and the cartoon character, Elsie the Borden Cow, who beat out an actor and a senator as one of America's most recognizable faces.

Currently still with us is *The Tonight Show*, which started as *Tonight* with comedian Steve Allen who predicted it would last forever. Allen was followed by a number of hosts, the most prominent of which were Jack Paar, and then "Heeeere's Johnny" Carson for thirty years (and they began calling it *The Tonight Show*). Carson started out "hosting" his own very funny local Los Angeles sketch-comedy show called *Carson's Cellar*, which I loved to watch, never dreaming of the magnitude of his future celebrity. Johnny was followed by Jay Leno who completed an approximately seventeen year run as host, and the show continues with Conan O'Brien. So far, Steve Allen is right.

* * * *

9

Triangles

I have a lot to learn … I'm also annoying.

Jenna Morasca

When I was 11 and in the 6th grade, my sister was three years older than I. She still is. It used to bother me, but now I'm okay with it. At 14, she was in the last year of junior high, which ran three years from 7th through 9th grade in our school system, and she had a boyfriend named Cliff who had a Salsbury motor scooter—a used, dented, organgish-red, 6hp beauty with a boat-tail rear end and sleek cowled front. For some strange reason our state legislators allowed 14 year old kids to procure a license to ride motor scooters on the street. Cliff would come put-putting up to the house with his leather jacket on, his immobile pompadour oiled up with Wildroot Cream-Oil and the rest of his hair slicked back into a duck tail, the style of the day and, with that much grease, it was like a granite helmet in the wind. He was about the coolest guy I knew. I couldn't understand why he had any interest in my sister. My mother wasn't thrilled either and refused to let Shirley ride on the scooter, but she would let me. I've always wondered about that.

Since Shirley continually found me annoying, I had a role to fulfill. I followed them everywhere when he was at the house.

What annoyed them most was following them when they would walk down the street at dusk holding hands. My usual distance was about fifteen feet behind, and one night, just as darkness was surrounding us, Cliff turned and motioned for me to come up to them. Thrilled that I was finally included, I rushed up and was promptly punched in the nose. I was so surprised, I don't remember whether it hurt or not. I do remember lying on the ground as they disappeared into the evening.

I didn't follow them anymore after that. I'm pretty sure I learned that lesson without the help of the Universal Forces. Then Cliff told me he was sorry he hit me and let me ride his motor scooter by myself down the block and back. It was scary, but I loved the incredible energy of that six horsepower engine. Cliff and I kind of became friends. I'm pretty sure that's why my sister dumped him.

When Shirley got into high school, she had two friends her age who lived next door to each other on the next street over, Ronnie and Alan. They were geeks, really smart and funny geeks. They constructed a radio transmitter in Ronnie's bedroom. It was amazingly powerful and they did their own broadcasts from it for a short time until their parents made them stop because they were certain they needed a license to do that. Even though the broadcasts terminated, that didn't stop them from having fun.

There was a very powerful radio station in Clint, Texas, a town in West Texas of about 500 people at the intersection of a railroad track, a state highway and a farm road, about 20 miles southeast of El Paso. The station had a broadcasting antenna that stuck up about two miles into the air, I think. During the day, its broadcasting power was pretty regular, but starting in the evening, it could legally jack up its wattage to something rivaling the power of Flash Gordon's ray gun which, I'm certain, if fired from my front porch could have put out the eye of Ming the Merciless standing on the planet Mongo. I don't think there was anyone west of the Mississippi, and maybe in the country for all I know, who hadn't heard that station, particularly after sunset. The deep Texas twangs of the announcers beat the drum for everything imaginable, including many religious products. They even played a record every once in awhile.

In any event, Ronnie and Alan would warm up their transmitter after supper and listen to that station, waiting for just the right moment in a commercial. It would be right after the announcer had directed the listener to send money in care of the station for a religious-related product. In the momentary silence that followed, either Ronnie or Alan, taking turns broadcasting from Ronnie's bedroom on the Clint, Texas station's frequency, would say in a hilarious Texas accent, "and also receive an au-tee-graphed foe-toe of Jee-sus Christ!" It just took a couple of seconds each time one of them did it, so the parents didn't catch on and the boys figured they'd never get caught.

After a few weeks, a big black sedan with a large rotatable antenna on top began frequenting the neighborhood in the evenings, parking in various places with two men inside rotating the antenna while, from time to time, laughing hysterically and pounding on the dashboard. Come to find out, the Clint, Texas, station had received a large number of unhappy complaints from listeners inquiring after the whereabouts of their autographed picture. So, the G-Men were sent to triangulate that illegitimate broadcast miscreated without the benefit of license.

Of course, the feds nailed the high-school perps and after the parents supervised the process of their sons dismantling the transmitting equipment, including the removal of the antenna they had secreted at the top of the huge tree in Ronnie's back yard, all in front of the G-Men, plus a promise from the boys never to do it again, coupled with the obviously-sincere parental assurances that the young men were grounded for the next six months, the feds were satisfied and left, still chuckling.

Who knows, Ronnie and Alan may have spawned the earliest version of electronic hacking. I don't know where they are now, but Shirley suspects they may be the true brains behind Microsoft.

10

Journalistic Bombardiers

Every instructor assumes that you have nothing else to do except study ...

Fourth Law of Applied Terror

On the subject of youthful exuberance and trouble, Tucker and I met early in grammar school and we goofed around together a lot through the grades, both during and after school. The *second*-to-the-worst trouble we got into at Lincoln Elementary wasn't really our fault. It resulted from unintended consequences while we were in the 5th grade. Striking out as young entrepreneurs, Tucker and I published a mimeographed newspaper with school news and gossip, selling it for a penny. Our first, our only, issue was quite a success because we published a featured human-interest article on our 5th grade teacher, Miss Thompson, who was young, very attractive, very nice, very popular and on whom every boy in the 5th and 6th grade had a crush. Since she was always happy to answer our questions in class, we felt certain she'd be pleased to answer anyone's questions at any time and, in passing, included her home telephone number.

On the third morning after publication and perhaps an aggregate of forty calls from students received by Miss Thompson at home in the previous two evenings, we were summoned to the

Principal's office and instructed to bring any remaining copies of the newspaper, together with the mimeograph master we'd so laboriously typed, one peck at a time, making very few mistakes on the non-erasable stencil (no whipping it out on the computer and hitting "print" in those days).

After he committed the atrocity of ripping our remaining papers and the mimeograph stencil in half before our very eyes, Mr. Quick commended our enterprising nature while explaining several things to us. One, the publishing of Miss Thompson's home phone number was an unacceptable error on our part. Two, we could not sell or distribute a newspaper on school grounds. Three, if we ever did anything like that again on the school grounds, or off school grounds if it included a teacher's personal information, our lives would be very unhappy. Even though our journalistic careers had been substantially shredded, we steadfastly hung true to our principles and refused to tell him how we got Miss Thompson's phone number.

Today, the whole matter would have a life of its own, litigating its way up to the U.S. Supreme Court at no cost to us through the largess of several non-profit corporations fulfilling their missions of protecting our rights, real or desired. We'd have lots of sympathetic TV exposure for awhile and the media would make an immediate shambles out of Mr. Quick's and Miss Thompson's lives, as well as those of our parents. Years later, about the time Miss Thompson would be getting ready to retire after marrying, having four children and seven grandchildren, a final Supreme Court decision would be coming down—maybe.

So anyway, several months later when Tucker and I reached 6th grade, in the first semester of our last year at Lincoln Elementary, we were both in Mr. Wilson's class and the *worst* trouble we got into wasn't really our fault either. It occurred because a maintenance ladder to the roof had been left up for at least a month at the back of the cafeteria. Reconnoitering, we climbed up one weekend and decided the flat roof surrounded by a parapet was perfect for tossing water balloons off and then ducking down behind the parapet wall which was about three feet high. We practiced on ourselves at Tucker's house and the big ones really stung when they hit, so we retained enough presence of mind to get relatively small balloons so no one would be hurt. Besides, they were easier to throw.

Furthering our plan, Tucker retrieved two of his older brother's abandoned canvas newspaper-route bags from his garage. A route bag had open saddlebags for carrying folded newspapers on each side, connected with a piece of canvas in the middle, designed so you could either put it over the rear fender rack of a bicycle or stick your head through a hole in the canvas and wear it like a sandwich board. Some kids put them over their handlebars, but the weight of a full load of papers made steering a little dicey, which in turn made it tougher to pump the pedals on our heavy, less-than-fancy, balloon-tired, one-speed steeds.

Anyway, the next Thursday after school, we packed each route bag with the maximum number of small water balloons filled to the bursting point, a matter on which we had become experts, rode them precariously on our bikes to the back of the cafeteria after everyone had left, stuck our heads through the center holes of the bags, which were really heavy, and struggled up the forgotten ladder to the roof, leaving the bags there and creeping away.

On Friday when the final bell rang, we sprinted to the cafeteria, scrambled up the ladder and over to the bags, taking care to duck down behind the parapet. It was perfect. All the kids had to walk past the cafeteria to reach the main entrance and leave. However, the identification risk was too great to look over the roof and aim, so we decided we would just lie on our backs and lob them over the parapet since the sea of bodies had to come down the walkway in any event. We waited for the first wave and lobbed several over, rapid fire and high so they'd all be in the air before the first one hit.

The screams and yelling started. They couldn't tell where it was coming from and they couldn't hear our laughter over their own commotion. It was great. We pelted wave after wave of kids that way. Pandemonium would ensue and we could hear them running toward the main gate trying to get out of launching range of wherever the balloons were coming from. That played right into our hands. The next wave coming around the corner was always unsuspecting.

When we'd lobbed the last balloon, we grabbed the route bags and sprinted for the ladder, intending to disappear like the infamous Shadow. No ladder sticking up. We thought maybe in our euphoria we'd forgotten where it was and ran back and forth on the roof at the back parapet. Panicked, we looked over. In his slacks, white shirt and tie, Mr. Wilson was standing there smiling, but not a really friendly smile. It was a 'gotcha' smile.

Silently, he put the ladder back up and beckoned to us. After we descended, he watched while we picked up every minuscule scrap of rubber from all the broken balloons, putting them in the route bags around our necks. It took a long time. He told us to tell our parents that we'd be staying late after school for the next couple of weeks, and have them contact him if they had any questions. We told them we were playing softball after school. The last thing we wanted was for them to find out, since retribution would be rapid and effective.

For the next two weeks, each day after we finished sweeping the classroom, emptying the wastebaskets, cleaning the blackboards and picking up all the papers around the outside of our classroom's wooden bungalow, we'd go back in and fill the blackboards with a sentence suggested by Mr. Wilson, "I apologize for throwing water balloons on my unsuspecting schoolmates." That would be left up through the next morning until the class finished the Pledge of Allegiance and then we'd erase the blackboards.

We were overjoyed that our parents never found out. We'd have been grounded for a minimum of a month, tacked on to Mr. Wilson's exercises. (Today Mr. Wilson's discipline would generate a lawsuit by the perpetrators' parents against the school for such an abuse against their poor little boys who certainly shouldn't suffer such severe punishment for bombarding their classmates with premeditated glee.) At a point during our blackboard writings, Tucker and I jointly decided we never wanted to see another water balloon for the rest of our lives, and saw no reason why we would.

Just before the end of that semester, Mr. Wilson advised the class that we were going to celebrate it by having a water balloon fight the last day and to dress appropriately. He'd supply the balloons and the water. Then he looked at the two of us and smiled. If the maintenance guy just hadn't left that ladder up in the first place.

I know that the Universal Forces put a broader lesson in there, but I wasn't paying attention and it would take several more arrangements of events until I did.

* * * *

11

We Want You

Be Prepared ... by previous thinking out ... how to act in any emergency so that [you are] never taken by surprise.

Robert Baden-Powell
Founder of Scouting

I WAS A CUB SCOUT while in grammar school. I'd joined at the beginning of the fourth grade and Mrs. Trimble, who lived a couple blocks over, had always been my Den Mother. I promised "to do my best" and made many things out of bars of soap in her backyard while preparing for my future in the Boy Scouts, which was every good Cub's goal. That would apparently come to fruition in the second semester of 6th grade because we learned toward the end of that school year that the next Friday evening, the Boy Scouts were going to put on an evening presentation in Lincoln Elementary's auditorium-lunch room to entice us to join them.

I thought that peculiar since I'd been programmed to become a Boy Scout ever since I started Cubs three years before with my dark blue shirt, little blue beanie-like billed-cap with yellow piping and wolf logo, and my yellow neckerchief with wolf-cub slide to hold it around the outside of the collar of my shirt, but no Cub pants. Being wartime when I'd started, regulation Cub pants weren't available in my area. What the war had to do with

Cub pants wasn't clear to me. We saved scrap iron, rubber and newspapers, but not pants.

In any event, no enticement was necessary to attract me to the Boy Scouts, but I'd heard they were going to put on an Indian snake dance with real snakes, which I thought incredibly brave, and I was anxious to see it. All the boys were invited and most of them in the 6th grade, together with their parents, were going to be there. It was a big deal.

I got there plenty early so I could get one of the folding chairs in the middle of the first row, right in front of the stage. The Boy Scouts were there, all spiffed up with their khaki uniforms, red neckerchiefs and lots and lots of merit badges all over their merit-badge sashes. Very impressive, particularly the mature Scouts who were in high school. Slung over their shoulders and chests like bandoleers, their sashes seemed to be made entirely out of merit badges.

The auditorium was jammed. There were many introductions, three-fingered Boy Scout salutes (Cubs could only salute with two) and talks about how terrific it was to be a Boy Scout and how it prepared you for life, all of which I already believed, but I wanted to see the snake dance with the live snakes, which they left for last because they knew it was the *pièce de résistance.*

Finally, they rearranged the stage, removing the chairs, flags and displays, and setting up a couple of teepees, a fake campfire and some fake bushes, leaving space in the middle for the snake dancers. I pulled my chair forward right up to the stage, which was just the right height so I could put my elbows on it and rest my chin in my hands. This was great—right on top of the action.

A tom-tom beat started from off-stage somewhere—BOOM boom boom boom, BOOM boom boom boom, and then the Indians came out. Well, they were Scouts with reddish-brown paint all over their bodies, war paint on their faces, leather loin cloth things which I thought were kind of gross, black wigs with pigtails, and barefooted. There were two of them and only one had a snake. They were making Indian yells and jumping around, doing toe-heel steps which looked kind of like the ones I'd seen

Indians do in the cowboy movies, and generally making a lot of noise. I didn't know anything about production values then, but it seemed pretty lame. Of course many years later, it would also be pretty politically incorrect.

Notwithstanding that we'd been more imaginative during our playing of Cowboys and Indians in the neighborhood, I got swept up in it after awhile—just five feet away from the action with my chin on my hands, the constant beat of that invisible drum and mesmerized by the guy with the snake. I didn't know much about snakes except if they bit you, the poison would kill you within three minutes unless someone sliced you open and sucked most of your blood out, and then you'd almost die anyway.

The fearless way this guy was handling the snake was a marvel to behold, like he wasn't afraid of being bitten at all. The thing was about three feet long and looked like a killer to me. You could tell the climax was coming. They really started yelling and jumping and the drum was going faster and faster and louder and louder, and then the guy started swinging the snake around his head. He had hold of it right behind its head and was swinging it around so it was virtually out straight. That, combined with the circle's arc, put the end of the snake about a foot from my face every time it came around.

I was certain all eyes were on my back to see if I'd flinch. I thought the "Indian" with the snake was actually trying to get me to flinch too. So, I made up my mind that even if it flew out of his hand and fastened itself to my nose, I would not move. It was the first, but not the only, time in my life I decided I'd rather die than look like a fool. Well, the snake didn't come out of his hand, but its contents came out of it, suddenly and without a hint of gastric distress. It relieved itself all over my face. I've always been a mouth breather too.

I've pushed out of my mind whether or not any of my friends became Boy Scouts. I had liked the idea of joining an organization of my peers with common interests, but found I rapidly lost interest in groups that crapped on me.

12

It's a Dry Heat

It's lovely to live on a raft . . . . It was kind of lazy and jolly,
laying off comfortable all day.

Huck Finn
The Adventures of Huckleberry Finn
by Mark Twain

BEFORE AND AFTER THE BOY Scout snake incident, I did spend time learning about nature. Every summer for two or three years while I was in the latter part of elementary school, my father would bring us over to Rancho Feliz, a dude ranch in the middle of the desert about ten miles west of his Southwestern city. The last summer was between grammar school's sixth grade and junior high's seventh grade. Our dad would come out to stay on the weekends, and during the week, he'd drive out every night for dinner and stay for a couple of hours afterwards.

It was so unbelievably hot in the open desert that time of year, only a father who wanted his kids to be near for the summer would pay to indulge them in such an extended and warm privilege. Thus, Shirley and I were the only full-time summer guests at the ranch and the summer skeleton staff consisted of the couple who owned the ranch, the maid, the wrangler-handyman and the chef.

Shirley and I each had our own cabin, both of which were about a quarter mile from the main lodge, but not right next to each other because all the cabins were fairly well spread out (a convenience not often seen these days in modern resorts). They were constructed of natural stone and sunk half-way into the ground as their only mechanisms for staying cool, having been built a number of years before at a time when evaporative cooling was a very unusual convenience, and refrigerated air conditioning was essentially unknown in such an application.

We didn't mind the heat. At least, I know I didn't. No one told me the heat should bother me, so I never even thought about it. There were too many things to investigate. I had the run of the ranch and the closest neighbor in any direction was six miles away. Lots of ground to cover with lots of things to look into, around, over and under. So long as I checked in with someone every once and awhile, I was golden.

The owners were happy to have us. They didn't want to lose the core employees and would have paid them over the summer in any event just to keep the ranch and horses maintained. Oh, now and again, a few guests would come, but after roasting for several days, they left. Some were interesting though. Kathy was a cute blond a couple years older than I and, in that last summer before junior high, she sparked a budding awareness that I may have a certain appeal to attractive "older" women. For that reason, I was particularly sad to see her go, but her mother thought she was much too fair for that environment.

No matter. Shirley and I usually had the swimming pool all to ourselves, and often I had it and the adjoining recreation room all to myself because Shirley had other interests such as reading in the shade or the boys her age who would stay there from time to time. I discovered an old wind-up Victrola in the "rec" room, and one 78 rpm record, but no needle for the tone arm. I knew they were just large, straight steel needles that were held in with a set screw, but none were to be had on the ranch. So, brushing against a Saguaro cactus shortly thereafter, I had an epiphany, got a pair of pliers and pulled a big needle out of that desert giant and put it in the tone arm. It worked like a charm for about five plays with an infinite supply of cactus needles right outside.

The lone 78 rpm record had been chucked into an old cabinet. On one side was a song, "Ain't Cha Ever Coming Back." The flip side was unplayable, but I didn't care. I had a Victrola and a side. I played it over and over and over and over again. It's a wonder that giant cactus survived. I've since learned that plants have feelings and I hope it was happy to contribute to my musical development.

Anyway, I didn't know I was listening to one of the greatest jazz singers of all time, but I knew I not only loved the song, I'd fallen in love with that sweet velvet voice and Peggy Lee. Many years later I learned she was accompanied on the guitar by her then-husband, Dave Barbour. They met while they were with the Benny Goodman Orchestra. Much later I learned that Frank Sinatra had also recorded that song with the Pied Pipers right around the time Peggy did. I think it's the only instance where I've decided Frank came in second.

Listening to Peggy wasn't the only thing to do on the ranch. There were horses to ride. I'd never ridden a horse before I got there, so "Sarge," the wrangler, told me Leppy was my horse. That steed's main attributes were important ones. Every summer he was breathing, upright and had a nice little cradle in his back for the saddle. I felt quite secure, even when he moved. Leppy and I got to be good friends. Together we were a finely tuned unit. I seldom had to pick up the reins and it didn't bother him at all that I grabbed onto his mane from time to time. He just seemed to go wherever the other horses went. I felt it was the subtle signals I gave him by changing the pressure on his sides with my knees.

Shirley said he was so old that all he could do was follow the other horses around, so long as they didn't trot. I don't think that was accurate. Leppy did exactly everything I expected of him. He didn't go too fast, he never ran off, he always stopped when everyone else did and he wasn't constantly nervously prancing around. It was a beautiful example of communication between a boy and his horse. Of course part of that was brushing, washing and cleaning up after him, but I'd had a lot of experience with our big, red dog, Prince. As I recall, they were both about the same size.

Leppy's nerves of steel paid off one day, and, of course, that's why the Universal Forces selected him for me. One afternoon, Sarge, Shirley and I were out for a ride in the desert a couple of miles from the ranch when a sudden desert thunderstorm enveloped us. It can happen quickly in the summer. It was pouring buckets and lightning seemed to be everywhere. Before we had a chance to listen to instructions from Sarge, a bolt of lightning hit the desert so close it kicked sand on Leppy and me, and the clap of thunder was so loud and sharp it left me senseless for a few moments. It occurred so fast, I didn't realize what had happened. Then I remembered I'd heard a crackle just before the bolt appeared, and the big bang came right after that. Lightning bolts are *very* big when they're that close to you.

Sarge's horse threw him. I think Shirley's is still running. I can see her now, hanging on to the saddle horn for dear life, bouncing up and down yelling "Whoa, whoa." I can't repeat the things Sarge said while sitting in the rain on top of a small cactus. Leppy didn't move a muscle. What a horse.

We finally regrouped. No one was hurt. Well, Sarge's rear was a little sore and he scraped his arm, but he was a WWII combat vet and told me that a lot worse things had happened to him on Iwo so I shouldn't be concerned. The lightning stopped, but it rained hard all the way back to the ranch. They were waiting for us with dry clothes and hot soup. I couldn't understand why they were so worried. We knew we were okay. Actually, a desert summer rain is quite refreshing, particularly if you're riding in the open and it's about 105° in the shade when it starts, and afterwards, the desert is pristinely clean, even a little steamy in places. It's marvelous. I can feel it still. Of course, riding a horse a couple of miles in wet Levi's isn't much of a thrill.

At Rancho Feliz, there were lots of desert creatures around. Rattlesnakes, scorpions, Gila monsters, tarantulas, black widows, brown recluse spiders, coyotes and deer to name a few. I heeded the early warnings to keep my eyes and ears open and never put my hands anywhere I couldn't see. I never did see a Gila monster. They apparently don't hang out much at all, but I'd be doubly careful in my cabin when I reached for something because the scorpions are hard to see and don't make noise. They just get on something, for instance, a wall, a table, behind a curtain, next to a drinking glass, in the folds of clothes you left lying on the slate floor, and they hold unusually still with their tails up, which look like a bunch of little tiny sausages stuck together with a stinger on the end, and they won't move unless you touch them. Very disconcerting when your hand is on the way down and you realize it's about to connect with a scorpion. I developed extremely fast reflexes. Every night, I'd always check the bed sheets and once or twice it paid off. It's kind of interesting now that I think about it. Instead of trying to exterminate every living thing in the desert within a one-mile radius, trying to make my life perfect in every way, they taught me to be careful—with consequences if I wasn't.

Even though it'd still be daylight when I'd leave for supper at the main lodge, I'd always turn on the lights in my cabin because, since my dad would come to eat and then spend time with us at the main lodge after dinner, it'd be dark when I'd get back, making it risky to feel around on the wall for the light switch. Of course, if there was no moon on the way back to the cabin, the desert would be pitch black and definitely potentially dangerous. So, I always carried my Cub Scout flashlight even though it didn't seem to illuminate much of the desert or anything else, but it was official Scout issue, shaped like an upside down "L" with a belt clip.

One moonless night after dinner, we were outside chatting with Marion and Mary Marion, the owners, walking carefree toward my dad's car in the dark. He was hugging us goodbye when the unmistakable buzz of an angry rattlesnake went off. It's unnecessary to have ever heard that sound before and, instantaneously, everyone froze. No one could see a thing. I slowly eased my trusty Cub light off my belt and pointed it at the sound. About two and a half feet from us, specifically from my dad's leg, was a six foot Diamondback, coiled and ready to strike.

All of us except Marion, and my flashlight hand, remained frozen. He carefully backed off, picked up a huge rock from those lining the parking area and dispatched the snake, which we measured *after* that. Universal Forces were obviously still with us, but Marion and I were hailed as the group's heroes for being prepared and taking quick action. I'd never known anyone with the same first and last name before and, blissfully unaware that it was John Wayne's real first name, I'd never heard of any guy named Marion. And unlike "Duke" Wayne, Marion Marion didn't have a nickname. It hit me that not everyone fit into the box of my knowledge, and years later when Johnny Cash recorded "A Boy Named Sue," these memories buzzed back into consciousness.

Well, with that episode over, I return to my lighted cabin and fueled by my triumph (it's like I'm right there again), I burst past the screen door, slam the regular door, toss my flashlight on the bed, and a giant black creature catapults from the floor straight up in front of me. It keeps doing this rapidly, over and over, inching closer to me each time it lands. Yelling my head off, I propel myself backward, blocked by the closed door. Behind me, my fingers tear at the door handle as I watch incarnated horror close in with each vertical leap. Finally pulling the door open, I turn to run and smash into the screen door, but blast my way outside. Reacting violently to the force applied to it, the spring slams the screen door shut and, bruised and terrified, I've escaped the creature.

Then I realize I'm out in the pitch black without a flashlight, a quarter mile from the lodge and surely no one can hear me because the stone walls of every building are at least a foot and a half thick. The heroic snake-rescue momentum no longer operative, on some level I begin to understand what my mother means when she says it's only "now" that's ultimately important. Evading death and cactus in the darkness, I stumble over to Shirley's cabin, which must have been moved three times further away just before I tried to get there, and breathlessly tell her of the fuzzy black monster jumping around in my place.

Characteristically concerned for her annoying little brother's welfare, "I'm not going outside to get bitten by a rattlesnake on the way over there and then get eaten by your creature. Here's my flashlight. Go find Marion or Sarge." She pushed me out and locked the door.

I see a light in Sarge's cabin down by the corrals. It's a tossup for that or the main lodge and I can't see any lights there. Breathlessly, but carefully, I pick my way to Sarge's. It's a hot night and through the screen door I see Sarge dozing on top of his bed. I bang on the door as I yell his name through the screen.

He springs, red eyed, off the bed and lands in a crouch, his eyes darting around the cabin. Then he sees me with my nose against the screen and slowly straightens up, his hands trembling as he buttons his shirt, "Boy, for a second or two there, I thought I was back on Iwo. This better be *real* good."

"Sarge, there's a black furry monster jumping up and down in my cabin. It tried to kill me!"

Sarge pulls on his boots, opens a drawer and extracts an honest-to-goodness king-size six shooter, spins the barrel and straps it to his hip. Putting on his well-worn Stetson, "Since yer eyes are bugged about two feet out'n yer head, let's go see what it is."

Sarge's giant flashlight is a lot better than Shirley's and we trudge up to my cabin.

He looks through the screen door, "I don't see nothin', Chip."

"It's in there. I know it. It couldn't have gotten out."

"How'd it get in?"

"You've gotta go in and see if it's there."

"What'd you say it looked like again?"

"It's black, furry, has big teeth and big eyes, it's huge, can jump straight up about six feet and almost got me."

In the light coming through the screen door, Sarge inspects my face, loosens the pistol in its holster, his eyes start scanning double-time and steps in. I stay outside.

Through his laughter, "How big you say it was?"

"Huge."

"Com'ere."

I gingerly step into the room. In the middle of it is crouched a motionless black tarantula perhaps four inches across. I stop.

"Here's your monster."

"This can't be it."

To my dismay, Sarge stamps on the floor. The big black fuzzy spider's legs uncoil another four inches and it jumps about three feet straight up. I freeze, expecting Sarge to shoot it. He starts laughing again.

"Chip, these're really ugly aren't they? Did you slam the door or somethin'?"

"Probably."

"If you startle 'em like that, they'll do what you saw. They're scared, but they don't attack. No big deal." He reaches down with his hand.

"You'll die!"

The tarantula crawls onto his arm. Speechless, I wait to see it jump onto his face and suck the life out of him. He opens the screen, puts his arm outside and shakes the big fuzzy spider off.

"Aren't you going to kill it?"

"Chip, it's a creature of nature and we're in its desert. We're invading *its* space, which is why we don't try to kill things on our rides out in the desert. We just leave 'em alone if they do likewise. Now while these tarantulas can't really hurt us, if some really dangerous critter that can do a lot of harm comes into what's become *our* space now, like black widows, brown recluses, scorpions and rattlesnakes, we can't reason with 'em about leavin' and then stayin' out, so we kill 'em for a little insurance against comin' back."

He chuckles and grabs me by the back of the neck, "I don't know what the critters call it, but we call it the advance of civilization."

He gives my neck a friendly shake, then leaves to go back to his cabin and his own thoughts. A few steps away, he turns, "Oh, try not t'bang on my door like that again when it's dark and I'm sleepin'. It puts a fright in me somethin' fearful."

I slept hardly at all that night. I had to keep turning on the light. I felt like things were crawling on me. In the morning, I sleepily downed my breakfast while enduring Sarge telling Mary and Marion about my close encounter with the aerodynamic arachnid, then threw on my bathing trunks and went down to the pool. No one was around and only the sun and the desert sounds were invading my space. I grabbed a raft, jumped on and, bobbing up and down softly with no critters in the water except me, I fell asleep to the sounds of quail calling through the Manzanita.

I woke up in the late afternoon. I was really thirsty, but felt rested. I went up to the lodge with a nickel to get a pop out of the refrigerated Coke vending machine. It chilled those hour-glass bottles so they were icy-cold to the very last sip. Can't be beat on a terrible-hot day.

Mary looked at me, "Chip! You've obviously been in the sun a long time. I think you should've protected yourself with some baby oil mixed with iodine."

Looking down at my white stomach, "Whaddya mean?"

"Your back and legs are scarlet."

We found a mirror. She was right. Then I noticed the tops of my arms were like that too. When I pushed on the red part, it would just turn white there for a second.

"It doesn't hurt."

"Oh dear. It will."

By the time my father showed up that night with a doctor friend and an assortment of ointments, I was in my underpants lying on top of my bed on my stomach with my skin doing the red-hot chili pepper thing. They talked about me as if they were examining a piece of raw meat.

"I don't know, Joe. I've never seen anything like this from the sun. How long did you say he was out in it? The only thing we can do is have him drink plenty of fluids and rub this ointment on his backsides."

Out of the corner of my eye, I saw my father put a glob of white ointment on his finger and reach for my back. As the outer layer of ointment molecules touched the fissioning outer atoms of my flaming skin, I made a loud and horrible noise.

"Chip, we've got to put this on or it'll be even worse."

"Let me die without it."

Unfortunately in those days, there were no sprays to waft onto my mega-sensitive skin. It was rub it on or nothing. After what seemed like hours of agonizing pain, they were satisfied they'd finally covered the back half of my body.

In the morning, I could scarcely move except to endure the excruciating pain required to attend to the necessities of life, a giant, hunched, red crab moving sideways in slow motion between the bed and the bathroom. I looked in the mirror as I sidled by and thought of the Saturday morning movie serials at the Lincoln Elementary auditorium (the venue of the Boy Scout snake-relief incident). After Billy Batson yelled "Shazam" and the lightning turned him into Captain Marvel wearing his very red suit, he'd combat The Scorpion, an unrecognizable person scrabbling about. As an amalgamation of the two, I knew I was the world's reddest, semi-crouching, crispy critter, *La Cucaracha Llameante (*The Flaming Cockroach).

In about a week, after the sadistically repeated twice-daily ointment applications, I could rise to move around for other purposes, but it was fully three weeks before I could stand up completely straight. The process was akin to limbering-up burnt chicken. I crackled when I walked. Then for two or three days, I was a beautiful golden brown. After that, I started peeling. Shirley wouldn't get near me, complaining I kept flaking on her.

The Universal Forces? Well, at Rancho Feliz, not only did Peggy Lee broaden my love for jazz that had started when I was a little kid (more in a later chapter) and the desert experience enhance my affinity for horses and nature, but the sunburn kindled an important and beneficial lesson. Later in life, I spent many summers on local lakes boating and water skiing with my family under the hot Southwestern sun, and I made certain we were always well protected from the sun (but not with baby oil and iodine), which is certainly paying important dividends for everyone today.

* * * *

13

Strung Along

The man who has no imagination has no wings.

Muhammad Ali

THE NEXT SCHOOL YEAR, SHIRLEY started high school, the 10th grade, and I started junior high, the 7th grade. Our house wasn't all that big. In fact it wasn't very big at all since it was primarily the two bedrooms and the one very small bath I've described, 900 square feet in all, on a lot 50 feet wide and 100 feet deep. The lot seemed even smaller than that to me since the narrow driveway on the side of the house took over the rest of the width and the detached garage took up much of the back, especially when combined with the big wire chicken pen we'd constructed next to it during the war.

While Shirley and I had originally been in the smaller back bedroom with the bunk beds, at a point my mother put us in the front bedroom which was slightly larger. The bunk beds were transferred in there and unstacked so we each had a twin bed on opposite sides of the room. Like in the back bedroom, we shared a small closet. As time went on in the "big" bedroom, Shirley continued the mindset that I was messy, being particularly annoyed because my stuff seemed to be getting into "her" half of the room all the time. I couldn't figure that out. It looked okay to me.

At one point, I spent the night next door at Bobby's house and the next day when I came home, there was a string taped at intervals down the middle of the room. She'd done the same thing to the closet. Assuming it would aggravate her to no end, I didn't say a word and pondered what to do next for a few days. Then came one of the most beautiful ideas I've ever had.

I always got home from school earlier than she did, so every day I'd move the string over to her side of the room a little—the width of the string each time. I'd moved it quite a way before she caught on, and then there was hell to pay. She was furious with me for string tampering and even madder at being duped. It was great.

My mother finally intervened. She made Shirley take up the string and instructed me in no uncertain terms to keep my stuff picked up. Then, so I could have my own room, she chatted with our friend and weekend hobby-handyman neighbor across the street about enclosing our small, covered, back patio, essentially a rectangular box with one open side, formed by an extension of the roof, plus the outside walls of the hall, living room and kitchen on three sides. Mr. Brunghanel, always willing to help, said he could accomplish the task in an extremely economical fashion—no cost—with items from his home-project scrap pile, and he'd be over the next weekend if his lumbago wasn't acting up.

The existing patio roof remained exactly the same, as did the three outside rough stucco walls. My new "life-box" was formed by enclosing the side open to the back yard with a framed wooden wall that had a window at one end and an outside door at the other. On the inside of the room, the new wooden wall was an unfinished matrix of scrap 2x4's, and the other three walls were, of course, the same rough stucco walls that used to be the outside.

The outside of the 2x4 matrix was covered with Mr. Brunghanel's scrap wooden siding which he stained a dark brown to cover up myriad spurious nail holes, saw cuts and marks that had resulted from being scraped, thrown around or initially used for something else. The door to the backyard was a narrow, old 24" wide, wood-framed, glass patio door he'd long ago removed from his house because it was too narrow and impractical, and the window was its matching twin, turned sideways and elevated at the other end of that wall of much-traveled wood. The resulting space was a tunnel five feet wide and ten feet long.

Access to the house proper was at the "window end" through the original patio door from the living room, and the only electricity was the porch light at the opposite end over my bed. The bed was my half of the bunk-bed set and ran lengthwise down the room, taking up more than half its length and four-fifths of its width. That forced me to shuffle sideways to get into it or to reach the backyard door which, fortunately, opened to the outside.

But the best thing of all for my mother, it was free. The best thing of all for me—it was all mine.

The Universal Forces were looking out for me.

* * * *

14

Mmmm ... Waffles

Do not be ... influenced by what you see ....
You live in a world which is a playground of illusion.

Shri Sai Baba

WITH ROOM-SHARING SKIRMISHES A thing of the past, a few months later our mother had to go out of town for a few days and our good, long-suffering and always reliable friend across the street, the wonderful German-American wife of the always helpful German-American gentleman who constructed my stucco tunnel, said she'd keep an eye on us and feed us breakfast and dinner. So, on one of those mornings, Shirley and I were at the small chrome-legged dinette table with the fake mother-of-pearl top (just like ours) in Mrs. Brunghanel's kitchen, eating her incredible French toast with Log Cabin maple syrup, the kind that came in the little tin cabins with the screw top which seemed like a chimney to me.

Mrs. Brunghanel was proudly telling Shirley that one of her married daughters had stopped working because she was "in a family way" ("pregnant" was a little too clinical and graphic for those days, and almost all employers required women to leave their jobs the *moment* they started to "show"), and then she busied herself putting some coffee grounds in her Percolator at the other end of the kitchen.

With Mrs. Brunghanel otherwise occupied, Shirley started indulging in one of her favorite sisterly pastimes, softly and incessantly carping at me about the way I ate. My opinion of my eating etiquette differed from hers and my new tactic, which I was finding successful any time she offered her thoughts on how I should conduct my existence, was not to react, except for looking at her every once in awhile with a barely perceptible amused smile. It finally got her. She picked up a piece of French toast with that Log Cabin syrup on it and silently mooshed it into my face, twisting it back and forth several times, then dropping it on my plate, just looking at me with a barely perceptible amused smile on her face.

I discovered a universal principle. That look had the same effect in reverse. I picked up a cup of cocoa and poured it on her head. That was the only thing Mrs. Brunghanel saw. A thin film of Log Cabin syrup is transparent on one's face so, just like in sports where the one who retaliates for a foul gets the penalty, "She started it" had no mitigating effect on our generous neighbor, and the rest wasn't pretty.

The lesson that stuck with me—never make a nice German lady mad.

* * * *

15

It Is Thicker than Water

Love your enemies ...

Jesus

ONE AFTERNOON A FEW WEEKS later, still in my first year in junior high, I was on our somewhat poorly manicured front lawn (that was my job) listening to Shirley do her cleaning chores with our old Electrolux vacuum cleaner that looked like a horizontal oxygen tank on four wheels and had a motor whine that would require industrial ear protection these days. I was idly passing a football to myself on the lawn because Shirley objected to my throwing it in the house, and there weren't any of my friends around to play catch with. I'd throw it forward, lobbing it in the air high enough so I had time to run under it and catch it. I was imagining myself Notre Dame's Heisman Trophy winner, Johnny Lujack, with the crowd screaming adoration at my quarterbacking prowess, when an older boy I'd never seen came sauntering down the street.

He was half-again my size and took my football, shoving me around as I tried to get it back. I was getting worried because footballs were hard to come by, this guy was kind of mean, I didn't want to get beat up, my mother wasn't home and none of my friends were there to help me. The whine of the Electrolux had stopped and I thought I saw Shirley by the window gleefully watching him pound on me. It hadn't been all *that* long since the string incident, not to mention the French toast and cocoa.

I was wishing in vain that an Avon Lady would come down the block selling her wares, maybe scaring him off, when, just as things seemed totally hopeless because I was lying on the ground where that malicious jerk had knocked me and it looked like he was getting ready to stomp on me, Shirley came out of the house with my baseball bat. I'm sure I was more stunned than that high school bully. I don't think anyone in our neighborhood had ever even considered teeing off on someone with a baseball bat, much less my sister who could slice you with scalpel-like precision through well-chosen words, but definitely wasn't a physically violent person.

Thus, it flitted through my mind that maybe she was going to hand the bat to him. But, to my astonishment, she told him to give the football back and leave me alone. He began walking toward her, offering for her consideration an extremely inappropriate and socially unacceptable remark. It was clear that phrase solidified her negative view of him and, even though he was too stupid to realize it at that moment, he'd definitely made an intractable mistake by saying that to a five-foot tall female with a bat who happened to be my mother's daughter. She raised the bat and repeated her request, but he kept coming. Good reflexes saved the day. As the bat swung in his direction "with bad intentions," a phrase we'd learn many years later from heavyweight champ Mike Tyson, the bully dropped the football and sprinted all the way down the block, never to be seen in our neighborhood again.

Shirley went back in the house without another word. I lay there, but nothing would compute. My in-house mortal enemy had just saved my life. It was so confusing that I simply stood up and started playing with my football again. Neither of us ever mentioned it after that and we pretty much resumed our skirmishes, but I never forgot it and tried to return the favor in different ways from time to time after we became adults. Meanwhile, in junior high I confined myself to activities like turning the coins in her penny loafers—tails up.

16

Fist

No act of kindness, no matter how small, is ever wasted.

Aesop

JUNIOR HIGH WAS THE CONSCIOUS start of my struggle for identity, at least with the guys, probably no different from every other kid in those days. It was exacerbated by being a December birthday boy. I was 11 when junior high started right after Labor Day in September, and at 12 in December, I was still one of the youngest, and as a result smallest, kids in my class. One day in gym class, Coach Ware (all the gym teachers coached something and were called "Coach"—he coached baseball) decided we were going to have a push-up contest. The rules were simple, you mutually agreed to partner with someone, he made a fist and put it vertically on the ground with the little finger curled on the bottom and you did as many push-ups as possible, measured by your chest touching the fist and then getting your arms straight again. After that, the partners reversed the procedure.

While it might have seemed incongruous to my sister, I was almost always nice to people. I found life naturally more pleasant that way and the Universal Forces were about to show me it could produce unanticipated rewards. Bertram was a big redhead. I mean he was *huge* and had fists the size of catchers' mitts. He was the biggest kid in the class by far and maybe in school even though he was only in 7th grade, but then he may have been held back a year or two at some point as he was on the downside of the Bell Curve in intellect and also physically slow. Most of the guys in class made fun of him at one time or another, calling him Clem Kadiddlehopper and other pejorative names, thinking the way to pull themselves up was to put others down. Few took the time to find out that he was a very nice and kind person. I always thought that being mean to someone over something that couldn't be helped wasn't right, so I went out of my way to be nice to him at gym, which was the only class I had with him.

For obvious reasons, all the guys wanted Bertram to be their partner. He looked around, saw me, pointed and smiled. He lost his part of the push-up contest by a wide margin that day trying to get his big body down to my comparatively minute fist, but, of course, winning wasn't why he picked me. When my turn came, he plopped his giant hand down on the ground and curled it into a gargantuan fist. I had only to go down about two inches for my chest to touch it. I stopped at 85 push-ups because the next closest person did 32 and the school record from any grade was 51. All the kids who had wanted him for their partner were complaining to Coach Ware. I remember exactly what he said.

"Boys, the rules apply equally to everyone, but because you're all different, they don't guarantee an equal result."

Imagine that.

* * * *

17

The Dancer

Any publicity is good publicity.

P. T. Barnum

BEING THE PUSH-UP KING OF Martindale Junior High my first year there was kind of cool and it put a brick into my confidence structure, but it didn't do much for me with girls. In fact, I'd never even been on a date or had a girlfriend, except for Susie MacAdam in the first grade and we didn't even live in the same state anymore. To make matters more challenging, at the school dances in the gym, which combined all three grades, the boys would line up on one side and the girls would line up on the other.

It struck me as odd that, primarily to preserve the gym floor, we were required to wear tennis shoes in gym class, which was just about the only place at school most kids wore them, but the dress code required us to wear our regular shoes at the dances in the gym unless it was a sock hop. Most of the 7th grade boys would have on the highly desirable wedged leather wingtip brogues with taps on the heels and toes and, sadly, the accessory of store-bought argyle socks since we had no steady girlfriends to knit them for us.

But I did procure my wingtips from the only shoe repair shop in our area that could wedge wingtips properly. It consisted of taking the heel off the shoe and adding built-up layers of shaped leather under the sole so in effect the shoes were leather wingtips with a leather wedgie sole. Then they added the taps, one to the toe and a large metal plate in the shape of a horseshoe that covered most of the bottom of the heel.

All very smooth fashion-wise and an absolute necessity if I was going to have a chance at wider acceptance. But the best part, in addition to the sound they made when I walked, they added at least an inch to my height. Since Levi's (generally the only acceptable daily wear besides corduroy trousers) weren't allowed at dances, I usually sported my Sunday pleated gabardine dress pants and a decent shirt that buttoned, plus, my hair was combed.

The girls had on their obligatory sweaters with "portable" white dickey-collars. The sweaters were cashmere if their parents could afford it, but few in our area could, so most of the girls had on Lanamere or Wondermere sweaters, the fake cashmere. Of course, those with ponytails had little scarves tied around that bouncy shock of hair. They also wore Lanz skirts, hopefully for them the real ones with the heart-shaped buttons, and not the knock-offs with the round buttons. Their preferred footwear was bobby sox, with Angora tops if they were really steppin' out, and either two-tone saddle shoes or almost any model of Joyce shoes. A girl could spot a Joyce knock-off three or four hundred yards away, and the most popular model of Joyce's was called "Little Indians." You could name shoes things like that then and no one seemed to be on the warpath over it.

The music would start over the loudspeakers, Peggy Lee's "Mañana," Nat King Cole's "Nature Boy," Doris Day's "It's Magic," Frankie Lane belting out "That Lucky Old Sun" or "Mule Train," and Perry Como's "Some Enchanted Evening." The boys would just stand on one side staring at the girls on the other. Well, a few of the highly advanced boys in the 9th grade, wearing their *hand*-knitted Angora argyle socks, would dance very slowly with their steady girlfriends, particularly to Vic Damone's "You're Breaking My Heart" or Sammy Kaye's "Careless Hands," but they were way out of our league because they had the maturity to be *in* love.

We just wanted somebody to notice us and we stood there gawking and thinking, "Pick me, pick me," while subconsciously hoping they wouldn't because we weren't sure what to do if they did. They call it an approach-avoidance conflict these days. Some of the girls would start dancing with each other and the boys would continue to stand there, staring. Finally, a girl would start the flood by crossing the floor to ask a boy to dance.

Even though I was fairly certain I looked really smooth at my very first dance in 7th grade, and it looked to me like regular dancing was just hanging on to each other and sort of walking around, I'd never done anything more than square dance in the 5th grade. I desperately wanted some female to pick me, but I couldn't pluck up enough heart to bell the cat myself. Asking a girl to dance and being rejected would be too much to bear, particularly with everyone watching and, believe me, they watched *everything*. The result was playing it safe by just standing around looking smooth and being a confirmed gawker.

Tommy Dorsey's "The Hucklebuck" came on and suddenly, as a result of knowing no one was standing behind me, I froze. The first girl to walk across the floor was clearly and purposefully walking straight at *me*, and I knew she was in the 8th grade! She was incredibly mature-looking and really attractive. All eyes were on her. As she reached me, she gave the command, "Let's dance," turned around, reached back without looking, grabbed my shirt and started pulling me to the middle of the floor.

She thought she had my shirt. She'd grabbed the crotch of my pleated, gray gabardine pants, pulling me off balance, and I was bent backwards like Gumby with a string attached, running after her on my tiptoes with my arms flailing behind me to keep from going down. As she heard the collective gasp from the crowd, she turned in mid-stride and focused on the bundled-up crotch of my trousers in her hand.

I wish I could patent the shade of red that instantaneously covered her face. Then, just as fast, her green eyes went back to normal size, lit up and she burst out laughing. In a very slight

Southern drawl, she said, "Well now, we've either gotta dance … or get married." It turned out that Lee Ann's family had moved into the house directly behind us in our subdivision and was on our telephone's party line—I recognized her voice.

No romance developed and I'd still never kissed any girl other than Susie in the first grade, but we got to be good friends and had a lot of fun. It helped immensely to have confirmation that another good-looking older woman besides blonde Kathy at Rancho Feliz in my dad's desert thought I was cute. So, another brick went into my confidence structure. What's more, after that episode, people at school I didn't even know nevertheless knew my name, waved "hi" to me and even talked to me after that. It didn't have anything to do with my wedged wingtips and horseshoe taps.

Were the Universal Forces trying to teach me that any publicity is good publicity? Surely not, but it's pretty clear they were helping me out.

* * * *

18

Stand-Up Guy

Rather than love ... give me the truth.
Henry David Thoreau

When I got into 8th grade, there was a girl in my class that I really liked. Her name was Linda and she was very cute, but above that, she had soft, kind eyes and always seemed interested in just me when we talked. That was nice because the only prior dating experience I'd had toward the end of the 7th grade, which I'll describe in a later chapter, pulverized one of the bricks in my confidence structure and I just couldn't bring myself to ask Linda to go out with me.

But the big year-end school dance was coming. Not one of the usual periodic, self-segregated, gender-gawking arrangements in the gym, but a really nice dress-up dating dance on those same hardwoods, an entirely appropriate occasion to ask a girl out. So once again, I summoned up all the pre-rejection defenses I could think of and asked her. Incredibly, she said yes. What a day!

The dance wasn't too far into the future and I busied myself with making sure things were going to be just right, learning about various types of corsages, stressing over whether it should be wrist or pin-on, and concerning myself with the details of sartorial splendor, to include getting a haircut. Throughout all this, my mother kept reminding me that the lawn needed mowing badly, and I'd put off cleaning out the garage even though I had assured her that task would be finished a couple months before.

Finally she said, "Chip, you've got to come back to real life if just for a day. If the lawn isn't mowed and the garage isn't cleaned out by the day of the dance, you're grounded. No dance. I mean it."

"No problem."

Every day my mother reminded me and every day I responded, "No problem."

In the late afternoon on the day of the dance, I was putting a shine on my wedged wingtips equivalent to Mt. Palomar's telescope mirror and my mother said, "Chip, we've got a problem."

"What?"

"Take a look at the yard, then open the garage door."

The blood drained from my body, so I whipped out my best, and usual, defense.

"I forgot."

We all know that doesn't work with the tax man, and it didn't work with my mother either.

"You're grounded."

"That's not fair!"

"Let's think about this. Your responsibility is the lawn. You also took on the responsibility of cleaning the garage, and for good reason, because almost one-hundred percent of the mess in there is comprised of your stuff. You've failed to fulfill your responsibilities, even in the face of clear and continuous warnings about the consequences, all of which were within your control, and you knew that if those consequences occurred, your lollygagging would be calamitous for you. Explain to me what's not fair."

Clear-thinking parents are a curse to the dilatory. I couldn't talk. I knew she wouldn't relent and promising to do it tomorrow wouldn't work. Of course, I'd be doing it tomorrow, but I wasn't going to the dance tonight, and it was all due to the choices I made. Today they'd call it "tough love," but I could only think of the catastrophic humiliation of having to call up Linda after all of the courage it took to ask her out, and tell her a few hours before the dance that I couldn't go because I hadn't done my chores. How lame is that? I popped the cap off a bottle of Nehi orange soda and went out to the backyard to pace up and down and think.

After about twenty minutes, it became obvious to me that I'd actually used up all my courage asking her out. I just couldn't call Linda and tell her, but she had to know. Then my eyes fell on the loose board in the fence that divided our backyard from Lee Ann's on the next street over. We'd become such good friends since our dance incident the year before that whenever I wanted to go over there, I'd just slip through that board and knock on her back door. And I did because I was so flustered that I couldn't even remember the word-prefix to her telephone number, which was the same as ours.

Praying she was home, I knocked. She yelled for me to come in. She knew I had been very excited about the dance, but then I started to tell her my sad story. She was getting ready to go to the dance too, but I was so distraught that she simply sat down until I was finished, the expression on her face changing with each passing word.

"Wow! Linda is going to be very, *very* unhappy. I'll bet she has a new dress for the dance and is looking forward to it as much as you are. She'll be devastated. I would be. This is terrible. Should I ask why you didn't do what you were supposed to?"

"I forgot."

She looked at me like the incomparable boob I was, "What are you going to do?"

At least I could remember Linda's phone number and wrote it on the pad by the phone, "Will you call her?"

The next look she gave me announced that, at least in this particular instance, I was a pathetic excuse for a human being, which I knew, but I couldn't call Linda.

After looking at me silently for some time, "Get out of here. I'll do it. You'd probably mess that up too. But if she says anything, I'm not telling you. If you want to know, you'll have to hike up your shorts and ask her." It was clear she wasn't identifying with me.

The next Monday, Linda would not look at me in class and it was obvious that, for her, I no longer existed. Diving into the ostrich technique, I didn't have the guts to go up to her and apologize. This went on for a few days until I finally got it together, cornered her and told her how sorry I was. She told me that she had indeed bought a new dress for the occasion and, quite properly, I felt like an even bigger jerk, assuming that was possible. I tried to smooth it over and we talked for a while, but things weren't really okay. Those soft, kind eyes were wounded.

The Universal Forces were giving me a swift kick in the behind, but what could they have had in mind for Linda?

* * * *

19

Shine

A smile is an inexpensive way to change your looks.

Charles Gordy

When I'd started junior high, I'd casually noticed that there was a big space between my two big front teeth, and the tooth next to one of them was almost completely behind that big tooth. Not only that, my eye teeth were way up above the rest of my teeth so that I looked like Dracula when I smiled. I didn't discover until years later that I might be related to the original Dracula, Vlad the Impaler. Funny thing though, other than a casual notice of how my teeth were arranged, I'd never thought much about their appearance and it never kept me from smiling, which I did a lot. No one else seemed to notice at all or ever made fun of me about them, I think because in those days crooked teeth were usual. Having braces on them was unusual, and even more so for boys. These days braces seem to be *de rigueur* for all kids and many adults, but sporting them then was uncommon, particularly in our area of town, which was nice, clean and well kept, but not the high-rollers' end by a long shot, and dentists who straightened teeth were quite expensive.

During Spring Vacation in the latter part of the 8th grade, I was visiting my father and he asked if my crooked front teeth bothered me. I told him nobody cared, so I didn't really care. He said he cared and he wanted a friend of his who was in town to look at them. I told him that was okay with me so long as he wasn't going to drill on them. Dad said he wasn't that kind of dentist.

What kind of dentist doesn't drill on your teeth? It turned out, the "dentist" was Dr. Charles Tweed, one of the leading practitioners of modern orthodontia at that time. His method of straightening teeth wasn't accepted by all orthodontists and was imaginatively distinguished from other methods by calling it, "The Tweed Method." Comparatively few orthodontists around the country were trained in it at the time.

Dr. Tweed looked at my eye teeth and immediately threw on a garlic necklace, arranging his fingers in the sign of the cross. Just kidding. He said I was a good and "challenging" candidate for his method and gave my father a recommendation for a "Tweed" orthodontist in my area when I got back home. He confirmed there would be no drilling and I was happy.

If I was a descendent of Vlad the Impaler, then my new orthodontist was an appropriate choice since he must have been related to the Marquis de Sade. The first thing he did was to have four of my teeth pulled, one in each quadrant of my mouth to make room for the straightened teeth. Then, the day after 8th grade ended, he fitted a metal band to each tooth left in my mouth. He did that by holding the slightly-too-small band at the bottom end of the tooth and then hammering on it so it was rammed tightly around the middle of the tooth and would not come off.

He'd have me make a fist and push up on my lower jaw when he pounded them onto my bottom teeth. That kept my jaw from flying off my face and cushioned some of the blow. But, when he hammered them onto my upper teeth, particularly my eye teeth, it wasn't so happy an experience. The shock wave from each blow traveled up my tooth, through my brain and out the top of my head, putting me into an altered state, popularly referred to as semi-consciousness.

That was the good part. Apparently, the only way he could get teeth to move in a non-precipitous manner was to connect all of them with wires wrapped around small appendages on the metal bands, and then *twist* the wires tighter. I knew right away my teeth were resisting. And just when I'd think he was done and start to relax, he'd give all of them one more twist for good measure. I think he gauged the number of twists by how far my eyes were rolling into the back of my head.

Then he'd be done. Nope. There was an additional way to get my teeth to move excruciatingly slowly, contributing to my mouth being so sore I couldn't chew for a couple of days—rubber bands. On each of the metal bands on my two Dracula teeth, there was a little hook. A very small but very strong rubber band was slipped over it and then stretched over a similar hook on my lower teeth. Even when my mouth was shut, the rubber bands were pulling, and pulling and … drilling was beginning to look pretty good.

When school started after the end of that first summer of wearing my braces, my first-period 9th grade home-room teacher, who had also been my 8th grade first-period home-room teacher, Mr. Cassara, checked out my appliances and told me he thought it was terrific I had them. He said, wistfully, that his folks didn't have the money for orthodontia and he had always wished his own teeth were straighter, but he was very happy for me.

In any event, even though I didn't think it was pleasant at the time, the Universal Forces were determined to help arrange events for my future, so my wires were tightened every week. At least, it seemed like every week. It may have been every two weeks. I've kind of pushed it out of my mind. Anyway, I'd get that done after school and the next morning, Mr. Cassara could tell by the look on my face that I'd been there again and he'd check the progress, always remarking how well they were coming along. After awhile, his interest and kindness actually got me excited and happy my teeth were going to be straight.

I hope wherever he is now, his teeth are straight.

* * * *

20

Prez

Why should we be in such desperate haste to succeed ...
If a man does not keep pace with his companions,
perhaps it is because he hears a different drummer.
Let him step to the music which he hears,
however measured or far away.

Henry David Thoreau

As 9th grade started, one of the first items on Martindale Jr. High's agenda was the election of class officers, including the school President who was always a 9th grader. That was the last year of junior high and they needed the maturity in that highly responsible position. In light of that, I'm not sure how my name got on the candidates' list. Some of my friends must have managed it somehow as a joke because I didn't do it. Many of my friends were prone to doing things like that. I don't know why people like that gravitated in my direction. Anyway, since it was a *fait accompli*, I thought I could have some fun going along with it.

The list of students who were interested in the job was rather short and composed of people who weren't really like me. It's not that they didn't like me; they just weren't like me. You know, they were kind of serious young people who knew what was expected of them, recognized those expectations were beneficial, internalized them and diligently tried to follow that course, while I seemed to be internalizing something which was slightly different and less reverent as it related to the establishment. It's hard for me to put my finger on, but it did seem to have something to do with having more fun than I thought they were having.

Everyone knew the desideratum of the principal and other staff members was certainly not me; it was Myrtle, who was mercilessly perky, very smart, very proper and had worked her way into their preferences by doing all the things they wanted a proper young person to do, which were all the things a proper young person should be doing. Nothing wrong with that. In fact, it's a highly desirable path and the probabilities of it working out for her were definitely higher than the probability curve for my path which was close to the antithesis of hers in junior high. Oh, I was pretty smart and, like Myrtle, I was in the Scholastic Honor Society, but the primary object of my cerebral energy and effort was enjoying life as much as I could in my own way—oh, certainly hers too, she just enjoyed her life in a different way.

So, in the Martindale Junior High school assemblies for candidates' speeches, I told my fellow students that I would work hard to shorten the school day to four hours and expand the lunch period to two, which counted against the four, and we'd also have an ice-cream break in the morning and the afternoon, all ice cream to be supplied by the school. That and other nonsense produced wild cheers, juxtaposed against polite applause for my opponents who, as I was to observe later in life, violated the first canon of electioneering—they were realistic.

While I'd had my fun prior to Election Day, I presumed I had no chance since Myrtle should have it wrapped up. When I got to school the morning after Election Day, people started gathering around telling me I'd won and Myrtle was second. I didn't believe them until some of my closest friends dragged me inside to the bulletin board and showed me. More than a little surprised, I turned to Tucker and said, "What do I do now?" Many years later, Robert Redford copied my line almost word for word in the movie, *The Candidate*.

At first-period home-room, Mr. Cassara said he thought the Principal, Mr. Smurt, would probably send a note to one of my classes asking me to come to his office so he could tell me what he wanted me to do. By the time I got to my last class of the day, algebra, no message had arrived. Things had been a little boisterous in my classes all day because of my surprise win, and my classmates were carrying on with congratulations and "wise" remarks.

I got caught up in the spirit of things and by the time algebra arrived everyone was having a lot of fun and talking and laughing more than usual. My teacher, Mrs. Breaker, a very prim and proper lady who thought only the perfect should be allowed in church, and who had never been a big fan of mine (we attended the same church), kept telling me to be quiet. She didn't tell anyone else, just me. It would work for a few minutes and then various people in the class would start in again and I'd get caught up in it again, and she'd shoot her attention at me again.

At the end of that fifty minute hour, Mrs. Breaker asked me to come up to see her. She said she was sending me to Mr. Smurt for talking during class and he would be waiting for me in his office. I hadn't seen her leave the classroom and wondered if they could read each others minds. I took the slip she filled out, signed "B. L. Breaker," to his office and he asked me to come in, close the door and sit down.

I thought that was actually a good sign since he apparently wasn't going to admonish me for talking in a way that others could overhear. Mr. Smurt scarcely looked at the slip Mrs. Breaker had filled out, or at me. He primarily stared down at his desk and said he understood I had been acting up in my classes all day long. I acknowledged everyone was a little happier than usual because, surprisingly, I'd won the election. Then, in a very somber tone, still staring at his desk, he told me that was inappropriate conduct for a School President and he was removing me from office.

I'd been warming up to the idea of being President as the day went along and was stunned that I was being removed for what seemed to be a minor and perfectly understandable infraction that probably wasn't going to happen again.

"So that's it? No warning? No anything?"

Still staring at his desk, "Yes."

He got up to open the door and I couldn't resist, "Is Myrtle waiting outside?"

Still not looking at me, he sat down, red faced, and started shuffling through the papers on his desk as I left.

It certainly wasn't apparent to me at the time, but the Universal Forces were teaching me important life lessons about the milieu in which one marches to the beat of his own drummer and how it should be done. Lessons that would become clearer as life went on.

* * * *

21

The Joy of Riding

As it is, the quickest of us walk about well wadded with stupidity.
George Eliot

My friend Tucker, of water balloon infamy, grew like a weed when we got into junior high and by the 9th grade he was tall and looked several years older than 15, which turned out to be for our benefit, in a certain way. We all wanted to drive cars, but none of us had legitimate access to a car at that point, nor did we have driver's licenses at that age. Toward the end of our first semester that year, Tucker was still riding his bike to school and on the way home, he rode by a particular gas station every day and noticed that an old Packard coupe had been parked in the back for several days.

Since he would be eligible for a Learner's Permit in the near future, he wondered if the car were for sale. He inquired and the gas station owner told him it had been left there after closing one night a couple weeks before and being a small businessman flexible enough to recognize a possible opportunity, he presumed the owner would be back at some point to get it and, hopefully, pay him to fix it if that were necessary. The owner took the keys, but was apparently kind enough to leave the doors unlocked in case the proprietor needed to push it elsewhere on the property.

Now, as you know, when Tucker and I got together, common sense often left. Since Tucker knew how to hot wire cars from listening to his father, a police detective, talk to his police buddies, we decided Tucker should see if the car started. That's all, just see if it started.

That gas station closed at dusk. So after dark, we rode our bikes down there and went around back. After Tucker did his stuff with a small screwdriver, the ignition wires were hanging down below the dashboard. Tucker's dad had explained to him how to drive a car, but Tucker had never driven one, so he said, "Get in, we'll just rev it up a little." So I got in. Tucker grunted from the effort of shoving the clutch pedal to the floor with his left foot and, satisfied he'd found neutral after grabbing the knob on top of the gearshift rod, which was sticking up about three feet out of the floor, and jerking it around a few times, he twisted the loose ignition wires together, pushed the starter button on the dashboard and, lo and behold, the old girl coughed into life as Tucker pumped the foot feed, which Tucker's dad quite progressively told him to call a gas pedal (we call it an accelerator now). Then, he reached for the emergency brake lever sticking a couple feet out of the floor, pushed the button on top, gave it a little pull back to release the tension on the ratchet and shoved it forward. As the car started to roll backward, he ground the floor shift into some gear, pushed on the gas pedal and started letting out the clutch.

This was contrary to the representation he'd made about what we were going to do, but before I knew it, the car had jumped forward about five feet and the engine was still running because Tucker had pushed the clutch back in. He immediately let it out, a little better this time, and we jerked out of the gas station onto a side street as he fumbled around on the dashboard and pulled the headlight switch knob. While my brain was on pause, Tucker got better and better at driving the car, even ultimately realizing the high beams were on and, without looking down, he felt around on the floor with his left foot for the dimmer switch and stepped on it. Finally, I suggested we take the car back before we got into trouble. He agreed, but before I could suggest a less obvious route, he confidently swung onto the main thoroughfare toward the gas station almost a mile away now.

About three blocks from it, the car ran out of gas and Tucker coasted over to the curb. It occurred to me that might have been the main reason the car was left at the gas station in the first place.

Being one of the two joyriding novices present, I asked, "What now?"

Tucker surveyed the situation, "We'll just have to push it back so it'll be there in the morning."

It's good Tucker was big because those old Packard coupes were heavy. Tucker was pushing with the front door open and steering at the same time. I was pushing from the back, giving it everything I had. After about a block, I was exhausted and Tucker wasn't much better. Just as we stopped, a police car with two policemen in it (all police cars had two policemen in them in those days) pulled next to us.

"What are you guys doing?"

I did my best imitation of a deer in the headlights, and Tucker calmly responded, "We ran out of gas. Can you guys give us a push up to that gas station so we can get some gas in the morning?"

They looked at us for what seemed like half an hour. Then one of them said, "You and your kid brother get in the car. We'll give you a shove."

When we got to the gas station, they gave a little extra push, honked, swung into the other lane and drove on. We coasted to the back of the station and stopped. The car was facing the wrong way, but we just jumped on our bikes and peddled as fast as we could.

A couple of days later we were at Tucker's house and his dad said to him, "You remember Charlie Barnett? You met him last year when he was over. He said the more he thought about it, you've grown a lot, but he's pretty sure he gave you and your little brother a push the other night when your car was out of gas."

I reprised my deer in the headlights expression. Tucker casually shifted his weight so he was in front of me and, again, calmly responded, “Impossible. I don’t have a car, and you know I don’t have a little brother.” He turned, winked, nudged me into his room and very slowly shut the door.

I’m not sure the Universal Forces authorized that episode.

* * * *

22

Close Acquaintances

Date sideways, never up or down,
sideways is usually a more comfortable position ...
any significant height difference ... is minimized.

Julianne Balmain

IN THE SUMMER AFTER 9TH grade, there came a certain real mobility, automobility. While I was still approaching 15, Tucker and Don (a friend you haven't met yet) were each old enough to get a driver's license at the beginning of the summer. They were both smart so I don't think they were held back before I knew them. They probably just started school later. Anyway, Don had a girlfriend across town named Dee Dee who went to a different school, the one where all the girls wore cashmere sweaters. Dee Dee had a girlfriend named Lina who had braces. Girls who had braces were a lot more self conscious about it than boys, perhaps because they matured faster. Boys didn't really care. Braces were just a nuisance, particularly if you got hit in the mouth playing sports because it created an imprint of them on the inside of your lips.

Even though my teeth were getting pretty straight and my Dracula teeth were almost down, my braces were still in full bloom. Don and Dee Dee decided that since Lina and I were both metal-mouths, we'd be a good match even though she was taller than I and probably outweighed me by about fifteen pounds. Don and Dee Dee planned our first date. She'd invite Lina over and Don would pick me up in his car, a nifty '41 V-8 Ford De Luxe Tudor Sedan, and we'd go over to Dee Dee's to drink Cokes, listen to records and even dance, you know, hang on to each other and walk around a little.

Dee Dee had a lot of records and we danced and listened to popular tunes cut on all three current popular formats, the traditional ten-inch 78 rpm made from easily broken shellac material that had one tune on a side, Capitol Records' relatively new twelve-inch 33⅓ rpm made from virtually unbreakable vinyl that had many tunes on each side, and RCA Victor's new seven-inch 45 rpm on a stiffer vinyl-like material that originally had only one tune to a side, but increased the number as their techniques improved. While the other two formats had the traditional small hole in the middle, the 45 rpm records had a big hole in the middle about the size of a 50¢ piece that required a separate player with a big middle spindle, but kids initially bit on that marketing ploy anyway. Later on, turntables with the traditional small center spindle pole came out that had all three speeds, along with inexpensive small-holed plastic adapters that could be snapped into the middle of the 45's, or else pulled up from the middle of the turntable. Some even had a big spindle you could slide over the smaller one.

Dee Dee also snuck some 78 rpm records out of her brother's room that were banned from airplay on the radio, like Dean Martin's "Wham Bam, Thank You Ma'am" about a guy with a broken heart, and early R&B legend Bull Moose Jackson's "Big Ten-Inch" about a 78 rpm record of his favorite blues. We couldn't see what all the excitement was about.

The four of us had a lot of fun, laughed a lot and always double-dated because Lina's father would not allow her to go out with any boy alone. One night toward the end of the summer, Don and I scraped up enough money to double date to the drive-in movies in style—no one had to hide in the trunk. The drive-in idea was good because every time we went over to Dee Dee's and Lina and

I started dancing at some point, the height and weight difference made it tough for me to lead.

Don drove to the drive-in, of course, and Lina and I were in the back seat. After awhile Don slid across the bench seat and he and Dee Dee started necking. The herd instinct kicked in and Lina and I started too. Things were going just fine until I felt a click. A click with a certain finality to it. Lina and I were fastened together at the teeth. We silently tried to unhook ourselves. It only made it worse.

"Don. We're kind of thtuck."

"What?"

"We're thtuck"

Don and Dee Dee both turned at once and then burst out laughing.

When you're physically that close to somebody and it's become involuntary, and you're each breathing into each other's mouths because that seems like a better choice than breathing into each other's noses, and then you realize you're not sure you know each other all that well anyway, and … well, you don't think there's a single thing amusing going on.

Don put his hand over Dee Dee's mouth so we could hear him over her laughter, "What do you want me to do?" as he cracked up again.

"Thumthing. Get uth apart."

He climbed halfway over the front seat and tried to pull our lips apart so he could see. "It's too dark here. You're probably fused. We'll have to go to the fire station."

With no practice, Lina and I yelled in perfect harmony, "No, no, no, *no!*"

Don and Dee Dee both folded up again, "Okay, but it's too dark. We'll have to go back to Dee Dee's so we can see. Do you want to see the end of the picture first?"

In unison, "*Now!*"

He put the speaker back on its post and started the car. At the first bump, "Gaaaaa. Thlow down for the bumpth, pleath."

"Try to keep your lips shut. The sparks are ruining my upholstery." They continued the wisecracks all the way to Dee Dee's.

When we arrived at Dee Dee's house, we discovered that it would be impossible to exit the back seat of a two-door Ford with our faces locked up like that. One twist and someone could lose some teeth. So Don went into the garage and came back with a flashlight, a pair of little needle nosed pliers and a small screwdriver. He climbed in the back seat on one side and Dee Dee on the other. It was cozy, particularly with both of them simultaneously trying to pry our lips apart and diagnose the situation.

Once they got a good look, Dee Dee involuntarily blurted out, "Oh dear."

"Hurry up. My backth thtarting to hurt."

With Dee Dee holding the flashlight in one hand and our lips apart with the other, and Don operating with the pliers and screwdriver, they got us apart. There were so many wires sticking out of our mouths, we looked like we'd each tried to swallow the same baby porcupine.

Since it was only a couple of days until my regular orthodontic appointment, I had Don snip mine off with a pair of electrical pliers and bend the ends in. My orthodontist took one look, "Got stuck, didn't ya."

Lina went home with her wires sticking out and I never saw her again. Her father forbade her to have contact with me, of any kind.

I don't know what was up with the Universal Forces on that one. Maybe they'll tell me when I get back.

* * * *

23

A Leg Up

In motivating people, you've got to engage their minds .... motivate ... by example.

Rupert Murdoch

My braces came off two weeks before I started high school. I was thrilled to run my tongue over my teeth and feel nothing but smoooooooth. They looked great too. Straight as a picket fence, both uppers and lowers. No more Dracula for me. An additional bonus was that my retainer didn't have the tell-tale wire around my upper teeth. Mine had a tendency to move in rather than out, so the retainer was just a pink plastic plate in the roof of my mouth—invisible. I'd never stopped smiling while I had braces, but now it blinded people and I received a lot of unsolicited comments on how nice my teeth were. It was terrific. One more brick in the confidence structure, thanks to Dr. Tweed, the Marquis de Sade, of course my dad, and I know the UF are in the mix too.

While I had a great set of pearly white choppers to start high school, I didn't have a car, and it was definitely un-cool to ride your bicycle, which became a forgotten relic in the quest to grow up as fast as possible, or at least attempting to look like it. So, in the beginning, I rode the bus to school and home. It was fun and

I made a lot of friends, which seemed pretty easy for me to do. I think it's because I always smiled and said "Hi" first, intuitively sensing that a lot of kids were a little tentative about reaching out since all of us were more than a little unsure of our ground, particularly on the first day of high school.

Most of us from the West Side had never set foot on the campus, and departing from the bus that first day to walk through the entrance arch into the huge grassy quadrangle was a breathtaking experience. Pearson High had 3000 students and I felt like an ant, an anonymous ant, but it was a delectably strange, new place, filled with the unknown and alive with possibilities all of us anxiously wanted to experience.

Somehow, I found my way to my first experience, Social Studies. All of us newbies were sitting in class jabbering away when the bell rang. Silence was instantaneous, followed by the realization that we had no teacher even though "Mr. Sprong" was written on the blackboard. We started staring at the teacher's desk in the left front of the room as if that would materialize him. It worked. Suddenly a very large man who appeared to be in his early 60's burst into the room with a gait that was slightly off. His receding gray hair was short, his complexion ruddy, his spectacles almost round and he was puffing from the rush to get to our class on time, having been delayed in a teachers' meeting he said. A sheaf of papers was in his hand and after he dropped onto his long-suffering chair with some effort, he began matching our faces to his list of names.

When he was done, "We're not going to do any work today. I'm going to give you some pointers about high school so that when I'm finished, you'll have a leg up. That's figuratively speaking of course." He gave a push on the desk and his oak teacher's chair rolled several feet to the side while he knocked on his leg as if it were a door.

"Because literally, I don't have a leg." He pulled up his trouser leg and there was a wooden leg, not like a pirate's, but it was definitely made out of wood. "The original occupant of this space weighed twenty five pounds."

I'd never seen anything like that before and I'm sure the other kids hadn't either. We were slightly in shock and he'd accomplished his real purpose. I never heard anyone joke about his leg or the way he walked after that. He was a good teacher too, but I don't know what else he said that day.

From there, my class schedule said I was to go to chemistry which was across the quadrangle. Older students pointed and told me to follow my nose. I found it easily enough. It was a large room with desks in front and student lab stations in the rear, each complete with a Bunsen burner, a small sink and other paraphernalia. There was also a larger lab station at the front of the room for the teacher. I sat down at a desk, stared at the huge periodic table of the elements taped to the blackboard and sniffed the myriad unfamiliar, unpleasant chemical scents escaping from closed containers in the back.

A pudgy kid with thick glasses was sitting next to me expounding that the way you smelled something was the result of the fact that little pieces of it, obviously molecules floating through the air, attached themselves to the inside of your nose and your body did the rest. While I was trying not to dwell on logical extensions of that concept, he told me he'd heard Mr. Sprong lost his leg in an accident at school. He was about to tell me the gory details when Mrs. Hames came into the room .

She was a fairly large bespectacled gray-haired woman in her sixties with her left arm in a full cast extending from her shoulder to her wrist and bent upward at the elbow, raising her hand a little higher than her head because a rod came down from the elbow to her waist to keep the cast in the air. From the front, she looked like a woman with a large, white, reversed "L" sticking sideways out of her left shoulder, waving hello. I'd never seen a cast like that and while I was furiously and silently speculating on how that happened, I missed the explanation of how it happened.

After she'd matched faces to names, she said she was going to do a simple, but interesting experiment so we could see how much fun chemistry actually was. There was a large glass container of water, perhaps eighteen inches across and six inches deep on the counter of her lab station at the front of the class.

With her good arm, she picked up a rubber-stoppered test tube, about an inch in diameter and seven or eight inches long, loosely filled with many large chunks of a solid substance submerged in a liquid. She explained that it was pure potassium obtained by electrolysis because it was always combined with some other substance in nature, and it was stored in kerosene in the test tube because it oxidized very rapidly in the air. Other than that, she said, it didn't really do much of anything except for what she was going to show us.

Looking up, she put the test tube into the raised hand sticking out of the cast, gripped it tightly with some effort, grimaced, and got the rubber stopper out with her good hand, careful to hold the test tube upright. Then she looked down at the large bowl of water and we realized simultaneously with her that she couldn't see the bowl and the test tube at the same time because her left arm was sticking up, immobile. She backed up a little and bent over at the waist with some effort until she could see both the water and the test tube by bending her neck back and up as far as a sixty-some-year-old can, then looking up and straining to see out of the tops of her glasses. One has to marvel at the dedication of teachers.

With a probe in her good hand that had a tiny spoon on the end, she finally managed to break off a piece, maybe the size of a small tomato seed, eke it up to the top of the test tube and drop it into the water. The instant it hit the water, it looked like a piece of fire buzzing and dancing all over the surface. Very unexpected and impressive indeed. All that lilac colored flame, smoke and action coming from a piece we almost couldn't see.

The class was thrilled and she happily asked if we'd like to see it again. We all yelled "Yes," and she started to repeat the process, bent from the waist, reaching out with the probe to her almost immobile hand at the end of the cast with the test tube between her thumb and forefinger, neck bent back and eyes rolled up. It was clear she was tired from her first effort which required contortions Mrs. Hames obviously wasn't used to. Some in the front row volunteered to help her but she said the school wouldn't allow students to handle such volatile materials.

Trying to repeat her earlier success and redoubling her efforts, she forged ahead in an activity that would tire a much younger person. Unsuccessful, she started bobbing up and down in ever increasing arcs from all the physical effort required. It was sadly comical. She looked like a malfunctioning Bill the Bird, those novelty hollow glass birds, filled with a chemical and articulated in the middle, that bend over, dip their bill into a glass of water, pop back up and then repeat the process ad infinitum.

All coordinated finesse having vanished from the effort, as she bobbed down, the probe jammed down hard to the bottom of the test tube and she instinctively jerked it out while she involuntarily bobbed up. Oooops. The mechanics of that episode ejected the tube's entire contents into an upward arc, first the potassium and then the kerosene. Reacting faster than Wonder Woman's grandmother, she bellowed "*Run!*" while those sixty-year old legs started sprinting for the front door, the chunks of potassium still in the air.

Having witnessed the first demonstration, we needed no further urging. Some followed her for the front door, and some, including me, instinctively bolted past the student lab stations for the back door. I was so curious to see what all that potassium and kerosene was going to do when it hit the water that I started running backward. I might've made a good soccer player (and that sport didn't depend on size), but virtually no one in this country had heard of it then.

Everything was going in slow motion. I saw Mrs. Hames get to the door which fortunately opened out to the hall, but because she tried to go through it squared up, she momentarily wedged herself and the cast in the doorway, at least until the wave of following students flushed her, clanking, into the hall. I couldn't help stopping to watch the potassium shards flying toward the water, followed by the globs of kerosene racing after them. There was a mighty purple explosion which rose to meet the speeding kerosene. The resulting conflagration was hugely colorful and delightful. Someone grabbed the back of my shirt and I was yanked out the door.

Except for Mrs. Hames bruised ego and perhaps a cracked cast from running into the door jamb, no one was hurt and those of us who saw it blow were excitedly painting the spectacle to our more prudent classmates as, concurrently, male teachers rushed into the classroom with those hand-carried fire extinguishers that looked like metal milk cans and were filled with water. They had a circular handle ringing the top and a small rubber hose with a little nozzle sticking out the bottom. The water exacerbated the problem. The building was still being evacuated as the fire engines rolled up.

It seemed like high school was a dangerous place—a teacher who lost his leg there and the chemistry teacher's lab station on fire. It was announced that classes in other buildings would continue, which is how I found myself in Mr. Fuster's geometry class. Now, Mr. Fuster was no spring chicken and the rumor was that he'd been "shell shocked" in the First World War, the significance of which wasn't clear to me because I didn't know what that term meant, but we heard he was a strict disciplinarian.

When we entered, he was seated at his desk in the front left corner of the room. We silently watched him for some sign of shell shock, whatever it was. As the bell rang, he rose stiffly from his desk, leaned forward slightly from his hip joints and slowly walked fossil-like to the center of the room, all the while turning his flinty body until his head was pointed in our direction, staring at us with that reptilian gaze older folks sometimes develop. Then, while rotating his shoulders slightly so he could look into each set of eyes seriatim, he began to address the class directly and slowly in measured words, spoken with a quiet Southern accent and a voice that seemed it once might have been deep and robust, but was now less so. Perhaps as a result of being shell shocked.

"Y'all know of the atomic threat facing our country today?" The vowels were drawn out longer than any Southerner I'd ever heard.

We nodded "yes" in unison. We were all aware that since the end of the Second World War a few years before, the Russians wanted to blow us to kingdom come.

"Since I've previously been in the armed services of our country, I'm the head of Pearson High's Nuclear Defense Training Committee." He inspected us with leaden eyes, "Have y'all heard of 'Duck and Cover'?"

We looked at each other, confused.

He continued in his very slow Southern drawl, "Well, in the event of nuclear attack, which will be recognizable by an extremely, and I do mean extremely, bright flash, I will yell 'Down' and y'all will immediately, and I do mean immediately, drop down to the side of your desks in a kneeling or similar position and cover the back of your heads or necks with your hands. If you are able to do that and also get at least your head under your desk, do so. You see, if you're not down and under your desks and the windows get blown in, you'll first be sliced to ribbons and then burned to a cinder. When the audio visual projector operators make it around to this classroom in a few days, we'll have a picture show on this subject. It involves Bert the Turtle showing you how to duck and cover. Why they didn't use a duck, I don't know. Are there any questions?"

It was ominous. No one spoke.

"Well, in that case, *Down*!"

Not realizing that the command would be yelled without a nuclear flash, we flopped around or froze in place, failing the test miserably. I was wondering why he yelled "down" instead of "duck."

His drawl continued, "Well, most y'all have just been burned to a cinder. I may yell that command at any time. Any of your other teachers may do so also. You must be prepared. Ready? *Down*!"

We dropped, ducked and covered in unison.

"That was much better. The next time I won't ask if y'all are ready, but I'm sure y'all will do much better, now that you have a leg up on the procedure."

We smiled weakly, but never deduced from the "burning to a cinder" part that if there actually were a nuclear attack, we'd most likely be meeting our maker while in the Duck and Cover position.

"Oh, there's just one more thing. Is there anyone disabled or otherwise infirm in this class?"

No response.

He continued, obviously not joking and looking slowly at each of us, "I thought I'd inquire since if there is a true emergency of any kind, including a nuclear emergency, I'm going to be the first person out of the room."

Oh … *that's* what they meant.

And that was my first day at Pearson High. I was shell shocked.

* * * *

24

Ice Cream Sodas

The challenge of social justice is to evoke a sense of community . . .
Marian Wright Edelman

As a freshman, I didn't have a car then, nor did any of the girls. They just didn't. As was the case with a lot of their mothers, many of the girls had not learned how to drive, and it was essentially unknown for a girl to receive a car as a sixteenth birthday present. The males drove and, fortunately for me, Tucker now had a car, a dark green '39 Pontiac Silver Streak Deluxe 6 Four-Door Sedan. He didn't drive it to school much, but he did on dates and was after me to double date with him and his girlfriend, Connie. My desire to pursue that invitation was mitigated by the facts that I didn't have a girlfriend, didn't know a lot of girls at Pearson High and of those I knew, I thought there was a much smaller number who might go if I did ask them. Actually, that number was close to zero. It was a cinch Linda wouldn't go out with me after standing her up for the 8th grade prom in junior high.

But, there was a cute little brunette, Pamela, in one of my classes who was kind of shy and seemed really nice, so I reached out to her and we became friends. In fact, I started to think she liked me as much as I had started to like her and I desperately wanted to ask if she'd like to double date to the movies via Tucker's car. But, at that point in life, it was still the continuing problem of my confidence structure being assembled one lonely brick at a time, and not a lot of solid mortar for reinforcement.

Rejection by a female was still a fearful thing. So fearful that sometimes the question was never asked, and if my courage was mustered to speak, the expectation was to hear "no," so that my face wouldn't look too crestfallen when that answer came. And if it did, I'd mumble, "Oh, okay, thanks" and skulk away, certain that everyone within a two mile radius had heard the conversation.

So, it didn't register when she said, "I'd really like to," and I must have short circuited for a few moments because that was followed a short time later by, "Chip … Chip, when do you want to go?"

"Oh … uh, I'll have to check with Tucker and let you know."

"Okay. I'll have to ask my dad, too, since I've never been on a date in a car."

Unknown to her, that last sentence instantaneously caused my autonomic nervous system to drive my blood pressure up while simultaneously constricting my throat because the mention of a parent, an automobile and a date in the same sentence triggered an overwhelming sense of dread. It happened three years before in the 7th grade on the very first date I ever had with a girl. The young lady involved, who I'm certain would prefer to remain nameless, wasn't in any of my classes and I'd pined for her from afar. Since I'd never been on a real date and didn't know her very well, asking for the first time in my life would take all the intestinal fortitude I could call forth.

One day, I finally blurted out a jumbled request that she accompany me to the Saturday matinee double-feature at the neighborhood theater. Awhile later, after recovering from the euphoria caused by her assent, it dawned on me that we lived on opposite edges of the Martindale Junior High district, a significant logistical dilemma. Thinking it would be kind of neat to pick her up in a car, I asked my mother to drive us.

When my mother and I arrived at her house to pick her up, the two mothers started giggling about how cute we looked and it went on and on and on as if we weren't present, culminating with her mother deciding to ride with us so she could witness the darling little couple being dropped off at the picture show. When we finally escaped that humiliation and got into the theater, the movie hadn't started, the lights were still up and ninety nine percent of the kids were from Martindale. Since we had never been seen as a unit before and gossip was a cornerstone of social structure, all eyes were on us and the place fell almost silent.

Don was there and, as we were trying to find a seat in his row, he asked me how we got there. Like a fool, I told him. The next thing I knew, he was yelling to Tucker five rows back, "Hey, Tuck, Chip's mother drove him here with his lady friend!" Less than three nanoseconds later, those who didn't catch what he said had been informed. Beet-red and mortified, we were wondering, silently and simultaneously, if we could fit under the seats.

That double feature took as long as ten movies, particularly with Don inquiring from time to time concerning how the love birds were doing. But the best was yet to come. Many gathered to watch and wave goodbye as my mother pulled in front of the theater to pick us up. That poor girl never spoke to me again and disappeared whenever I got within a hundred yards of her at school.

Back to Pearson High. The next day, Pamela said it was okay with her dad, but he wanted us to come inside so he could meet all of us before we left, and then he wanted us to come right back there after the pictures, which usually were double features. I didn't have a problem with that. After all, the object was to see the movies, right?

Well, Tucker wasn't all that thrilled with the arrangement, but I told him she said there was a soda fountain in her house and we could all have ice cream after.

Tucker's response, "Holy crap. What kind of house does she live in that has a soda fountain in it?"

"I don't know. Here's the address. She wrote it down for me. We're supposed to be there at 6:30 Friday night."

"Do you know where this is? It's the ritziest part of town way over on the East Side. All the houses have big columns in front of them and those statues of little guys out on the lawn!"

"Big deal."

Tucker mentioned it to his police-detective dad and informed me the next day that her father was in the State Legislature, very high up on the social scale and characteristically hobnobbed around with the most powerful politicians in the state.

"Tuck, we're not taking *him* to the movies."

So, at the appointed time, Tucker, Connie and I pulled into the circular driveway through the big trees and up to the huge house with the manicured lawns, little statues and Corinthian columns supporting the two-story high porte-cochere. We rang the doorbell, heard at least three choruses of Chopin played on a set of chimes deep within the edifice, then the butler opened the door, smiled and invited us in. He turned out to be Pamela's father.

Pamela was nowhere in sight and he congenially chatted with us about how old we were, how long Tucker had been driving, what grade we were in at Pearson, how we knew Pamela, what pictures we were going to see and what time he could expect us back for ice cream. Then he wanted to see Tucker's car, ostensibly because he hadn't seen a 1939 Pontiac for some time. Fortunately for us, Tucker kept it spotless and in perfect condition. It looked like it had been suspended in time from the day it was manufactured and you could eat off the engine. Tucker was proud of it and showed him every detail.

Dad was very impressed and said he'd go upstairs and call Pamela. As she came down the stairs, she stared at me in disbelief. We'd passed the interrogation! As we drove away, he reminded us what time we were supposed to be back, and smiled. I guess he figured we were harmless, which was pretty much the case, and that Tucker took such good care of the Pontiac he probably wouldn't go racing around in it—correct again.

Pamela wanted to know everything that happened and we gave her a general summary. She was astonished. Then, when Tucker turned into the drive-in movie, she got a little nervous.

"Is this where you told my dad we were going?"

Tucker grinned, "Well, I told him what pictures we were going to, but I didn't exactly tell him where it was." Pamela didn't say anything. Sensing some apprehension, Tucker took the oblique, "We'll be back on time. It won't be a problem."

The four of us had more fun than a barrel of monkeys and laughed all night long. We got back on time so we could get our ice cream. Pamela told us to follow her, and it seemed like we walked forever. They even had wall-to-wall carpet in the *halls*. She threw open a set of double doors and we were ushered into a very large, wood paneled recreation room that contained a ping pong table, a pool table and a jukebox, none of which we'd ever seen inside a *house*, and it indeed had a full soda fountain, complete with stools. We'd never seen or heard of a soda fountain anywhere except in a drug store, much less in a house, and Pamela's house at that. We were flabbergasted.

We punched in Johnnie Ray's "The Little White Cloud That Cried," Pamela gave us scoops and we started constructing our concoctions. What a deal. Anywhere else, it'd be five cents a scoop. She put six big scoops of various colored ice creams in a big ice-cream soda glass, the tall kind that are small at the bottom and expand to a wider mouth at the top. She stuck her glass under the soda spigot and pulled the handle, but nothing came out so she fiddled around under the counter, twisting some dials.

"That should do it."

She showed us how she was tipping the glass toward her a little and slightly to the side so the soda would run into the holes around the scoops of ice cream, and then she pulled the handle on the spigot. No soda. We heard a momentary hiss and then a huge blast of compressed air which turned the glass into a mortar tube, blowing the ice cream past Pamela's head and up, way up. All six scoops blasted into the twelve foot high ceiling and stuck there, creating a multi-colored slow-motion waterfall that dripped, and dripped and ....

We laughed and laughed standing under it trying to catch the drips on our tongues to the racing rhythm of Les Paul and Mary Ford's "How High the Moon" when, all of a sudden, it all let go and came hurtling down. Lots of laughing again and then, as we realized it was all over us, our clothes, the ceiling, the floor and the tops and bottoms of our shoes, the humor ground to a halt and Connie started to worry about the late hour. Pamela said she'd clean up the mess. We asked how she was going to get it off the ceiling. She just made a face and said she'd tell her dad about it in the morning.

I figured after he saw that, it would be the last time we'd be there, but he seemed to take it in stride, happy to know where we were I guess, and all of us went out again several times to the movies. At a point on one of those trips to the drive-in, Tucker and Connie started necking, so Pamela and I exchanged a few tentative kisses too. Then Tucker suggested from the front seat, "Let's all French kiss," and he and Connie apparently started in.

I looked at Pamela inquiringly and she half-apologetically whispered in my ear, "I don't know how to French kiss."

"Shoot, me either. I was hoping *you'd* know." We cracked up and decided French kissing wasn't for us, particularly after Tucker explained it.

Pamela and I were developing a very nice relationship on our double dates and one weekend the four of us went to a single feature sit-down theater instead of the drive-in in order to see *Bwana Devil*, the first color stereoscopic 3-D movie feature. Still wearing our cardboard 3-D glasses with one red and one blue cellophane-like lens, we got back to Pamela's house earlier than usual.

We started in on the soda fountain and hadn't been there long when Connie started feeling ill, apparently from all the Coke, popcorn and candy she'd scarfed down at the theater, and Tucker thought he should take her home so her mother could give her some castor oil, lamenting that sometimes she'd lose control when she had too many goodies and if she did, it wouldn't be a pretty sight.

Singing the jingle, "Gimme a package of Beeman's Pepsin Chewing Gum please," Pamela gave Connie a stick saying it might help settle her stomach on the way home. As I was telling Pamela goodbye, her father got wind of the difficulty and said he'd be happy to drive me home later. Problem solved. Tucker left and Pamela and I fooled around at the soda fountain and played ping pong to the strains of Tony Martin's "There's No Tomorrow."

Time to go. I hopped in her dad's big Caddie and the two of us were off. Wow, it was like riding in a living room on wheels. It took awhile to get to the West Side and I was telling him to turn here, turn there and so on as we were talking. Finally I said, "Okay, right here," and he brought the car to a stop. Our street had no street lights and he was squinting trying to see our house. It would have been easy for him to miss if he were by himself since I'm sure it would've fit inside his living room. And, of course, I hadn't mowed my old nemesis the lawn for awhile either. He said in kind of a surprised way, "Is this it?" I said it was, thanked him profusely for taking me home and he drove off.

The next week at school, Pamela seemed a little subdued, but said everything was all right when I inquired. Except, after that, whenever I suggested we go to a movie or something, she seemed sad and always had some prior commitment that prevented our going out. After awhile, I was pretty sure we weren't going to go out anymore and it made me sad too. I just didn't get it.

I get it now, of course, and that's what the Universal Forces were looking for.

* * * *

25

Connie's Hurricane

The proof of the pudding is in the eating.
By a small sample we may judge of the whole piece.

Miguel de Cervantes

IN THEIR EFFORTS TO LIFT me out of my Pamela-melancholy, Tucker and Connie took me down to the amusement park one night. We played the pinball machines, ate enormous quantities of popcorn, hot dogs, French fries and salt water taffy, all washed down with lemonade and Coke, smashed each other around with the bumper cars, walked all over and did lots of other things. We ended up at the Hurricane Racer, a huge wooden Erector-set-like structure supporting a roller coaster that went higher and higher, then almost straight down and fast, fast, fast around the curves. Connie wanted to go on it.

Tucker, "No way. I'm not going on that thing."

"But Tucker, I *want* to. I've never been."

"And I never will. I'll do anything but that."

Apparently she'd hit Tucker's Achilles' heel, so Connie swung around and looked at me with pleading eyes. They hadn't let me pay for anything all night and were basically doing this for me, so I couldn't refuse even though I disliked roller coasters almost as much as Tucker.

I gave it one last shot, "Are you sure you want to do this? When you get up there, it's even with the top of the Martori Building and that's awfully high."

In a pleading whine, "But I've never *been*."

"Okay, okay, but you have to let me buy the tickets. Sure you don't want to go, Tucker?"

We were first in line for the next set of cars. They were actually more like a set of about eight or ten articulated benches hooked together on wheels, two riders to a bench. I told Connie she could have her choice of the very front seat or any of the others. Even Connie knew the front seat would probably be more than she could take, "The very back." So we climbed into the back row while the other patrons filled up the rest of the rows. I was feeling a little full of all the junk we'd eaten and wasn't thrilled about doing this, but …

The coaster jerked into life and went around several escalating curves, rises and dips before it started up Hurricane Hill. I believe it was over 120 feet high, about twelve stories. A big chain under the cars ratcheted it very slowly up the "hill." Clunk, clunk, clunk, clunk, and we were going higher and higher. Soon we were much higher than most of the downtown surrounding buildings and still going up. Clunk, clunk, clunk, clunk. I kept looking over at Connie because she didn't look so good. I was afraid to say anything.

As the coaster reached the top of Hurricane Hill and started to go over the other side, it hesitated just a moment so that everyone was looking almost straight down, twelve stories. During that pause, I glanced at Connie again and her face reminded me of the ice cream on Pamela's ceiling—red, green, yellow, brown, purple and white. Just as the car released and right before it started shooting downward, things started in slow motion, as often seemed to happen to me.

Connie spouted the entire contents of her tummy in projectile fashion, and she'd obviously eaten much more than Tucker and I put together. Her voluminous ejection was propelled in front of the now-plummeting coaster cars, forming a high, hanging canopy. Shooting down the steep grade, the cars pulled under that descending, viscous, perfectly-timed awning of many-colored chunks, and the passengers' immediate destiny was apparent. Their joyful screams turned into guttural cries of anguish as Connie's Hurricane hit.

Then some of the passengers in the front started to spew, causing others to do likewise in a mighty chain reaction lasting for the entire twelve stories. The blowback was terrible. When the cars finally slid to a stop at the end of the ride, no one was a pretty sight. The formerly-joyous revelers shot out of the cars and ran screaming from the coaster in such bad shape they didn't even take time to curse at Connie. The brake attendant standing on the platform took one look and a whiff, "Oooooooooooh my God," then yelling to someone out of sight, "They all blew, fire hose, PDQ!"

Somehow, I'd managed not to barf, but being in the rear seat during that juicy maelstrom at 60 miles per hour in the direction of hell made me think that's exactly where we'd been. When Connie erupted, I reflexively flipped around as much as I could and sunk as far toward the floor of the car as possible, but nevertheless, the back of my shirt, which happened to be green, was soaked and had things on it I'd never seen before. There was something in my hair too.

Tucker, waiting at the passenger exit, took one look at the pandemoniacal scene and laughed so hard he started gagging. We took Connie over to one of the outdoor shower stations by the huge swimming venue and hosed her down, as well as rinsing my shirt and sticking my head under the faucet. When they dropped me off that night, shirt in hand, all I could think of to say was, "Thanks you guys. I really appreciate it. And you know, Connie, you look good now, a little thinner I think." Tucker broke up, Connie started whacking him in the head and I cackled all the way into the house.

I guess the UF felt I just needed a good laugh.

26

Public Service

Only a life lived for others is worthwhile.

Albert Einstein

I WAS FORTUNATE TO HAVE friends like Tucker and Don with cars when I started high school, but I wanted desperately to drive a car myself. The closest I had come so far was driving my mother's Oldsmobile back and forth in the driveway. Since I couldn't qualify for a Learner's Permit until later in the school year, she wouldn't let me take it on the street and neither Tucker nor Don would let me drive theirs.

However, when Shirley went to college, I had inherited the back bedroom, and Tucker, the only expert among the three of us at joyriding, had a plan to help me. I would sneak out at two o'clock in the morning and the three of us would push the Olds out of the driveway and down the block before we started it. Our neighborhood would be like the Hall of the Dead then and it should be a snap. Then I could drive as much as I wanted and Don and Tucker would be there to give me instructions, which is how they justified this venture—a public service.

My mother had retired earlier in the evening and I slipped the keys in my pocket before I went to bed at 10:30. I was fully dressed and, afraid of the noise my alarm clock would make if I set it, I struggled to stay awake the three and a half hours until 2:00.

I kept falling asleep and jerking awake. By 1:30, I was wondering if it was worth it. I thought I'd check the backyard, so I stuck my face up to the venetian blind and pulled up a slat. Two inches from my eyes were two eyes staring back at me. I jumped back, knocked some stuff over, tripped and fell onto the wooden floor. Great, now my mother would wake up and that would be the end of the escapade.

Hoarse whisper from the other side of the window, "What the hell's the matter with you?"

Hoarse whisper back, "Me? What the hell are you doing trying to scare the b'jesus out of me like that?"

Tucker explained he was just about to tap on the window when the slat went up and my eyes got as big as saucers. In the telling, he fell to the ground trying to stifle his laughter with Don pounding on him trying to keep him quiet, which only made him laugh more. Once that settled down, I listened carefully for about ten minutes to see if there would be any activity from my mother, which would be easy enough to hear on the wooden floors. Absolutely nothing. Whew. I raised the venetian blinds and they dragged me head first out the window of the back bedroom, and we went over to the car.

The Olds was, as usual, pulled up to the closed garage door in the back, but not into the garage because it contained all my "stuff," always inappropriately referred to as "crap" by Shirley. The car being outside was a good thing because the springs on the garage door, a double-wide heavy wooden giant that swung upward, always groaned like the Gates of No Return. In any event, we had to be extremely careful because the driveway was on the left side of the house and Bobby's mother's bedroom was actually closer to the dastardly deed than my mother's, and neighborhood moms had an excellent communications network—they talked to each other.

I had taken the precaution of removing the overhead light and leaving the passenger door slightly ajar. We stealthily pulled it open and I slid across the bench seat, planted myself behind the wheel, firmly gripped the shift lever on the steering column and, without the necessity of stepping on the brake which was a safety precaution not yet invented, slowly slipped the Hydra-Matic Drive out of reverse and into neutral. In those days there weren't any seat belts either. Safety was embodied in the idea that the car was built like a tank and its inertia would plow through anything it might hit, unless it was at least a similar car of course.

Don and Tucker started pushing it backwards, an easy task because the driveway slanted slightly toward the street. They got it going pretty good so when it got to the end of the driveway, I'd have enough momentum to swing it parallel with the street and then let it coast to a stop, again no brake lights. An excellent plan. I turned the wheel perfectly and it coasted backwards to a stop in the street, right in front of my mother's bedroom. Everyone froze. No activity. Her venetian blinds remained motionless.

Don came around to the driver's side, I turned the crank and rolled the window down. He whispered, "You idiot."

"You never said which way to turn."

"Should I have to?"

"Well, it's the first time I've been out of the driveway."

His eyes rolled back, "Alright, we're going to push you forward to the far end of the block before we start it."

A 1941 Oldsmobile Dynamic 6 Cruiser Four-Door Sedan must weigh close to 3400 pounds, and the end of the block was about 150 yards away. They got it about 60 feet. Don came up to the window, "You're going to have to help push."

"Who's going to steer?"

"You are. Push on the door post and stick your right hand through the window when it needs it."

I got out and assumed the position. Don and Tucker got behind the car. Tucker whispered, "one, two, three," and in unison, we shoved with all our might to get the metal monster rolling. The only thing that happened was that Don farted. We fell to the street in silent laughter. Collecting ourselves, we finally got it about 50 yards from my house and were sweating bullets, exacerbated by the fact that it was a cool night and we had our jackets on. We couldn't go any farther.

Tucker came up, "Okay, we can't leave it here, so we'll just have to chance starting it. I'll drive it down around the corner and then you can drive."

We got around the corner, Tucker stopped in front of his own parked car and put the Olds in neutral. He moved around to the passenger side to supervise my driving and I slid under the wheel. Don was hanging over the seat from the back.

After all this trouble, I couldn't believe it, "I can't touch the pedals."

"Who was just driving the car?"

"You were."

"Slide the seat up." I did.

"Now we should turn on the lights." I did, and then sat there.

Impatiently, "Okay, put it in gear and let's go."

Going back and forth in the driveway on those very short and repetitive, but authorized, trips, I gauged my forward progress by looking up at my basketball hoop over the garage door. Now I realized I couldn't see the street over the dashboard of that steel behemoth. So, the three of us removed our jackets, piled them up under me, adjusted the seat a little more and I was good to go, thankful it was a Hydra-Matic.

We drove around for about an hour and I felt like I was getting the hang of it real fast. Going back toward my house, I hit a pretty good dip at about 40 miles an hour. Don was sitting in the back and shot up into the air, his vertical travel soon interrupted by the car's cloth headliner and about one-eighth inch later by the car's metal roof, a good advertisement for why seat belts should've been a requirement in those days. It was clear he was still conscious because he said the "f" word, forcefully, followed by a few choice phrases aimed at my driving prowess. Tucker looked back at him, "Chip, make a note. Next time we'll practice slowing for dips."

As we were coming to my street, Tucker said, "Okay, let us out at my car. You get it going, shut off the engine a few houses down and coast up your driveway."

The Universal Forces kept me from tumbling off that turnip truck, "Noooooo, nooooo, nooooooooo, no. You guys have to stay with me until I get it into the back yard." A brief and lively discussion followed, and, based on what they'd seen in the past hour, they decided to stay with me.

I got it going about 30 miles an hour toward the house, shut off the lights, put it in neutral and shut off the engine. As we got closer, Tucker started saying under his breath, "Too fast, too fast, too fast." I stepped on the brake pedal and as we were almost at the driveway, Tucker started saying, "Too slow, too slow, too slow." I whipped the wheel left and very shortly thereafter, it became clear the car was going to creep to a halt about half way up the inclined driveway. Tucker and Don instinctively jumped out, very quietly I might add, and started pushing for all they were worth. Just as they dropped to their knees, that metal beast rolled to a stop at its designated resting place and I popped it into reverse, the "Park" gearshift position of those days.

We examined Don's head closely and deemed it okay. They shoved me back through the bedroom window and that was that. Except for the small permanent bubble in the top of the torpedo roof over the back seat, which my mother never did notice, Don and Tucker's altruistic public-service mission was a success.

I'm not sure if there was a UF lesson there, but I did learn how to drive, and they apparently arranged it so we all stayed in one piece, including Don, even though he may have been a teeny bit shorter.

* * * *

27

The Relationship Between Jazz and Cars

There is no such thing as chance or accident; the words merely signify our ignorance of some real and immediate cause.

Adam Clarke

At the same time I had started high school, Shirley had started college out of state, but her high school boyfriend, a very nice guy, still dropped by from time to time to visit with my mother and me. Tommy liked me and had never punched me in the nose. Of course, having had that experience once, I was careful not to have it repeated.

He had his own car and it was a really cool powder blue (not the original color), four door, 1939 De Soto Deluxe 6 with a Syncro-Silent three-speed transmission, a Handy-Shift lever mounted on the steering post, electric overdrive and electric windshield wipers (a modern innovation when the car was made) and a screened, push-up (by hand) outside fresh-air vent between the windshield and the hood (an air vent or two and the windows were essentially a vehicle's air conditioning feature in those days). But, best of all, it was *customized* with a fur-lined glove compartment. It was the greatest car I had ever ridden in. Even better, in my opinion, than Pamela's father's Cadillac.

At a point later in the school year, Tommy said he wanted to sell it in a few weeks when he'd saved the rest of the money he needed so he could buy a foreign sports roadster, and if I had enough money by the time he was ready to sell, he would let me have the De Soto for $300 even though it was worth significantly more. That was a kind gesture, but unreachable for me since the savings from my pre-Pearson High summer jobs, which consisted of a paper route and a sweeping gig at Mr. Hendelman's hardware store, were rapidly dwindling due to my recreational expenditures. My funds had only been extended to this point by pocketing my lunch money from time to time and hitching rides to school periodically instead of taking the bus, plus my mother would give me small sums for the movies from time to time.

However, the Universal Forces had already been arranging some important things for my benefit, starting when I was about six years old. My mother had one jazz record in her small record collection. It was a single number by the Benny Goodman Orchestra that was so long it filled both sides of a 78 rpm recording with an extended version of the bombastically energetic tune for which Goodman's 1938 Carnegie Hall Jazz Concert is most remembered. I'd heard my mother playing that record often, and in my sixth year she showed me how to work our RCA console which combined an AM radio and a 78 rpm record changer, the grandest piece of furniture we owned at the time.

After that, I played "Sing, Sing, Sing" with Gene Krupa on the drums at every opportunity, instinctively appreciating why it's arguably the most famous tune ever to come out of the Swing Era. I would get my head as close to the speakers as I could, turning them up as loud as Mommy would tolerate. She witnessed my joy and, over the next few years, that kicked off presents of recordings with solos by Buddy Rich, followed by Louie Bellson. They were the triumvirate of big band drummers in that day. Starting with Gene, those sounds were my inspiration and are still in my head now.

So that particular planning by the Universal Forces came to fruition in my fifteenth year when my dad came to town for a visit as he did often when he wasn't transporting Shirley and me to his city for a visit from time to time. But this time he was accompanied by his much-cherished brother, my Uncle Sam (yep, that was really his name), whom I'd heard of many times but had never met. He and his wife were as nice as my father, and they were quite well off, the latter fact unknown to me then because those types of observations weren't within the universe of my thoughts.

Similarly outside the penumbra of my perception was the fact that my father also made a very nice living. I didn't know that at the time, primarily because my mother was very independent, a women's rights advocate (many years before the term "women's liberation" was popularized and probably before anyone had even thought about coining it) and, as a result when they divorced, she had refused to take any money from him. That was over his strenuous objection since he sincerely wanted to support all of us in a much grander style, and she ultimately consented to his giving us presents, which included buying us clothes. That's why we were the best dressed kids on the block and I had a football uniform no one else would let me use. Like I said before, I never wondered why some things were the way they were, they just were.

While I always had those Krupa-Rich-Bellson sounds running around in my head, I didn't have a set of drums because the price was way too much for me to afford at the rate I earned money and, so far as I believed, way too much to even ask for from anyone in the family, not even as a Christmas gift. So I made do. For a couple of years before Uncle Sam's visit, I'd kept a little bench in my room with several different thicknesses of magazines on it to represent different sized drums. Somehow, I knew the right way to hold the drumsticks, but that was all. The rhythms I made on those magazines were my best approximation of the Krupa-Rich-Bellson in my head. I don't know what the three of them would have thought.

My drum bench started when I was in my stucco tunnel bedroom. When I moved into there, Shirley returned to the back bedroom, to which I then subsequently migrated when she left for college. Liberated from my elongated tube, the great thing about being back in my original bunk-bed abode, sans the bunk, was that it had electrical outlets and I could play my magazines to the radio. "Just a Song at Twilight" with Gene Krupa licks sounded okay to me.

In any event, my father, my uncle and my aunt stayed for a week in one of the downtown hotels. Even though I was only fifteen, I drove them around town in my mother's Oldsmobile, an act legalized so far as I believed because I'd just acquired a Learner's Permit and a licensed driver would be in the car with me, most of the time anyway. I sort of discounted the time when I was driving to the hotel to pick them up and after I dropped them off.

Uncle Sam chatted with me from time to time during the week about what I liked to do, and in a natural progression asked me what I would like to do that I had never been able to do. So, when they came over to the house, for the first time I'd disclosed it to anyone not living with us, I showed them my drum bench and, even though I felt really stupid with them watching, I played the magazines and told them my Gene Krupa jazz-record story. In passing, I described the set of white pearl Gene Krupa Deluxe Radio King Slingerland drums in the window of Rodney's Music Store, which I pined over every Sunday after church, but they were $600 which was more money than I'd ever seen in my life, and apparently a lot more money than other aspiring drummers had because that nifty and highly desirable set had been in the window a long time. My uncle let the subject drop.

On the day they were leaving, we were all in my uncle's hotel room and I was telling the three of them goodbye. He casually mentioned my desire to play the drums and asked if I'd really stick with it if I had a set. I reminded him of my drum bench, but said it didn't matter because they were just too much money. Drums being something out of reach, I thought he was simply making pleasant conversation. He smiled and, with his eyes twinkling a little more than usual, he looked at my aunt and dad who were smiling also, pulled out his wallet, peeled off six brand new one hundred dollar bills, handed them to me and said whatever I made out of them was up to me.

The feelings I had are not describable (I'm tearing up as I write this) and of course I thanked my uncle and his wife profusely. It gave them and my father great joy to see how happy I was. And, since my uncle said it was up to me, I made good use of the money too. I got Rodney down to $300 on the drums and, Universal Forces having been busy arranging Tommy's finances, I bought his De Soto with the other $300, promptly naming it "Speedball Baby" after a powder blue, Indianapolis 500, wind-up toy racing car I'd had in grade school.

* * * *

28

Cyclonic Connection—Track, Rhythm, and Blues

I have a dream ....

Martin Luther King, Jr.

IMMEDIATELY, I MADE A DEAL with my mother and the neighbors. With my mother that I would set the drums up in our detached garage, and with the neighbors, concentrating the most on Bobby's mother since her backyard was bordered on one side by our garage, that I would stop playing promptly at 9:00 p.m. if they wouldn't complain. I kept that promise and it was perhaps a minor nondisclosure that with my new car, I would be able to rush home after school and start playing at 4:00 p.m., which I ultimately did, breaking only for a quick dinner. My mother wasn't happy with that, but she was happy to know where I was. Oh, I "solved" the Learner's Permit problem by taking Tucker to school with me and back, coupled with the same discounted-time method to and from his house.

But, I had a couple of significant pre-existing problems. I didn't know how to play the drums and I couldn't afford lessons. I'd never even hit a real drum before I got my white pearl Gene Krupa Slingerlands with the Radio King snare drum, and they definitely didn't sound like the magazines. So, with the Krupa-Rich-Bellson sounds bouncing around in my head, I just sat down behind those beauties, whose accoutrements included a set of Avedis Zildjian cymbals, and I pounded on them almost five hours a day, much longer on weekends, every day for three months straight. Not much was happening except cacophony. Then, one day, the *gestalt* closed and what was in my head came out through my hands and feet. I can still remember Bobby's long-suffering mother asking me the next day, "What happened?"

So now that I could make my hands and feet do what I was thinking and feeling, I needed to play to some music. I purloined three small AM table radios from the house and put them on makeshift stands, one on each side of my head and one in back of it. The forerunner to rock and roll (not yet a musical genre) was rhythm and blues, one of the major types of listening pleasure for my peer group. I dreamed of playing that, but the only program I could get in the garage that came in clearly enough and loud enough on all three radios was Frank Bull's Dixieland Jazz.

Static-free FM could be found in some very expensive console radios containing several broadcast bands, but what commercial FM programming there was primarily broadcast classical music, and in any event, combining FM and AM tuners in small table radios, so common today, was essentially unknown then. So I cranked those static-laden AM radios up as high as they would go and learned to play drums to Dixieland—Ray Bauduc, Nick Fatool, Art Tatum, Bob Crosby, Louis Armstrong and me. I loved it. I was playing. But there were no Dixieland bands at my high school nor would any of my peers consider that cool.

Even though the Universal Forces hadn't arranged the kind of music consistent with my rhythm-and-blues dream, I kept dreaming the dream and one day during track-team practice at high school, one of my track mates, nicknamed "Cyclone" because he was extremely fast (they continued to call me Chip), said he'd heard I had a set of drums. He asked me to play with the rhythm and blues band he was forming, the Blue Notes (I know, the name wasn't original, but it *was* high school). I figured I'd better level with him and tell him I could only play Dixieland, played by ear, couldn't read music and I'd never actually played with *people*.

Cyclone's response, "That's great, man. Come on over after school." Fortunately, my band mates were patient and encouraging with me, the only white face in the Blue Notes, and my dream was becoming reality.

We played together a lot. All of our school gigs were frequent dances in one of our high school's two recreation canteens, the one Cyclone went to all the time. The Blue Notes never played at the other canteen. While it may be difficult to believe in the present day and age, originally I was so clueless that I thought the Pearson High kids who came only to the canteen we played at did it because all the black kids, and the few white kids who came, were on the cutting edge of hip and that they liked dancing to rhythm and blues a lot better than to recordings of Patti Page singing "Tennessee Waltz" or Teresa Brewer singing "Cotton Fields." Since I was still at the stage in life where most, if not essentially all, my thoughts revolved around *me*, it never registered that I'd never seen a black kid in the other canteen.

Up to that juncture in my life, the only time that discrimination based primarily on what a person looked like had previously touched my experience, and I didn't recognize the implications of it then either, was when Japanese Americans began enrolling in Lincoln Elementary a few months before the end of the war. I was in fourth grade as I recall when I saw a person of Japanese ancestry in the flesh for the first time. Conditioned by WWII combat movies, I was amazed to learn there were Japanese people who were *Americans*, and the reason I'd never seen them was that all those in our area had been segregated in camps by our government (euphemistically called "relocation" camps) shortly after WWII started when I was in kindergarten. Not recognizing the import nor the broader ramifications of that information, I didn't ponder why our friends the Brunghanel's across the street, whom I knew were Americans of German ancestry, hadn't been in a camp, nor did I wonder about the Colombo kids down the block who were Americans and their parents came from Italy.

In any event, our Blue Notes band had a blast. Cyclone had a little trick he used that heated it up toward the end of the evening. We'd start an "up" tune a little slower than usual and Cyclone would have me progressively increase the speed of the beat, hopefully imperceptibly, over the next few minutes until the tune was charging about three times faster than when it started. The saxes were wailing, the kids were screaming and the energy level could propel a bus. It was a lot of fun, but a bad habit for a drummer, particularly when I started playing jazz a few years later.

I'm telling you, I think the kids at the other place who didn't come to see the Blue Notes lost out by dancing only to Patti Page and Teresa Brewer records. They never got to hear our rhythm and blues covers of Big Jay McNeely, the king of the honking tenor saxes, and of the superbly talented Earl Bostic growling on his alto.

My clueless state ended awhile later when one of my closest friends since junior high, the incoming Editor-in-Chief of the Pearson High newspaper and one of the white kids who came to hear us play, carefully explained the segregated facts of life to me, astonished at my naïveté. I couldn't believe it. It all seemed so stupid. MaryJean clearly thought so too, vehemently. And as incoming Editor-in-Chief, she was going to have access to the press.

In those days, high school newspapers were filled with what the bowling and Latin clubs were doing, as well as similar polite tidbits of the day. But, MaryJean was hearing her own drummer loud and clear and stood everything on its ear. She didn't have the time to wait for the U.S. Supreme Court to finish deciding Brown v. Board of Education. Before she was done, there were fist fights among adults at the city's school board meetings, which was perhaps the best way for a bad thing to occur since it was adults, not the kids, who made that policy and enforced it at the other canteen. But in the end, the canteens were officially desegregated.

Of course, as a matter of the heart, Cyclone's canteen had always been integrated because all were welcome to listen and dance to the really good stuff. Oh, and MaryJean, she was honored with a major regional social service award.

And the Universal Forces? They were providing me with several extremely important first-hand examples of awareness, character, heart and courage.

* * * *

29

Synchronous Filament—Baseball, Movies, and Track

There are no loose threads in the web of life.

Lenny Flank

You know, I may never have gotten to know Cyclone in high school, with the results that I would play rhythm and blues and also be a first-hand witness to the important related lessons I've just described, if the Universal Forces hadn't made arrangements for a couple of necessary steps to set the stage for our meeting. The initial step in those arrangements was the "family jewels" baseball game back in the fifth grade which resulted in distress I couldn't possibly see was for my benefit at that time, but caused me to decide to play second base in the future.

Consequently, by the time I reached my last year in junior high, second base had become my position on the baseball team after considerable effort on my part and the second step had begun. Well, I was a second-stringer and hadn't started a game all season, but I did get to sub a few times. In fact, we never knew if we would start until just before a game, but I'd learned not to clutter my mind with remote possibilities.

We had a big game coming up Saturday morning; however, since I wasn't concerned about being a major force in it, I decided to go to the horror picture marathon at an all-night downtown movie theater with some of my less mindful buddies on Friday night, unconsciously including myself in their loosely thought out mindset. In order to do that, I had to sneak out of the house after bedtime, which was easy because in junior high, I was still in the stucco tunnel and the door to the backyard was right next to my bed.

At that particular point in my life, I'd never really done anything like that, much less stayed awake that long. My most extended evening foray had been yelling and pounding pans outside at midnight on New Year's Eve and then going straight to bed, a relief because I was sleepy and it was boring waiting around to have that much fun. Anyway, at the appointed time on Friday night, I snuck out silently, a fun-seeking ghost in the mist, met my buddies at the bus stop and we rode that belching behemoth downtown to the movies, gleeful in our surreptitious freedom.

When we got out of the theater, we discovered there were some disadvantages to living in the "Now" in a mindless way. It was a lot colder than when we arrived and to our chagrin we found that our regular bus didn't run that late and the all-night busses didn't run anywhere near our neighborhood. We started walking home in the dark. It was surprisingly scary downtown that time of night and we often thought we saw nefarious figures in the shadows but, with a lot of juvenile bravado, we made it back, arguing most of the way about whose bright idea it was to go to the movies.

I got home just in time to do my paper route, which I remembered in the darkness as I was sneaking up the driveway. I really disliked getting up early to do that, but I needed the money. Anyway, what luck, I was already up! Engaging in that permissible predawn activity, I grabbed my route bag and bike and headed for the drop point to fold my papers.

As I finished my route, I realized it was almost time for the game. I sped to the baseball field and arrived just as Coach was calling everyone together, but I'd forgotten my glove. No matter, I wouldn't be starting anyway and if I went in, I could use Clay's since he would be coming out. Coach Ware spotted me. "Chip, you're starting." Right at that moment, I realized I hadn't had any sleep in more than twenty four hours, I had a headache and my eyes were blurry, but what a great opportunity! If I did well, who knows what could happen. I borrowed Clay's glove and stumbled onto the field.

We were the home team and my legs felt like lead from my movie-walk as I stood on the infield that first inning, the sleepy guardian of second base. Before I knew it, they'd scored a run and there was a man on third with two out. Luckily, I wasn't involved in any of those plays. When our pitcher (as we loosely referred to him) started his motion, I bent my knees and assumed the ready position, staring blurrily at the strike zone so I could be moving the instant the bat contacted the ball, a little trick of mine.

The hitter struck the ball and it was bouncing on the ground straight toward me. Something wasn't right. I saw two baseballs. I stuck my glove down for the one on the left and the ball bounced into it. What luck. Since everyone was screaming "First! First!", I spun toward the base as I pulled the ball out of my glove. Things still weren't right. I saw two identical first basemen. I threw to the wrong one. After the ball had sailed into the next county, the run had scored and the batter had stopped at second, Coach pulled me out.

Right then and there, I decided I'd try *track* when I started high school next year.

Gotta love those Universal Forces.

* * * *

30

Even Cars Need to Eat

How people treat you is their karma; how you react is yours.

Wayne Dyer

AFTER AWHILE IN HIGH SCHOOL, I didn't spend all my spare time playing the drums. I couldn't. There were other important things, a job to support the car, girls, and I wanted to save enough money to get a motorcycle. Through a friend at church, I got a job in a cafeteria downtown. It required multiple skills. I peeled vegetables in the "prep" room, bussed dishes and washed the windows as necessary. Washing windows was a little inconsistent with the initial job description I was given, but I thought it made sense to gain as much work experience as possible. You never know what could be important in the future.

And washing windows was the most difficult part of the job because the owner, Giovanni, had me do it exactly at the beginning of the lunch-hour rush so the ingesting hordes could witness our attention to cleanliness. While I washed the windows, he bussed the dishes and chatted it up with the customers. He was a marketing genius. Consistent with his view of me as an idiot high-school kid who, among other things, hadn't learned the value of saving money wherever possible, he advised that it was a waste of money to buy a bucket for me when I could use an old stainless steel container that appeared to have something to do with the steam tables in its former life.

It was about eight inches in diameter, two feet deep and had no lip around the top, essentially a stainless steel tube with a bottom but no handles. I was instructed to fill it almost to the top with a strong solution of half ammonia and half water, which made it heavy in addition to being very slippery when wet. Giovanni also had an eighteen-inch rubber squeegee with a very short handle that, held by the end as Giovanni instructed, could be completely dipped in the solution in one motion, saving time and effort. That made Giovanni very happy, as did the fifty percent ammonia solution which would cut rapidly through whatever was on the windows. He was oblivious to the side effect of the fumes, which scrubbed the membranes of my eyes, nose and throat.

Because the ammonia came in a big, heavy glass bottle (no plastic bottles in those days) and Giovanni didn't want the idiot, vegetable-peeling busboy carrying big, heavy glass bottles around through the customer area or outside, he instructed me to fill my two-foot stainless test tube at the big sinks behind the steam tables and then carry it outside through the rapidly-filling customer seating area. Once outside, and in accordance with his very specific instructions, I would place it next to the hose by the big plate glass windows, turn the hose on, open the hose nozzle and spray the windows with only enough water to wet them, turn the hose nozzle off, turn the hose off, dip my squeegee into the ammonia solution with a single motion and squeegee the windows, standing on the low bottom sill to reach the tops, pulling the rag from my back pocket to catch the places I missed.

When I finished, I stuck the rag, followed by the end of the foot and half squeegee, into the back pocket of my Levi's, coiled up the rubber hose next to the building, picked up my now-really-slippery stainless tube with about a foot of 50% ammonia solution left in it, and worked my way through the crowded customer tables toward the sinks in order to empty the container. Giovanni didn't want me to dump the remains in the gutter because it smelled like, well, the pungent ammonia solution it was and might deter potential customers, nor did he want me to wash it away in the gutter because it wasted water he had to pay for.

One particularly busy day after doing the windows, I carefully negotiated my way toward the back of the crowded room to reach the steam-table sinks. There was just one more table to get past with my wet, slippery, stainless tube in those tight quarters. "More tables, more people eating," as Giovanni would happily say.

Speaking of more, to make it more difficult, there was a hefty middle-aged patron hot on my heels going for the empty seat next to her friend at that last table. Just as I reached it, the abdominous lady behind me called out to her friend who turned and knocked her dessert dish off the table with a beautiful piece of untouched chocolate cake adhering upright to that flying saucer. As was becoming a usual occurrence during pressure packed events in my life, things started to go into slow motion.

Like an idiot high-school kid, I stopped quickly and started to flip the container to my left arm so I could catch the dessert plate with my right hand. Being unable to control the forward inertia of her considerable bulk, the corpulent lady closing in on my backside cracked the edge of her tray into the "funny bone" of my right elbow just as the flip was commencing, causing the ammonia container to rise high into the air and drop directly down onto the top edge of the seat-back on the empty chair right next to the seated friend, the concussion turning the tube into a stainless steel cannon that propelled a large ball of ammonia water back into the air.

Simultaneously with those events and having set my intention about two quarks before the tray chop to my elbow, I bent over to snare the chocolate cake dish screaming toward the floor. That caused the squeegee in my back pocket to vault the tailgaiting woman's tray into the air, spinning it upside down at its apex, the centrifugal force dispersing the contents of that very hungry woman's extremely full tray in a manner reminiscent of Connie's Hurricane.

A vortex of coffee, creamed corn, gravy, roast beef, chicken, string beans, soggy bread, butter, jelly, green Jell-O and other assorted chunks started to descend onto the unlucky patrons nearby as well as the tailgater herself, eerily coordinating with the stainless steel cannon's concussed ammonia-water ball which came down on the head of the seated friend who was still watching her cake glide toward the floor on top of the porcelain UFO.

Through that quick action and the miracle of slow motion while pandemonium reigned around me, I caught the dessert plate with my left hand, my right rendered useless by the funny-bone-cracking tray.

My search for a new job commenced that afternoon with my verbal description of the cafeteria work experience as my sole résumé. It must have been my smile. I landed a job at the most exclusive restaurant in town. My new duties were table setups, pouring water and bussing the used dishes when they were finished. No windows. It was in a much nicer part of town than the cafeteria. I had to wear black trousers and a white shirt, and the clientele were often the cream of the crop, the kind of folks who came in furs and evening gowns on Saturday night to dine before the opera. You know, the kind I'd never seen before. Well, maybe except for Pamela's dad.

I liked the job and, as was the desire of the maître d', Martín, I worked hard at doing it quickly, efficiently and attentively, particularly since part of my job was to keep the patrons' water glasses filled when I wasn't clearing tables and rushing dishes out to the kitchen in my bussing cart. I got so good at water-filling that one Saturday night, an "opera night" to be precise, a regular, very-demanding and arrogant opera-night patron flipped me a quarter as he was leaving. It was so unusual, particularly from him, that I wasn't expecting it and missed the quarter.

He seized that opportunity to make loud, thoughtless and demeaning prognostications about my future in connection with handling money, and his wife joined him in laughing uproariously at my embarrassment. At that moment, I wanted to flip them something too, but having matured somewhat in connection with employment, I smiled and went back to the kitchen. My car had to eat too and I needed the job. But I didn't need that *particular* quarter and I left it on the floor.

Opera night had special significance for me after that and I was ready to catch anything flipped my way. Then one opera night a few weeks later, who came in but arrogant Demeaning Man and Laughing Wife. They sat on the aisle at a table for two in another busboy's area and, as I needed to make the turn to the kitchen with my cart several tables before reaching them, they didn't have the opportunity to again use me as their foil. Not that they would have; they almost knocked me down going to their table and there wasn't a scintilla of recognition.

As was usual for the opera, they were really decked out. He had on the obligatory tuxedo, looking like the shirt collar was choking him to the point he wouldn't be able to eat, and she was resplendent in pearls, a perfect coiffe and a long, white silk gown which she carefully arranged around her chair like a bridal train as they were seated. Standing at my station, he was facing toward me and she had her back to me, her gown flowing perilously close to the aisle. No matter, everyone was trained to step around such things at all costs, and I didn't have to go near them anyway.

As they had clearly forgotten about me, probably about the time the valet brought their car that first mean-spirited night, I decided to forget about them since they wouldn't even be a footnote in the book of my life. Starting right then we got so busy that I did completely forget about them since it was not only opera night, but a large cat show was going to start just down the street and those folks were streaming in for dinner. I was rushing around so much there was no time to dwell on annoying people.

One of the popular house specialties was a Plank Plate, a round two-inch thick wooden plate twelve or fourteen inches in diameter with a ring of mashed potatoes around the outside, a ring of peas just inside that, a rib eye in the middle and a thick house sauce poured over everything. The people who went to the opera never ordered it, but other people did. It was crazy with waiters and busboys rushing around everywhere, but Martín was calmly directing the operation like the European pro he was, assuring everyone individually that they would be finished in time to attend their respective events.

My cart was piled to the brim with dishes and I was rushing down the isle with it, about to make the left turn into the kitchen when, on the fly, a waiter popped an almost intact Plank Plate on top of all my dirty dishes. I started the turn and looked at it wobbling on its precarious perch. Someone had eaten the steak out of the middle but everything else was as untouched as the moment it left the chef's loving hands. As I flew around the turn to the kitchen, the slow motion thing started again. The Plank Plate failed to make that left turn and began floating off the cart toward the floor. Then, like a coin on edge, it rolled down the aisle, shooting sauce-laden peas into the air like a Gatling gun.

The patrons toward whom it was headed got wide-eyed, including arrogant Demeaning Man. Seeing his expression, arrogant Laughing Wife turned in her chair as the wooden disc rolled toward her, saucy peas flying, flecked with mashed potatoes. Spinning closer and closer, it started going slower and slower and, just before it reached Laughing-Wife-now-frozen-with-fear, the peas stopped popping off and just stuck to it as it rolled right up to the edge of her furled gown and stopped. Her eyes looked heavenward and she relaxed with relief.

Of course, she couldn't see that in slow motion it was wobbling ever so slightly. Then it shuddered and fell face-first onto her gown. Brown sauce, peas and mashed potatoes never looked so good on white silk. She screamed. He recognized me and started yelling and pointing. Martín materialized behind me and told me to go into the kitchen immediately and wait for him. I willingly complied as they directed their angry energy at Martín about how their evening was ruined, not to mention the cost of her gown. I was in the kitchen for twenty minutes or so wondering if Martín might give me a recommendation for my next job. He finally came in.

In despair, "Well, I guess that's it for me."

Expressionless, he looked at me for a few seconds, "I command you to work every Saturday night and, if fortune smiles on us, then those insufferáblè jackásses will never eat here again." A big grin broke through his accent.

Universal Forces were obviously still at work, on all fronts.

* * * *

31

The Road from Fur to Bondo

You cannot love a car the way you love a horse.
Albert Einstein

Oh?
SW

My cash flow was pretty good when the busboy money was combined with the allowance my father had started sending me, having been impressed by his visit. I had enough to support the car, go on a few dates, and even had some left over to customize the car so I would be cool enough that dating might take place at a higher frequency than sporadic, and it might even be possible to acquire a steady girlfriend—a mark of maturity leading to expanded social acceptance.

And, since Speedball Baby already had a fur-lined glove compartment, completing her customization was appropriate, if not necessary. I started frugally, and wishfully, with a "Necker knob" (also known as a spinner or suicide knob) that I attached to the steering wheel so I could turn it with one hand while I had my arm around my non-existent girlfriend which I hoped the car would help me acquire. Then I sprung for a set of whitewalls. Well, not really. Whitewalls cost a lot of money so I bought a can of rubberized whitewall paint at Pep Boys. I believe Manny, Moe and Jack were still alive then, so you know there was no such thing as skinny whitewalls, just the big fat ones that covered most of the tire. As a result, it took the entire can of the thick, rubberized whitewall paint, dashing my hope of saving some in case I scraped a tire.

Even though I installed a set of spring-wire curb feelers at the bottom of the right-side fenders and took great care not to scrape the tires on curbs, my un-scraped whitewalls soon became a Frankenstein's Monster. The paint turned yellow within a month and yellow whitewalls attracted negative attention, so I had to buy another can and keep touching them up because the touch-up would turn yellow, and the paint in the can was hard on the top each time I opened it, so it ran out quickly and then I had to buy another can and ....

After learning to live with that, I acquired a set of tear-drop rear fender skirts and installed them, completing my four-door De Soto sedan's nifty streamlined look. But something still didn't look right, so I bit my lip and sprung for the bucks to have the skirts painted the same color as the car. That was the touch.

Then I realized that all the really cool cars had deep, throaty, dual mufflers and dual tail pipes with chrome tips, one on each side of the car. After getting the skirts painted, there was no way I could afford the entirety of that custom modification, so I hunted around until I found a muffler shop that agreed to do just what I asked, after they stopped laughing. Because, as usual, my funds were low, I bought their cheapest new and very noisy muffler. Then I fished around in their junk pile for some tailpipe scraps and had the shop make a "Y" coming out of my new muffler and run a tailpipe to each side of the car, a novel and apparently humorous idea in those days.

After that, I bought a new chrome tip and fastened it onto the end of one tailpipe with the set-screw, then did the same with my existing chrome tip on the other. It sounded mellifluous, very similar to our neighbor's new Buick Dynaflow; that is, like a tank on rubber tires. The crowning touch was adding a set of fake wire-wheel hubcaps to the front rims. I was well on my way to becoming a motorized Casanova.

As my finances allowed, I Frenched the nose, rear deck lid and doors by removing the hood ornament and other pieces of chrome, trunk handle and outside door handles on all four doors. Then I filled in all the holes with Bondo body putty and sanded it down, covering the puttied areas with grey primer until the time I might be able to afford to have the entire car repainted. There were a lot of high school kids' cars running around with the spotted-primer paint scheme.

Once I'd accomplished the Frenching operation, I realized I had a problem. There was no way to lock the trunk (a "luggage locker" in the car's original advertisements). Worse, if I shut all the doors with the windows closed, I wouldn't be able to get back into the car—luckily figuring that out while one of the windows was rolled down. So, I started inquiring about what others did with a Frenched car. They used electric solenoids with hidden switches to open the doors and trunk. Well, I couldn't afford that luxury, so the trunk was never locked, but it looked great, and even though you could just lift it up by the edge, there was no visible means to open it.

I also left one of the little front door "wing" windows unlatched, so I could push it open, contort my arm through the hole and open the door from the inside. Not impressive on a date but I got pretty slick at it. So my car always looked locked, and anyone knowledgeable enough to look for my hidden nonexistent door and trunk solenoid switches would never be able to find them. The security tactic for wire-wheel hubcaps on the front revolved around the fact that I was apparently the only person in the world who wanted just two of them.

When coupled with the Universal Forces looking out for me, it was an effective system.

* * * *

32

The Battle

I coulda been a contender. I coulda been ***somebody***.

Marlon Brando,
On The Waterfront
(Tennessee Williams)

THINGS WERE STARTING TO DEVELOP. Not only was I playing with a rhythm and blues band, but right after I started playing with Cyclone, the Universal Forces arranged for Billy to transfer to my high school, a fellow drummer and a devotee of Gene Krupa, Buddy Rich and Louie Bellson. We had an instant friendship and Billy came over soon after we met and we chatted about drumming, taking turns playing my drums. I played all the licks I'd thought up or that I'd mimicked from music I heard, and Billy did likewise.

He said he'd heard our high school talent show was coming very soon and suggested we do a drum battle like Krupa and Rich. It sounded like a great idea to me, but there wasn't enough room in the garage to set up his drums too, so we never got a chance to practice together. We just talked about what we were going to do and practiced on my drums in the little time we had left. Our plan was basic, alternate solos two or three times and then both play together for the furious finish.

The big day came. The talent show was a much-anticipated event and the school auditorium was filled to capacity with students. Both our drum sets were in the middle of the stage behind the curtain. Billy was on my left and we'd decided we would both play "time" on the cymbals while the curtain was opening and then he'd go first. We were announced and the curtain slowly opened. The crowd roared at those two gleaming white pearl drum sets with our first names on the front of our bass drums. All eyes were on us. It was like getting pulled across the junior high dance floor by the crotch of my pants, only in a good way this time.

I nodded to Billy and he took off. He was playing my licks! I couldn't believe it! So, when it was my turn, I played his licks. Then he played his licks. Then I played my licks. For the finish, first we both played his licks together, then my licks together. The crowd was crazy and our reputations were made. Billy said he just couldn't help it. He had those sounds in his head when the curtain opened and that's what came out in his hands and feet. I knew the feeling.

And finally, I was *somebody*. All thanks to my Uncle Sam—God bless him. He was obviously in cahoots with the Universal Forces.

* * * *

33

Chicken Yard

Chicken one day, feathers the next.

Anon

EVEN THOUGH I HAD NEWFOUND confidence, I still wasn't nearly as fast as Cyclone in track even though I kept trying. I was too light to play football, too short to play basketball and I didn't have good memories of baseball. The two-first-basemen fiasco, particularly when combined with the family-jewels incident, just didn't leave pleasant feelings.

Because of all those things and the fact we had an all-male cheerleading squad in high school, I decided to try out for cheerleader. It looked like a lot of fun and I'd have an on-the-field seat for the games. Cheerleaders were picked by popular vote after demonstrating their skills by individually leading a cheer in a school assembly. I signed up and started practicing in secret.

Having watched previous tryouts, I'd noticed that all the participants merely led their cheers and exited the stage. My strategy was to add a little extra so the voters would be certain to remember me. Thus, I decided I'd tell a joke before I started. Now, you have to remember, this was back in the days when there was still civility, still societal rules concerning what you should not say in public, particularly within the confines of the youthful halls of learning, even though those rules were often developed after the fact and applied as if they had previously been in existence. I think the guideline in effect then was the question, "What would offend an unreasonable prude with no sense of humor?"

When the big day came, my turn was around the middle of the lineup of hopefuls. Having already seen me in the auditorium during the drum battle, the crowd yelled and whistled when I walked over to the microphone.

I smiled, "I couldn't decide between a couple of cheers today. The one I decided not to do was called, 'I lost my gum in the chicken yard and thought I found it three times'."

Pandemonium ensued. The whole place fell out. They must have laughed and hooted for five minutes. When they finally quieted down, I did my cheer and left to thunderous applause.

My votes were never even counted. The faculty supervisors disqualified me for "inappropriate conduct." Not in my view. I had a blast.

The Universal Forces were still teaching me to find the optimum way to march to my drummer, but it ate at me.

* * * *

34

Cleanliness

... the rain ... a wonderful feeling, I'm happy again.

Arthur Freed

I HAD A CLOSE FRIEND, WARNER. He had a nifty little 1929 Ford Model A Coupe painted royal blue with black spoked wheels. The top was chopped down so the roof was several inches lower than stock and the gearshift lever on the floor had been similarly shortened. The engine was the original four-cylinder and it ran pretty well.

Warner and I had a lot of fun chugging around in it as fast as it would go and blowing the aooga horn, but our specialty depended on the weather. We'd noticed that right after it rained and the sun came out, people would get their cars washed at a car wash on a corner not far from Warner's dad's business establishment. There was only one exit from the carwash, followed by the patrons often being forced to wait for the traffic light on the corner.

After a rain, there would always be a fairly deep puddle about eight feet wide and ten feet long in the right-hand lane at that light, so of course, any sensible driver would pull his spanking clean car into the left-hand lane, leaving the right open. We got a bright idea, the type of idea that seems to be peculiar to young high-school boys with too much time on their hands. It was to wait almost a block back and get so we could time the light perfectly after accelerating the Model A as fast as it would go. We figured we'd be hitting 35 or 40 miles an hour by the time we hit the puddle just as the light changed to green.

Of course, in a Robin-Hoodesque flair, we decided to pick only on Cadillacs and Lincolns, particularly if they sported the spare tire in a color-matched Continental kit mounted between the back bumper and the trunk lid—the quintessential luxury accoutrement in those days. Even so, we knew that blasting water all over some well-to-do businessman's just-washed new luxury automobile would have a predictable negative effect on his emotional temperament, and we realized that if we continued to drive straight after the puddle, there was no way that Model A four-banger was going to outrun a Lincoln or Caddy V-8. It also occurred to us that the Model A would flip like a pancake if we tried to turn right at 35 or 40. Putting on the brakes just as we hit the puddle wouldn't work either because the instant those mechanical brakes got wet, they were almost useless.

However, this escapade was several months in the planning, and not just any dumb high school kids could pull it off. It took great attention to detail, an aptitude that has served both of us well as we've gotten older. In our initial practice runs, not only did we perfect our timing, but by trial and error during rainy day practices, we discovered that the hydro physics of a Model A hitting a big puddle and causing cascades of muddy water to explode sideways also slowed the Model A down sufficiently to make a right turn. In fact, it slowed so fast, I banged my head against the passenger-side windshield the first couple of times. I think the tires were too skinny to hydroplane. The engine would usually sputter from water splashing up, but she never failed us and always caught again.

Once we had that perfected, we christened Warner's car, "Poseidon," and made our first hit. Our victims couldn't see through the muddy water on their side window and it took them awhile to calm down enough to turn on the windshield wipers so they could see out the front. So, we were always at least a couple of blocks away before they recovered and made the turn to chase us. At three blocks away we'd turn right again, then shortly right again down the alley and pulled Poseidon out of sight behind Warner's dad's business which fronted on the street. Then we'd hurry in and grab a Coke just in time to watch a muddy Lincoln or Caddy shoot by several times looking for those damned high-school perps, the latter an easy call because high-school kids were the only species known to drive Model A's those days, and no adult would be gooning around like that.

Experience taught us it was imprudent to do it more than twice on any one puddle-day because by the third time, the car-wash people were on alert to run out to try to catch us just as the engine was sputtering. That wouldn't have been good because the car had running boards they could leap onto, and the doors wouldn't lock.

Somewhere around twenty hits, Warner's dad casually inquired about our activities, having heard talk from other businessmen in the area describing pluvious incidents involving a blue Model A. Innocent faces prevailed and Warner painted the retired Poseidon gold.

We've chuckled a lot about that over the years, and the Universal Forces haven't forgotten either. The other day, some smart-ass high school kid went by me about 50 miles an hour in his daddy's Mercedes and drenched my spanking clean car. I think the little @#$% looked back and laughed.

* * * *

35

Mystique

Public opinion is a weak tyrant
compared with our own private opinion.
What a man thinks of himself, that ... indicates, his fate.

Henry David Thoreau

Now that I had a car, was drumming and had gained more than a little recognition for the Chicken Yard incident, one of the "men's" fraternities at Pearson High took an interest in me. They were loose copies of college fraternities on the surface, but had no 100-year traditions behind them. However, it was another way to be "in" and, all in all, the fellows in them were pretty nice guys and the more popular kids in school. For instance, Warner was in one, was a great guy and was one of my best friends.

When they asked me to pledge, I was flattered. It was another step up the "somebody" ladder, an ultimate status accomplished by doing nothing except becoming a member and basking in the mystique. So, I became a Delmus pledge. That meant for some weeks I had to do whatever I was told by an active member, no matter what, and at the end of it endure an initiation into the fraternity, the details of which were unknown to the uninitiated other than it was extremely unpleasant and nauseating. But, following that, I could wear the fraternity's pin which would signify to all the world, or at least to some folks in our high school, that I was, in fact, "in."

The things we had to do for the "actives" as pledges amounted to getting them food, washing their cars, mowing their lawns and similar tedious tasks. Not much else happened at all, except one important thing, getting to the football games early and saving several rows for the active fraternity to sit. Having been to the games the prior year, I knew as the season wore on there would be a lot of dew on the long benches that comprised the seating in the high school bleachers. With that foresight and trying to always be prepared even though I passed on joining the Boy Scouts, the first chilly Friday evening I brought a large beach towel, anticipating an order to get the water off the benches. Since we were required to look spiffy at all times, I'd also purchased a brand new pair of Levi's that afternoon, just in time to slip them on before I left for the game. The creases from the folds in the pant legs were still showing.

Like a Centurion, I stood guard over several rows of benches, protecting my end of the rows with singular diligence. One of the first actives to show up was Marty. He was one of the cooler guys in school. I think because he looked and acted cool, since I was never able to discover any other abilities. Anyway, he was a pretty nice guy, as nice as cool-acting guys could be, but he showed up without his girlfriend. They'd been in an argument that afternoon and he didn't look happy. He barked at me to get the water off the row he wanted to sit in. I took the beach towel from under my arm and started wiping.

"No."

I looked at him quizzically.

"Sit down and slide along the bench."

"Marty, my Levi's are brand-new (no stone-washed jeans in those days—just dark blue Levi's, period). If I do that, my legs will be blue for a week and I'll freeze to death during the game. That's why I brought the towel." I held it up.

"Sit down and slide down the row."

Well, this was my Moment of Truth. How far was I willing to go to be "in?" What would I do to bask in mystique?

"No."

"What?"

"No. It doesn't make any sense."

"If you don't, you're out."

I took the towel with me. He'd see how he liked a wet butt.

Early the next week, they had a meeting about me. No pledge had ever done anything like that before. Since the heat of the moment was over, I wondered if common sense and cooler heads would prevail. They didn't, except for Warner and a couple other guys who were in there pitching for me. But I was out.

Funny thing, it seems getting axed made me more popular after that, even with some members of the fraternity who voted me out. They thought I "acted like a man." That's what every high school boy wants isn't it—to be a man?

* * * *

36

My Basketball Career

The invention of basketball was not an accident.
It was developed to meet a need.

Dr. James Naismith

NOW THAT I WAS A junior, I began to survey my life. While I was having a lot of fun with the guys, my track record with the girls could be charitably described as abysmal. Recognizing this, Warner fixed me up with a cute little sophomore named Anne and we got along well for a fairly extended period of time, a month I think. One night she said she wanted to go steady. Overtaken by surprise, I said okay and went home in something of a quandary.

When I saw Warner the next day, I told him what had happened and that I had two problems. I liked Anne and would like to keep dating her, but now that I actually had the opportunity, I wasn't sure I really wanted to go steady with anyone, and even if I did, I owned no jewelry whatsoever, so I had no ring she could wear on a chain around her neck, a customary signification of that elevated commitment at Pearson High if you didn't have a school letterman's jacket.

Warner thought for a minute and then with a big smile and a chuckle, "Okay, I've got it on both counts."

"What?"

"If you say 'no' now, she'll be so upset she'll dump you. So, look at it this way, it's not like you're getting married. Give it a try and if you don't like it, there's nothing to keep you from breaking up with her. Shoot, the average eternal relationship around here lasts about six weeks, doesn't it?"

"So, it's like a lab experiment?"

"Well ... don't look at it that way. Let's just say you're giving the relationship a fair chance." Then he chuckled again.

"Great. So, what do I give her to wear? Dating's expensive enough. I don't have the bread for a gold ring to put on her neck."

Chuckling some more, "Well, this is the great part. No dead presidents necessary. I've got a gold basketball my team won in an Optimist tournament last summer and it's on a gold chain. Give it to her to wear. It doesn't have to be a ring."

"Terrific, I've got to be the worst basketball player in the world. She's not going to buy that."

"Trust me. She doesn't know what you did last summer. It'll make her happy and solve your problem."

So I did it. Anne didn't say much but, as I fastened it around her neck with the gold chain, she seemed quite pleased with that small gold basketball sporting a big, raised, enameled "O" on it.

She was so pleased, she wore it twenty four hours a day. After about ten days, she hopped in my car after school and I drove her home, which had become our custom. As I shut off the engine, I turned to say something to her just as she was closing her purse. She had a funny look on her face so I didn't say anything, feeling certain she was about to say something. She opened her hand. It held a gold chain and a green basketball with an enameled "O" on it. Next, she showed me the green place on her skin where the symbol of our possibly eternal connection had caressed her neck.

Then, just before she got out of the car, she held the basketball up by the chain and, clairvoyantly, I held my hand out. She dropped that less than exquisite piece of not-so-fine jewelry into my hand with a final look reminiscent of the exploding potassium in Mrs. Hames' chemistry class. It was kind of a relief that at least I didn't have to sprint backward. And then it dawned on me. From the time she got into the car until the time she left it, she hadn't said a word, and neither had I.

Warner couldn't stop laughing. He told me he wanted the gold chain back and I could keep the basketball because he wouldn't get near a piece of junk like that, *but* I shouldn't be discouraged because I had increased the total time of my relationship with a female to five and half weeks, a personal best which was just short of his estimated average.

I think it was the Universal Forces' turn to have a good chuckle.

* * * *

37

The Lesson

And if my heart be scarred and burned, the safer, I, for all I learned ...

Dorothy Parker (*Incurable*)

Billy told me Gene Krupa and Buddy Rich were coming to our area to do one of their famous drum battles, but his date lived so far in the other direction, we wouldn't be able to double. I was really excited and wanted to share it with somebody, preferably a girl. Having long since recovered from the inhibiting scars of the distressing end to my pursuit of Pamela, and having gained some empathy as a result of my relationship with Anne, I thought this event was significant enough to make amends to Linda for my boneheaded conduct in junior high. She had always been nice to me after I had apologized about standing her up for the dance, but she was clearly somewhat reserved. So I thought I'd try again because I still really liked her. To my happy surprise, she accepted.

This was going to be a great evening, Gene Krupa, Buddy Rich and Linda. It couldn't be better. I was ready for it all and agonized over whether to wear my powder blue Zoot Suit with the over-broad shoulders on a jacket that narrowed precipitously at the waist, continuing that way almost to the knees, together with matching trousers sporting pegged pant cuffs that I could hardly get my foot through, topped off by my leather brogue wingtips with mirror shine, or to wear my pegged charcoal gray wool flannel trousers with white bucks, half-inch wide white suede belt and electric-fuchsia faux-silk long sleeved shirt. I ultimately opted for a sport jacket, dress shirt, tie, slacks and chukka boots. My wardrobe was sufficiently varied because my dad was still springing for the clothes.

Speedball was all cleaned up and I felt terrific as I pulled up in front of Linda's house, hopped out and knocked on the front door. Her brother answered. He looked and sounded kind of funny when he told me she wasn't home and he didn't know where she was. In response to my somewhat stunned questions, he said she'd gone out about an hour before and said she wouldn't be home until much later.

I walked back to my car totally confused and sat there for a few moments. I didn't know any girls who weren't required, as a bare minimum, to tell their parents exactly where they were going and when they would be home, all of which had to be approved. As I drove away, it brushed my mind that someone had been peeking out one of the windows when I drove up. Then it hit me—payback time. I didn't like it, but felt I deserved it and it put me so down in the dumps that I never went to see Gene and Buddy that evening. I just went home and played my drums. That works when you're happy and helps when you're sad.

At school the next Monday, Linda looked quite contrite when I walked up to her. Before she could say anything, I said, "I guess I had it coming." She said it was her turn to apologize, which she did profusely and confessed that she wanted *me* to feel what it was like, but her brother had gotten so mad at her afterward for making him do it that she realized it was wrong and she really was sorry. Those soft, kind eyes told me it was true.

We ultimately agreed to let bygones be bygones, not to try dating again and just be good friends—and so we were, and still are. Of course, that result is part of what the Universal Forces were trying to accomplish all along since different plans were in the works for both of us.

38

Buddy and Me

Drums are not a percussive instrument.
They're a musical instrument we play with rhythm.

Jeff Hamilton
Clayton-Hamilton Jazz Orchestra
Jeff Hamilton Trio

IN CONNECTION WITH THE LESSONS the Universal Forces were teaching me in relation to Linda, I had prevented myself from seeing Gene and Buddy, together and in person. But, since the UF set me up with the drums in the first instance, they must have felt sympathetic because they subsequently fixed half of that void twice, and then threw in some extra things, so I guess that adds up to something between less and more than the whole. I'll explain.

Billy and I had a drumming friend, Sonny, from a different high school who was the student protégé of a well-known and highly talented big band drummer, Jack Sperling with Les Brown's band. We used to go up to Sonny's house and all three of us would fool around on the drums and Sonny would show us what his guru was teaching him. We had a lot of fun and used to go see Jack play with a combo in one of the well known jazz venues in the area when he wasn't out with Les Brown.

Jack got them to let us in with an educational plea and we drank only Cokes. Then we'd sit and chat with Jack and the other musicians afterward, soaking up all the knowledge and jazz ambiance we could. One evening during one of those chats, Jack said that Buddy Rich was going to be playing with Harry James' big band in a big public ballroom nearby and he inquired if we wanted to go when it happened. We were jumping all over ourselves.

When the big night arrived, unfortunately Billy couldn't go, so Sonny and I went with Jack. It was incredible. It was the first time I'd ever seen or heard a big band like that live and in person. The music seemed to swell up from some place inside the earth. Buddy was blazing, and so was Harry James who, as the UF had previously cleverly arranged it, was playing trumpet on that seminal two-sided 78 of Benny Goodman's orchestra with Gene Krupa doing "Sing, Sing, Sing," the performance that got me excited about the drums in the first place.

During one of the band's breaks, Buddy came over to our table to chat with Jack. We hung on every word and finally we were introduced to Buddy. He asked if there was anything we wanted to know. Sonny asked him a couple of questions and then Buddy looked at me.

I squeaked out, "Mr. Rich, I've noticed that Louie Bellson has used two bass drums playing with Duke Ellington, and I've heard of a drummer named Ed Shaughnessy who's doing it too. I was wondering if you're going to do it."

He looked at me with abundant amusement and flashed those snow-white teeth through his patented smile, "Crap, kid, I can do anything with one foot they can do with two." Jack Sperling's eyes were smiling as Buddy left. We watched Harry James' band in rapture the rest of the evening.

Well, that was the initial half of the fix by the UF. You're thinking that Gene Krupa's the next half. Nope, I never did get to see Gene in person, the guy that started it all for me. So, the UF worked the Buddy angle twice. A number of years later, after I'd completed my education, had a family and was actually working for a living, which was also a few years before Buddy passed, big band jazz had a loyal following, but was no longer in its heyday and his big band was one of the few hanging together and going on tour. He came to play two shows in a one-night concert at one of the jazz clubs in my city, a venue much smaller than that big public ballroom. The club's tables had been removed and the entire floor was wall to wall with folding chairs for the audience *and* Buddy's band, all packed liked sardines on the same level.

Jimmy, one of my best pals (and still is), owned the city's leading drum shop and procured tickets for both shows in the first row, strategically just a little to the right of Buddy whose drums were in the front of the band in that setup. It was excellent. We could see his hands, his high-hat foot (left) and, importantly, his bass-drum foot (right). Things were so packed, we were not more than five feet away from those hands and feet. We could see perfectly and we could hear just fine. That's a little joke. If big bands can be anything, they can be *loud*, and by the end of the evening we were not only half-deaf, but our eyelids were sunburned from the klieg lights reflecting off Buddy's teeth.

Buddy was energy personified. He seemed to be twice the size he actually was. The sweat pouring off his face was a waterfall as he put 250% of himself into every tune. He obviously lived to play and played to live. I watched that right foot constantly. He did things with that bass-drum pedal I can't even dream of doing on a snare drum with both hands and drumsticks. Buddy was still at the top of his game, churning on "Readymix," taking no prisoners on "Mercy, Mercy, Mercy" and wailing on "West Side Story."

Our wives and some of our other friends were with us and between shows the wife of one of my long-time pals, in her high heels, climbed up on the sink in the ladies room, removed a poster for the performance from the ceiling and gave it to me. I was sitting there wondering out loud to Jimmy if I'd be able to get Buddy to sign it after the performance. He said he knew one of Buddy's roadies and he'd go chat with him. Jimmy came back and said, "No luck."

Oh well, we were getting to see it up close and it was a great evening still in progress. The second show exceeded the first. Buddy was even more energetic if that were possible. When it was over after a couple of encores demanded by the screaming, cheering, whistling crowd, Buddy and the band disappeared quickly. I didn't even get a chance to rush that five feet and ask him to sign the poster. No matter—a terrific time and I had the poster.

As we were waiting for the room to clear so we could get out, Jimmy put his hand on my shoulder, "I've got a surprise for you, buddy."

I smiled, "Your roadie friend will sign my poster? And don't call me Buddy."

"Fifteen minutes alone in the band bus with Buddy, buddy."

"Right."

"C'mon. I go in after you." He started dragging me by the arm out to the bus parked in front of the club at the curb. An unexpected rain had started and the bus was dark. We stayed back under the lighted portico of the club to keep from getting wet. Jimmy waved at the roadie standing by the bus door with an umbrella. The roadie motioned and Jimmy shoved me at him. The roadie pulled the door open and pointed inside the unlighted bus.

It was all very mysterious so I figured I'd play out the joke and let Jimmy have his fun. At least I'd be getting out of the rain. I went in. The door closed. As my eyes started to adjust from the bright portico lights, I looked around. The bus seats were empty. I was alone. I was about to open a window and yell something appropriate to Jimmy when, about half way down, I thought there might be a small figure hunched in one of the seats.

I moved slowly down the isle. It was Buddy! He was sitting there silently, all scrunched up in a thick, white terry cloth robe with the collar up around his ears. He seemed deflated to half his normal size. The robe looked way too big, like the life force had been drained out of him and every ounce of energy in his body had melted into his drums. They say the drums are the heartbeat of the band and, obviously, they were Buddy's too.

He spoke very softly, "Sit down." He slid to the window and motioned for me to sit next to him. I thrust my hand toward him and introduced myself. His hands were much bigger than I expected and surprisingly soft for a karate devotee. He scarcely moved. I described that night many years before when I'd met him in high school and how I'd also missed the drum battle with him and Gene (who had passed to the Big Band in the Sky by this time).

His eyes had been fastened directly on mine from the beginning, but I couldn't detect a reaction. Then I told him what an inspiration he'd been to me as a young drummer and how his playing had always inspired me to do my best. His eyes sprang to life and there was a little smile. I don't remember what else we talked about during those fifteen minutes, but they went very fast. As I was getting up to leave, he took the forgotten poster from my hand and signed it, saying he enjoyed our talk. Then he reached out and shook my hand.

Jimmy went into the bus and came out fifteen minutes later. Come to think of it, I don't think I've ever asked him what they talked about. It's not that I don't care. It's just that every time I think of that night, I can only think of Buddy and me. Jimmy and I were still standing under the portico a half hour later because it was raining cats and dogs, we had no umbrella and the car was two blocks away. All the band members had piled onto the bus. Buddy had never left it. The bus started and I felt eyes on me from somewhere. I looked up and Buddy was looking at me. The bus started to pull away and his eyes stayed on me. I gave a small wave. His head moved slightly in acknowledgement, and he was gone. The poster is still up and framed in my drum room.

Some might think the Universal Forces had definitely evened it up with Buddy twice, but they were still going. They arranged for a friend of ours to invite us to a charity event featuring Harry James and his big band. His band played all the tunes identified with him, including "Ciribiribin" and his classic schmaltzy versions of "You Made Me Love You" and "All or Nothing at All." After the performance, I met Harry, who as you may remember had been married to WWII's most famous pin-up girl, Betty Grable, and I told him the story of seeing his band in high school and what Buddy had said that night. He laughed a lot, saying, "Vintage Buddy," and then signed my program. It's also up in my drum room.

In retrospect, it's clear that the UF *always* keeps on keepin' on. The third member of my inspirational triumvirate, Louie Bellson, came to town to perform and it turned out that he was a friend of Jimmy's! After the performance, which included a terrific rendition of his most famous drum solo "Skin Deep," the three of us had a marvelous dinner together and Louie, with the naturally-earned reputation of being the nicest person anyone could ever hope to meet at anywhere or any time, graciously signed one of his posters for me. Yep, it's up in the drum room. That was a number of years before Louie passed on February 14th in the year this book is copyrighted. I was at a large jazz concert that day where one of Louie's friends, Jeff Hamilton, whose quote is at the beginning of this chapter, sadly told the audience of Louie's passing and said it was only fitting that one of the sweetest people ever to be on Earth passed on Valentine's Day. Then Jeff played Caravan softly on the drums with only his hands in one of the nicest musical tributes I've ever heard to a fellow jazz drummer.

Of course, the UF never intended to stop with Louie either. The way I've figured it, they're always putting in motion planned sets of seemingly random separate events that years later coincide, appearing to come together by happenstance, but they're synchronous from the beginning. For instance, back in the year of the

Krupa-Rich drum battle that I missed, the UF arranged for Jeff Hamilton to be born, and not just so I could put that drumming quote at the beginning of this chapter.

Close to that same time, the UF also arranged for my drum-shop-owning pal, Jimmy, to be born, and then for Jimmy and Jeff to be separately, but irretrievably, captivated by the drums as kids and, at a point a few years later in their lives, for them to become good friends, which is one of the reasons Jeff would come over to our state from time to time and give "drum clinics" to help Jimmy get his drum shop started. Right about that time, Jimmy and I got to be friends because, as a counterpoint to the demanding pressures of my "day job," I was constantly going into his shop whenever I could and we would always chat at some length about drumming, music, new equipment and other rhythmic matters.

One weekend during that period, my wife and I went to a relatively new annual "jazz party" in town. A common form of jazz parties is perhaps 25 up to 60 or more world-class jazz musicians, ranging from the highly talented younger musicians to the more mature with more established reputations, who are mixed and matched during a weekend or longer. A number of "badges" equaling the number of seats available, usually at tables in a hotel ballroom, are sold to jazz fans for all or part of the time, and the musicians play much of the day and half the night for the length of the party. Whoever has a badge showing can come and go as they please; thus, the price of a badge can be shared with friends. However, most come to stay the entire time because it's not often musicians of that aggregate and individual caliber and talent come together to play in various combinations in a setting where the audience arrives to *listen* to the music, rather than chat with each other during it. The musicians love it.

In any event, the next day after the jazz party was over, and knowing Jimmy hadn't been there because his drum shop was open all weekend, I went in and said, "I just saw a drummer this weekend who plays like I think, but can't play."

"Oh, you've gotta be talking about Jeff Hamilton. Now the jazz party is over, he's staying at my place the rest of the week to do some vacationing and a drum clinic for the shop. It got so many RSVP's I had to move it into that giant tent they're putting up in the parking lot. Come on over tonight for dinner. We'll see if maybe he'll give you a private lesson while he's here." I don't think Jimmy was aware that if that happened, it'd be the first drum lesson I ever had.

We all had a great time at dinner and since we didn't live far from Jimmy's house, Jeff said he'd like to see me play my own drums the next day. He came over and after he told me three or four truly hilarious jokes (a common start to any chat with Jeff), I sat down behind my kit and pulled out every Gene Krupa lick I knew.

"Chip, that was great. Really great. You might win any Krupa contest I can think of, and may the Big Bandleader in the Sky bless him. The only thing is, if you played that way with a mainstream jazz group these days, they'd be looking around for a different drummer. That was a different era and just as it always does, the music has evolved. We're not rejecting in any way what's gone before. It's wonderful music by legendary players, a vital foundation. Without it, we couldn't do what we do now, which is incorporate the best of what those players did and then build on it with our own talents. They did the same thing in their day."

After he played a few demonstrations of what he was talking about, including the difference between mechanically playing patterns on the drums versus making music with them, he put the drumsticks down and talked to me for approximately an hour and a half about the way I should *think* about playing drums within the context of how I should *listen* to the music, because my playing should flow from the latter.

Then he showed me two seemingly simple mechanical things—slightly changing my grip on the right hand stick so it was free to bounce and essentially play itself instead of me playing it, and the lateral angle at which I should hit the snare drum head when

I played with the brushes (you know, the things with the wires sticking out the end).

That, coupled with the quote at the beginning of this chapter, and lessons whenever he was in my town or I was in his, improved my playing at least 300%—in my estimation. I've never solicited Jeff's opinion, but he always seemed happy with my progress. And in all the lessons I've had with him, he's never said, "No, don't do that." It's always been, "Okay, let's try this." And the desired result would become self evident.

Oh, you may remember that Cyclone taught me how to speed up during a tune when we were playing rhythm and blues in the high school canteen, and I lamented it was a very bad habit for a jazz (or any) drummer to get into. Well it is, as a habit, but a couple of days ago, I heard Jeff's trio play a new arrangement and they sped up on purpose. So, the music does evolve—certainly what goes around comes around.

And on the synchronicity front, it's interesting to note that my first-born child arrived on an anniversary of Jeff's birthday, turned out to be a natural drummer and some years later, she took lessons from him. Further, curiously enough, ever since she was born, the two of them always celebrate their birthday on the same day of the year. (Sorry, my friend Jimmy suffers from being the master of the world's corniest jokes and somehow I caught it.)

After my family, the drums have played such an important part in my life and Jeff has expanded the joy of my playing experience so much, I'm compelled to give him some brief kudos. The list is very long but just to name a few things, before I met Jeff he had played with, among others, the Tommy Dorsey Orchestra, Lionel Hampton's big band, and Woody Herman's big band—The Thundering Herd. After we met, he played with the Count Basie Orchestra, Ella Fitzgerald, the Ray Brown Trio, the Oscar Peterson Trio and also musicians who are still alive as I write this, such as the phenomenally successful jazz singer-pianist Diana Krall.

He also co-leads the Clayton-Hamilton Jazz Orchestra (CHJO) with both his multi-talented musical partner, conductor, composer, arranger and former Basie bassist, John Clayton (also his best friend and best man at Jeff's wedding), and with Jeff Clayton (John's brother) who's played the slowest, sweetest version of Duke Ellington's signature tune, "Take the A Train," I've ever heard come out of an alto saxophone. To my way of thinking, the CHJO is the way Count Basie's music may have evolved if he were still down here leading his band today.

Among many awards, the CHJO has won the DownBeat and the Jazz Times Readers Polls, Jeff's won the Modern Drummer Readers Poll twice, John's a Grammy winning arranger and has been voted Best Arranger in the Jazz Times Readers Poll, and both Jeff and John were jointly honored as Musicians of the Year by the Los Angeles Jazz Society. During this time Jeff also formed the Jeff Hamilton Trio, the tightest and most inventive jazz trio I've ever heard, evolving the music and tradition of the great jazz trios while remaining true to the lineage of traditional mainstream jazz. (Please help me, I've been captured by a jazz-critic.) Suffice to say that jazz publications often refer to Jeff these days as a "Master Drummer," a description with which anyone who sees him play readily agrees. Oh, and he's also been on hundreds of recordings up to this point.

Of course, it's now been over twenty five years since we met, and Jimmy, Jeff and I have been great friends all that time. Thanks to the UF, through the both of them, I've met and become friends with a number of talented jazz musicians including the terrific jazz drummer, Lewis Nash, who grew up in my city, went to New York and has bowled them over ever since, having been referred to as Jazz's Most Valuable Player when he appeared on the cover of Modern Drummer.

Someone took a picture of Jimmy, Jeff and me back close to the beginning and we've managed a picture with the three of us at the end of approximately each ten years since (yes, they're up in my drum room) and while we've, oh, perhaps changed just a little in that time and my hair may have gotten a little grayer (being a little younger than I, the other two claim they look exactly the same), in all of those pictures, everyone's eyes sparkle with what I view as the boundless joy received and expressed through playing the drums.

That can be said about playing any instrument, and I always marvel at jazz musicians in, for instance, their eighth or ninth decade of life here. They might be bent over a little and shuffle, limp, hobble or have help getting onto the bandstand, but once they start playing, they're fifteen again and you know you're privileged to be sharing a peek into their soul.

While sometimes I'm tempted to think in my musical instance that the Universal Forces arranged the best for last, I'm happy to say it's not over yet and I'm eagerly looking forward to the joys that will come. *God bless my Uncle Sam.*

* * * *

39

Trig

There may be times when we are powerless to prevent injustice,
but there must never be a time when we fail to protest.

Elie Wiesel

AFTER THE CHEERLEADING-DISQUALIFICATION EXPERIENCE at Pearson High, it dawned on me that teachers were people, people who might not see everything my way. That epiphany was reinforced when I met with my Pearson High faculty counselor, Mr. Carrion, to plan my schedule for the following semester. Things were going well and the only thing left was picking two elective courses to which I was entitled. Before I had a chance to express my choices, he filled "Trigonometry" into one of the slots.

"Wait a minute. That's not what I want to take."

"Calculus then?"

"No. I want to take Drama and Radio Workshop for my two electives."

"Look, you're a straight-A math student. Those are too easy, so pick only one of them."

"But I finished my college math requirements by not taking an elective this semester. That's why I'm entitled to two. I don't need any more math. I don't plan to be a mathematician and electives are supposed to be something *I* want to do, not what you want. I shouldn't have to pick between your choices."

He wrote down Radio Workshop and Trigonometry.

"What does 'elective' mean?" I asked.

"Trig."

When I told him I wouldn't go to trig no matter what he wrote down on my schedule, he explained that if I was not in that class, he'd have me picked up by the truant officer. Those days, that meant a trip to "Juvie Hall" at police headquarters, and since Mr. Carrion was also the Dean of Boys, I knew he was serious.

So, at the beginning of the following semester, I reported to Mr. Sigurd's trigonometry class. After three or four days, he noticed that when the class was doing an assignment, I was sitting there quietly, somewhat unusual for me in any case, and doing no work. He asked me to speak with him after class.

I had been in his advanced algebra class and knew this big, soft-spoken Norwegian in his 50's was a nice man. He inquired calmly, "Chip, I noticed you're not doing any work in class."

I explained what had happened with Mr. Carrion.

"Well, you know Mr. Carrion. He's not going to change his position. So, as long as you're here, why not do the work? You're an "A" student. You're planning on college. It can't hurt you."

"Mr. Sigurd, this just isn't fair. I'm supposed to be able to choose a class and Mr. Carrion is forcing me to be here. He can make me do that, but it's not right. I'm not bothering anyone. Just let me sit here and give me an "F" at the end of the semester."

"Chip, I actually sympathize with you, but I can't let you sit with the class and not do anything. If I don't do something, it's going to undermine my authority with the other students."

"I don't want to cause you a problem, sir, but I'm not being treated fairly by Mr. Carrion. I shouldn't be here and I'm not going to do the work."

"Chip, I don't want to cause you a problem either and I understand this is a matter of principle with you. Tell you what. I won't report this and I'll give you an "F," but you can't sit in class."

I saw unexpected light in this situation. He was going to let me loose and I'd have a free hour. Not a bad trade.

"So, you'll have to sit in the storeroom during class, and the only thing you can have with you will be the course textbook and course materials. We'll pull a desk in there."

Now, the storeroom at the back of the classroom was really a glorified closet, five feet by six feet at the very best, but lined with shelves for supplies which made it much smaller. We couldn't fit a desk into the remaining space. So, Mr. Sigurd put a wooden chair in there, just enough room for me to sit and that was it. Each day I would go into my self-imposed prison and close the door. For fifty minutes, I sat there holding the course materials, pissed for 3000 seconds every school day for a semester. Too bad I didn't know about meditation then. But, we'd apparently created the prototype of today's "time-out" room in school.

To this day, I can't do simple math problems without a calculator. And before small hand-held electronic calculators came into existence, I'd always offhandedly ask someone else for the answer to simple math issues, which I still do sometimes today, much like a friend of mine describing his challenges with dyslexia. I guess I developed mathmadia. I never took another math course. Much later in my life, my father told me that in the beginning, he'd always wanted me to study engineering. My response, "Why didn't you *say* something?"

Since Universal Forces were always arranging events, they must have figured being an engineer wouldn't be for my benefit.

* * * *

40

Radio Workshop

I admit thoughts influence the body.

Albert Einstein

PERHAPS MR. CARRION WAS IN league with the Universal Forces when he wrote down Radio Workshop for me instead of Drama class. Radio Workshop was not an electronics course, but a radio performance class reputed to be equipped with the latest in reel-to-reel tape recorders. Since it was an elective, there were Juniors like me in the class as well as Seniors. We sat at small oblong tables instead of desks, two to a table. Apparently the UF also arranged for our teacher, Mr. Siriani, to randomly construct a seating chart so that sitting with me was one of the prettiest and unintentionally sexiest girls I'd ever met.

Penny was slender, lithe might be a better description, had hair toward the red end of auburn, huge blue eyes, and lips to die for. But she was a Senior. Just my luck. Romantic mixing between classes occurred with Senior boys and Junior girls, but not between Senior girls and Junior boys. It just wasn't done. Oh well. I could have been sitting next to a guy instead of her and, besides, she was really nice to me. So we had a lot of fun together in that rather *laissez faire* class for the first few weeks.

And, of course, there was always the slim thread of hope that she might evidence more than a platonic interest in me. Along that line, I was sitting next to her in class one day, lost in daydreams dangling from that hopeful thread, when I heard a voice from far away, very far away, accompanied by Penny's tinkling laughter, "Chip ... Chip ...." It kept getting louder and louder, interfering with the newly-learned Samba beat I was idly practicing on the desk while immersed in trance-like thoughts imagining Penny whispering sweet nothings in my ear, like Katharine Hepburn and Spencer Tracy, Lauren Bacall and Humphrey Bogart or Betty Grable and Harry James.

Dancing among the theta rhythms of my daydream state, I thought it was strange the laughter sounded exactly like Penny's, but the voice sounded like Mr. Siriani's. Slowly retreating from my Latin reverie, I opened my eyes and saw him standing over me. The unrequited dreams of Penny plummeted into the Hopeless Abyss when my slim-hope-thread snapped under the weight of the class clapping a Latin rhythm to my desk Samba and yelling "Ole!" as I stopped. It was followed by uproarious laughter, including Mr. Siriani who invited me to join the real world.

After the class settled down and Mr. Siriani began droning on again, some unknown force suddenly caused a miracle and things started to happen in the present.

Penny puts her hand on my arm, pulls me a little closer, brushes those beautiful lips against my ear and whispers, "Do you want to go to a movie this weekend?"

I almost lose consciousness, "With who?"

"Me."

"Who else?"

"No one, silly."

I'm in stun. Could this be happening? Here is one of the most beautiful *Senior* girls in school asking *me* to go on a date with *her*. Things start scrambling through my mind. It isn't Sadie Hawkins Day. I'm awake. We'll be going alone! Is Speedball Baby finally paying off? Is it my drumming? I flash back to my platonic relationship with the older Lee Ann in junior high, but that was ages ago and I'm taller now. Could this casually self-assured, gorgeous redhead be interested in just *me*? I become paralyzed. Universal

Forces come to my rescue. I hear the word "Sure" come out of my mouth. I'm positive it isn't me speaking.

"Great." She smiles, flashes those perfect teeth and writes out the directions to her house. "Seven on Saturday. Okay?"

"Sure" comes out again, from somewhere.

I tried to be casual the rest of the week and not mention the date. Actually, I was afraid to mention it because it would give her the opportunity to say something had come up and she couldn't go. That Friday, she said, "Seven tomorrow. Remember." I assured her I would.

Speedball Baby had never been so clean. What a chariot! Saturday I put on my best pegged Levi's, fourteen and a half inches at the bottom of the cuff, my leather wingtips with mirror-like spit shine, and a pullover shirt with a collar. I ditched the Wildroot Cream-Oil and bought a tube of Brylcreem, "a little dab'll do ya," and my hair was combed to perfection. I noticed that without so much grease on it, it was kind of naturally wavy. Not a bad look and it really worked well with my ducktail treatment in the back.

I popped a stick of Clove chewing gum in my mouth and showed up right on time. Her father owned a successful business and they lived on the other side of town in a really nice brick two-story house with a very green lawn and big trees. He opened the door and seemed like a very pleasant person for the seven seconds or so we spoke. Penny was right behind him and whisked me away.

As we walked to the car, it was impossible not to notice how terrific she looked in a cashmere sweater buttoned up to her neck, just the right shade of beige to complement her hair, such long auburn eyelashes surrounding those marvelous big blue eyes, eyebrows delicately and perfectly shaped, a wonderfully understated shade of red lipstick defining indescribable lips orbiting perfect pearly whites, those shimmering red-auburn locks framing a creamy, baby-like complexion with nary a freckle or blemish, her hair so lusciously thick with bangs cut exactly the right length to flow into the sides and back which fell briefly toward her collar, changing midstream to soft, thick waves of delicious feathered curls brushing the neck for-which-I-have-no-adjective.

I wouldn't have been able to say that on one breath even then, much less process those sensory kaleidoscopic blasts in one mind-chunk, and I think I was just about to demonstrate the feeling I was experiencing by jumping up and clicking my heels when it dawned on me, "What movie do you want to see?"

She looked at me casually, "What's on at the drive-in?"

As I deftly slid my hand through the wing window and opened Speedball's passenger door, "I don't know."

Her eyes started to twinkle a little. Her hair bouncing as she plopped herself on the seat, she looked up at me smiling, "Well, let's go see."

Of course, I knew full well why most high school kids went to the passion-pit, but being stupefied that Penny even wanted to go out with me, I was equally certain that particular scenario wasn't going to apply to this situation and figured the twinkling smile was just putting me on a little, kind of like the briefly-known older Kathy at Rancho Feliz and the not-briefly-known Lee Ann when I was in junior high. Perhaps all older women were the same. I wouldn't know since this was only the third time in my life one of them had evidenced any kind of interest in me whatsoever.

When we got within sight of the drive-in marquee, she said, "Let's watch it." I was so thrilled that this incredible specimen of humanity wanted to go somewhere with me, I had no idea what the marquee said. I paid and we parked. I cranked the window down, pulled the speaker off the post, hooked it inside the window and cranked the window back up since it was kind of cool and a little damp.

Sitting like a statue behind the steering wheel with Penny a mile away on the other side of the car, I'd been staring at the movie a short while when Penny said effortlessly, "Why don't you slide over here and put your arm around me? I'm chilly." Unable to speak, I willingly complied. She slid down a little in the seat so it was a perfect fit. I was suspended in time by her scent. So light it was almost imperceptible, but unmistakable. She must have sprayed a little in the air and run through it. I'd seen my sister do that.

I closed my eyes and just breathed in. As I was lost in near space, she turned a little, reached up and gently pulled my head down to those incredibly luscious lips. I started floating through outer space. One thing naturally, and I mean naturally because I had no experience at this, led to another and I found my hands under the back of her sweater trying to unhook her bra.

Now, I'd seen my mother and sister around the house in their "unmentionables" (brassiere, slip and underpants) and I knew where the hooks were, but after I fumbled around for fully two or three minutes with no success, she laughed softly and started unbuttoning her sweater, an act that caused severe hyperventilation on my part. "It hooks in the front, silly." Even with that knowledge, I developed an instant case of hot-dog fingers and couldn't get it unhooked. So she did it for me. I didn't know anything could be that soft and was in hyperspace now.

"What's going on in there?" The sound of a metal flashlight was banging on the window. It was the drive-in-movie-decorum police. I'd heard about these sadistic college students who worked at the drive-in and loved to go around ruining romantic encounters.

"We're watching the movie."

"Every single window in your car's fogged up. You can't see out and I can't see in."

That was a relief. I reached up and rubbed a little circle in the windshield. "We can see the movie now. Go away!" His footsteps crunched away in the gravel. I glanced at Penny. She was calmly looking at me with a kind of Mona Lisa smile. The rest of the movie was marvelous, I guess—whatever it was.

When we got back to Penny's house, the front was dark, "We'll have to go around to the back door." We tiptoed around to the back but the porch light there wasn't on either. Penny was fumbling around trying to find her key when the light snapped on and the door opened. There was her dad.

The electricity of "The Now" went through my body like a thunderbolt. I didn't look quite like I did when I picked her up.

My hair appeared to have suffered the effects of a minor explosion in my skull and, wrinkle-free clothes being unknown, my shirt seemed to have been removed, wadded into a tiny ball and then put back on, without being tucked in to boot.

Penny looked a little worse for the wear too. I'm tempted to make a joke that her sweater was on inside out, but it wasn't. She didn't have any lipstick on though, her hair was no longer perfectly coiffed, not by a long shot, and both our faces had the slight suggestion of an understated red tinge, the color of the lipstick she started the evening with.

He smiled. I wasn't sure what was coming next, but I could run pretty fast and figured this was my last date with Penny.

"Hi, did you kids have fun? Chip, do you want to come in for a little while?"

Penny whirled toward me with a look of moderate apprehension in those big blue eyes.

"Oh, no thanks, sir. It's getting late and my mother will be expecting me."

"Well, you're certainly welcome to come in for a minute or two."

I must have looked like I was wavering, because those baby blues were now much wider than usual with little energy-spears shooting out at me.

"I need to be getting along. Thanks anyway. Goodnight, sir. Night, Penny."

"Night, Chip," and the twinkling eyes with the mischievous smile were back.

Penny and I dated from time to time for the rest of the year and, since I was a year younger and to many in high school image is everything, I think she may have suffered some opprobrium from her peers, but Penny wasn't listening to their drummer. To my peers, it was something of an astonishment. To Penny and me, it had nothing to do with social status. We just genuinely liked each other and enjoyed each other's company. To the Universal Forces, they were arranging events for my benefit since, from that time forward, I've always been comfortable with beautiful women of any age by just being myself. It's worked out great.

I'm certain the Universal Forces intended some benefit for Penny, but I don't know what it was. She went off to college the following school year and I ran into her when we were both home from different universities a couple of years later. She was engaged and we had a nice chat. I've never seen her again and I do hope she's had a wonderful life.

* * * *

41

The Orange

> The public may be willing to forgive us for mistakes in judgment, but … not … for mistakes in motive.
>
> Robert W. Haack

THE BIG GRASSY QUADRANGLE RIGHT in the middle of Pearson High was perhaps fifty yards square. At lunch period, most students would congregate around the edges and socialize after they finished their noon repast, leaving the middle relatively empty until the bell rang.

One day, Mr. Carrion was strolling through that empty space and an orange came in his direction from the perimeter. It was thrown high, really high. It seemed to go up forever, and took even longer to come down. All eyes, except Mr. Carrion's, were fixed on it. When it became clear the trajectory would end right on the Dean of Boys, everyone fell silent. As it smashed on the back of his shoulder and splattered all down his coat, the crowd let out a collective whoop followed by much laughter. That is, until he collected himself and whirled around. At that point, a door slammed on the laughter and a thousand students stood silently uttering a prayer for his victim. His eagle eyes went into motion, darting from one student to the next looking for the perp.

I presumed word of my math rebellion had ultimately gotten back to Mr. Carrion, but I didn't really know until the Eagle's eyes stopped on me. His arm came up with the claw pointed in my direction. It started beckoning at me. I cupped my hands to my mouth and shouted, "I didn't do it." He kept beckoning and it was clear he wasn't going to walk over to me. When the Dean of Boys commanded, the student genuflected, a ritual I'd failed to perform in connection with the Trig Incident, so I thought I'd better engage in an act of contrition now. After all, I had nothing to fear because I didn't do it.

As I slowly walked toward him protesting my innocence, the crowd started chanting, low at first and then with increasing volume, "He didn't do it. He didn't do it." I could still hear it as I sat down in his office and the door shut.

"Why'd you do it?"

"I didn't do it."

"Yes you did."

"No I didn't."

"Who did then?"

"I don't know."

"I could have been hurt."

"I know, sir, that's why if that orange had been mine, I never would have thrown it."

"Fess up. It'll go easier with you."

"Look, sir, the first time I saw that orange, it was on its way up. I mean really high, and then it started down toward you and ..." Re-visualizing the trajectory, I tried to stifle my amusement, but failed.

"I'd suspend you from school, but that would be too much like your trig class."

I knew it.

"So, you've got study hall after school every day for the next month and you *will* study. Are your parents going to be home this weekend?"

"It's just my mother, sir."

"Tell her to expect a call."

I explained to my mother what had happened and that Saturday morning, the phone rang. She answered. In between whatever was said to her, her responses went like this. "Yes, I know he did that last semester. That was supposed to be an elective course." ... "Did anyone say he saw him do it?" ... "I'm not surprised, because he said he didn't do it." ... "Dean Carrion, he may not see the world like you do, but he doesn't lie." ... "I can't stop you from doing that, but I believe it's not the right thing to do." ... "Well, if you're going to insist, I'm sure it'll be one of the least harmful ways he can experience injustice first-hand." Apparently Mr. Carrion didn't want to speak with my mother anymore because the conversation ended shortly thereafter.

I did my month's penance in study hall, actually studied, was educationally the better for it, and that was that, at least from my perspective, but in retrospect, I think the Universal Forces must have had something in mind, perhaps a lesson that assumptions are shaded by one's point of view and if the beholder's belief in them are strong enough, in his mind they take on the aura of facts. But they aren't facts. They're only proof of his state of mind and, without more, produce evidence of his motive, but seldom an appropriate result.

* * * *

42

Green Hornet

"What are you rebelling against?"
"What've you got?"

Marlon Brando,
The Wild One

WITH SPEEDBALL BABY'S CUSTOMIZATION COMPLETE except for the spotted grey primer on baby blue paint scheme, I turned some of my attention to motorcycles. Tucker got me interested in them before Speedball Baby and before the drums because, in addition to his nifty '39 Pontiac sedan, he had a big, used, 72 cubic inch Harley Hog his uncle, a motorcycle officer, gave him on his 16th birthday. I hadn't quite turned 15 at that time and didn't even have a Learner's Permit.

On Tucker's Harley, we had a lot of fun together, as usual, and had a blast going all over town on it. In those days, there were comparatively few motorcyclists and whether they rode Harleys, Indians, Triumphs, Ariels, Vincent Black Shadows, Nortons or any thing else, the popular conception was that riders were outlaws who would kill you for drunken sport. Not entirely true. We certainly weren't like that, but because we were on a motorcycle and had on leather jackets with short-billed cycle caps and light-blue tinted "rock" glasses (functionally named because they kept rocks and bugs from hitting us in the eyes), we struck fear in the hearts of motorists everywhere who were certain we were young savages. But, we were just having fun.

After I arrived at licensing age and had acquired Speedball and the drums, I finally achieved enough affluence to afford a motorcycle and Tucker had been looking around for a used 45 cubic inch Harley for me. He finally located one at a small motorcycle shop for $150. He assured me it was a good deal. It was either a converted WWII Army bike or the civilian version of it and smaller than Tucker's big Harley, making it just my size. It was hopped-up with only a toggle switch for the ignition and Tucker said the shop's owner told him it had been used for racing with the engine bored out to around 61 cubic inches. That thing went like a scalded dog.

It had no front fender, a bobbed back fender with a small pillion pad on it used as a passenger seat for those who could take it, and it was painted racing green with black tiger stripes. I named it, "Green Hornet."

In those days, the usual Harley had a hand gearshift on a steel stalk on the left side, requiring the removal of one hand from the handlebars to shift. To balance that, there was exactly one noticeable safety feature on the usual Harley, a foot-operated "rocker" clutch pedal, also on the left side, which was like a teeter-totter and would stay in whichever position it was rocked, forward or back, to engage or disengage it. Hey, the number of safety features on the bike could have been zero.

At least that's what the usual clutch arrangement looked like to me then. I wouldn't know because the scariest thing about the Green Hornet was its "suicide clutch." At some point in its life, I assume from racing, the Green Hornet had acquired the safety-absent suicide option. The clutch pedal was just like a car's. It had a spring on it, you pushed it down and held it to disengage the clutch and let it up to go.

That meant I owned, concurrently, two vehicles with a suicide feature. Speedball Baby's rear doors opened from the front edge and hinged at the rear. Thus, if the door latch popped loose for any reason while the car was traveling at speed, the wind immediately flared the door open like a clamshell, placing a rear passenger in significant peril because, as with virtually all cars then, there were no seat belts. So naturally, they were commonly called "suicide doors."

The Green Hornet's suicide clutch made for very fast shifting, but sitting stopped as the first in line at a traffic light or stop sign was dicey because you had to remove your left foot from the ground to push the clutch in while removing your left hand from the handlebars to work the gearshift, coordinating that with shifting your weight to your right foot to steady the bike.

After the moment you pulled the shift into gear, if your foot prematurely slipped off the clutch for any reason, it popped the bike and you into the cross traffic—hence, the suicide feature. Believing myself immortal, coupled with never being certain when the light would change or an opening would appear in traffic, I always sat with the clutch held down and the bike in gear so I could be "gone" instantaneously, not recognizing the double entendre. Despite my impatience, my foot never slipped. Those Universal Forces were always mitigating my youthful exuberance.

Compared to today, there were few bikers on the roads in those days and every motorcycle rider you met was an instant friend no matter what the age, make of bike or any other difference, sticking together against the slings and arrows of an un-adoring public. I met and became friends with a lot of interesting folks that way. Smiley, in his early 30's and nicknamed for his great teeth and smile, was 6'6" and well tanned with dark wavy hair. He rode a bright yellow 61 cubic inch "knucklehead" Harley, named for the appearance of the cylinder head covers. It was hopped-up, had a suicide clutch and Smiley prided himself on being able to make it do a 90 degree jump turn by popping the clutch while shifting into second gear as he was pulling into traffic from a side street.

One second he was pulling into it and the next he was going the same direction as the traffic. Most of the time he'd wait for a space for his motorcycle to fit in.

Smiley is how I found out how fast the Green Hornet could go, and the Universal Forces kept me from finding out how stupid I was. Late one night, Smiley and I were riding up the very first freeway in our area not long after it was completed. There were no cars, just long stretches of concrete. We decided to see how fast we could go, but my bike had no speedometer. You'd think for $150 they might have thrown one in, but the shop had to reinstall a headlight because it had been used for racing. So Smiley told me to get it going top speed and he would match my speed.

The Hornet was screaming with everything it had and there was Smiley right beside me. He indicated with his fingers 101. It didn't dawn on me until much later that it required him to remove one hand from the handlebars. Then he cranked it hard and pulled away in front of me. When we finally pulled over to the shoulder after that, he said he had been doing over 120 but his bike was vibrating so badly toward the end he couldn't tell exactly.

That was so much fun, we decided on the way back we'd get going as fast as my bike would go, we'd both extend our little fingers, he'd slowly move over and we'd see if we could keep them touching for at least a mile. The Universal Forces must love me, and Smiley too. We did it. I don't know where he is now, but I'm still here.

One day Smiley and I were riding along a small street and pulled up behind a car at a stop sign waiting for heavy cross traffic to clear on the boulevard. The car was driven by a young woman who appeared to be about Smiley's age so far as we could tell from the back. Smiley's front wheel was about 6 inches behind her bumper. Mine was a little further back. Hearing the rumble of our idling bikes, she kept looking in her rear view mirror and it was clear our presence made her nervous—stuck at a stop sign with two killer bikers behind her and not wanting to act frightened by rolling up her window. Since car air conditioning was virtually unknown then, almost everyone drove with at least the driver's window down on warm days.

At a point, she started an abortive crossing attempt, but with her clutch in, she rolled backward slightly, lightly bumping Smiley's front wheel. She knew it instantly. Smiley broke into, what else, a big smile, turned to me and said, "From here she looks like she's pretty cute. I should tell her she didn't hurt my sodamycle." That's what he called it. What can I say? He reached over, shut off my bike, then shut off his engine, popped his kickstand down, unrolled his six and a half foot frame from his bike and with boots crunching on the debris in the street, walked slowly up to her open window whistling High Noon.

He bent down, way down, and just like Gary Cooper, "Ma'am."

Looking straight ahead, "I'm so sorry. You won't hurt me, will you?"

"Of course not, Ma'am. I just want to tell you there's no damage and not to worry about it."

She turned and looked at him with disbelief.

Not being able to resist, Smiley continued, breaking into another big grin, "But I would be more careful. If you'd tapped my buddy's bike back there, you'd be tapping on death's door." Great, now I was a killer.

I don't think she picked up that he was flirting and she definitely didn't get the humor. Grateful to have escaped the Two-Wheeled Reaper, she asked us to please go around her. Then she rolled up her window.

I guess that's why a lot of people thought bikers weren't very nice. But in my experience, they were all really nice, so long as you didn't upset them. When they did get upset, it was kind of a different story. One day about ten of us were riding down a main artery in the city. At the head of the pack that day was a huge redhead named Woody, with a beak to match, and he rode a big, red Indian bike. I just happened to be right next to him. Oblivious of the staggered single-file safety formations used today, we always rode double file in one lane.

A man in an expensive car a little way in front of us hit a dog, glanced back at it and just kept driving. The dog was lying in the middle lane, hurt and crying. It seemed like everyone knew instinctively what to do. Woody blasted off after the car and I followed him, curious to see what his plan might be. The rest of the group surrounded the dog with their bikes and directed the traffic around it.

When Woody caught up to the perp, he was a well-dressed middle-aged businessman in a suit who, amazingly in that situation, had left his window down. Woody swung over next to him, very close next to him, reminiscent of my little-finger stunt with Smiley.

"Hey!"

The man continued to look straight ahead.

"You just hit a dog."

No response.

The gas feed on an Indian is operated by the twistable left hand grip, just the opposite of a Harley, so Woody reached through the driver's window, grabbed the man by his coat and bellowed, "Look pal, I saw you look back at the dog. Now pull over real nice or you're coming out this window and then we'll talk."

His car outweighed Woody's bike by quite a bit and the driver could have done a lot of things, none of them good for Woody, but the motorcycle mystique was still working and he slowly pulled over. Trying to be useful, I motioned traffic around from the back. Woody didn't have much trouble convincing the gentleman to return to the scene, put the dog in his car, now surrounded by the bikers, and take it to the vet I knew not far away who had saved my cat, one-eyed Willy. Fortunately, particularly for the perp, the dog did not have life-threatening injuries, the driver wrote a check (no credit cards then) for the vet's bill on the spot, and the owner was contacted from the information on the dog's tags. So, riders aren't such bad guys, are they?

In fact, a WWII vet I knew, Smokey, was a very nice guy. He was reputed to have been a member of the POBOB's which I understood had become the Hell's Angels. Whether he was a Hell's Angel or not, I really don't know. He didn't talk about it, but based on their reputation then, he was scary looking enough to be one because Smokey had gone over a mountainside on his bike several years before and lived. But the result to his face and head was, unfortunately for such a nice person or anyone for that matter, a frightening sight to behold. In any event, Smokey and all the other riders I knew, except Tucker, were much my senior, but they liked Tucker and me for some reason and we rode with them more or less as mascots.

Even though Tucker was a big guy and looked much older than his age, they wouldn't let us ride with them if they planned to go out to drink, usually on Saturday nights. That was okay with me. I knew I was out of my element in bars and the atmosphere kind of scared me. But one Thursday night we were all out riding and they spontaneously decided to stop at a beer joint that consisted of a huge, dimly lit, WWII Quonset hut with lines of picnic tables placed end-to-end and sawdust covering the floor. I said I'd stay outside and watch the bikes, but they said this place was no problem and I should come in with them. So I did.

The only light was from small candles in glass containers sparsely placed on the tables. Any more than a foot away from a candle and it was impossible to see anything clearly. The waitress came down the tables in our line taking everyone's orders. Coming up behind me, she asked what I wanted. I'd only had beer once before and didn't like it. I really wanted a Coke, but being with the big guys that night, I squeaked out in my best sixteen-year-old biker's voice, "I'll have a beer." She promptly asked me for some identification. Smokey, sitting directly across the table from me, stretched down the table with his best arm, grabbed a candle, pulled it under his face, rolled his eyes up at her and growled, "Give the kid a beer."

I received the beer promptly from the waitress' trembling hand, and of course under those circumstances, I drank it. I had a slight buzz from it and it's the only time in my life I've ridden a motorcycle after drinking an alcoholic beverage, but the UF were watching out for me, and I'm sure the statute of limitations has run on all counts by now.

* * * *

43

My First Time

One reason I don't drink is that
I want to know when I am having a good time.

Lady Astor

THE FIRST TIME IN MY life I'd ever had any beer occurred a few months before that Thursday night motorcycle ride. Tucker and I were in Don's car one evening, just aimlessly riding around on the other side of town where his girlfriend, Dee Dee, went to high school. Then, Don decided to pick up a couple of friends he'd met at her school. Tucker and I didn't really know them very well and I didn't feel right about these guys after they got into the back seat with me. They immediately wanted to go get some beer. Don liked the idea and Tucker and I didn't, but they kept insisting and talked Tucker into it, saying it was time everyone learned to drink a man's drink. I continued to protest and Don said he'd drop me at my house, but they were going to pick up a six-pack on the way.

That problem defused somewhat, Don's friends directed him to a liquor store they'd heard was pretty loose and picked Tucker to go in because he was the biggest and looked the oldest. Tucker had never tried to buy beer before and since his father was a cop, he was feeling the pressure, but he didn't want to lose face. Fortunately for my face, I'd finessed that particular issue by objecting in the first place.

A discussion ensued between Don's two "experienced" beer-loving high school juniors about whether to get bottles or the relatively new cans.

"Let's get cans."

"Beer in cans tastes like the can."

"Light through the bottle kills the beer."

"Canned beer still tastes like metal."

"But there's no deposit, no return on cans."

"Good thought."

When we got to the liquor store, there was a wino hanging around outside with a bottle in a paper bag and Tucker managed to wiggle out of his face-saving problem by talking the wino into going in and buying it for us in return for a twenty-five-cent stipend. Tucker said he'd watch the guy's booze bag while he was inside. It all happened and we were off, five of us with our own paper bag containing a six-pack of Falstaff, "The choicest product of the brewers' art." It was also the cheapest.

Since it was a half-hour drive across town to my house, the other four in the car decided they needed a beer right away. Tucker was in the front passenger seat and I was sitting right behind him. A little peeved that I had opted out, he reached back over his shoulder and dropped the paper bag with the six-pack on the floor at my feet, "Here, since you're not going to have any, at least make yourself useful and open us some beers."

Not wanting to make a federal case out of it, I hoped there was no beer-can opener in the bag (no aluminum pop-tops in those days, just steel punch tops), but, unfortunately, the wino made sure one was included. The twenty-five-cent fee wasn't exactly pocket change to him and he probably wanted to make a good impression, hoping for return business.

I usually drank Coke or RC cola out of bottles and used the kind of opener that just flipped the top off. I'd only tried the pointed steel "church-key" openers on the new Royal Crown Cola cans a couple of times. I wasn't good at it then and I wasn't good at it this time. I couldn't get the little hook thing to stick under the lip of the can so I could lever the sharp pointed tip into the top and slice that inch or so triangular puncture hole. So, I just tried to force the pointed end into the top by grabbing the opener and shoving it and the can against each other as hard as I could.

I struggled with the can and made little more than a pinhole puncture in it. Because the beer had been jostled by both its drop to the floor and my efforts to get the can open, beer started shooting out of the hole and the can slipped out of my hand during my panic try to make the hole bigger. Everybody in the back seat was grabbing for it, shaking it up worse, and it flipped up in the air spraying the car and everyone in it with that Falstaff artful-brewers choice product.

"For crying out loud! Here." One of Don's friends shoved the now three-quarters-empty, but quiet, can into my hand, grabbed the opener and opened mine right, then he opened one for each of the others in the car. They took a sip and then looked at me. "Go on, take a swallow for cripes sake." The beer permeating my clothes didn't smell so good, but I was a little curious to see what it actually tasted like. So, thinking it would be something like Coke with a different flavor, I took a big gulp from what was left in my can.

Mistake. I'd never had anything alcoholic before, or anything that pungent carbonating around in my mouth. It burned my tongue, throat, everywhere it went beyond that, bubbled out my nose and I think out my tear ducts. My eyes were burning and I was coughing, choking and sneezing. It became clear to me why both my parents quietly declined anything with alcohol in it. They were a lot smarter than I gave them credit for.

Everyone in the car was laughing uproariously and deriding me severely, as those with "experience" are sometimes wont to do with a neophyte. All this was happening while Don was driving down a major city artery heading for my side of town. Don's boneheaded friend in the back seat behind him chugged the rest of his can, gave everyone a manly "ahhhhhhhhhh," burped and tried to crush his can, but couldn't even dent it (those steel cans were tough).

So, to cover his embarrassment, he leaned forward, stuck his arm part way out Don's window and made a left-handed hook shot over the top of the car just as we were stopping at the crosswalk for a red light at a major intersection.

At the same instant, a car was coming up on our right in the curb lane. The driver obviously saw the can in the air and screeched to a stop. The can caromed off that car's hood onto the sidewalk, rolled diagonally across the corner, fell off the curb of the cross street and clattered to a stop at the foot of a motorcycle policeman sitting on his police Harley, waiting for red light runners with his partner. The cops had whirled upon hearing the screech and were watching the white can roll with its Falstaff shield spinning over and over. Then, wonder of wonders, they looked straight at the driver of the car next to us. She was a little gray-haired grandma who pointed directly at us, clarifying the situation immediately.

The blood drained from each of us. Don had already become a stone sculpture muttering, "Change … change …," but the light still hadn't changed before one of the cops appeared in front of our car in his khaki jodhpurs, spit-shined knee-high jack boots and black-billed policeman's cap with badge on the front. He was in a wide, unmovable stance with both hands on his hips, glaring at us. The other was opening the driver's door shining his flashlight around the inside at each of us in turn. Of course, whenever I'm around Tucker and the cops appear, I do the deer-in-the-headlights thing.

"What's going on here?"

Don, hoping against hope, "Nothing."

He leaned down into Don's face, "Well your car smells like a brewery."

Still hoping, "Really?"

The other cop moved to the passenger door and opened it, "You four get out and go over to the curb by our motorcycles. Young man, pull your car into the parking space by our bikes. Don't *anybody* entertain even a little *tiny* thought about doing anything else." The pistol in his holster must have been a foot long and his hand was resting on it. In those days, if you ran from the police, *you* assumed the risk.

"Yes, sir."

There didn't appear to be any damage to the little old lady's car and she left after they took her information. When they finally strolled over to us, both cops were taller than Tucker, twice as solid and obviously tough, really tough. Standing next to them, we looked like a bunch of babies—not far from the truth.

"All of you stink. Look at yourselves, you've got beer all over your clothes. Let me smell your breath (the acid test, no breathalyzers then)." Our breath failed, but none of us were even slightly drunk, except maybe for the chugger. "I suppose you boys are aware that at 16 and 17, you're just a little shy of the legal drinking age by, oh, maybe four or five years?" We all did the deer thing then.

Pretty soon two black and white squad cars with the single big, round, red light on top showed up with the customary two officers each, also with big guns on their belts and big Billy-clubs they kept tapping on their palms as they listened to the motorcycle cops. They searched Don's car and preserved the evidence. One unopened can of beer, one opener, my almost empty can, three cans about two-thirds full, and added the empty basketball-substitute can that rolled up to the cops. They made a note of all that and poured the beer from the open cans into the street, tossing all of them into our soggy bag along with the torn-open cardboard of the six-pack, all of which they placed in the trunk of the squad car transporting Tucker and me, the other three riding in the back of the other squad car.

Along with the evidence, we were delivered to Juvenile Hall where we were interrogated by the dreaded "Juvies," plain clothes officers assigned to deal with and straighten out young neer-do-wells like us, that is, juvenile delinquents. We spilled the beans and told them exactly what had happened including the beer spraying all over us and the hook shot off the hood of the car. We also detailed our not-so-vast drinking experience, which didn't take long.

They sent us out into the waiting room alone while they shut the door to their room to call our parents. In that respect, the first thing Tucker had done was to plead with them not to tell his dad because he'd never been in trouble before and his dad, being a cop and all, would be really mad at him. Since they knew Tucker's dad, they said they'd call him first.

We sat in the waiting room speculating on what it would be like to be in jail. The furniture in the waiting room consisted of some ugly brown chairs and a double-ugly brown couch with big cushions, all of which had to be at least older than we were and, from all appearances, had never been cleaned. Just having to sit on that couch was punishment enough. Trying not to touch the exposed surfaces of the cushions, I idly stuck my hand between my cushion and the back of the couch, a place I presumed had never seen the light of day, and pulled out a twelve-inch hunting knife. I held my surprise prize up in the air for the rest to see just as Tucker's dad walked in. His eyes bugged out at the knife as he started to reach inside his coat for his weapon. Then he saw it was me.

Exasperated, "Chip, what in the holy hell are you doing?"

"Honest to God, it was behind the cushion and I just accidentally pulled it out. I swear."

"Well stick it back there quick and forget about it or you'll spend longer than you think in jail."

I complied immediately. He gave a knock on the Juvies' door, walked in and shut it behind him.

We heard muffled voices and we thought we also heard laughter. After awhile, they came out. They gave us a long talk about our stupid and potentially dangerous behavior and we were extremely contrite, hoping against hope we wouldn't be spending the night in the drunk tank with a bunch of winos. Ultimately, Tucker's dad said, "Chip, your mother's so mad she told us she's not coming to get you and to toss you in the hoosegow and throw away the key."

Well, I was going to spend the night in the tank for sure.

"So, I'll drop you at your house before Tucker and I go home. His mother wants to have a chat with him in the worst way. Perhaps I should come in while you chat with your mother?" He smiled.

"No, sir. That won't be necessary. Just drop me off at the curb. And ... thank you, sir."

As we got in his car, Tucker's dad said, "Chip, come on over this weekend. I'll give you some church-key lessons using RC cans. After that, you and Tucker can work on getting a little more air under your hook shots." He chuckled to himself all the way to my house.

I don't know which was worse, that experience or the one a few months later after we started thinking it would be cool to smoke because everyone we idolized in the movies was doing it, including then-actor Ronald Reagan who appeared in print ads bearing his signature with a Chesterfield hanging from his smiling lips, "I'm sending Chesterfields to all my friends. That's the merriest Christmas any smoker can have ..." Even Santa had a cigarette between his fingers in a Lucky Strike ad, hawking "A Gift of Pleasure." Of course, there were no health warnings on cigarette packages in those days.

Even though the future United States President (elected more than 30 years after that ad) was touting Chesterfields, I decided Herbert Tareyton Cork Tip Modern Size was my cigarette, very distinguished. The "genuine cork tip" always stayed "firm and fresh."

With a lit Tareyton hanging at just the right angle out of my mouth, I was driving alone one very nice afternoon with my windows down. Without touching the cigarette with either hand and just clamping it between my lips, you know—like the real men did, I took a big drag just as I was pulling up to a stop light and inhaled—I admit I inhaled. With the cigarette still between my lips and no hands, I turned my head to the right as I exhaled forcefully in a very adult way, unintentionally blowing the smoke over into the face of the driver staring at me from the car stopped on my right. It was my Sunday School teacher.

The Universal Forces must not have wanted me to drink much, because I don't. And, as you might suspect, I don't smoke either.

44

The Color Purple

Courage is a special kind of knowledge . . .

David Ben-Gurion

ONE OF THE FRIENDS I met riding my Green Hornet Harley was a biking Irishman named Mike Madigan. Naturally everyone he knew called him Irish Mike. His Harley was his only transportation and he didn't call it anything except "my bike." He was a WWII vet and the manager of an Earl Scheib car painting shop. I used to let him borrow Speedball Baby when he needed a car and since the painting facilities weren't used on Sundays, he determined to show his gratitude by painting it for me, remedying my primer-mottled paint scheme. He said he could mix any color I wanted.

Speedball was too special a car to be painted just any color. It needed a color no one else had. So Mike and I fooled around mixing paints until we came up with a purple that was vibrant, even fluorescent, much niftier than the purple on Gorgeous George's Cadillac. It was perfect. I was certain it was the first "pulsing purple" car in the world as Mike called it, and according to the Juvies who constantly stopped me and searched my car after that just because of Speedball's color, it definitely was. Fancy that, somebody making decisions on the basis of color. That was one of the most senseless things I could imagine.

Everyone connected with our high school who hung out in the evenings did so at a drive-in restaurant we called "the Clock." It had a big clock on top of it, duh, and lots of neon lights. The main building was on a corner and it had some booths inside with those little miniature juke boxes on the wall at each one so you could select a song for a nickel from your booth. But the main attraction for us was two long rows for cars to park in a semicircle around the building. What really made it great was a driveway in front of each row so you could cruise slowly in front of every car before you parked, showing off your car and acting really cool. It was the forerunner of kids hanging out at the mall these days.

The carhop would roller skate out, take your order and bring it back on a tray she hooked to your window. They had little carhop hats, short skirts (for the time) and nice white professional-type skating boots with rubber-wheeled quad skates on the bottom, a far cry from the non-booted cheap metal-wheel quad skates we used as grade-school kids on the sidewalk. Those metal wheels were riveted onto a flat metal plate you fastened onto your leather shoes by turning the metal skate key as hard as you could to tighten metal clamps that grabbed the front of the leather sole on your shoe on both sides, plus a prayer they'd stay on. You'd wear the key on a string around your neck. The back of the skate was pulled tight against the heel of your shoe with a leather strap that buckled around your ankle.

The four metal wheels would grind down the sidewalk, catching on every pebble and seam in the cement, causing the clamps to eventually work loose when you were least expecting it and your foot would fly off the front of the skate. You'd end up flat on your stomach—no protective gear, just you kissing the sidewalk with the skate dangling from your ankle by the leather strap.

Anyway, we survived and made it into high school to travel by car to the Clock. For each person jammed into the car, we usually ordered a cherry Coke. It had a real maraschino cherry sitting on top of the crushed ice and you'd smoothly offer the cherry to your girlfriend, if you had one, holding it by the stem and dropping it into her mouth like fish food into a guppy. A large order of fries would be shared by all, consumed over a period of at least two hours.

Since hamburgers were about 30¢ at the Clock, we'd often stop first at a little drive-up joint named "Ken's" where you got out of your car and bought them in a sack at the window. It was kind of like eating cardboard with ketchup on it, but they were only 11¢. We'd heard of a new place called "McDonald's" that sold better burgers for 15¢, but it was fifteen miles away, so we never went there. After all, gas was 29¢ a gallon for regular and everybody would have to chip in. Funny how things change, Ken's isn't around anymore.

In any event, my car was now magnificent, and even though their members were at least a year or two older than I was, I decided I wanted to join "Headers," which was the coolest car club in town. A number of my friends wanted to join it too. Car clubbers then had a small metal plaque hanging from two short chains on the back bumper. The plaque had the name of the car club along with its logo and would drag on the ground every time you went up a driveway from the street, or vice versa. That sound was one of the great car-club things, as were the jackets with the club name and logo stitched into the back.

One of the subtle-head-turning events that would happen at the Clock was when a member of the Headers would come cruising through, the plaque would scrape as he pulled in and you'd hear the rumble of his exhaust pipes as he slowly moved down the rows, checking everyone out and being checked out. Then he'd slowly back into a parking place in the front of the second row so he could see everything that went on. The Headers virtually owned the Clock from the car-club perspective and no other car club ever cruised through there.

My idea was that I would get in the club and that would be the foot in the door for my friends to get in, one by one. But, the Headers rejected Speedball. What fools. They said it wasn't nifty enough. An oscillating purple car with fake dual pipes and a fur-lined glove compartment? C'mon! I didn't agree with that decision any more than I did with the chicken-cheerleading deal or Mr. Carrion's orange view of things. So, undaunted, my friends and I started our own car club. Fittingly we thought, we called it "Rebels."

What a great day when the jackets and car plaques arrived. Our Rebel band of twelve clustered together on a Saturday afternoon, installed our bumper chains and hung our plaques. That night after our spy was sure the maximum number of Headers members had arrived, we paraded through both rows of the Clock and left. It created the desired effect. Instead of ignoring us as insignificant wannabes, they gave us substance by letting everyone know they were furious. We rubbed it in every night at the Clock, parading, backing our cars in as slowly as we could and walking around in our jackets with "Rebels" embroidered across the back while talking to friends in the other cars there, which was almost everyone there because our high school was the engine of the Clock's economy. Of course, we didn't chat with any Headers.

A couple of weeks later while I was alone in my car at the Clock, Brick, the president of the Headers came over and said he wanted to meet me exactly one week hence at 8:00 p.m. in the big vacant lot in back of the Clock to teach me a little car clubbing lesson. Brick, a year ahead of me at Pearson High, was bigger than I was and kind of mean. In a fight a couple of months before, he had actually broken the rib of a fellow I knew by kicking him when he fell down. The protocol for his type of fight was to bring all your friends with you, the opponent would bring all his friends with him and it would ultimately turn into a free-for-all with people getting more than bumps and bruises, sometimes a lot more. I think he picked on me less because I was president of Rebels, and more because I would chat with his girlfriend from time to time and, probably thinking I was bird-dogging his steady, he definitely didn't like that.

Now, I'd never been in a *real* fight where there was an appointed time for the blows to begin, and except for splitting Irving Grodeman's lip with a lucky punch in junior high because he was trying to hit me—after I accidentally shot him in the ear with a rubber band—I hadn't been in an actual fight with anyone since the third grade when Dickey Dunlap pounded the bejesus out of me after school because I put his name on the blackboard for talking while our teacher was out of the room. Being class monitor had its responsibilities.

That wasn't much of a fight since Dunlap was twice my size and I spent all my efforts unsuccessfully trying to keep from getting hit. My friend Ralph Alltalk was with me and he said that if Dickey had hit me one more time, he was going to run and tell my mother—just as fast as his black high-top canvas P-F Flyers with the white rubber soles could take him I presume. I couldn't connect the dots on that defensive strategy since my house was over a block away.

But, the worst part of it was that I'd dropped my big sock full of marbles. I usually tied a big knot in the end of the sock, but I'd been showing Alltalk the new shooters, marbled boulders, clear peeries, steelies and aggies I'd won playing "keepsies" with the other guys at lunch hour. We'd drawn a pretty big circle in the dirt for the contest that day too, and I was pretty happy until Dickey started pounding on me and then he kicked my marbles as hard as he could after they spilled out of the sock. It took me a long time to find most of them again because Alltalk left shortly after proclaiming his loyalty, saying he had to get home, but I did find my lucky cream-colored shooter with the red stripes.

You were able to take a big heavy sock full of marbles to school then and no one even remotely thought of it as a weapon (and certainly not me or I might have won the fight). It was just a bag of marbles you had to put inside your desk during class time so they wouldn't clack around. Today they'd get you expelled, and if you had an aspirin in your pocket too, you'd be banished from the city. Oh, yeah, getting pounded on with only your pride hurt by Dickey Dunlap was just about the most dangerous thing that would happen to a kid walking to or from school then.

But being in a fight with Brick was another thing entirely. So, I stewed almost twenty-four hours a day for a couple days about what to do. He could really hurt me, and if I told the other members of Rebels, they would come and could really get hurt. I finally decided to go by myself, give it everything I had and maybe get the crap kicked out of me, but at the end of the evening I would want him to know he'd been in a fight, and it wouldn't be by the Marquess of Queensberry rules either, since I knew they were meaningless to him.

I should have just relaxed and turned it over to the Universal Forces because they were already planning my defense. Two or three days before the big fight, my track teammates and I were suiting up in the locker room when one of them said, "Hey Chip, Bobby tells me you're pretty good in the neighborhood boxing matches, why don't you and Two-Fast Frankie spar a little?" Great. Two-Fast Frankie was my size, but he was a city Golden Gloves Champ and everyone knew it. They called him Two-Fast because he was lightning on two feet and lightning with two hands.

"I'm not an idiot, he'll kill me. You do it."

He pulled Frankie over, "No, no, he'll take it easy on you, won't you, Frankie?"

So now there's most of the track team crowded around Two-Fast Frankie and me, chanting with rhythmic clapping for a sparring session.

Realistically confident, Two-Fast said, "Look, I won't hit you very hard and you can try to hit me as hard as you want."

He put his hands up and started dancing around. I put mine up and didn't do anything except dance around too. The spectators became restless.

Getting a little peeved, he said, "Look, if you don't come after me, I'm going to come after you."

Knowing a little bit about counterpunching from the neighborhood bouts and watching Sugar Ray Robinson on TV, I knew Two-Fast wanted me to take the initial shot, but I thought doing it would be my first mistake with him, so, brilliantly, I said, "Come on."

He sprang at me like a cheetah.

Once again, everything went into super slow motion—for me anyway. He threw a left hook and I knew it before he started, saw it coming very slowly and blocked it. He threw combinations. The same thing happened and I blocked them. I knew what punch was coming every time and it moved like molasses. The crowd started exclaiming in amazement and he redoubled his efforts, really going for it. No matter what he did, I blocked or slipped those slow motion efforts easily. Finally, he dropped his hands in embarrassment. Disgusted with himself, he walked away mumbling. The word went around the right circles like wildfire. Without ever having thrown a punch, I was *somebody* for a second time. Marlon Brando would have been proud.

Fight night with Brick and the Headers arrived. It was 7:45 p.m. I was sitting in my car alone, looking at the big clock on top of the Clock and counting off the minutes to 8:00. I heard Irish Mike's bike rumble to a stop behind me somewhere. Shortly, he hopped into my car and asked "What's up?" So I told him of my impending doom. He said he'd parked his bike back in that dirt lot and wondered what all those high school kids giving him the once-over were doing there.

Then he looked at me for awhile like I imagine you might look at a kid brother and said, "Chip, I don't usually talk about this because word gets around and then people just want to take a turn at me, but I boxed in the Navy. I was good. I had 30 fights and won 29 of them, 22 by knockout. Only lost the first on a close decision and nobody ever wanted a second go at me. Why don't I just hang around the fringes and if they start ganging up, I'll help you out a little against those jalopy boys?"

I really should have guessed it from his build and the looks of his nose. In any event, I started feeling just like I had when I sparred with Two-Fast Frankie and, all of a sudden, I *knew* what was going to happen in a few minutes with Brick and the Headers.

Promptly at 8:00 p.m., the two of us walked over to the vacant lot. Irish Mike hung back in the shadows and Brick didn't see him. Brick was sitting on the fender of his car with his girlfriend and a passel of his car club buddies standing around on either side. Only you or your girlfriend, if she was a really good one, could sit on the fender of your car.

I walked up without hesitation. About three feet away, I looked straight at him, "Here I am, let's go."

Surprised, "Where are your friends?"

I heard Irish Mike step out of the shadows behind me.

"I brought this one."

Looking around at his friends, he sneered, "The two of you are going to gang up on me?"

"Nope, he's here to keep your friends off me."

Then Brick took a good look at Irish Mike. His eyes widened almost imperceptibly and, just for an instant, I saw fear and confusion flicker through them. Then I literally heard his thoughts, 'He's ready to go at me by himself. And behind him is a mean looking *real biker* who's here to keep my guys from helping me. I've gotta go solo against the guy that Two-Fast Frankie couldn't lay a finger on. I could lose in front of all my friends—and my girlfriend!'

Brick's eyes closed slightly, "I think I'll just let it burn in my mind for awhile."

Not inquiring into the precise meaning of that sentence, I knew it was my cue to leave. I spun on my heel while deftly replying, "Your call." As Irish Mike and I walked away, he said under his breath, "Way to go, kid. I'm not real sure I could've taken all those high schoolers at once."

I never had a problem with Brick again. I don't know what the Universal Forces arranged for him after that, but for me, just like my experience with Two-Fast Frankie, they fixed the fight so I didn't have to throw a punch.

* * * *

45

Burger Flippin'

Speed, it seems to me,
provides the one genuinely modern pleasure.

Aldous Huxley

THE REBELS CAR CLUB FLOURISHED after the incident with Brick and the Headers, but whether or not you were in a car club, a usual occurrence was street racing. Most of the time a drag race happened at a stop light when another "enthusiast" pulled up next to you and wanted to go, usually signaled by a look and some slight motion with the head.

Less often, but a lot more exciting, were the "planned" street drag races between two souped-up cars with lots of talk, reputation and mystique behind them. The word would travel at light speed and at the appointed nighttime hour on a deserted stretch of road, up to perhaps two hundred kids would line the sides to watch. Of course, all drag racing on the streets was (and still is) inherently dangerous to the participants and anyone else within the range of their boneheadedness. Injuries and deaths were definitely not unknown. However, those of us who participated in some capacity considered only the possibility of an apprehension by the "fuzz," being otherwise certain we were eternal and invincible.

In an effort to get racing off the streets and combat youthful exuberance (generally an age range through the mid-30's including younger vets of World War II), the police, the more responsible car clubs which included some of those same vets, and concerned citizens, began talking about legal, organized drag racing, and some of the talkers actually did it. We heard about it and, enamored with our club's self-perceived success, we decided to hop-up a car and take it to the recently-organized drags at the old airport. The drags were held every Sunday from eight in the morning until dusk on an abandoned runway (actually an abandoned taxiway but we didn't know the difference), which afforded plenty of distance to race a quarter mile and have room to stop, plus other areas to park and tinker with cars. We could race as much as we wanted without glancing continuously in our rear view mirror.

Baby Huey, our largest member whose real first name we didn't know, said his dad had a beat up '41 Ford flat-head V-8 Business Coupe in the back yard that didn't run, and he talked his dad into giving it to us, letting us work on it there and using his dad's tools so long as we were strictly accountable for cleaning and inventorying them at the end of each work session, promptly replacing any that were lost or broken. I think Baby's dad was just relieved to know where his lumbering son was going to be most of the time, coupled with the fact that his dad was a former dirt-track racer.

Some of us, and often all of us, were working on that car almost constantly. We all chipped into a fund for necessary parts, most of which were procured at junk yards from wrecked Fords, including a pretty good V-8 engine at a great price, but that almost exhausted our budget. No big deal. The mechanics in our group got the car into slick shape, beefing up the clutch and the 3-speed syncro transmission, and otherwise modifying it as much as our funds and the results of begging for parts allowed. With genuine gratitude, and not being completely oblivious to the realities of the situation, the members elected Baby Huey as the head mechanic, recognizing "Dad's tools, Baby rules."

Baby's dad, who could have done everything himself and always gave advice freely when asked, intervened at one point for safety reasons, which were matters that really didn't concern us.

Out of an abundance of caution accumulated from his dirt track experience, he installed lap and shoulder harness restraints for the driver and welded big roll-bars forming a cage protecting the driver in case the unwanted occurred. He was also going to put in a stripped down bucket seat to offset the weight of the roll-bars, but he learned that if the car didn't have its normal seats, it would take it out of the stock-gas class at the drags, and we definitely needed to be in the lowest class we could get into. But, in the course of that endeavor, he also found out that the Ford Business Coupe was originally sold stock without a back seat; it was an optional accessory. So at least we could avoid that and its weight.

While I knew enough to impress the girls and hold my own in casual hop-up talk, it was all bloviating, as was also the case with the remainder of the spurious mechanics. So our group of poseurs decided the car's body needed to look slick too. We sanded, Bondo'd, sanded some more and, with some free primer from Irish Mike, primered it completely gray over the next couple of months.

As the last act in building the car and since the overall organizational responsibility was mine as President, I delegated the task of buying some brand-new 6.00x16 tires to one of the guys who said he could get us a really good deal on tires that size. Even at that, the purchase was going to blow out our budget; thus, we couldn't afford wider tires for more grip off the line, much less wider rims to mount them on, all of which rendered moot our unending debate concerning whether bigger tires would take us out of the "stock" class.

Then, after some discussion at our regular Tuesday meeting, we named our finished beauty "Rebelina," and even though she was completely finished, we decided not to start her engine until the following Saturday so we could have a little party and celebrate. When Saturday came, we suddenly realized the success of the party hinged on the engine starting. A couple of months' hard work was hanging in the balance. Baby Huey made sure the six volt battery was completely charged and he primed the dual

Stromberg carburetors with a little high-test ethyl gas. Somehow we never wondered whether the Strombergs would take us out of the stock class.

Baby lumbered around to the driver's seat, pushed in the clutch, flipped the toggle switch we'd installed for the ignition and put his finger on the starter button. Everyone crowded around the car and we all counted, "One, two, three!" Baby pushed the button. Dead silence. I wondered if we'd forgotten to fill it with oil, but only for the first second or so because we'd shaved the heads on that V-8 and the compression was pretty stiff. Then it turned over once, then several times in rapid succession and burst into life. Boy, did that thing sing. We were cheering and jumping around and Baby was gunning the engine which sounded like a true screamer because the covers to the cut-outs were unbolted to let the exhaust run straight out instead of routed through the mufflers. The cut-outs were a necessary option because the car was to be driven on city streets to the drag strip and we had to bolt the covers back on to avoid a ticket.

Not many cars were towed to the drag strip anyway. These drags were the forerunners of today's modern events and didn't come close to approaching them in spectacle, cost or safety. They were started in order to get people like us off the streets. The cars in your classification just pulled up to the line in two queues and you raced against the car at the head of the line in the lane next to you. You checked your time when you were finished and if you were fast enough, you could keep moving up in the standings against the other fast vehicles. But regardless, for fifty cents you could run as many times in a day as you felt like going around and getting back in line to wait, at least until the time arrived for final eliminations for the fastest.

Fear of anything negative that could possibly be imagined had not pervaded each aspect of daily life in those days and the drags were relatively informal, which also included overlooking common-sense dangers. Many of the spectators parked their cars on the sides of the quarter mile run and just milled around them, watching. Many would also stand on the sides close to the starting line and watch. Often they would go back in the area behind the starting line designated for work on the cars, and then sometimes a number of the folks in the car-prep area would run right up behind the cars on the starting line to see a particularly interesting race take off.

Anyway, after Baby started the engine for the first time and we stopped congratulating ourselves, we realized no one had been selected to drive Rebelina. Baby would have been the driver, but his dad, mumbling something about his dirt track experience, wouldn't let him do it, which was a disguised blessing because Baby Huey weighed 235 blubbery pounds if he weighed an ounce. The rest of us, not focusing on Mr. Huey's not-so-subtle message concerning self-preservation, engaged in a lively discussion about who the driver should be. A majority could not agree, primarily because almost everyone wanted to be the driver.

Finally, I exercised my prerogative as President and said we were going to draw straws. That provoked an even livelier discussion because some who wanted to drive weren't perceived as drag-driving material by a majority of the others, and we all agreed we wanted Rebelina to do the best she could do. So I set a time limit of ten more minutes to decide or we wouldn't be going to the drags the next day.

It's apparently true that necessity is the mother of making decisions, because with no further help from me in that ten-minute period, they decided I was to be the driver since I was the only person who'd raced there before, plus I could speed shift really fast and at the right time, resulting I think from drumming—good ears, coordination, reflexes and timing. I don't know if they'd taken into account that weighing 117 pounds was also an asset. In actuality, my experience of running at the drags before with Speedball was scarcely a notable racing accomplishment since anyone could if he paid the fifty cents and passed the safety inspection, that is, the tires looked okay, the windshield was clean and the brakes stopped the car at the inspection station which had a big sign, "RACE AT

YOUR OWN RISK." Hey, still a better situation than racing on the street.

The following day showed up, as we felt sure Sunday would, and we caravanned to the old airport with Rebelina in the lead. It was the first time anyone had driven her and she was sweet. The shift lever was on the steering column just like Speedball's and I blew off from the stop signs, practicing speed shifts all the way. She sprinted like a gazelle. We'd put only a quarter tank of high-test in her to keep the weight to a minimum. If we ran low, there was more available at the drags from a 50 gallon barrel with a hand crank.

We got to the old airport and there were all manner of vehicles around, most gunning the engines with the drivers acting like they were too cool to notice if anyone was watching, but we all knew peripheral vision was being exercised overtime. Many of the younger drivers and "mechanics" were walking around with their T-shirt sleeves rolled up, often trapping a pack of cigarettes inside, and doing their best to look manly, swaggering with arms held a few inches out from their sides as if they were ready to draw six-shooters from imaginary holsters.

When I pulled into the classification station, the gentleman said our car looked real nice, particularly the big, flashy red-lettered script "Rebels" that Baby's sister had painted on the rear deck lid. He looked inside the car and then had me pop the hood. He looked at the engine and asked if it had been bored out and had oversize pistons. I told him not a chance, we couldn't afford it. He didn't inquire if the heads were shaved and neither the sight of the dual carbs nor the cut-outs bothered him. He wrote on a sheet of paper, handed it to me, and then with white poster paint put "136 s/g" on each of the rear side windows. I looked at the sheet. It had the date and "1941 Fd Cpe #136 stock gas" together with his initials. He told me to leave the marks on the windows and not lose the sheet in case we won a trophy. I think there was a little tiny smile as he said it, but we were official racers now.

Well behind the starting line, which we were sure was up there somewhere, we pulled Rebelina to a stop in a jumbled mass of other competitors' vehicles doing the same thing. Since, our class wasn't supposed to come up for awhile, we excitedly busied ourselves with unbolting the covers from the exhaust cut-outs without burning our hands, last minute checks, adjustments and, of course, lots of bloviation. A few racers even came over to look at our car and we swelled up even more.

There was everything there—bone stockers, sports cars, supercharged roadsters, supercharged chopped coupes with Roots-type blowers blocking most of the driver's vision, "Jimmy" blowers scrounged from WWII GMC landing craft engines, mean sounding engines with the familiar exhaust lope of Iskenderian cams, Edelbrock intake manifolds and aluminum heads, the whine of McCulloch's new model supercharger which few serious rodders could afford, cars simply stripped to the frames, and "thingies" which were little more than four tires, engine, steering wheel, bucket seat, gas pedal, small gas tank, transmission and rear end, all delicately fastened to an anemic set of steel rails. There was even a Ferrari, and a late model Cadillac with a lady in a straw hat at the wheel. We heard she was the wife of the starter.

Finally, the cobbled-together public address system announced our class and I started for the queue, but not before Baby's dad popped a goofy looking helmet on my head, fastened it, checked my lap and shoulder restraints and told me in a forceful way to leave everything on even though none of it was required. As I got closer to the start, it still looked the same as it had when I raced Speedball. For about seventy-five feet or so behind the starting line, there was a clear space separating the start from the competitors area with its jumbled hodgepodge of cars, racers, mechanics and millers-about. That jumble spread around to the sides and up the runway a ways before the more orderly "guard-rail" cars took over, parked with nose toward the runway and extending down each side of it for much of the remainder of the quarter-mile racing length between the start and the timing traps at the finish line.

Those guard-rail cars belonged to the spectators and not only did that help solve the parking problem, but those cars served to protect those who were sitting in them, on them or standing around them watching, and presumably quick enough to jump behind them and duck if an out-of-control racer started heading for them. The runway itself was perhaps 80 feet wide with a white line down the middle serving to delineate the two racing lanes.

My queue kept moving up through the car-spectator jumble and I finally penetrated into the short open space behind the formerly-white starting line, now almost obliterated by a layer of rubber from cars peeling out. The starter, a guy in a straw fedora with a cigar in his mouth, straddled the center line and motioned for Rebelina to come on, he pointed to the left lane and I pulled up to the line. As I closed in, I couldn't really see where the line was supposed to be, but he motioned for me to inch forward and then slit his throat with his finger. I stopped and looked over at a yellow Chevy pulling up in the right lane.

We stared at each other until the starter backed up a few feet, still straddling the white center line. He was casually holding the bunched-up flag in his left hand and he pointed his right index finger at me. I already had Rebelina in first gear with the clutch in and revving the engine to just the right rpm, all by ear since we had no tachometer. Relying on my previous one-time racing experience, I gave him the thumbs up, adrenaline coursing through my body. He pointed at the other driver who was watching me and did the same thing. The starter quickly switched the flag to his right hand, pointing it and his other hand to the ground as he bent his knees, hesitated a second, then sprang up with the flag shooting over his head.

I let Rebelina roar. It was perfect. I blew off the line with a hint that three more rpm and the tires would spin. Speed-shifting into second gear was magical and I heard the tires give a little chirp as it popped in. Just as I heard the rpm's start to top out, I punched in the clutch for third, slammed the gear shift down a picosecond later, then popped the clutch out in the next consecutive picosecond. The speed shifts were a smooooth 1-2-3, just like playing a triplet on the drums, left-right-left in lightning succession.

As the tires chirped into third, I was almost to the quarter-mile timing traps operated from a car at the side of the runway. I looked at the lane on my right for the yellow Chevy. It was nowhere in my field of vision and my victory yell was lost in the roar of unbridled exhaust. As I turned my head back toward the front, I heard a funny noise, kind of like a zipper. Then, the steering wheel jerked out of my hands as the right front fender dipped and the rear of the car yawed into the air. I blinked my eyes and I was lying on a stretcher about a hundred yards past the finish line.

I still had the helmet on and Mr. Huey was looking down at me, "Damn good thing I put in the shoulder harness 'n the roll-bars or you'd a been ground beef. What the hell did you guys buy *retreads* for? They don't do no damn good that fast." He glanced toward a fire truck guarding the remains of Rebelina a short distance away. She was upside down and the right front tire was shredded away. All the body work was squashed, squished, crushed or gone, except the roll cage. I looked at myself. There wasn't a mark on me, everything moved and I didn't hurt.

With characteristic medical acumen of the day, the ambulance drivers asked me if I was okay. I sat up, Baby Huey's dad pulled me to my feet, I slipped the helmet off and said, "Yeah, fine." Going to the hospital for observation wasn't even a consideration until many years later. The ambulance drivers retrieved the stretcher, jumped into their ambulance and sped back to their position with lights flashing. Then a totally insensitive bulldozer operator unceremoniously pushed Rebelina into a field.

When I got back to the spectator area, the guys all ran over.

My only inquiry, "Did I cross the finish line?"

Baby Huey was bouncing around, undulating like the giant cartoon duck he was nicknamed after, "That was unbelievable! You were goin' over n' over, flippin' like a hamburger for at least a football field. Pieces was flyin' off it like hot grease off'n a griddle! Hee—eell yes you crossed the line!" Then, looking at me more closely, "Are you sure you feel okay?"

"I'm great. Are you sure you guys aren't pissed?"

They were all grinning. “It was beautiful, man.” “Worth it, man.”

The next day, my entire body felt exactly like a finely-ground flipped burger, and on reflection, I knew there had been at least one hot-rod-equipment-purchasing task I should not have delegated. Retreads—I couldn't believe it. While taking care to protect me, the Universal Forces were teaching me to check *all* the details. That would work out well for me later on in life.

* * * *

46

The Graduate

I have never let my schooling interfere with my education.

Mark Twain

SOMEHOW, I FINALLY MADE IT through high school with good grades and graduation day arrived. My graduation class had eight hundred students in it and almost everyone knew almost everyone else by at least their first name, or in my case by my nickname. Most everyone just knew me as "Chip." Why would you need to know more than one name anyway?

We were all in our rented caps and gowns, with the gold tassels on our mortar board hats still on the right, ready to be flipped to the left—or was it the other way around? Anyway, it was in a large auditorium downtown so all our proud parents and relatives could be accommodated for this momentous occasion. The faculty sat up on the stage looking academically regal in their robes.

The nascent graduates were not regal. We were all yelling brilliant and erudite comments at each other like, "Hey, Chip, did you bring a bag of oranges for Carrion? Are you close enough to nail him?" "Hey, Chip, are the drums on the back of your motorcycle?" "What color did you paint your car for graduation?" We were generally causing a large number of separate mini-hysterically-happy commotions.

All eight hundred of us sat down together in front in no particular order. The drill was to file out of our row when the proctor directed us to do so, climb the stairs at the side of the stage, hand a piece of paper with your name *legibly* printed on it to a man with a microphone standing there, walk in a ceremonious manner to the center of the stage to receive a fake diploma with your left hand from the Principal who mumbled congratulations each time into his own microphone while he shook your right hand, then place your tassel on the other side of your cap, exiting at the stairs on the other side of the stage and going back to your row. A pretty slick setup, and the cap and gown people made out like bandits.

All-in-all, as a group we felt that recognition for our accomplishments while in high school was entirely appropriate, particularly if one took into account our collective, spurious, extracurricular accomplishments, because those took large amounts of otherwise-unused creativity and ingenuity, energy every student should exercise.

About 400 students had filed up to Microphone Man who droned out each's name as he or she walked across in his or her own ceremonious way, students yelling out personalized messages to the graduate, generally messages that had nothing to do with graduation, and the relevant family cheering and whistling for their student who, particularly if male, threw up his arms in a victory salute when he reached the other side of the stage.

Despite this joy and goodwill, people were starting to get bored by the time I went up the stairs, handed my paper printed with large and easily readable letters to Microphone Man and started my ceremonious saunter across the stage. "Hey, it's the Wild One." "Look out, Mr. Carrion—incoming!" Sitting on the stage, Mr. Carrion did not look pleased. Microphone Man looked at the paper and boomed out, "George Charles Carroll, the Third." Eight hundred students erupted with unified hilarity. It turned into absolute chaos.

The Principal turned and looked at his Dean of Boys. Mr. Carrion rose in his cap and gown and started to approach the

Principal's microphone. As he did so, very low at first and then with ever increasing volume, "He didn't do it. He didn't do it. He didn't do it."—and on and on. By the time Mr. Carrion got to the microphone, no one could hear him. I stood smiling at the side of the stage, basking in this unexpected, if not infamous, celebrity. The Principal walked over to me, which caused rhythmic clapping to start accompanying the chant.

Before he could say anything, I yelled so I could be heard over the din, "I'm not the one chanting, sir, and that *is* my real name!" Well, except that I was not the third person in my family with exactly that name.

He looked at me with exasperation, speaking slowly and distinctly, "Stop smiling. Do not wave to the crowd. Do not make a face. Do not gesture. Do not do anything right now except go back to your seat, sit down and look straight ahead. Understood?"

"Yes, sir."

I heard that still, small voice in the back of my head telling me to do it just like he said. The Universal Forces wanted to make certain I got out of high school and into college.

* * * *

47

Gut Feelings and Crickets

The first step to getting the things you want out of life is this:
Decide what you want.

Ben Stein

PRIOR TO MY GRADUATION AND shortly after the Orange Incident, Mr. Carrion assigned me to a new class counselor. Perhaps Mr. Carrion thought his being my counselor was a conflict of interest at that juncture, and also that it was somehow poetic that my new counselor should be my math teacher, Mr. Sigurd, who had always been sympathetic to the trigonometry plight that got me on the wrong side of Mr. Carrion in the first place. Of course, Mr. Sigurd knew that I was almost finished with fulfilling all of my college requirements (other than actually graduating), and like my parents, he felt it was important for me to go to college.

So, starting several months before my graduation from Pearson High, he helped me make an application for admission to a large, private, prestigious and well-known university in our state. It wasn't an easy university to get into, but my mother wanted me to go there and my father agreed. It's the only place I applied. Mr. Sigurd mailed the application with a cover letter I never saw.

For reasons still unknown to me, I was accepted, and during the summer after graduation, I got a letter from my university faculty counselor setting a date for me to go up to see him in order to arrange my course schedule, a dorm to live in and other details necessary in connection with my freshman year. He emphasized he was quite anxious to meet me. Interesting. I've always wondered what Mr. Sigurd said in his cover letter.

Now that the reality was upon me, it was a problem because that university had twenty thousand students and I'd never felt truly comfortable about going there for that reason. My parents would be happy, but I'd be an ant again, surrounded by nineteen thousand nine hundred ninety nine other ants. Shirley had gone to a much smaller university in the neighboring state and city where my father lived, the only university in that state. She had always liked it, said everyone was very nice *and* it had fewer than five thousand students. I thought about it a lot, but couldn't decide where I should go.

In the end, I decided to trust my gut feeling about the matter. So, I didn't go see my university faculty counselor and, after waiting awhile to make sure I still felt the same way, I threw everything important to my survival away from home into Speedball Baby—one suitcase and my drums. Then I kissed my mother goodbye, told her I would break the news to my father and set out for his city in the desert.

The drive was boring. That was before the interstate highway system we know today and, once out of the city, most "highways" were simply long stretches of two-lane roads punctuated only by "poke and plumb towns" (poke your head outta the car and you're plumb outta town) and ubiquitous Burma Shave signs every few miles, that series of several white on red, small wooden signs with a verse ending in "Burma Shave," a brushless shaving cream which accelerated the demise of shaving brushes. I understand the Smithsonian Museum has a set of original signs that reads, "Shaving brushes—You'll soon see 'em—On a shelf—In some museum—Burma Shave."

Of course, that was prophetic for those large round shaving brushes that were dipped in water and churned around in a cup containing hard shaving soap, all in order to whip up a lather that's brushed onto a poor recipient's face. "Poor" because he then had to shave either with a lethal straight-edge razor or that Gillette two-edge "safety" razor that sponsored the *Friday Night Fights*, either of which could and usually would slice you to ribbons, precipitating the decoration of your face with little pieces of toilet paper stuck to the cuts. By the way, my childhood next-door neighbor pal, Bobby, still whips up lather with a shaving brush and is adamant that all other shaving methods are inferior.

When I got to the state line, which was in the desert a little over half way to my destination, it was midnight and it was hot, really hot. It wasn't hot where I'd been, but it was here and I'd been warned there was a heat wave, unusual even for the desert this time of year, and that's why I was driving at night, car air conditioning being essentially unknown as you may recall. It was definitely hot in the car because only the screened outside center air vent was open, my windows being rolled up because of the wind noise at 50-55 mph highway speeds. Since I was very low on gas and really thirsty out here in the middle of nowhere, I was praying there'd be a gas station open, and all of a sudden, one appeared around a curve in the highway. It had a small service building with an attendant inside, the usual two pumps, regular and ethyl, and was surrounded by what appeared to be new black asphalt, with the area lit by several very bright flood lights on poles.

I didn't want to get new-asphalt spatters on Speedball's paint, but reluctantly pulled off the "highway" with the tires crunching across the fresh asphalt which seemed more like sticky black gravel than anything, and I pulled up to the pump for regular. The guy inside was reading something, did not look up and seemed in no hurry to come out and fill the tank (self-serve was unknown then). I could hear a motor or air compressor making a screeching noise so I figured he didn't hear me pull up.

Finally, I opened my door, hopped out and slammed the door behind me in one motion. No wonder he couldn't hear patrons. Opening the door, the screeching noise was about five times louder. It was 800 billion crickets chirping, give or take one or two crickets. The "crunchy gravel asphalt" was a living mass of three inches of crickets *everywhere*. I realized all this in mid-air after jumping out. Landing on top of them made them insane and they started flying and leaping up, around, over, through and into every cubic inch of airspace surrounding me, including every crack and crevice in my clothes. They were going up my pant legs, down my shirt, trying to get in my nose, eyes and ears, and getting stuck in my hair. Crazed, I ran toward the light, burst through the service shack door and slammed it behind me.

The attendant looked up in surprise, "Oh, sorry, I was reading and can't hear anything over that damned chirping. A bajillion of 'em swarmed the place about an hour ago. It must be the heat wave and the lights. I've never seen so many of 'em this late in the year. If I'd a seen ya, I'd a waved you off. Sorry about that."

I already had half my clothes off shaking crickets all over the floor and the attendant started stamping for all he was worth with his big, thick-soled work boots.

"I couldn't have left anyway. I'm almost out of gas."

"Well, I'm not goin' out there now, 'n if you try it yourself and manage to get your gas cap off without being eaten alive, the crickets'll be down that filler pipe 'n in yer gas tank 'fore you can swear at yerself for makin' that mistake. They'll go away in a few hours. Always do. Just grab a Coke and relax. Can't get television out here, but tune the radio to anything you want. Course, this time a night, 'bout all my little AM will pick up is that nine trillion watt station in Clint, Texas. Say, are your windows shut?"

At about ten the next morning, I arrived at my dad's office. He was sitting at his desk absorbed in something. I stood in the doorway until he glanced up. I'll never forget the look on his face as he froze in place. After he'd decided there was really a human being who looked exactly like his son standing there, and that it actually was me, only his lips moved, "What are you doing here? You're supposed to be in college—at home."

I smiled a very genuine smile, "This *is* my new home. I've decided to go to college here."

Still without moving, "Do you realize that it starts here in three days?"

"No ... but I'm going to go to school here." There was no doubt in *my* mind. I knew it was going to happen, and not in slow motion either.

He just looked at me as only a father can when he knows the son he loves is not only adamant in the absolute, but reacts to purported obstacles in the same manner as a cat. Try it. Stand directly in the path of a cat moving with purpose. It doesn't change demeanor, doesn't miss a beat and doesn't stop. It simply walks around you.

Three days later, I'd been admitted and was in Freshman Orientation. My dad had picked up the phone right there and called one of his best friends, the best source he knew about getting into school, the University Registrar, who said, "Don't worry about it, Joe, I've been contemplating creating procedures for situations just like this one. One more candle in the room just adds more light, doesn't it?"

So, taking action on my gut feelings when the path isn't otherwise clear is what the Universal Forces, who were responsible for those feelings, wanted all along. And they had obviously anticipated arranging this particular situation for my benefit many years before, because that's when the registrar and my dad first met, just by chance.

* * * *

48

An Ant Again

From the outside looking in, you can never understand it.
From the inside looking out, you can never explain it.

Anon

MY DAD HAD ARRANGED FOR me to stay in the home of Mrs. Williams, who had been our housekeeper when I was a very little kid. She lived only three blocks from the university and she was grateful for the extra money. After going to class for about a week and a half, I was gradually learning my way around. I'd also been wearing my Freshman Beanie. I didn't like wearing my beanie, but the problem was that any group of students who were not freshmen were authorized to throw you in the University Fountain if they caught you not wearing it, and they were delighted to do it. (Think of the legal proceedings these days—assault, battery, hazing, criminal charges, compensatory and punitive damages, and those are the easy things to think of. But, one would be protected from tradition and the horror of getting wet.)

If you couldn't produce a student picture identification card that said you were a sophomore or above, or convince them you were simply a visitor, you were in your next class dripping wet. If a freshman laggard could think of claiming he was a visitor when accosted, it didn't work well after a week or so because with fewer than five thousand students, almost all of whom were on campus most of the time, it wasn't all that much bigger than my high school and faces started becoming familiar, particularly those with the cherubic and confused countenance of a freshman male. Females were exempt from dunking, simply too delicate.

Looking back, wearing the beanie under threat of dunking for failure to do so had a very important beneficial aspect. While I was an ant again, I was an ant who clearly belonged in the colony.

Of course it seemed like a pretty good-sized colony at first and while the shared experience of participating in university traditions put a pretty good dent in it, the feeling of anonymity wasn't completely assuaged, so as a result of chatting with me about it, my father called another good friend who was our next door neighbor when I was first born, the university's long-time and highly successful baseball coach. Coach said he had an idea that might help.

Then my father said I should sign up for fraternity rush. I was reluctant and recounted my unpleasant high school fraternity experience, saying that, with some exceptions of course, I wasn't sure that, in the main, fraternity people would be the kind of friends I could count on. He countered, saying that if Coach was any example, I was wrong.

"I helped get you in school quickly, so trust me on this one. Try it. These fraternities are all national fraternities with histories that go back a hundred years and they have local chapter houses at colleges and universities all over the country. While I'm sure you have high-school classmates who have fond memories of their fraternities, even the one that booted you out because of … let's say … the courage of your convictions, these are different from the ones there, and I'm only asking you to put yourself out there and see what happens. If you don't like it, you can vote with your feet just like you did in high school."

So, I signed up for first semester organized rush, became a "rushee" and was given a schedule of the times I was to visit the fraternities I'd put down on the form with some help from my father. We were allowed to remove our beanies when "rushing" at a fraternity house. It was a whirlwind deal for the first few days. I'd rotate among the fraternity houses, staying at each for the allotted time while talking to the active members, the idea being to see if, preliminarily, you liked them and vice-versa.

If they weren't interested, you wouldn't be invited to the next round. If you weren't interested, you wouldn't go if invited. I liked everyone I met and a lot of them seemed to like me. Of course, at first I would look like a lost puppy standing around fingering my name tag until someone would come over to me and introduce himself and start a conversation. It wasn't until a number of years later that I learned, out of professional necessity, how to really work a room.

The first round was the most taxing because I was finding my way around and meeting everyone for the first time, and my story about where I was from and so on started boring even me after awhile. The Sigma Iota house, one of the oldest and most well-known national fraternities and one of the top houses on campus, was the last house for the evening and I kind of wanted to get back to Mrs. Williams' place and hit the sack.

When I walked in the door, the member who was greeting everyone had a name tag on that said, "Rush Chairman," with his name underneath it along with the fraternity's crest. He said hello to me as he glanced at my name tag, turned, looked briefly at another member across the room and before I knew it, I was talking to two of the friendliest "actives" I'd met so far, and they seemed to know a lot about me. Their fraternity pins looked really cool on their pressed cotton dress shirts that complimented their pressed cotton pants and highly polished cordovan loafers. They all had short haircuts and many of them had flattops—buzz cuts that were absolutely, perfectly, flat on top. Very collegiate. I felt stupid with my pompadour and duck-tail. It was big at Pearson High, but obviously not here. Oh well, I'd just let my personality shine through.

"Hi, Chip. We hear you play the drums."

"News really travels fast. How'd you know that?"

He smiled, "Oh, we have our sources. We also understand your grades are pretty good, too."

"Well ..."

"Do you play any sports?"

"Oh, I played a little baseball, ran track and boxed a little." Hey, it was true.

"Great, we've won a number of championship banners in university intramural sports and want to keep up that tradition."

"Well ..."

"About those drums, were having a little rush party this Friday night. Would you bring them over and play with some of our guys. We've got a Sigma Iota Dixieland Band with a great piano player who's kind of a combination of stride, ragtime and boogie, and we also have a bass player, clarinet, trombone and coronet player, but no drummer. It'd be fun."

Incredible. I'd cut my drumming teeth on Dixieland and, for the first time, I was finally going to get to play with real live musicians who played it. These were *college* guys and I hoped I was good enough. "Sure, I'll come over with my drums and give it a shot."

"Come over about an hour early. You can meet the guys and they'll help you set up. Then you can play together a little before the party starts."

Wow. This could turn out to be really good. I was getting invited back to an evening rush party by one of the top houses on campus, which is what every rushee desperately hopes will happen, *and* I was going to get to play my drums.

On Friday, I showed up in Speedball and pulled up to the front of the fraternity house. "House" is misleading. It was like a medium sized adobe two-story hotel with big Greek letters "ΣΙ" on the front for Sigma Iota. It contained a large number of rooms for the actives and pledges, kitchen and dining facilities to match, a library, a card room and, where the entertaining took place, a really huge living room with a very high beamed ceiling, not to mention the side yard with basketball and volleyball facilities, plus a large parking lot in back. The rooms had closets and study desks, but no beds because everyone slept on a large, open "sleeping porch" in metal bunk beds virtually identical to the arrangement of those in an army barracks, except three of the "walls" were primarily floor to ceiling screens, which was a fairly typical fraternity or sorority setup there. It could get warm at night in this desert city and only the ΣI living room, dining room and kitchen had cooling, an add-on at some point because this grand Southwestern structure had been built at a time when cooling was composed of thick adobe walls and prayers for a breeze on the sleeping porch.

Since most cars were calm variations of black, brown and green those days, several curious actives immediately came out to see the fluorescent purple, fender-skirted vehicle with fake-wire-wheel hubcaps. Upon discovering it belonged to the rushee who played the drums, they promptly had three pledges take the drums into the living room. While the pledges were helping me set them up, I asked them how they got to be pledges when rush wasn't over yet. I discovered they were the three pledges who hadn't made their grades the year before. While their grades were good enough to continue in school, they didn't meet the fraternity grade standards for initiation into active membership, and they were being given another chance. Hmmm. That was a little different from the Delmus philosophy I'd experienced at Pearson High.

The band members came down to the living room immediately and were very impressed with my Gene Krupa Deluxe Radio King White Pearl Slingerlands, very impressed. The piano player, whom they'd nicknamed "Bumps," sat at the piano and started in while I was setting up next him. Man, he was good, no sheet music and played totally by ear, just like me. He was spanking those ivories. I couldn't wait to pop my Zildjians on top of the cymbal stands. I did it, spun the wing nuts, flipped on the snare, picked up my hickory 7A's and fell right into the groove.

"Swede," the bass player, smiled, picked up his instrument and started walking it down, "Casaba" cut in on the coronet, "Lone

Pine" jumped in on the trombone and "Shadow" on clarinet came right through the back door. It was drummer Ray Bauduc and the Art Tatum All Stars reincarnate (except some of them, including Ray, were still alive). There aren't many times in your life when you sit down with a group of musicians for the first time and play with one mind, but it was happening to us that night.

Soon the whole fraternity was in the living room, then the rushees who'd been invited came, then the girls in the sorority across the street came over with their rushees. The word was traveling down Greek Row and soon students from the other fraternities and sororities down the street started filtering over with their rushees in tow, but there wasn't any more room inside, so all the doors and windows were thrown open. The campus police came, but nothing was happening except people standing around enjoying themselves and listening or dancing to the music, so they just stuck around and started tapping their feet too.

We were wailing. At a point, Bumps nodded at me and mouthed, "Take it." We were on a natural high, particularly me. (Actually, when we got high, we were always on a natural high because we'd seen the movie *Reefer Madness* and it scared us.) I was having so much fun, I was in another dimension. I started a solo and when I finished, all the kids were yelling and screaming, inside and outside, even the cops were cheering. Swede was pointing to his watch and yelling at me, "Thirteen minutes. You did thirteen minutes!" That was interesting, for me it was timeless, which is kind of a drumming pun because the basis of drumming is keeping time.

For the rest of the brief rush season, the Sigma's wouldn't let me take the drums out of the house and had me come over every day. As you might suspect, I accepted a ΣI pledge button which qualified me to be "strongly urged" to, first, get a free flattop, which I did—complete with a complementary stick of "butch wax" so it would stick up and be flat on the very short top and, secondly, to move into the house and spend five nights a week in our mandatory Sigma dining room study hall for pledges, which

I did. Of course the latter was for my benefit even though I didn't realize it at the time, and was offset in my mind by having earned a nickname right away, something that ordinarily could be at least a year down the road. "Sticks." Pretty original, eh?

I didn't learn until much later from Bumps that Coach, who had been initiated into Sigma Iota many years before my appearance, had phoned the Sigma's Rush Chairman and had a little chat with him about me. Bumps said it was the first and only time Coach had ever recommended anyone who came through rush and, coupled with the fact that the ΣI's had two All-Americans on the baseball team, it was like God calling.

Well, I'd be willing to say it was certainly the Universal Forces at work again, and they'd obviously started planning this one many years before too, not only by having Coach move in next door shortly before I was born, but also by arranging it so that Dixieland was the only station I could get on my three little portable radios in my garage, an event that didn't seem to be advancing my interests at the time. Yep, those drums did a repeat. I was no longer an ant. I was *somebody* again. God bless my Uncle Sam.

So, at that point, there had been at least two watershed events in my life. The first was, of course, getting the drums, and joining ΣI was definitely the second. In my view, that time was the apex of the Greek system in the 20th century for college fraternities and sororities and, as in other national fraternities, the older members of Sigma saw it as their mission to instill in the younger "brothers" the character to think right and do right.

Consequently, the group never lost the perspective that we were there to prepare for our lives to come, not only personally but to shine our light on others in the best way we could. When I was initiated into membership and they pinned the Sigma badge to my chest after my first freshman semester, I willingly took an oath to follow those ideals, the same types of ideals I'd seen through my parents' example, and it made an indelible impression on my young and influenceable life. Ever since, I've always tried to use my best efforts, under whatever the circumstances at the time, to fulfill that promise, sometimes more successfully than others of course, but the goal has always been to direct my thinking forward and upward. I made friends there who shared that common perception and they are still old friends today.

* * * *

49

Good Food Equals Strong Muscles and Quick Reflexes

I swear it upon Zeus, an outstanding runner cannot be the equal of an average wrestler.

Socrates

THE ENDING OF THAT LAST chapter doesn't mean we didn't have a lot of fun in Sigma Iota, and notwithstanding my experiences in high school, I even drank some beer once in awhile, lordy, lordy. Of course, there were some brothers who, despite everyone else's best efforts, lost focus from time to time, but in the main, it was just good clean fun and by today's societal standards, we could have qualified as choir boys.

All of us ate the evening meal in the large main dining room, the most cherished feature of which was located high on the walls just below the very high ceiling and out of harms way—the numerous banners the fraternity had won for the yearly overall championship of the university's intramural sports competition. Located on the floor were rows of long tables at which the actives and pledges sat to feed. The food for each table was carried in from the adjoining kitchen by the "house boys," fraternity members working their way through school who were paid for that service.

In rooming-house style, an identical set of bowls, each containing its part of the meal, e.g., mashed potatoes, gravy, salad, vegetables, meat, were placed at each end of a table. Then we stampeded in as dinner time was gonged on a huge metal triangle to the shout of, "Chow time, anybody hungry out there?" The bowls weren't touched until the ΣI Grace was said in unison, and any announcements were finished, usually made by the President who stood so all could hear. When the announcements were done, the moment the President sat down, the piranha-like feeding frenzy would begin as the bowls worked their way toward the middle.

From time to time before the gorging started, an announcement would be made about one of the brothers who had been awarded a special honor for some service to the university or the community. As the announcement would finish and the brothers were indicating hearty approval, every once in awhile someone close grabbed a large handful of mashed potatoes or other food substance from a serving bowl and anointed the honoree in one swift motion, just like getting pasted in the chops with a cream pie. Instantaneously, the cry "*Food Fight!*" would ring out and the contents of all the serving bowls filled the air, painting the rest of the brothers, the pledges, the walls and the floor, but nary a drop on the intramural banners.

When we ran out of food to throw, it didn't take long to realize that youthful exuberance had its price. No one would have anything to eat because the cook had standing instructions from the House Manager, also one of the brothers, to lock the kitchen doors from the inside at the first sign of that non-gastronomical celebration, foiling any raid on the next day's food. So, the actives were left with the choice of cleaning themselves up and going out to get something to eat, or just going hungry.

The pledges had the unified choice of cleaning up the mess, which had a chilling effect on our evening study hall that otherwise would take place in the dining room. In turn, that would generate a lecture by the President and other officers at the weekly chapter meeting of the actives (pledges could not attend those meetings, of course) about the foreseeable consequences of food fights and, as a result, everyone was generally safe for several weeks.

As a 5'8", 117 pound pledge in my first semester, I wasn't big enough to play any level of college football and the track team was too fast for me. Cyclone I wasn't. I took one look at the guys on the boxing team, saw that they gave new meaning to washboard abs, and decided that wasn't for me either. My only real skill on the hardwoods revolved around the gold-turned-green Optimist basketball in high school and, by their very existence, the All-American baseball players in ΣI were a reality check in connection with that sport.

Rusty, my roommate in the fraternity house who was studying for his Ph.D., was an NCAA National Wrestling Champion as an undergraduate, having originally been initiated into Sigma at a Southern university. The house needed someone to wrestle in intramural sports at my weight, and Rusty, in his slight Southern drawl, volunteered me.

Now the only wrestling I'd done was in the neighborhood in grade school and junior high where the object was to get your opponent's neck in the vice-like crook of your arm, pull your vice shut with your other arm and force him to submit instead of passing out. Not exactly consistent with collegiate rules. Rusty said he'd teach me everything I needed to know in order to do well, at least in intramurals against the other fraternities. That consisted of two wrestling moves, which was good because wrestling started the next day.

The first move was "Rusty's Clapper," a thing of beauty. If you've seen collegiate wrestling, you know the opponents start out standing and facing each other, a whistle toots and they go. The move is this: As soon as the whistle toots, you clap your hands right in front of the opponent's face, he reflexively shuts his eyes and, continuing in one motion after the hand clap, you drive your head into his stomach, simultaneously dropping your hands to the back of his knees, pulling forward and up. He's surprised, of course. His eyes open as his upper body is flipping backward toward the mat and his legs go up in the air. It's fair to say he's somewhat disoriented at this point.

Still in a continuous motion as he's in the air, you shift so that your chest is over and crosswise to his, your left arm goes over and around the back of his neck in a swimming motion, more or less clamping his head in your armpit as your right arm goes between his legs with your hand in the small of his back. As he's hitting the mat on his back, you pull up with your right hand for all you're worth, rolling him up on his shoulders (the contact point for the count). He's basically confused and helpless with no leverage, the referee counts to three and the match is over. The whole thing should take less than five seconds. No stamina required. We practiced it a couple times.

The second move is in case the first hasn't worked and, due to your ineptness and his skill, you find yourself somehow on the bottom. You "bridge." That is, using the back of your head and your feet as contact points, you arch your legs, hips, back, neck and shoulders so the latter aren't touching the mat because you're bent backwards in a semicircle, a bridge. Then you figure out a way to get back on top. We didn't practice it because it's really hard and the first move seemed a lot better to me.

As I'd come to expect, the next day arrived. Rusty had a class and couldn't go over immediately, so I walked over to the gym by myself. The matches were a single-elimination affair and the intramural champion in my weight class would be crowned that afternoon. I was sitting on a bench waiting for my first match to start, hoping to get a clue about how everything worked, when a freshman my size from another fraternity came over and sat next to me. He was a nice guy and said he'd been tapped by his Pledge Father to wrestle and was my first opponent. We chatted a little and he disclosed that he had never wrestled in his life.

Then he said, "How about you?"

"Oh, I've been wrestling since I was a kid." That was true.

"Where at?"

"YMCA competitions mostly."

Okay, that wasn't exactly true. All right, it wasn't true at all, other than I used to go to the Y a lot to swim. But when I said I'd wrestled since I was a kid, I saw the same flicker in his eyes that I saw in Brick's that night behind the Clock, so I figured I'd play it out. When I made the second comment about the competitions, I knew I had him. The match was over in three and a half seconds. He never knew what happened.

Fortunately, all of the competitors wrestled at the same time in a round-robin sort of deal, so no new opponent had seen Rusty's Clapper and I continually advanced until I was going to be in the championship match. Rusty had arrived several matches before, had seen my opponent wrestle and had asked a few questions.

"Okay, Sticks, this kid isn't like the others. He's been wrestling in competition since he was eleven."

That was my line. I felt myself flicker.

"So, you've got to be doubly fast and hard when the whistle blows. Give it everything you've got on that first move. I mean everything. Drive your head straight through his stomach until it clanks on his backbone. You've got the move down perfect. You can do this. He'll never know what happened."

Rusty had me psyched. I was ready. The whistle peeped. I clapped and sprang like a wildcat. My head hit his stomach like a pile-driver. I almost broke my neck. He was exactly my weight, but about 5'1" and a living boulder. He didn't have any knees and didn't budge. He got me in a bear hug and we were staggering all around the mat for, I'm certain, approximately a millennium, and it was exhausting because he was so short that I was the one bent over while his arms were locked around my back. Even though there wasn't an ounce of fat on my seventeen-year old body, drumming was not keeping me fit enough to wrestle effectively for more than about six seconds.

All of a sudden I was on my back and he was inching his petrified-wood-like bulk up toward my shoulders. He succeeded. As the referee's hand was on its way down to slap the mat for the count of one, I heard Rusty at the edge of the mat drawling,

"Bridge … bridge!" Now, using your neck to elevate yourself into the air *and* 117 pounds of rocklike opponent stuck to your chest like a leech is a good move in the abstract, but when you're a drummer lying exhausted on the mat, it doesn't happen. As the ref's hand came down for the count of three, I heard myself yelling at Rusty, "Easy for you to say!"

But, Rusty was proud of me. He said I had actually lasted around fifty seconds with that guy after his Clapper didn't work, *and* we got second-place points toward the intramural banner—very important. I've still got my runner-up medal. It's in the form of a key chain with a bas-relief wildcat on it.

While walking back to the house, Rusty asked me, "Have you ever fenced?"

"Naw, I've only been a busboy and a waiter."

He smiled his kind of Southern drawl smile and gave his kind of Southern drawl chuckle, "Think Errol Flynn."

"Is the house doing a pirate musical for the Christmas Capers? They'll probably want me to play the drums for it with Bumps and the guys."

"Toward the end of next semester, fencing is going to be an intramural sport. We want the points."

"You can teach me fencing too?"

Another Southern draw chuckle, "Fencing 101 can meet your Phys. Ed. requirement for next semester. By the time it comes up in intramurals, you'll be Zorro. Consider yourself volunteered."

So, I enrolled in Fencing 101 at the beginning of the second semester. I was relieved to find out they did it with full head masks and padded chest and private parts protectors. I wanted the opportunity to start a family. I also found out they did it with three kinds of swords, a foil, an épée and a saber. You could hack people with a saber and the padding wasn't all that thick, but you could only stick them with the épée and foil and the ends were blunted. Since the foil was much lighter and smaller than an épée, I chose it.

It turned out that having very quick hands and feet from drumming and neighborhood boxing translated to the foil. I picked it up quickly. After learning the basic moves, executed rapidly in coordinated succession just like the drums, it was a matter of sensing the area to strike, reflexes when attacked and footwork. I was good at it, understood it and it was fun. I found that if I intently, but fuzzily, zoned on an area from my opponent's stomach to his neck and just followed my instincts, the "Force" was with me as I learned many years later from the *Star Wars* movies, and my thrust, parry and riposte seemed to be guided from outer space.

During that semester and just a few weeks before intramural fencing was to start, I was initiated into Sigma Iota as a full-fledged active member, a *very* big day—no longer a pledge, but an "Active!" For some reason, that propelled me into the idea that beyond just fencing individually, with careful teaching of some basic moves, I could train an entire Sigma Iota fencing team and we could surprise a few folks in that intramural sport. But, I found there was no one in ΣI who was interested in fencing. However, there were some who had an interest in sword fighting. The house sprung for the equipment and I taught those five guys, who thought practicing sword fighting was fun, how to fence well enough that we won the foil team championship.

And a really interesting thing happened too. Fencing requires a smooth combination of rapid perception, thought and reaction, and I discovered that developing that ability applies to everything else. I just seemed to think faster. School work was easier and my drumming was better. Those five other guys noticed it affected them in similar ways too.

Well, the Universal Forces were reinforcing for me that superficial moves may get you into the fray, but to come out on top takes study and practice. However, they didn't bother messing with the food fight. Throwing away your dinner is definitely a self-limiting exercise.

* * * *

50

Bikes and Gas Stations

Expecting a positive outcome from negative input is like expecting to be paid for work we didn't do.

Jonathan A. Baker

AFTER THE END OF MY freshman year in college, I drove back home in Speedball for the summer. At first, Bobby's mother failed to recognize me, a bona fide fraternity man with a flat-top crew cut, but she was overjoyed to find out my drums were still at college. I was overjoyed to pull my two-wheeled Green Hornet out of the garage. I gave her some minor maintenance, fed her some gas and primed the carburetor. With no electric start in those days, it was all jumping on the foot pedal attached to the crank, all the while hoping the engine wouldn't backfire and break your leg or vault you over the handlebars. She loved me. She cranked right up.

The next morning, I put on my leather jacket and billed cap, hopped on the Hornet and took off to see if I could find some of my old riding buddies from the year before. Sure enough, I ran right into Smiley, Tucker and Irish Mike. They were going to hook up with Smokey and a couple guys he knew and ride up the highway a few miles to visit Steamboat.

Now Steamboat was aptly named. He was seven feet tall, very square boned and huge, but not fat. He was so large, his banged-up dirty-white '41 Indian Chief looked like a Scout underneath him. He wore the biggest unblocked moth-eaten gray felt Stetson known to man. It was tied onto his head with a leather chin strap which pulled it straight down to the top of his eyebrows and ears. The brim looked like it stuck out from the hat by a foot and a half all the way around except the front, which was permanently turned up by the wind. Essentially, it was a Paul Bunyan-sized Gabby Hayes cowboy hat. Roy Rogers would've been impressed.

Steamboat had a Galloping Goose Motorcycle Club insignia on the back of his leather jacket. From a distance, it could be mistaken for a hand with the middle finger extended, very naughty in those days, but up close, it was a goose, and Steamboat himself was kind of a paradox. He had short blond hair, a low, soft voice, and large, piercing, robin's-egg-blue eyes that looked straight at you but focused nowhere, not in front of you, not on you, not behind you. He was very spooky, but always quiet and even-tempered. No one had ever seen him mad, and no one wanted to be the first to do so.

When all of us got to Steamboat's house, the garage door was open, no one was home and Steamboat's old 1941 Indian Chief was gone, presumably with Steamboat on it. However, inside the garage was a beautifully refurbished 1948 Indian Chief. It looked showroom new with those signature skirted-fenders, the front one topped by the traditional Indian-head fender light, beautifully chromed spoke wheels, a magnificent glistening maroon and grey two-tone color scheme reminiscent of a late '30's Indian Four, and a marvelously painted Indian Chief's profile with gold feather headdress flowing behind, one on each side of the gas tank. It looked like real gold flake had been mixed into the paint.

It also sported a huge, long, leather "chummee seat" with a low, ornate, chrome-bar hand-hold all around the back of it in the event of a passenger aboard. The rider would slide forward and his girlfriend would sit behind him and either hold on to him or to the chrome bar. Had it been Indian's main competition, a Harley, it'd be called a "buddy seat." Steamboat's gorgeous bike also had a chrome luggage rack over the back fender, beautiful new leather saddlebags, full whitewall tires, twin chrome mirrors, a brand new crystal clear windshield without a scratch and three heavily chromed headlights in a single row in front—one big light in the middle and a slightly smaller one on each side. The 3-speed hand shift was on the right side of the gas tank and the hand-grip throttle was on the left side of the handlebars, typical of Indian and just the opposite of Harley (brand identification you know), although Indian would reverse them as an option.

Tucker was exclaiming, "Man, this is cherry, really cherry," and we were all admiring every inch of it while we waited for Steamboat to come back.

Smokey referred to one of the two bikers who came with him as "Weasel." I didn't know him, but you could easily understand from his countenance and demeanor why he had that nickname. Anyway, Weasel boasted that from time to time he'd helped Steamboat bore out and rework the engine and otherwise resurrect the bike, saying he didn't even know if Steamboat had tried it out yet because they'd just finished it a couple days before, except for installing the tubular chrome "crash bars," which would stick out and help protect the bike if it went down, which should never happen to a machine as marvelous as that.

Weasel took the gas cap off, took a sniff and the tank was dry, so he looked around, found a can of gas and filled the tank, saying he'd crank it up and get it humming for Steamboat as a surprise when he came back. It had a manual spark advance and he twiddled around with it and the distributor for awhile, left the bike on the kick stand and jumped up and down on the crank pedal with his full weight, maybe 140 weasely pounds, for all he was worth. The stiff, newly overhauled engine finally sputtered to life and he monkeyed around with it some more until it sounded pretty nice. We'd been there almost an hour at this point and Weasel swung his leg over the seat while he continued revving the engine and said, "No tellin' when he'll be back. Let's take it out for a test spin."

Irish Mike, who had helped Steamboat paint it, quickly said, "I don't think I would. Steamboat's awful proud of that bike. Since it's taken him the better part of a year, piece by piece, I think he should be the first to ride it."

Weasel's eyes shifted back and forth, "Naw, I want it runnin' real nice for him when he gets back."

Smiley smiled, "It's your funeral."

Smokey's eyes rolled at him, but Weasel took off on the bike. We jumped on our bikes, including Weasel's buddy, Stumpy, and followed him. He went about three miles down a narrow back road, goosing the bike pretty hard, and then slowed down and pulled off onto the dirt shoulder. We were behind a ways and when we pulled up, it was pretty clear the Chief wasn't running. The bike had a small tool kit attached to the lower front of the left rear fender skirt and Weasel was taking the top off the distributor.

"Damn! The points broke. Ain't that just my luck and I know there ain't no spare set in them saddle bags."

Smokey and Irish Mike just looked at each other and shook their heads. Smiley started whistling the Funeral March through his smiling teeth. Tucker and I gave each other looks that said this didn't seem like a real good thing to have happen so far away from Steamboat's house, and Tucker whispered to me, "Maybe he could have just taken it up and down the street a little?"

All of a sudden, Weasel had an "Aha" moment. He pushed the bike to the other side of the road, pointing back in the direction of Steamboat's house, and said, "Hey, there's some rope in the saddlebags! I'll tie it to the seat of the Chief and the other end to Smokey's seat so he can tow me back."

Smokey's lips didn't move, "Not to my bike, pal."

Weasel looked over at Smiley questioningly. Smiley just kept smiling and whistling.

Irish Mike shaking his head, "I told you not to take it out."

Weasel looked at Tucker and me. We froze.

"Leave 'em alone—too young to die." Irish Mike saved my tail for the second time since we'd known each other.

There was only Stumpy left and Weasel stared him down. Stumpy said, "Wouldn't it be better to …"

Weasel angrily, "Look, I know how to do this!"

"But if you ..."

"Just tie it like I said and let's go," Weasel barked.

Not wanting to set the erratic and hard-headed Weasel off any more than he was already, Stumpy shrugged and tied it between the seat posts of the two motorcycles. This whole thing was Weasel's show. The rest of us watched. The rope was about fifteen feet long and Stumpy pulled forward slowly to take out the slack. Weasel yelled, "Not too slow, we won't be able to stay up." So Stumpy goosed it a little and almost pulled both bikes over because the rope was tied to the seats and the physics of that Einstein-like towing setup put Stumpy on the asphalt road and the silent Chief to the right rear on the dirt shoulder, always pulling somewhat sideways against both bikes. Although worrisome, at least Stumpy had the good traction under power and after a little fishtailing, wobbling and cursing, things settled down and they got going at a steady low speed, at least when they were going straight.

The paved part of the road was not only a narrow one-lane, it curved in places. So far, all the curves were to the right and they seemed to have gotten used to the shaky low-speed dynamics of doing that. Then the road curved to the left for the first time. Motorcycles (and bicycles for that matter) counter-steer when executing turns when traveling at cruising speeds. Thus, it's the customary practice when steering into a left hand turn at high speed, to counter-steer by turning the front wheel away from the turn while leaning toward the turn and that's what Weasel unconsciously did in his somewhat distressed state.

But, that's the opposite of the right thing to do in a left turn at low speed, exponentially exacerbated by being pulled sideways toward the turn with the goofy towing setup Weasel insisted upon. Deftly sensing the problem, Weasel quickly reacted by steering into the turn (correct), but, sadly, continued to lean into it instead of shifting his weight to the outside. Thus, he succeeded in reducing very-little-chance-of-any-positive-result to absolute zero.

Following the motorcycling adage of "look where you want the bike to go," Stumpy was looking ahead and to the left around the curve as Steamboat's 1948 magnificently reconstructed Indian

Chief went down in the dirt and gravel of the shoulder while Weasel simultaneously jumped off. By the time Stumpy realized that the principles of Newtonian physics were the underlying cause of that horrible sound he was hearing behind him, he'd dragged the downed Chief at least twenty yards on the asphalt road.

That's what the dynamics of everything looked like to me. Following Smokey's lead, the rest of us had been about fifty yards behind. When we got up to Weasel and dismounted, he was brushing himself off. Since no one wore helmets in those days, he was lucky he hadn't hit his head, and thanks to his boots, Levi's, leather jacket and gloves, he and his clothes had a few scrapes, but he wasn't too much the worse for wear. The same thing couldn't be said for Steamboat's formerly-exquisite Indian Chief.

Starting where Weasel was standing, all the way to where the Chief was resting on its side, there was a trail of small, mangled parts and chrome pieces—a mirror and its stalk, the air cleaner cover, buckles off the saddle bag, one of the three headlights, pieces broken off the windshield, pieces torn off the leather seat and its chrome rear sissy cage, the cover to the tool kit, tools, and a long swath of maroon and grey paint on top of the asphalt, flecked with gold from the Indian headdress that used to be painted on the side of the gas tank.

As we helped Weasel pick up the mangled pieces on the way over to the downed Chief, which had come perilously close to sliding into Stumpy's Harley, Weasel lamented, "Damn, I wish those crash bars had a been on there." Smiley and Irish Mike lifted the Chief onto its kickstand. Its right side looked great. The left side looked like a crazed buzz saw had a grudge against it, to include big ugly scrapes in the white sidewalls. But the front forks weren't bent, nor were the wheels bent even though their chrome rims were roundly scraped. The bike would roll fine and, of course, it didn't need the left handgrip gas feed which was dangling by a cable from the handlebars.

As we dumped all the parts we could find into the good saddlebag on the right, Weasel said, "Okay, Stumpy, check the rope and let's get going again."

Smokey looked at him with disgust, "Why don't you save the grief of trying to get the bike back and let me give you a ride to Steamboat's house. You can say your Rosary on the way because the second he finds out, you won't have a future."

"No, no, I can't leave it here, Steamboat'd kill me for sure."

Smiley wasn't smiling, "Kind of like whistling *Dixie* while you're picking between the gallows and the electric chair, isn't it?"

We followed them and they made it to Steamboat's place without going down again. He still wasn't home. Weasel rolled the previously pristine 1948 Indian Chief into the back of the garage with the good side facing out, said he wasn't feeling so well, climbed on his bike and left.

Stumpy told us what we all knew. He'd been trying to tell Weasel to run the rope tied to Stumpy's seat post straight back to the post between the front wheel and the handlebars on the Chief so it would tow directly behind Stumpy's Harley. Silently, we just looked at each other knowing none of us wanted to be there when Steamboat got home. We all split.

I put the Green Hornet in the garage and used only Speedball Baby for the next few weeks. Steamboat had never seen my car and I didn't want to be the one who had to tell him what happened. One night a short time later, still a little spooked about maybe running into Steamboat, I pulled into a gas station not far from Pearson High and out of the corner of my eye, I caught a figure walking over to my car. Whipping my head around, he had a jellyroll-ducktail haircut and wasn't big enough to be Steamboat, so in a few seconds, my hands unclenched from the steering wheel.

It was Marty from Delmus. You know, the guy who wanted me to get the dew off the benches with my new Levi's. He was the station attendant. After he recognized me with my flat-top crew-cut, we chatted. He said he'd started there full time shortly after he graduated from Pearson and was making pretty good money, but he didn't like working nights because everything got damp if it was chilly, like that night. When we were done, I asked him to fill 'er up with regular and to please get the windshield because it had gotten coated with dew while we were talking.

Oh, I never did see Weasel around anymore after the catastrophe, and no one knows what happened to Steamboat either.

However, the Universal Forces, knowing I'd be a recreational Harley rider for many years to come, were trying to make it clear to me that I should never, ever, ever, never, ever even think about touching another guy's bike. Just leave a motorcycle that isn't yours alone and stay healthy. I think it's a good idea.

Oh yeah, the gas station with Marty—the UF obviously tossed in a quick demonstration of the Golden Rule, which as we all know is freely translated as, "What you send around, comes around." In some circles, they call it Karma.

* * * *

51

Rushing Around

Before you go Greek, know who the Gods are.
All-American Al

THE SUMMER WAS OVER AND it was time to get ready for the start of my sophomore year in college and prepare for the new rushees who'd be in the same position I was in the year before. I drove back across the desert, careful to avoid cricket-infested gas stations, and finally arrived at the Sigma Iota house. School hadn't started yet and there weren't many bro's at the house. So first thing, I retrieved my drums from the attic, set them up in the living room and played a long, quiet solo by myself. The tears in my eyes told me how much I'd missed it. I noodled around for a couple of hours and then went out to get a hamburger with Rusty who'd been tending his Ph.D. experiments all summer

Within a couple of days, the full membership was back and we started reviewing, systematically and in earnest, selected new rushees recommended from various sources ranging from fraternity alumni and friends of the fraternity to the actives and pledges who knew outstanding prospects behind them in high school. Beside these "recs," there was another category, the "legacies," rushees coming through who had a relative who was a Sigma Iota in the past, usually a father and often including a grandfather.

In any event, at least one, and often two people were assigned to meet every rec and every legacy to talk to him and report on him.

There could well be desirable rushees unknown to anyone connected with the fraternity, so all the other rush applications with their brief resumes were carefully reviewed, initially by the house Rush Chairman for persons of interest, for example, student body presidents, talented athletes, top students, and individuals who had distinguished themselves in one way or another such as an editor of the school newspaper or who came from an incredibly wealthy family (just telling it like it is—alumni contributions are important).

However, decent grades were always a priority in the qualifications, and a rec, legacy or interesting person who didn't have them was grilled in as subtle a way as possible concerning why. A person who ultimately did not make his grades could not be initiated, so it made little sense to invest time and energy into a pledge who didn't seem like he had the potential to make grades for whatever reason, whether a behavioral problem or just poor academic aptitude.

It was a grueling process. Attendance for the entire active membership was mandatory and we were up into the wee small hours of the morning reviewing potential candidates for pledgeship in as much detail as possible. By the time rush started, we knew the rushees we specifically *wanted* to look at and the ones whom we *had* to look at, such as a legacy who had done nothing to distinguish himself in high school. Concerning rushees outside that envelope, that is, those of initial non-interest, we were aware that, no matter what the gaps in the resume, there were people who blossomed after high school and it applied to enough of us so that we always took that into account.

Since we knew who would be arriving in each rush group, specific actives were assigned to each person of interest, as well as to each person we didn't think we'd be interested in since, with respect to the latter, the pre-rush evaluation was just our opinion based on very limited knowledge and we didn't want anyone to be ignored. We had excellent members who were proof that pre-judgments could be very wide of the mark.

Now I fully understood why there were a couple of guys I met immediately who knew all about me and seemed to become my instant best friends when I went through rush—all thanks to Coach—and why I was passed from person to person in such an easy and effortless way so that by the time the session was over, I'd talked to many in the room. It's probably good they got Coach's call before they saw my palpitating purple car.

In any event, at the end of a long day and evening of rush, the actives would gather in the dining room for a detailed evaluation of each person who came through that day. The tables were arranged in a large rectangle around the perimeter of the room and we all sat on the outside of a table so we could see and hear each of the others. The discussions ranged from calm to, shall we say, very, very highly spirited, depending on the range of opinion on a particular person. Some of the toughest were legacies we didn't want, or recs by highly influential alumni we didn't want either. And when that combination coincided in an individual some felt we *had* to take or lose significant and important support, principles and practicality clashed in purple-faced and very loud ways.

But no matter what the rationale for an opinion or the depth of feeling, it all came down to the vote, a procedure that had its roots in ancient Greek culture. Each active had a white marble and a black marble in his hands beneath the table. A wooden box with a hole in the top was started by the President and slid to his left around the table. As it reached each active, he put a closed fist, shielded by the construction of the box, over the hole and let a marble drop so all could hear he voted. There were no abstentions. The other marble remained in the closed fist of his other hand. When everyone had voted, the President unlatched the box and dumped the contents into a large, clear glass bowl. For a rushee to pass to the next round, the vote had to be unanimous.

One could see instantly the color of the marbles. A single black ball doomed a candidate who had, of course, been "black-balled."

Right after the voting balls had been revealed, the wooden box was passed again and each person's remaining ball was dropped through the hole. Those contents were also inspected and counted to be certain they were the exact opposite of the vote and matched the number of actives at the table. Under circumstances not clearly defined, but controlled by the President, if the balls were not unanimous, there could be further discussion and a "do-over" vote.

Of course, a single black ball in the bowl resulted in a furor, coupled with impassioned arguments from all those who felt compelled to do so. They could never be certain to whom their pleas should be addressed because the person who dropped it may have said nothing in the original discussion and the membership could not be polled concerning how it voted. If there was still a black ball in the box after a second vote, some actives might spontaneously combust, but I don't recall there was ever a third vote.

When we finally arrived at the tail end of rush, those potential candidates who had survived the intensive scrutiny by the active chapter to that point, which included behavior at rush parties and also outside the formal rushing process, plus a unanimous vote after each successive invitation back, were subject to one final winnowing vote. That last meeting could get doubly incendiary at times of stiff opposition, particularly if only one or two black balls had been dropped on a rejected candidate in his first vote that night, because members who had shepherded a particular potential pledge to that point were normally absolutely convinced he would be a good fit and, of course, just to be considered on the final night, the candidate had previously received a unanimous vote. But, no matter what, there was always strict adherence to the marbleized voting system.

After that final epic struggle, a resulting bid would be put in writing by Sigma Iota, but it was handed to the rushee in a sealed envelope by the staff of the Dean of Men at his office on Bid Day. Of course if a bid were extended, that didn't mean a rushee would automatically pledge Sigma Iota because, in the usual case, he would have been rushed diligently by other fraternities who thought he would fit with them as well, and several other bids could be expected to be in his envelope.

Those of us who were first-timers on the active chapter side of the process wondered out loud how we ever made it, particularly after listening to some of the discussions surrounding those who were black-balled at the final conflagration. But, after it was done—it was done, and because it was never known with certainty who dropped a black ball, unless the dropper ratted himself out which wasn't often, intense feelings were soon diluted and the brotherhood went on as normal.

Now all this is not to say that there weren't people whom the fraternity knew from the get-go that it wanted to pledge and, assuming they were ultimately willing, they would be pledged unless they turned out to be a Jekyll and Hyde, which virtually never happened. Those earmarked folks would also be in high demand by the other fraternities because, of course, they exhibited extremely desirable qualities in one or more areas. The competition for them was especially intense and it was necessary to fight fire with fire.

So at the beginning of rush, we came up with an ingenious plan to land all of those rushees. This resourceful, even inspired, plan had two general parts, *The Schmooze* and *The Close.*

The Schmooze. We would have at least two actives assigned to each must-have rushee for the purpose of being their buddies, constantly running into them "fortuitously," having breakfast, lunch or dinner, helping them with the nuances of being a freshman and just generally being all-around good guys, the kind of guys you'd want to spend the rest of your college career with. The thing was, after you spent that much time with them, it was usually a goal that turned into a close friendship and no longer an assignment. Freddy is an example of how we worked it and that's exactly what happened.

Swede and I were assigned to Freddy who had been Student Body President at his high school and also an All-State shortstop on its baseball team. Leadership and athletic skills, a highly desirable combination with a lot of potential for him and for

Sigma Iota. Swede had been teaching me the nuances of the high-powered rushing ropes and let me take the lead because Freddy was also an aspiring drummer and the two of us were becoming good friends.

Of course, we weren't the only fraternity hip to inventive techniques and it became an intense game to isolate a highly-desirable rushee like Freddy from the other hungry dogs as much as possible since it was far from a slam dunk that he would pledge any particular fraternity, including ours. Because it was within the rules for any fraternity to tell Freddy at any time there would be a bid from it in his envelope when he opened it, it was a certainty that he would be swarmed by members of other fraternities on the front steps of the Administration Building on Bid Day, both entering and exiting, since it contained the Office of the Dean of Men where the envelopes were handed out, and no one actively connected with a fraternity could go beyond those steps on that day.

Thus, Swede and I had made arrangements to pick Freddie up for breakfast on the big day and, of course, pumped him up about the bid card from ΣI he would find in his envelope, also telling him he would have all the time he wanted to make up his mind, but we were certain he'd enjoy the great surprise we'd have waiting at the house for him just after he left the Dean's office. Then, before walking him to the front door of the Administration Building, we suggested that in order to avoid the inevitable pressure by the other fraternities at the front entrance after retrieving his bid cards, he should exit by an obscure side door we described, known to Swede only because he had worked maintenance in that building during his first year in school. We were waiting there and Freddy, who had received bids from all the best (in our opinion) fraternities on campus, came out that door as we hoped and, before the Greeks out front could wonder why they hadn't seen him come back, we whisked him away to the Sigma Iota house for his surprise which was, of course, The Close.

The Close. Freddy was not only a Student Body President and an All-State baseball player, but, to our advantage, also a typical

1950's seventeen year old impressionable high school kid—particularly important for the closing, which would ultimately be to his advantage, of course. So, during the schmooze period, we told our sports-oriented rushees, including Freddy, fantastic, aggrandizing stories about both of our baseball All Americans, their athletic prowess and their exploits, but neither of these sports heroes, who legend has it could fly, ever appeared at a rush event or anywhere else the rushees might be. Upstairs in the Sigma house was a room with a sign on the door that said "All-American Room," but none of the rushees had ever been allowed through that always-closed door, even though it was often called to their attention while they were being regaled with the All-American stories.

This is so great, it's like I'm there again. After we arrive at the house with Freddy after he'd retrieved his Bid, we take him up and give a special knock on the door of the All-American Room, wait briefly, then enter the room and close the door. Inside the silent room is a curtained enclosure about the size of a phone booth. We face it. The name of Al, one of our two baseball All Americans, is fastened onto the booth. Unknown to Freddy at this juncture, Al, our six-foot-six All-American first baseman is standing silently behind the curtain. It's his turn to be in there. The two of them rotated as their services were needed.

I say quietly and reverently, "Brother Al, are you there?"

From behind the curtain, Al responds slowly in the deepest natural god-like voice he can muster, "Yes I am, Brother Chip. How may I help you?"

I respond with humbled veneration, "May I introduce Freddy to you? He's an All-State baseball player and he knows all about you."

All-American Al's arm extends through a slit in the curtains and shakes the hand of Freddy who's forgetting to swallow and his mouth is starting to stay open.

The arm withdraws to a place behind the curtains and All-American Al says slowly and emphatically in the same god-like voice, "Freddy, I've heard a great deal about you, particularly what a fine leader, gentleman and athlete you are. You are the kind of person who will bestow great credit upon yourself and this fraternity. You should know that no one is allowed to be a member whose heart makes only a four-year commitment to Sigma Iota, but I'm convinced you have the character and integrity that can meet the challenges and uphold the high ideals of our fraternity for a lifetime. I also want you to know that everyone in the house, every single person, including me, wants you to become a member of Sigma Iota."

Freddy's eyes have the look of rapture.

All-American Al's arm extends through the curtain again, "I'd be honored if you'd take this Sigma Iota pledge pin from me right now so I can come out and pin it on you personally."

Freddy is a goner. Mesmerized, he reaches up and carefully takes the Holy Grail, his eyes shining. All-American Al, with the biggest regulation Sigma Iota badge they make pinned on his jersey over his heart, comes out in his baseball uniform and cleats. Towering over Freddy, he takes the pin from Freddy's trembling hand and fastens it over Freddy's heart. Then Al flashes a big smile, clasps Freddy's hand and profusely welcomes him into pledgeship. While Freddy is still in the All-American-Bubble, Swede has him sign the bid card and pockets it. Pretty sweet, huh?

And what did the Universal Forces have in mind here? Well, obviously, they wanted to set the stage so the ideals of conduct and character embodied by Sigma Iota could be ingrained in Freddy over the next few years of his collegiate career, and the UF enlisted our assistance. And by the way, Freddy ultimately became one of the best United States Senators his state ever had, demonstrating unflagging integrity, character and common sense. Gosh, kind of makes you wish for the "good ol' days," doesn't it?

* * * *

52

Steppin' in the Chicken Yard Again

I can see clearly now ... I can see all obstacles in my way.

Johnny Nash

YOU REMEMBER MY DISQUALIFICATION FOR telling the Chicken Yard joke when I tried out for cheerleader at Pearson High? Like I said, it ate at me. So, at the beginning of my freshman year in college, I decided to try out for the Frosh Cheerleading Squad. These tryouts were much different. There was no assembly and school popularity vote. A committee which consisted primarily of the existing Varsity Cheerleading Squad, male and female, were the judges, and it wasn't a "good 'ol boy-girl" networking event either.

The frosh squad was going to comprise the candidates from which replacements were picked at the end of the year for seniors graduating from the varsity squad. They were looking for people they thought would be the best at it so the varsity squad wouldn't look like a bunch of doofuses when the replacements were picked. Anticipating rock and roll icon Little Richard's future release, through some judicious "Slippin' and a-slidin', peepin' and a-hidin'," I dodged the doofus tag and made it.

The Frosh Cheerleading Squad cheered for the basketball games and the Frosh Pep Band played for them. The Varsity Cheerleading Squad and the University Marching Band handled football. Obviously, basketball wasn't receiving the same emphasis from the university administration even though it was very popular and the gym was jammed to the rafters with vociferous students for every game, win or lose. Well, maybe a little more losing, although every once in awhile we surprised a really good team even though we never even got close to the National Championship Tournament, at least while I was there.

These days at the university, the varsity squad cheers at the basketball games, and the full marching band plays also, because the basketball team is consistently rated among the top teams in the country, virtually always plays in the National Championship Tournament and you have to kill to get a ticket. But, there's something to be said for the good old days. Then, the players graduated instead of jumping to the pros in two years, and it seemed like there was more sport to it. You know what I mean? It wasn't *all* about winning.

The baseball team was really good then, still is, but there wasn't any organized cheering for the team. Still isn't. You'd think it'd liven things up a little. I've gotten sidetracked again.

Cheerleading at the basketball games was a great time. It was better than a front row seat and I learned a lot about motivating the fans so they had fun while doing what we asked them to do. Of course, it wasn't fun when a player crashed into you, but we got good at anticipating that. At the end of the year, I was selected to join the Varsity Cheerleading Squad. At the end of my junior year, the squad unanimously picked me to be Head Cheerleader for my senior year and I hadn't even thrown my megaphone into the ring. I was just doing the best I could at something I really enjoyed.

Varsity cheerleading at football games in the '50's seems to me it was a lot more effective then than it looks like it is now. All the students actually participated in organized cheering then. Now in a lot of games I've been to and have seen on television, it looks like there are a group of people in cheerleading outfits, talented and spirited tumblers all (I think they call the men "holders" or "bases" and the women "flyers" now, or something similar), in the corner of the end zone yelling up into the crowd or holding up signs that say things like "noise." They're doing their very best of course, but not much collective organized noise seems to result, and the loudest cheers seem to start spontaneously in the crowd, although I hope what I've seen in recent years are the exceptions.

"Back in our day," the head cheerleader stood on a raised platform with a microphone on the fifty yard line. Our PA system ran from the twenty yard line to the twenty yard line, was separate from the public address system, and it was loud. The cheerleaders were spread out from the twenty to the twenty, as was the student section, pretty much from the bottom to the top of the stadium. It was a perfect setup and every student happily participated, thousands of them. At halftime there was a card section too. Each seat in the student section had a pile of cards under it (with instructions) that on cue from the PA system, the students held up to collectively create a series of giant pictures (like the dots do in newsprint pictures) or words that dynamically spelled things out in cursive writing to coordinate with the marching band on the field. The spectacle and the whole game was a blast, win or lose.

Of course, we had traditional school cheers which everyone knew, such as, "Hit 'em again, hit 'em again, harder, harder," or spelling out the school's name (which I inadvertently misspelled once and the crowd misspelled it right along with me) and we were also constantly trying to invent either new one-liners or relatively short catchy cheers the students would like. The one-liners the students got into most occurred when an opposing football player would clearly and obviously do something dirty to one of our players and hurt him enough that he had to be removed from the game for one or more plays.

Then, under our direction, the opposing player would hear his number from thousands of students, whispering at first, then slowly escalating until they were yelling in unison at the top of their lungs, "Get 54, get 54, get 54 …" The intention, of course, was only to encourage the team to block him solidly. This would go on ad infinitum, alternately escalating and lowering in volume, until either a concerned opposing coach would remove him from the game for a few plays, or our players removed him from the game for a few plays. When 54 went out, the roar was thunderous, and the opposition usually cleaned up its act. Can't do that these days, but compensating in part for that, there are jumbotrons and instant replays at the stadiums now.

A new catchy cheer we introduced one Saturday night was an instant crowd favorite. We waited until the game got to a really exciting point, and then, as always with a new cheer, I recited it twice to the crowd in the cadence we were looking for, which is all they needed to pick up the words and rhythm (they were college students, you know). It went like this, "Rah, rah, reeez, kick 'em in the knees; rah, rah, raass, knock 'em on the grass!" As I felt certain they would be, the crowd was inventive. Thousands screamed in unison, "Rah, rah reeez, kick 'em in the knees; Rah, rah, raass, knock 'em on their ass!" You may have heard a cheer similar to that many times over the years, but it was new to us then and definitely risqué for a college football stadium in the '50's.

The following Monday, I got a message to go see the Dean of Men. All of a sudden, visions of the Chicken-Yard episode exploded in my head and I knew my cheerleading fun would shortly be over. The dean invited me into his office, directed me to sit in the chair in front of his desk and closed the door. He sat down and looked at me, a really long, silent look.

"Chip, I know this is a modern world, but when directing thousands of students to cheer, with tens of thousands more listening in the stadium, not to mention the radio, many of whom are long-time alumni contributors, plus their wives and their children, it's very important to maintain a certain decorum."

It was the beginning of the end. Since I knew the excuse 'I told them to say it differently' would be nothing but lame, I'd already decided to take it like a man, "Yes, sir."

"So, please don't do anything like that ever again."

He rose and opened the door. I just sat there.

"That's all, Chip. Just give me your word that you won't do it anymore."

Rising with astonishment, "Yes, sir. I certainly won't. Thank you, sir."

"Sure, Chip."

I exited the room quicker than The Flash.

And the Universal Forces? They were refining my understanding of the optimum way to step to the beat of my own drummer, and knowing this part of the lesson could be gentler than the first time, they'd planned it so that in addition to the registrar, the dean had also become one of my dad's good friends many years before.

Even so, the UF wanted me to see clearly that often after you view things from your perspective, before you act it's good to consider there may be reasonable views of others with differing perspectives. I could see analogies to playing the drums. In many circumstances, it would be wise to take another look at the speed of my cadence, the direction of my march and, most importantly, the type of rebound that stick's going to have after I've hit the drum with it.

In my experiences since that lesson, I've found the Universal Forces have a pretty nice idea there. And even if I decide not to alter my march after focusing on my drummer's beat, I'm much better prepared for the direction of the stick's rebound, and there are a lot fewer surprises.

* * * *

53

God Bless America

There are good days and there are bad days,
and this is one of them.

Lawrence Welk

My dad, Joe, was born in Europe in 1895. His family emigrated to the United States through Ellis Island in the early 1900's and they were well aware that one of the best things a person could do for his own benefit was to get a good education. Joe and my Uncle Sam worked hard in grammar school and high school and did get a good education. They didn't wait for someone to give it to them; they actively sought it, got it and were grateful for it.

Joe was the eldest and when it came time to go to college, the family didn't have enough money to send him, so Sam, whose joy and generosity knew no bounds, insisted that Joe go and he'd work to help him with the costs until he finished. Thus, with Sam and everyone else in the family helping where they could, including Joe who got a job making umbrellas at a penny apiece, they were able to pay for the tuition, books and materials, and most of the time for the carfare. If not, Joe walked—a long way. Everyone was happy to pitch in. They loved this country dearly and the opportunities it offered to all those willing to work to achieve them.

World War I, the Great War, *the war to end all wars*, started in the summer of 1914 while Joe was in college, and the United States entered it in the spring of 1917, about six months before Joe's graduation. With a strong belief it was important not to let any power threaten the promise and freedom of this country, Joe enlisted as a private in the U.S. Army immediately upon graduation without a second thought.

He was assigned to the 3rd Division (Infantry), 6th Engineers, Company B, and in December 1917 was sent to construct bridges, trenches and other fortifications for the front lines in France. Because the engineers were usually some of the first World War I "doughboys" at the front, they often did their work under enemy fire, including blistering artillery bombardment. In addition to defending themselves when necessary, they were also used as offensive infantry troops if reinforcements, replacements or reserves were required due to battle casualties or other battle necessities.

All was not quiet on the Western Front and he was in the battles known as the Somme Defensive and in both the Aisne-Marne Defensive and Offensive. He was nicked two or three times by stray shrapnel but, mirroring his fellow soldiers, he simply pushed on with unflagging resolve until the day when the concussion from an exploding artillery shell knocked him unconscious and he rolled into a shell hole with some lingering mustard gas in the bottom.

Just at that time, by chance of course, an ambulance driver was approaching, saw it happen, slid to a stop and jumped out. At no small personal risk to himself, he scrambled down to get my dad, pulled him out and whisked him to medical attention.

Inhaled mustard gas isn't very good for your respiratory system; one thing led to another and Joe ultimately spent five years in the hospital after that. His breathing wasn't easy the rest of his life here, but he persevered and ultimately made it to the age of 95 before he went back "home." During all those years, he was always looking forward, and was extremely proud of his service to his country. Not once during our joint lifetimes here did I ever hear him complain about anything, except, of course, if someone disrespected *his* country. When they whined about not getting enough out of it, he'd comment they just weren't putting enough into it.

From my perspective, it's a good thing that ambulance driver happened to be around (those Universal Forces again) and that my dad chose to persevere, or I wouldn't be here; well, I wouldn't be *his* son. But fortunately I am and he set many positive examples for me. As a few results of those examples, I stuck with my studies in college and married during my senior year while earning a bachelor's degree, followed by a beautiful baby girl a year and a half later while I was earning my master's degree.

As another result during my college career, which should be easy to understand, I enrolled in the Reserve Officers' Training Corps (ROTC, we pronounced it "rotsee"), an undertaking that did not then have the opprobrium later heaped upon it by the anti-war movements of the Vietnam era and subsequently. When I joined ROTC, the timing of my birth placed me about half way between the end of the Korean War and the start of America's Green Beret "Special Advisors" involvement in the Vietnam War.

I progressed through ROTC and, in order to be certain that we were properly trained and occupied during the summer before my senior year in college, the Army issued orders to my ROTC classmates and me to report to a U.S. Army Post several states away in order to undergo basic combat training, that is, ROTC Boot Camp. So, four of my Sigma Iota brothers and I jumped into an old Chevy sedan and headed out. On the way, we pulled into a gas station in a little mountain town and the attendant, who'd obviously lost his left arm in some kind of an incident, perhaps in Korea, was having trouble getting the hood open. One of my bros, well-intentioned but without thinking, jumped out and offered, "Need a hand, buddy?" That lack of appropriate mindset before acting was the harbinger of the nemesis all of us would most need to overcome during that summer.

Now, I'd shot a bow and arrow at camp, a homemade slingshot, wooden rifles during our grammar school WWII "war games" in the neighborhood when I was a kid, a Daisy BB 1000 Shot Red Ryder Cowboy Carbine Air Rifle I'd smuggled into the garage when I was in junior high because my mother would not consent to my ownership (something to do with shooting out eyes), but never a .30 caliber M1 Garand semi-automatic military rifle. For the summer, we were each issued our very own M1 and bayonet, but no ammunition. I guess poking an eye out with the bayonet was okay, but they didn't want us to shoot ourselves. The combination weighed around eleven pounds, which felt like 111 pounds if you carried it long enough and far enough, which we often did, and sometimes while holding it over our heads as a result of failing to follow very simple instructions.

So, if the weapon was ever dirty in any respect (measured in nanospecks), except very briefly after proper use during an exercise, we would run laps around the company area holding the rifle high in the air with both hands until we understood how important it was to keep it clean and why. There were no exceptions; thus, we learned self-discipline and attention to the smallest detail very rapidly. It's amazing what one can learn, and how fast, when there are consequences.

Our customary dress was combat fatigues, heavy leather combat boots (unfortunately, long before the lightweight materials in use today), our M1 rifles and either a fatigue cap, a steel helmet or just its light composition liner, depending on the task at hand. In the morning we were normally afforded the mandatory opportunity to travel a couple of miles at a fast "double-time" shuffle with our M1's held at "Port Arms." That is, held diagonally a couple of inches in front of our chests, left hand toward the top of the barrel and the right hand toward the bottom just below the trigger housing. The morning "jog" was an enlightening experience as I became acutely aware of muscles I didn't know human beings possessed—but they developed, and developed well, as the days limped by.

Upon finishing the double-time, we were supposed to be lined up straight when we stopped, but after two miles of staggering in unison at Port Arms, we weren't even close, at least in the beginning. So, after several commands intended to put us in perfect alignment, we'd be at attention with the rifle at Order Arms—the butt on the ground by our right toe, pointing straight up along the right leg and steadied by the right hand.

After that, we were given the command, "Specshaa ... Humz!" The first time that happened, we had no clue what our drill sergeant was saying and involuntarily did an approximation of the Keystone Cops, banging into each other every which way. So, he clearly explained the intricacies of Inspection Arms for our M1's and loudly underscored that it was very important to get it right *every* time or the extremely unpleasant consequences that followed would be self inflicted, not from him, but by us.

For rifle inspection, the M1's were brought to Port Arms, then with a quick motion of the left hand the bolt on the rifle was pushed open, which took a really good, hard, sharp push on the small curved handle sticking out because the spring trying to keep it shut was very strong. After it caught in the open position you looked into the chamber quickly to make sure it hadn't received a cartridge and was empty, following which, your left hand was returned to Port Arms, leaving the chamber open for inspection.

If you didn't push hard enough the first time to get the bolt to catch open, you tried again, looking like a bozo now because you could well be the only one moving and clanking. Either way, once it was open, you started praying that the company commander, in our case a regular-army (RA) captain and West Point graduate, would not randomly pick you and inspect your rifle as he walked down each line. If he did, he'd stand directly in front of you approximately the length of his forearm away from your diagonally-held rifle, with his arms motionless at his sides. Moving only his head, he'd inspect you up and down.

Without warning at any point during the look-over, he'd bring his right hand up like a trigger spring and grab your rifle. In that instant, at least three things could happen, one of them good, the other two not good at all:

1. You could let go of your rifle with *both* hands at exactly the point when he touched it and then it would be in his hand, you'd be at attention and, continuing his grabbing motion, he'd inspect your rifle, which is how it's supposed to work.

2. You could let go of it in a timely way with your top hand, but a nanosecond too late with your bottom hand, causing the latter to become a fulcrum during that one billionth of a second you shouldn't have been holding it, and the butt of the rifle would instantaneously swivel into your private parts before he tore it from your grasp, leaving you with your eyeballs spinning and desperately trying to remain motionless at attention.

3. As you can see, rifle inspection demanded quick reflexes and precise timing, which enhanced the desire to precognate exactly when the captain would make his move. If your psychic abilities completely failed you that morning and both your hands opened before the captain's hand moved, the rifle dropped to the ground, causing you to have an *extremely* bad day indeed.

On the third day of our training, I was gasping for air, perspiring like the next horse in line at the glue factory, my feet were killing me, my vision was blurry and my eyes stinging from the sweat running into them (heaven help the cadet who moved a muscle to do something about that) and I think I may have been weaving very slightly in place when the captain came down the line, and went right by me. I started thinking it was going to be a real nice day. He inspected two or three other rifles and then the first sergeant gave the appropriate command to close the rifle bolts.

We'd received a lot of instruction on how to do that properly so it would be an automatic procedure, particularly if you were in the shape I was in that morning, because the spring is tough and the bolt slams shut hard. Here's how it works. Still at Port Arms, you use the edge of your right hand palm to press against the little curved handle on the bolt in order to hold it open, which you definitely want to do because you're going to put the thumb of the same hand down into the bottom of the space the bolt wants to occupy in order to push on the catch that fully releases the bolt, which you are still holding open with the edge of your palm.

Then, in exactly this order, you remove your thumb, stop holding the bolt back with your palm, and the bolt rockets forward, snapping shut, hard. All this is accomplished *very* quickly (in about the time it takes to say the first four words of this sentence), precisely and in unison with the other cadets after the command is given.

If you get the order of events wrong, and in its essentials there's only one way to get it wrong—the bolt slams closed on your thumb, trying to ram it up the barrel because it thinks your digit is a rifle cartridge. Notwithstanding that I was a drummer used to executing rapidly changing patterns, I made an error in the order on that third morning and, without looking, I knew I'd acquired the highly unpopular, and instantaneously excruciatingly painful, "M-1 Thumb," its most visible feature being a highly-machined red circle with a red dot right in the center, the latter courtesy of the firing pin I believe.

Upon executing that blunder, there are things you definitely don't do right away. You don't yell, flinch, curse or act like anything happened at all, or both the captain and the company first sergeant will single you out for a little chat in front of the entire company, asking you to display your thumb. Then later, you and your platoon sergeant, that is, your drill sergeant, will have another chat because it reflects poorly on him if you're not trained properly. I knew that already because by the third day, I was far from the first to do it. In any event, the pain lasts about a week and the symmetrical marks much longer. You need only do that to yourself once in a lifetime and you'll never do it again no matter what the situation—guaranteed.

The next thing I recall is firing an anti-tank weapon, the 3.5-Inch M20 Anti-Tank Rocket Launcher. Three and a half inches is the diameter of the two-foot solid fuel rocket that's fired from a six-foot launching tube that comes in two pieces which are screwed together. The whole package was called the "Super Bazooka," as compared to the smaller bazooka used in WWII.

It's fired from the shoulder, and it's not unusual to do it while you're on the ground in the prone position. There are bi-pod legs to support the front of the tube and a shoulder brace for its operator who supports the back. We wore steel combat helmets for this exercise and we got to use real rockets, but the business part of them contained no explosives, the concern being that we might hit something.

After appropriate instruction, I was the first to fire. On my stomach, the shoulder guard was firmly against my shoulder and the tube pointed in the direction of the target perhaps a hundred yards away. My firing buddy, one of my Sigma bros, loaded the rocket in the back of the launcher, made sure no one was in front or behind, armed the rocket, smacked me much harder than necessary on the helmet, barked "Up" and turned his head away.

Now, at those amateur meets where people build and fire their rockets into the air, there's a reason no one at all is allowed within about a hundred yards of the rocket when it's fired by remote control. And there's also a reason they called the weapon on my shoulder a *Super* Bazooka. I pulled the trigger, heard a click, a "ssssst," the beginning of a really big "whumpfff" and immediately thereafter an extremely loud noise that sounded like the word "bazoo-oo-oo" echoing inside a sewer pipe just before my ears went "kaaa."

The next thing that caught my awareness—my face was in the dirt, my bro had fallen on top of me, and we were in the middle of a twenty foot circle of smoke and dust, most of which I was inhaling. Over the ringing in my ears, I could hear my platoon sergeant trying to mask his amusement while chuckling, "It's always good to have a feel for the power of this weapon." The captain stifled a smile, "Perhaps next time you should give firing from the kneeling position a try. You know, it *is* one of the suggested alternatives."

Whereupon, my platoon sergeant broke into gales of laughter along with his fellow sergeants (NCO's—non-commissioned officers) who were there.

A few days later, we were engaging in an infantry-with-tank-support exercise. For reasons known only to him, the captain had appointed me as a platoon leader. Our platoon had its own tank for the purpose of engaging the "enemy" who was on the other side of a clearing in a wooded area. Each platoon in the company had its own area well away from the others. After some basic tactical instruction, it was left to the platoon leader to determine how the objective would be captured.

Calling on my extensive WWII neighborhood war games experience, I decided the tank would stay hidden behind some small saplings and brush on our end of the clearing while most of the platoon dispersed in the woods on both sides of the clearing, sneaking about half way up and stopping. A few of the men would stay behind to safeguard our rear from any surprises.

At my signal via walkie-talkie from a protected observation point behind a tree to the side of the of the tank's right rear, the cadets on the sides of the clearing would start firing in order to get the enemy to return fire so the tank commander could see exactly where they were. Then on my signal, the tank would scare the hell out of the enemy by charging from the woods as fast as it could, blasting and firing toward the other side of the clearing about fifty yards away, with the platoon also firing and moving forward but being careful not to get in front of the tank or into its line of fire. We actually had blanks in our M1's for this; the enemy had blanks and the tank had blanks in its machine guns and in its turret main gun. There would be a lot of muzzle flashes and noise; thus, it would be very cool.

The platoon was in position up the sides of the clearing. I spoke into my walkie-talkie and the platoon started firing from among the trees. Since this wasn't the real deal and he wanted a good view so his tank wouldn't run over any of our warriors, the tank commander was sitting casually in the open turret. The enemy started firing and he turned, looking down at me. I motioned for him to move out and he signaled the driver (by kicking him in the helmet I think) as I took a couple of quick steps to get behind the right rear of the tank for cover. Gotta love that drum training combined with fencing footwork—the timing was perfect. Just as I arrived behind that Sherman tank, the driver floored the giant 400 horsepower V-8 Ford engine.

The next thing—the walkie-talkie was no longer in my hand, I was flat on my back, the tank was at the far end of the clearing along with the platoon, and the captain was peering down at me shaking his head slowly. His voice sounded a short distance from laughing, "Good news, the mission was a success. Not such good news, you appear to be a casualty. My training advice—next time, jump behind the *other* side of the tank."

That was a good thought because, unknown to me, the exhaust for that Sherman Tank's 400 horsepower V-8 was hidden head-high behind a nondescript mesh grill on top of its right rear fender and blew straight back. When my spectacular timing put my face right behind that grill at the instant the driver floored it, I thought I'd been slapped in the chops with a flying pile of whale blubber. However, disregarding the injury to my military bearing, which at least the captain hadn't overtly laughed about, the only real casualty was the walkie-talkie, which in those days was a fairly heavy hand-held radio about a foot long. At the end of its airborne flight, it failed to survive its sudden stop against a tree.

For the remaining weeks, I decided a change in my subliminal "background" thinking was necessary, from "I *hope* I can do this" to "I *know* I can do this correctly and well," and I resolved to redouble my perseverance. After that, we were tested on our accuracy firing the M1 rifle from a standing and prone position. I qualified at the "Expert" (highest) level. Following that eagle-eyed accomplishment, the captain appointed me as a squad leader in one of our training exercises. My instructions were to take the squad to a designated place in the woods, wait three minutes for a "resistance fighter" to show up with extremely important battle intelligence for our regimental commander, and if he wasn't there within that three minutes, leave.

We left the muster point and snaked our way to the designated location. I checked my watch. The first minute went by and he didn't show. The second minute passed and he hadn't arrived.

A member of the squad whispered in my ear, "They're screwing with us, he'll show at the last second."

As we hit the end of the third minute, a little thought-voice in the back of my head said, "Leave. Leave now!" I motioned to the squad to pull out.

Whispers from the squad, "No, a couple more minutes. He'll show."

Thoughts in the back of my head quietly yelled, "Get out now!" I pointed back toward our muster point and emphatically mouthed five readily understood words I won't repeat here. We left rapidly. About fifty yards later, we heard rifle and automatic weapons fire (blanks of course) back at the point we'd just left. The captain appeared and personally congratulated me for following orders and avoiding the "ambush."

So, having changed my thinking, I was doing better. To add to that, at this late juncture in the summer, we were in outstanding physical condition. We'd had no choice, but it was amazing and the last time in my life I've been in that kind of shape. I also did very well in fixed-bayonet (rubber) hand-to-hand combat training. With my fencing experience, no one had a chance.

And then came the last exercise of the summer. We were on an enemy search mission with blanks in our rifles. They were really serious about this one and it was being graded by NCO's with clipboards at the ready, one to a squad. We were told they were invisible and to forget they were there. So, I did just that as we were sneaking through the woods on our mission when an "enemy" combatant started firing at us from about thirty yards to our left.

My neighborhood WWII war games training kicked in again. I jumped flat-out in that direction, aiming my rifle with my body in the prone position flying through the air like Superman. I fired just before I hit the ground, landing flat in the same prone position. In grammar school I was a lot closer to the ground and it didn't hurt nearly as much when I came down. But, unfortunately for the sergeant grading our exercise from a few feet away, he stepped right into my line of fire and the wadding from the blank hit him in the boot above his ankle.

His clipboard went into the air as he started hopping up and down and swearing. Simultaneously, I yelled, "Dammit, Sergeant, if you hadn't been in the way, I'd a had him!" The captain was watching. He walked over, picked up the sergeant's clipboard and scribbled something on it as he walked back to me, still in the prone position. He tossed it in front of me and walked off. Next to my name, he'd written, "Outstanding attitude."

So, thanks to the example of my dad's perseverance and to the Universal Forces who, among other things, obviously had my back at the "ambush," I successfully completed that summer—and my dad was proud.

* * * *

54

Sleep Soundly America

The most dangerous thing in the world is
a Second Lieutenant with a map and a compass.

Murphy's Law of Combat Operations

I think because I'd ultimately done well in ROTC Boot Camp that summer, at the start of my senior year, the colonel in charge of the program at the university appointed me the regimental adjutant of the ROTC Corps, solely a ceremonial position. I had no duties other than to be one of the two cadets who marched behind the cadet colonel in the annual Veterans Day parade. That was good because, other than that, I had no idea what a regimental adjutant should do. By the way, of the other two cadets in that marching triangle, one became a university president and the other a United States senator (it wasn't Freddy).

In any event, at a point in the school year, we had to put down our preferences for a branch of the army in which to serve and whether we wanted to be on active duty for six months or two years, which would be followed by service in the army reserves for another six years. The branch requirement was to put down three branches classified as "combat arms" and two classified as "non-combat arms" of the army. That paper would be sent to Washington, D.C., and somewhere deep in the Pentagon, after intense examination and deep thought, the selection would be made and the results sent back to our colonel who would relay them to us.

I put down two years for active duty, and for combat arms, I put down Armor notwithstanding the blast from that Sherman tank, then Artillery because I loved the sound of those big guns going off, and lastly Infantry. I liked the infantry, but I put it as my third choice because those leather combat boots just killed my feet after a few miles.

In fact, my feet are so flat that I rock when I'm standing still. I had to argue with the military doctor for the better part of an hour at my initial ROTC boot camp physical to keep from being tossed out and reclassified 4-F. My basic argument was that they were asymptomatic, which they were. They did not bother me, at least until I was issued combat boots. The boots were the perfect size for my feet, but they were designed for people with arches. So, I just endured each day until my feet went sort of numb and then they were asymptomatic again.

For non-combat arms, none of which I was interested in, I put down the Chemical Corps first, figuring I'd never be put there because I couldn't even work the chemistry set I got for my tenth birthday and I knew nothing about chemical, biological or radiological warfare. "Radiological" is what they used instead of "nuclear" then. I guess because people could pronounce it correctly.

And, since I was the regimental adjutant, I put down the Adjutant General's Corps (AG) for my other non-combat arm. The description said, "The Adjutant General officer's job is to plan, develop, and direct systems for managing the Army's personnel, administrative, and Army band systems." I liked the Adjutant General's red, white and blue shield insignia with white stars on it, *and* they were responsible for the army bands. Except for Glen Miller's unfortunate experience in WWII, it could be great to be a drumming army bandleader. I had aptitude for that and I didn't think it would be any problem to learn to read music. But AG was my last choice, so I'd never be assigned to that branch anyway. By the way, the Adjutant General's Corps is not to be confused with the Judge Advocate General's Corps which is a bunch of military lawyers. Because they went to law school, they have an extra letter, JAG.

On finishing my bachelor's degree, I was, of course, commissioned a second lieutenant in the Adjutant General's Corps, a shave-tail second louie, but maybe I'd get a band! Anyway, since I'd completed many of my master's courses during the last year of my bachelor's degree and only had one more year to go to finish my master's, the army let me do it, with orders to report promptly after that for a temporary-duty assignment, the two-month Adjutant General's Officers' Basic Course at an army installation just outside a fairly large Midwestern city.

So, upon finishing my master's degree, I kissed my wife and baby goodbye, temporarily, and reported promptly. The installation was a nice place, somewhat humid in the late summer, but pleasant. My officers' class lived in a fairly typical army barracks, except it was divided so there were only four of us to a room as I recall, instead of everyone elbow to elbow in one large room. The one thing that caught my attention was the big tornado warning sign in the "lobby." It told us that in case of a tornado, we should open the windows on one side of the building and close the windows on the other side. Someone had printed in large letters at the bottom, "Then run like hell."

Since AG is a comparatively small corps trained in mostly administrative work, much of our training time was spent in the classroom, with two separate exceptions, physical exercise and continued combat training. Not knowing what environment a soldier of any branch might be stationed in, everyone had to be prepared to engage in military combat, even though in a non-combat arm.

As an officer, I purchased my own uniforms, which on classroom days was light tan military khaki trousers, short sleeve khaki shirts, no tie, garrison cap (the flat one that's peeled open and looks like an upside-down envelope) and standard low-cut military oxford shoes. For combat training days, it was standard olive drab military fatigues and I also purchased a pair of leather combat boots that fit my flat feet. The oxfords fit too.

Concerning the physical exercise, on classroom days we had about an hour and a half of it right after lunch. I mean, *right* after the noon meal. Having eaten breakfast and gone to class very early in the morning, we'd be hungry and eat a big lunch. Immediately after that, we'd fall-in and march to the athletic field, fold our highly pressed khaki shirts neatly on the grass, leave our T-shirts on, put our caps on top of our folded shirts, leave the rest of our uniform on, including our oxford shoes, and double-time for two sunny, hot and humid miles around the field. I was grateful that at least it was without rifles or packs, but I'd always thought if you did that right after eating, particularly if it was hot, you'd throw up somewhere between a half mile and a mile.

A few did at first, but no one was going to be the officer who complained, so we got used to it. After running, we'd do pull-ups, then sit-ups and push-ups on mats so we wouldn't ruin our uniforms, and various other exercises. When we were finished, we put our shirts and caps back on, pulled out a handkerchief, dusted off our shoes and marched back to class for the afternoon. Don't ask. I can't explain it either, but I think maybe it was a test. We certainly learned we could function outside the box. It's just a matter of mindset.

There was a big, strong, brand-new (like the rest of us), second lieutenant in our class from the South, 6'2" and 195 pounds of solid steel. When he did pull-ups, knuckles facing him, he'd not only do them twice as fast as anyone else, he'd vault his upper body straight up every time so he finished each one with his arms straight and the bar below his belt line. We routinely made him stop at fifty because we couldn't stand being intimidated that way any more than necessary. It wouldn't do any good. He'd just jump down and crank off a hundred sit-ups to cool off.

The comparison wasn't any better in the combat training exercises. For instance, he was far and away the fastest and absolutely unafraid and unhesitant in the live-overhead-fire, belly-crawling exercises where if you panicked and stood up, you were history if you popped up too fast for the soldier firing the machine gun to stop (at least that's what they told us). He said he wrestled alligators back home for fun. We weren't sure we believed him until he morphed into a Death Eating Tractor in hand-to-hand combat training, chewing up anyone who took him on, including a couple of the less observant instructors. We nicknamed him "Bubba."

On combat training days, usually only a day a week and sometimes at night also, we'd wear our fatigues and often do things similar to those in ROTC boot camp except, as commissioned officers, we were treated differently and much of the emphasis was on leadership. One day, we were going to have gas mask drills in the tear-gas compound, but first they gave us classroom instruction about the various types of gases that might be used on the battlefield, particularly nerve gas.

Our instructor that day, an Infantry captain, carefully explained that nerve gas was a colorless, odorless gas and the first indication of it would be certain symptoms which he carefully delineated. If you were fortunate enough to realize you were beginning to experience those symptoms, you had something like less than twenty seconds to locate the place where you were carrying a small flexible metal tube, like the old metal toothpaste tubes, but about an inch long and half as wide. It had a hypodermic needle maybe a half inch long or so on the end which was shielded by a protective cover. The tube was filled with liquid atropine, the only antidote if administered quickly enough. If you were slow and blew your twenty-second window, you'd rapidly croak in a very unpleasant way.

He showed a short movie demonstrating how to pull the cover off and jam the needle forcefully through your fatigues and into the top of your thigh muscle, which squashed the tube at the same time and injected atropine into you, hopefully saving your life. Our instructor was, understandably, very serious about this and put two atropine tubes complete with needle and filled with a practice saline solution on each of our desks, telling us we were going to practice this twice.

Now so far as I know, no one in our class of forty three shiny-new AG ROTC officers had ever voluntarily jammed anything at all into any part of his body, much less blindly through his clothing. It was not a common thing to do in the circles we traveled in, and not in many circles at all in those days. It caused more than a little apprehension, and that needle looked at least three feet long. But once again, no officer was going to do anything except jam it into his leg—twice.

When the captain asked if there were any questions before we started the exercise, there was an eerie silence.

Then we heard Bubba's voice, "Not gonna do it."

Not sure what he'd heard, the captain responded, "What?"

"I'm not going to do it."

Still confused, "Do what?"

"Stick that in my leg."

The rest of us immediately implored him to do it, "Come on Superman, there's nothing to it. You won't even feel it."

"Yeah. How many times have you done it?"

The captain walked up to his desk and stared at him.

Bubba looked up and said calmly and matter of factly, "You can court-martial me. You can put me in front of a firing squad. You can throw me out of the army, but I'm not jammin' that thing in my leg."

"Lieutenant, in a combat situation, if you don't, you'll be dead."

"I know, sir. I'd rather die than stick that thing in my leg."

The captain said nothing and on the way back to the front of the class, he shouted, "Nerve gas!"

In a flash, each of us grabbed a tube, tore the cover off the needle and slammed it into our leg. The force of my hand banging into my thigh gave me a Charley horse and I didn't even feel the needle. Then we all looked at Bubba. Both tubes were still on top of his desk and we figured he was history. Slowly, he looked around at all the crushed tubes sticking out of our legs and then turned toward the front of the room.

"Please, shoot me, Captain."

The captain started laughing, "Tell me where to send the flowers, Lieutenant, because you just died." We all breathed a sigh of relief. Bubba wasn't going to be drummed out of the corps.

To celebrate Bubba's escape, several of us didn't study that night and took him into town to one of the local jazz clubs. One of our companions had gone to college with me and told the others that I was a drummer. After some celebratory libations for Bubba, he and the rest were insisting that I go up and sit in on the drums.

Now, I'd played a number of small jazz clubs just like that in college, and the last thing you want is a bunch of imbibers insisting that their buddy sit in on the drums because "he's a really good drummer." I did my best to stay in my seat, but Bubba picked me up, carried me up there and coerced the drummer, who seemed like a really nice guy, but a pacifist, into letting me sit in.

I apologized to him and sat down behind the drums which were remarkably similar to my set. His drums, and certainly jazz drums, had calfskin heads in those days and durability wasn't their best attribute. After all, you were pounding on a polished, tightly-tensioned piece of dead animal. Plastic heads were starting to come on the market, but no self-respecting jazz drummer would play one in those days because they didn't have the warm sound of calf. Synthetic heads that did wouldn't be developed until years later. The only other synthetic head I knew about then was a treated, tightly-woven, nylon-cloth head which lasted a long time, but sounded goofy, like you were playing on a piece of stretched nylon cloth.

Anyway, it's not unknown for a jazz combo to test, and punish, a guy whose buddies insist that he sit in, and the leader counted off an extremely fast, perhaps faster than a human can play, version of "Apple Honey," a tune composed by Woody Herman and made famous by his First Herd. The calf head on that drummer's snare drum was in the last days of its life. The edges were fine, but the middle looked like rough sandpaper had been taken to it, aggressively and often.

As it turned out, that head was actually in the last few vibrations of its rhythmical sojourn because I reprised the atropine exercise of earlier in the day when, just at the end of the first eight bars of the tune, I jammed the stick right through it. He didn't have a spare. I gave him some money for a new head, slunk off the bandstand and he unhappily played on his floor tom the rest of the evening. My buddies said it was great while it lasted.

The next week, our combat training took place at night because it was the Night Compass Course. We were divided into squads and each squad was given a paper with a number on it that identified us, plus a compass that glowed in the dark. That's all. No flashlight. No nothing, except we had to elect a squad leader who would memorize a set of compass azimuths that changed direction a number of times over two or three miles, plus the varying yardages we needed to travel on each separate azimuth. The squad I was in elected me. They'd all gone to college, but I was the only one in the squad with two degrees so they collectively decided I had the best memory and voted me the Night Compass Course Leader. Whatever. Mine was not to reason why. I was there to serve.

An NCO took me aside and carefully stated the azimuth coordinates and distances to me three times. Then he said we had two hours and turned us loose on a moonless night. We'd already been standing there with no light for almost an hour, so we could see enough not to run into any large object directly in front of us, but that was about it. All the squads were located around a quarter mile apart and forbidden to communicate with one another if our paths happened to cross, which would mean at least one group was screwed up.

We smashed into small trees and stumbled through brush, pot holes and anything else we could step in, fall over or run into, but we needed to make the best time possible in order to stay within the time frame. I'd repeated the compass information to everyone so that if, theoretically, an NCO appeared and told me I'd been exterminated, someone else would be able to take over.

The law of unintended consequences took over. Every time we stopped to sight a new azimuth with our glow in the dark compass, everyone remembered the information slightly differently. So, in order to make progress in some direction, I told them not to speak again and simply follow me unless I was tapped out by an NCO, a possibility that was mere speculation.

We didn't even know what was at the end of our journey. I felt like a blindfolded, rubber-legged scavenger trying to find an invisible needle in a flat haystack several miles square. We didn't know what it was, couldn't see anything and even though I knew the length of my normal gait, it was constantly changing because we were always stumbling, tripping, falling or stepping in a hole.

We never did run across another squad and an NCO never tapped me out. In about an hour and forty five minutes, within fifteen feet of the end of my last counted step, an NCO sitting on a chair behind a stake turned on his flashlight, congratulated us for coming out on a stake and asked for the paper with the number of our group. While the guys were cheering and slapping me on the back, he checked our paper against his clipboard, "The fact that you guys came out on a stake is very impressive, very impressive indeed … but this one is a half mile sideways from *your* stake." As we walked to the deuce-and-a-half truck to take us back, I endured many comments about the value of two college degrees, to which I responded with humorous thoughts on intelligently exercising the right to vote for your leaders.

We never did learn anything about army bands in our eight-week Adjutant General's Officers' Basic Course. They weren't even mentioned. But all of us graduated and we were turned loose to go to our respective army posts all over the country. I think the lesson the Universal Forces had for me in those two months was just to keep on keepin' on, and do my best at it.

* * * *

55

American Soldier—the Ultimate Weapon

They also serve who only stand and wait.
John Milton

AFTER BRIEFLY GOING BACK HOME to start the arrangements for the move of our meager family possessions to the East Coast before I had to leave for my permanent duty station, I kissed my wife and baby daughter goodbye again with the knowledge they were poised to join me as soon as I could arrange housing. I put a suitcase filled mostly with my uniforms in my 1959 Austin-Healey "bug-eyed" Sprite, my third car after Speedball Baby, and set out across country.

I'm sorry to say that during college, Speedball ultimately blew a seal and threw a rod while I was driving back to school across the desert one summer. Fortunately I was just pulling into the only gas station-junkyard in a tiny desert town. With barely enough money to get gas back to college if I had a running car, I was destitute in that 115° heat, and class registration for the semester was going to start first thing in the morning. I traded Speedball to the station owner for a Coke, a sandwich and a bus ticket, always intending to return and retrieve her if she were still there, but, swept up in the college life again, I never returned.

As Speedball's replacement, I acquired a used 1951 ice-box white, Studebaker V-8 Starlite Coupe, you know, the kind where you couldn't tell if it was coming or going. That Stude V-8 was an underrated engine in the first place and the guy who had it before me had hopped it up. I thought the rest of it should be as spirited as the engine so, with the supplement to my income through playing at jazz clubs and fraternity dances on the weekends, I Frenched the nose, deck and doors with the same treatment as Speedball, lowered it with a little alteration to the springs and redid the interior in a combination white and baby-blue tuck-and-roll naugahyde upholstery (I think many call it leatherette these days or, pejoratively, vinyl). Notwithstanding that the people who accomplished it for me thought I was crazy, the crowning glory was a completely chromed dashboard.

That car accelerated like a cat with its tail on fire, and touching the chrome dashboard on a sunny desert day was the same sensation. I traded the Stude in on a used 1956 Chevy Bel Air Coupe just before I got married so we could drive off on our honeymoon to Las Vegas in style. Then I acquired the Sprite while I was finishing up my master's degree.

You know, virtually any guy can recite everything about every car he's ever owned. Funny thing, though, I didn't give any of them a name after Speedball went to the Big Junkyard In the Sky. It just didn't seem right. I've always secretly imagined that someone discovered her there years later and now she's happily restored and motoring around in all her fluorescent purple, fur-lined glove compartment glory with a nice shiny antique-car copper license plate. I actually thought I saw her from a distance once, but couldn't catch up. It's just as well. Even now, I still can't bring myself to go back to look if she's still waiting for me in that hot little town's scrap yard. It'd be easy on one of our trips. I just can't do it.

The Austin-Healey Sprite successfully carried me to the beginning of my two-year active duty tour which would be spent on a large army post, essentially the size of a small city, on the East Coast, and my assigned Military Occupational Specialty

(MOS) was Army Personnel Officer, one of the main things an Adjutant General's officer is trained to do. When I arrived there, and even though I was married, I was temporarily housed in the Bachelor Officers Quarters (BOQ), a sort of a nicer barracks, with separate rooms, furniture, a closet instead of a locker, and a real bed instead of a metal bunk. I would be in the BOQ until I found a place for us to live. I presumed our first residence would be in the company-grade officers' housing on the post shortly after I received my assignment from the post personnel officer. Then I'd send for the family.

My appointment for that assignment, which I also presumed would be as a personnel officer at one of the units on the post, wasn't scheduled for several more days, and having never been that far from home, I was in limbo. I didn't know anyone and there was absolutely no one else staying in the BOQ. It was lonesome and I occupied myself by playing pool against myself in the BOQ's Day Room and by watching John F. Kennedy debate Richard Nixon on TV in the race for the President. JFK was articulate and confident. Nixon looked strangely stiff and uncomfortable, perspiration glistened on his upper lip and black and white television accentuated his five o'clock shadow. I wasn't surprised when Nixon lost.

When the debating wasn't on, I'd watch movies starring the quintessential American, John Wayne, who probably could have been elected President if he'd run. An actor as President? If memory serves me, I think Ronald Reagan developed some ideas on that subject a few years later. In any case, where *have* all the John Wayne's gone?

If he wasn't on, it was always great to find something with Elvis Presley doing his stuff. When I was in college, I remember all of us sitting in the Sigma Iota living room waiting for our glimpses of Elvis and his gross gyrations on *The Ed Sullivan Show*. In his first two Sullivan appearances, Elvis was shown full view and his wiggling from the waist down was outrageous. The young people in the audience went crazy and Sullivan said he just couldn't understand it. Today, it'd put a network censor to sleep, but in those days it was so shocking that on his third and last appearance on the show, almost every song was a ballad and, with one brief exception, Elvis was shown only from the waist up. Things have changed a little since then.

My meeting date at post headquarters with the post personnel officer finally arrived. Wondering what unit I would be a personnel officer in, I entered his office, saluted and the major invited me to sit down. We chatted a little and he asked me about my educational background. I told him I had two degrees in speech pathology and audiology, with a minor in the psychology of personality for both degrees, the cumulative effect of the latter essentially being a degree in psychology. He looked off into the distance and mused out loud concerning where to most effectively place me.

"Speech … speech … English … speech … English. We need … yes, we need an English teacher in the Specialist Training Regiment (STR). They do Advanced Individual Training right after a soldier's Basic Training. Yes, yes, your speech background qualifies you perfectly for that."

I don't think he noticed my jaw on the floor because I immediately said, "Sir, might I suggest the Post Hospital? It's quite a large facility and my training in speech therapy could be of significant benefit there with brain injured patients in particular, not to mention audiology with patients who've suffered hearing damage."

"No … I think the English would be a much better fit."

"I should also tell you that I'm a musician and might fit in well in connection with the post's Army Band program."

"English, English is the thing. Yes, you'll be a fine company executive officer (XO) in the Specialist Training Regiment's Company Clerk School *and* you can teach them English."

He scribbled some directions on a piece of paper, "Go down there and see the personnel officer, Lt. McGillan. I'll call him and he'll fix you up."

I stood, saluted, did an about face, went outside, and took a number of deep breaths as I found my way to the STR and Lt. McGillan, a big, strapping Irishman. He'd graduated from the

Adjutant General's Officers' Basic Course about six months before. As I told him what had happened at post headquarters, his laughter increased in frequency and volume, "Welcome to the army."

While I finished filling out around 12,000 pages of paperwork, he explained what I would be doing while teaching English (but not as a second language which might be a common assumption these days).

"First of all, as the executive officer of Company B which houses and teaches the privates how to be company clerks, you'll be the next ranking officer in the company, right behind Captain Spader who's the company commander. Among other things, that means you get to be in the company barracks when the bugle sounds *Taps* and the lights are turned out at night, just to make sure they're all actually snug in their beds, and when the bugle sounds *Reveille* in the morning you get to be there in order to make sure they get out of those beds. Then, during the day, you'll teach English to them in the English classroom at the Company Clerk School next to their barracks."

"How big is the class?"

"Oh, each hour you'll have a different group of about twenty. They'll rotate all day to different subjects like typing and paper shuffling, just like in college. Only this is their two months of specialist training which isn't *quite* like college. They'll have just graduated from boot camp so this will essentially be the start of their third and fourth months in the army and you'll have several basic types of students. In terms of size, the largest group will be draftees who wish they were somewhere else. If they finished high school, you won't be able to figure out how."

I was trying not to think until I'd heard the whole story.

"The next largest group includes a lot of high school drop-out delinquents, primarily from New York, New Jersey and Philly. They've been given the choice by a judge to either go to jail or keep their record clean by joining the army. But there's a bright side. The next group, which is smaller, is the enlistees. They actually want to be here.

"The smallest group will be Ivy-League-type grads who've been drafted. They'll be bored into a trance state because they learned the difference between a subject, verb and adjective in the first grade. You want to identify them early and make them your assistants when their hour in your class rolls around. They'll be eternally grateful for the small things you give them to do for that hour, and if they're going to be permanently assigned here for the rest of their tour, and if you're lucky, you can get one or two of them assigned to help you teach.

"I'll do what I can for you in that respect, but you actually have two assigned to you now, one's a Princeton grad and the other's a high school teacher from Philly, not an Ivy Leaguer, but he's a 230 pound ex-footballer who knows how to handle the folks the judges send to us. While he can't do it here, his technique in his particular Philly "Blackboard Jungle" class—did you see the movie?—was just to watch the total chaos awhile on the first day so he could identify the biggest, toughest, ringleader type in his class. Then he'd ask him to come to the front to participate in a learning exercise. With the entire class laughing as their boy sauntered up to make a fool out of "Teach," Teach'd hit him in the stomach as hard as he could without warning—no marks that way. He tells me he never had any discipline problems the rest of the year. You'll like him."

I stared at him dumbly.

"Oh, and there's absolutely no housing available on post, it's all taken and there's a long waiting list, so you'll have to find a place for yourself and your family off post. I can't help you there at all. I was lucky to get a place after the first three months. Availability is tight, *very* tight. You've got a week to find something to rent before you have to report to the company. Good luck, Chip." I was surprised to remember that my first name wasn't "Lieutenant."

He wasn't kidding. All the rentals in communities anywhere near the post were filled with military families and there was nothing, absolutely nothing, to rent. On the last day of that week, I finally found an "older" two bedroom house in a small community an hour from the post, advertised as "wears well." Even with a housing allowance, I could barely afford the rent for it on my second lieutenant's pay, but it was the first and only place I'd found that was available to rent. It had the added benefit that I was also able to get inside to inspect right away—the results of which I felt compelled to ignore.

All the floors were wall-to-wall black asphalt tile, I guess to help it "wear well" and reduce the cleaning effort because of the constant military-family turnover. Everything about the house was banged up and scarred from continuous use. Under any other circumstances, I wouldn't have walked through the front door, but I snapped it up in a second. I stayed in the BOQ until our furniture and personal possessions arrived at our new rental in the moving van, courtesy of the U.S. Army. After our stuff was there and in place, I called my wife and told her to hop on a plane with our daughter for the military life.

With domestic commercial air travel by jet still in its infancy, there were mostly propeller-driven airliners and, with our small daughter in tow, my wife flew all day long on the low, slow and noisy prop-jobs to get to the airport closest (about an hour away) to our very humble rental. In the last throes of dusk, I met them as they descended the stairs from the aircraft to the tarmac, about the only way to get on and off an airplane then. I could see that my wife was understandably exhausted, but my daughter was as bright eyed, active and excited as a one-year old on her first plane ride could be. Having had everything we possibly could previously shipped on the moving van, we collected one suitcase, the baby's bag of necessities, one-eyed Willy's cat-travel cage with him inside, crammed that, plus us, into the two-seater Austin-Healey Sprite and headed for our tattered little abode, which I had described as "acceptable" over the phone to my wife.

Luckily, it was dark when we drove up. We went in and, taking a deep breath, I flipped on the lights. As I carried my daughter in, my wife slowly looked around at the black asphalt floors, the walls and the counter tops. Then she sat down on a kitchen chair and burst into tears. But, my luck was holding, the little one had fallen asleep on the way "home."

The house had another significant drawback, its location. In order to make it to the company in time for reveille, I had to get up at 3:30 a.m. After the company's taps at night, I'd drive home, and if I got to bed by 11:30 p.m., it was a good day indeed. But, it was usually 12 or 12:30 a.m. With an average of three and a half hours sleep a night, I'd be facing students staring at me blankly all day while I tried to teach them the difference between plural and singular nouns and verbs, using very short sentences.

One day in the first winter, it was very cold and the troops were directed to wear their army issue pile field caps, olive drab beauties with a bill and fur ear flaps that would tie under the chin, much like a winter deer hunter's cap. Since it was even a little chilly in our sparsely insulated English classroom, they'd continue to wear them, but tie the ear flaps up across the top of the cap, ostensibly so they could hear me. I was busily teaching away when I noticed one of the students had on a civilian hunting cap with red plaid cloth that lined the earflaps tied over his head. An aardvark would know they were different from military issue.

"Stand up, soldier."

He stood at attention next to his desk, "Private Zupancic, sir."

"Everyone, please take a look at Private Zupancic's headgear. There are lots and lots of soldiers in the Army and we can't have everyone wearing whatever he feels like. You must all wear the same thing."

Another private stood in the back, "Sir, where can the rest of us get a hat like that?"

The sad part is, he was serious.

As the XO of Company B, I had a number of additional duties, such as being the Regimental Officer of the Day (OD) whenever it was our company's turn to do it on a rotating basis among the several companies in our regiment of about 3000 soldiers, including approximately 60 officers. That meant I'd get to stay up all night. As a kid, my mother would never let me do that and now I didn't want to. The regimental OD had several tasks, two of which were to check the food in the regiment's enlisted mess hall, and to be at one of the companies in the regiment at reveille to see if their troops got up on time.

My first time as OD, I hadn't been in the regiment long at all and having had dinner in the enlisted mess in the evening, it seemed a poetic segue to be at the company housing the cooks' school when reveille sounded to wake the troops in the morning. Because the reveille inspection was random, the company first sergeant wasn't expecting me and was just leaving on some other matter, so he handed his clipboard to a corporal and told him to accompany me.

The corporal and I were standing silently at the door to the barracks when reveille sounded. The soldiers started piling out of their bunks and stumbling for the latrine. I noticed there were soldiers who'd made no effort to rise. I walked up and looked closely at one on a top bunk. He was sound asleep. Outrageous. I began walking quickly through the barracks tapping the bunks of the sleeping men.

"Corporal, take that man's name and stand him at attention next to his bunk."

"Sir …"

"Corporal, take that man's name and stand him at attention next to his bunk."

"Sir …"

"Corporal, take that man's name and stand him at attention next to his bunk."

"Sir …"

I went through the entire barracks and had about twenty very sleepy privates trying to stand straight next to their bunks. I was about to turn to give them my thoughts on rising at reveille when the corporal caught up with me and spoke quietly.

"Sir, those are the trainees who've worked all night in the mess helping to prepare breakfast for this morning. They went to sleep at 0430 and are required to sleep until 1230."

I turned and in a commanding voice, "As you were, men," and strode briskly out the door.

The most important duty of the regimental OD and his company was to supply soldiers to guard various facilities on the post during the OD's duty night, and the facility that mattered the most was the post bank. So, of course, when I was OD, I had the duty to assemble, train and supervise the guards, comprised of our band of nascent company clerks.

While my first time as regimental OD was somewhat comical, I got the hang of training a reasonably effective guard force after a couple more times. So, the day before my next turn, I gave each of my prospective guardsmen a copy of their eleven General Orders for guard duty, which they'd previously been required to memorize in boot camp; thus, virtually all of them had it down pat by the time I inspected the guard in the late afternoon before their night protecting the post.

The inspection was important because we had to convince them they were engaging in serious business. The troops would be issued M1 rifles without ammunition. We didn't want them to decide they needed to shoot someone who failed to respond properly to the challenge, "Who goes there? Advance and be recognized." In addition to the loaded army issue .45 caliber M1911A1 semi-automatic pistol I was required to carry, I carried several clips of M1 rounds for them to use in case something really serious happened, but it never had. In those days, they were much more likely to become needlessly spooked while marching their posts by themselves in the middle of the night than be confronted with an actual situation. (Unfortunately, that's not true these days.)

However, the post bank had a lot of money in it and I was most careful where it was concerned and assigned four guards to it. The post commanding general had made it very clear that absolutely every precaution was to be followed in guarding the bank. So much so that, in addition to the General Orders, he had personally designed and approved a set of Special Orders to be used in doing so. There was to be no deviation from them whatsoever. So I always picked our best and brightest privates to guard the bank and emphasized the First General Order, "Take charge of this post and all government property in view," and the Eleventh General Order which read in part, "… to allow no one to pass without proper authority."

Then I went over the commanding general's Special Orders with the four bank guards in great detail, the most salient points of which were that they would lock themselves in the bank, they would have a notebook with the name, rank, serial number and current photograph of each person who was authorized to enter the bank and, *if* the guards determined it was safe to do so, only for those individuals would they unlock the door carefully and allow them to enter, immediately relocking the door. No one else was allowed to enter the bank on their watch at night, period. No exceptions.

Then I gave them an example I'd just thought up that afternoon to underscore the orders, "If the President of the United States arrives, wants in and his picture is not on the list, he doesn't get in. If there's a problem that involves the threat of violence, or violence, immediately telephone the Post Military Police, *then* me at the company or if I'm not there, get me on the radio (cell phones wouldn't be around for years). If it's a non-violent problem of any kind, call or radio me.

"If you let anyone into that bank who is not on the list, as the company XO, I have the power to conduct a Summary Court-Martial and I will personally sentence you to a month in the post stockade and dock two-thirds of your pay for that month. In short, the max. Is there any soldier who has the slightest doubt about what he's supposed to do?"

As usual, I spent much of that night sitting in my XO's undersized cubbyhole at the company chatting with Willy, the Jeep driver usually assigned to me for my OD tasks. Periodically through the night, Willy would crank up the Jeep and we'd check on the guards at various facilities spread all over the post. About 2:30 in the morning, I was at the company chatting with Willy and musing that the name Willy was appropriate for a Willys Jeep driver, when the phone rang. A very angry voice was on the other end. It was the post commanding general. He was conducting his own surprise inspection. They wouldn't let him in the bank. He said he'd wait while I called the guards on my other phone and set them straight.

I called them. One of my Ivy Leaguers answered. I asked calmly, "What's going on down there, Private? I've got the commanding general on the other phone and he says you won't let him in."

He replied equally calmly, "He isn't on the list."

"Tell me what happened."

"He banged on the door and wanted in. We looked in the notebook and he's not in there. The President's not in there either. If the President can't get in, then the general can't get in. He asked if we knew who he was. We responded in the affirmative. He demanded again to get in. We told him again he wasn't on the list. He asked for your name and phone number. Then he went away."

I'd be willing to bet that if I could have seen him, that private was smirking. In any event, I was starting to think the commanding general might be testing us and I didn't want to be the one to step in that bucket. If I was wrong, it didn't seem right to court-martial me for following clearly written orders he'd personally devised. I made a quick assessment and picked up the other phone, "I'm sorry sir, you're not on the list."

There was a long pause, "Look, Lieutenant, if the President of the United States showed up, would you let him in?"

I must have been psychic earlier, "Of course not, sir, he's not on the list."

There was another long pause, then a click as he hung up.

I told Willy we'd better go out and check on the other guards, starting with the ones furthest away. I didn't want to be there if the general should happen to show up at Company B.

The next afternoon, the regimental commander called me up to his office. I entered, stood at attention and saluted, "Good afternoon, Colonel."

He didn't tell me to stand at ease. It wasn't looking good.

"Lieutenant, I received a very unhappy phone call from General Reba this morning. Why didn't you let him in the bank?"

"He wasn't on the list, sir."

"He asked me to go over that situation with you."

"Yes, sir."

After surveying me for a few moments, "Consider it done, Lieutenant. That's all."

That's how my life went. I'd get four hours sleep on a really lucky night, be on duty at least 16 hours a day, drive at least two hours a day, and be eating, getting up or going to bed in the remainder of that time, except when I was OD. Then I got no sleep and was on duty forever. After seven or eight months I decided I was getting chronically punchy and my effectiveness at anything was drastically reduced. I realized this was nothing like the rigors of combat, but we weren't at war and I wanted to be able to do the best job I could.

So, I went up to regimental headquarters (HQ) to see the regimental adjutant, an AG major and a nice person. He was in charge of post housing for the regiment. He told me to sit down. I explained my situation and tried to make it clear I wasn't complaining.

"Sir, I volunteered to serve in the army and I'm happy I'm here. I'm willing to do whatever I'm asked to do, but I think I can perform my duties much better if I have housing on the post. It would certainly make my wife rest easier too; we're going to have a second child soon. The quarters don't have to be anything fancy, just close. We've tried to find closer housing off-post, but there's nothing available I can afford."

"I'm sorry, Lieutenant, there isn't any company-grade officers' housing available on the post, but I'll forage around anyway."

"Thank you, sir."

"You know, I've heard about you. You've caught the attention of the colonel."

He didn't elaborate. Surprised and somewhat confused, I thanked him for anything he might be able to do and left.

Nothing happened for several weeks and I presumed nothing was going to happen. Then one day, my company commander since the day I got there, Captain Spader, came into my cubbyhole and dropped a set of military orders on my desk, "Well, it looks like you're going up to regimental headquarters as Assistant Adjutant, and they're giving you field-grade quarters in the new Capehart housing. You're going to be living like a major. Congratulations, I haven't been able to accomplish that."

A short while later, I transferred up to regimental headquarters. To my surprise, the major was gone and an Infantry captain I'd never seen before was the brand new regimental adjutant. He wasn't new to the post, but he was new to the regiment and the job. While we were getting acquainted, he said the major had been transferred overseas and must have liked me because I was going to be living in his former house. Well, well, well. The Universal Forces were always hovering in the background arranging beneficial events. I'd be living five minutes away in a modern, furnished, three-bedroom, two-bathroom house with kitchen, breakfast area, dining room, living room and *carpets*.

Not only were my company XO duties over and I'd finally get some sleep, regimental headquarters was paradise compared to the company. I had a moderate-sized office and a private called "Beyondo" who would carry out my every wish if I needed something—paper clips, you name it. However, his primary activity seemed to be to keep my coffee cup filled at all times with hot coffee, all day long. My primary activity was to do whatever the regimental commander or the regimental adjutant asked me to do.

The first thing the colonel said to me after "Good to see you again, Lieutenant," was, "You know, Lieutenant, I've been walking around the regiment and I've noticed that all the butt-cans and their stands are green. Since soldiers are tossing lit cigarettes into them, they should be red."

"Yes, sir." I saluted and left his office.

Butt-can stands in the regiment were as ubiquitous as squirrels in an outdoor nut factory. They were made of 2x4's that formed a crude basket about waist high that a #10 tomato can was dropped into. It seemed like everyone smoked in those days and those stands were everywhere. Without delay, I went down to the regimental Utilities Section, which handled all the light construction and maintenance, and sought out Master Sergeant Mast who ran that outfit. I'd met him when I was with Company B. We got along well and it was clear to me early on that NCO's are the backbone of the army and if they aren't with you, nothing happens.

He was happy to learn I was in regimental headquarters and we chatted about different things for quite awhile, and then I told him about the butt-can stands. He laughed a good laugh. Apparently the stands and cans used to be red, but when the colonel's predecessor took over the regiment, he felt they should blend in more and had them painted green. Then we both had a good laugh and less than 48 hours later every single butt can and butt-can stand was red. The colonel was very pleased.

A lot of my regular duties involved writing detailed procedures and regulations for military activities peculiar to our regiment, either rewriting obsolete or unintelligible regs or writing new ones based on the colonel's desires. Writing was one of my natural aptitudes and, just to be factual, I was very good at writing regulations. One of the main reasons for that hinged on the fact that I spent a considerable amount of time talking to the people at all levels who would be affected by a particular set of regulations so I understood exactly what those folks needed in order to do what the colonel wanted.

The mechanics of writing regs was a little different then. It consisted of a bunch of #2 pencils, a pencil sharpener, a good eraser and lots of paper to write on. When I added or changed words, often instead of erasing, I'd write in all of the margins with arrows into the text. Beyondo would type triple-spaced drafts until I was done marking them up, and when I was satisfied, along with whoever needed to approve it, Beyondo would create a mimeograph stencil with the ribbon removed from the typewriter so it would punch clean letters into the special stencil paper. Then he'd lock the stencil onto the big rotating drum on the mimeograph machine, pour in stuff that smelled like embalming fluid, load in the blank paper and crank out pungent-smelling copies for the entire regiment. It reminded me of my newspaper venture with Tucker in the 5th grade.

All-in-all, it was a tedious process. There was no monitor screen, cursor, cut, paste, or delete, except with an eraser, glue or scissors. In short there were no computers; thus, no word processing programs. We had the old manual "hit the letter key which pushes a metal bar with that letter up to strike the ink ribbon while the paper carriage moves to the left one letter at a time" typewriters, and heaven forbid if you hit two keys at the same time, jamming the type bars. The revolutionary, very fast, IBM Selectric electric typewriters with all the letters on a single metal sphere the size of a golf ball and no moving paper carriage (it was the ball that moved) were just coming on the market and it was a cinch we didn't, and wouldn't, have one in the foreseeable future, much less a "correcting" Selectric which wouldn't be introduced until more than ten years later.

One of my other time-consuming tasks was to send the regiment's Manpower Utilization Report each month to the post Manpower Utilization Division (MUD).

At each unit in the regiment, the top NCO and his or her subordinates would spend hours and hours each month identifying, counting and classifying the people who fit into the various categories on the forms, done in quadruplicate, which required 7 sheets of paper to be inserted into the typewriter, three of which were carbon paper between the blank forms (no Xerox machines in those days). So typos were a nightmare to correct, erasing individually the original and each carbon copy, by hand, while trying to keep the pages aligned so the new strike would get the letter in the right place on each copy.

When finished, the units would send them up the chain to me at regimental HQ, together with any manpower utilization comments or suggestions they desired to enter in the blank box for that purpose. It was such a chore just to compile and type the report each month that no one ever made a comment; they just scrambled to get the main body of the report in on time.

I would then synthesize all the regimental-unit information into our regiment's report, have Beyondo type it in quadruplicate (he was grateful there was never anything in the comment box) and send it to MUD at post HQ where the five full-time military people up there would synthesize similar reports sent by every unit on the post into a report which was given directly to the post commanding general.

I got to wondering how much time was spent doing this every month by everyone, start to finish. Asking that question of our NCO's, I multiplied the per person average by the number of people I estimated were doing it all over the post, plus the time spent by the five military people doing it full-time at post headquarters. The resulting number of hours was astronomical, and even more shocking when multiplied by an estimate of the average cost per hour of each individual's time.

Then, after chatting about it with our personnel officer, Lt. McGillan, a good friend of mine by now, I realized that every personnel officer on post had the same information for his unit in a much more useful and condensed form because that was his job, and it was sent every month to the post adjutant general who, probably unknown to anyone until we figured it out, was not in the same chain to the general as MUD. The result, the commanding general was getting two reports about the same thing, one with information already at hand, and the other created from scratch every month.

So, the next month, in an attempt to unMUDdy the waters (sorry, I couldn't help it), I put all the information I'd discovered into the blank "comments" box on the Manpower Utilization Report, spilling over onto an additional sheet, and recommended in capital letters that "THESE REPORTS BE DISCONTINUED AND THE POST MANPOWER UTILIZATION DIVISION BE DISBANDED."

A few days later, Lt. McGillan called and told me that when the five people assigned to paper-shuffling-hell at Post MUD saw it, they gave their unanimous and unqualified recommendation of approval to the post commanding general. Not long after that, the regiment received a directive from post headquarters that the Manpower Utilization Program was discontinued, effective immediately. Several days after that, I came into my office one morning and it had been paneled in mahogany overnight by Sergeant Mast's Utilities Section.

Probably tired of me congratulating myself for putting my manpower thoughts in motion, the Universal Forces must have decided I could use a "grounding" exercise. The colonel called me into his office and motioned me over to the window which looked out on a large, grassy quadrangle behind the regimental headquarters building.

"Lieutenant, you see that tree on the grounds?"

There was a lone, kind of skinny tree in the middle of the quadrangle, "Yes, sir."

"See anything unusual about it?"

"No, sir."

"The sucker."

"Sir?"

"See that sucker growing out of the trunk about half way up before the branches start. Not good for the tree. It shouldn't be there."

There was a sapling-like branch about three feet long growing out of the trunk in that spot, "I'll handle it, sir."

I saluted, went back to my office and called Sergeant Mast in the Utilities Section. A few minutes later I realized someone was standing in the doorway of my office staring at me, clearly a dropout private who'd enlisted to keep out of jail. His mouth was open and he was staring listlessly at me with his arms hanging at his sides, a long handled pruning nipper in one hand. He'd forgotten why he was there. I called him over to my window, went through the "sucker" exercise with him and sent him out to cut it off.

About fifteen minutes later, I swung my chair around to see what the tree looked like with the sucker gone. The private was standing there staring at the tree with the pruning nipper dangling from one hand and the sucker still sticking out of the tree.

I opened the window and shouted to him, "The sucker, *cut* the sucker!"

He jerked back into consciousness, raised the nipper, cut the sucker and started walking away, the nipper dangling from his hand.

"The sucker, *take* the sucker!"

Now that I was in regimental headquarters, I set the schedule for the regimental OD's, but was no longer one of them; however, periodically I was the *Post* Officer of the Day. The post OD duties were important but nondescript since, basically, I was to be available to the Officers of the Day for all the subordinate units around the post, such as our regiment, in the event something occurred they felt needed to be handled at the post level.

I had a radio, a Jeep driver and a big notebook describing generalized procedures and contacts for a number of possible emergencies. I had developed the habit of always requesting Willy as my Jeep driver from the regimental Motor Pool because nothing much ever happened, he was an interesting guy and we'd chat most of the night while we were just sitting around or driving around inspecting things.

On my most memorable post OD night, my duties, as always, were scheduled to start at 6:00 p.m., or 1800 in the military vernacular. At 1750, Willy showed up and it was starting to snow, not a big event for that time of year and we started chatting about things, including the fact that we had a one-eyed pet cat named Willy at our house that I'd had since high school. He allowed as how people, and apparently cats, with the name 'Willy' were tough birds that never quit.

By 9:00 p.m., the snow was coming down in buckets, then bathtubs, then swimming pools full and the wind was blowing hard in steady swirls. I began getting calls from all over the post about people getting stuck. I called the post Motor Pool OD who was responsible for the snow plows, which were actually snow-plow blades attached to the front of standard army deuce and a halfs, big 2 ½ ton (carrying capacity), ten-tired, all-wheel-drive, diesel trucks. He said not to sweat it, he was just waiting for the snow to pile up a little more before sending them out. He wanted to conserve their fuel because it looked like it was going to be a long night.

In another hour the free standing drifts were about three feet high and those piled against parked cars and other vehicles were much higher, blocking them in. With the wind blowing the heavy falling snow, it was almost impossible to see anything and the only reason we were getting around was because when Willy got behind the wheel of a Willys, he became wonkers, but a beneficial wonkers if you really needed to get around, and we did.

He was fearless and had an unerring sense of where the road was and its direction even though we'd be driving straight into a white-out and couldn't see anything further than ten feet in front of us. Willy had great reflexes too, which was good because seat belts weren't in Jeeps, much less in most passenger cars those days (these days they're still not installed in most school busses, except for the driver—go figure), and I just held on to whatever part of the Jeep was available, usually the grab bar bolted to the outside of the Jeep at seat level for my right hand, with my left hand around one of the metal ribs holding up the canvas top, primarily to keep me from shooting through it when we hit a bump—recalling the dent Don put in the roof of my mother's Oldsmobile.

Soon, we were the only vehicle that appeared to be operating on the entire post and I called the post Motor Pool OD again on the radio.

"Why don't I see any snow plows?"

"The drivers are having trouble getting in."

"How many are there now?"

"None."

"When will they be there?"

"I don't know."

"Why not?"

"Some of them can't get out of their driveways, and the wives of others say they left in plenty of time to be here by now, but they're not." (As you recall, no cell phones then.)

I thought I'd ask, "Can you drive a deuce and a half plow?"

"Nope. Nobody else around here can either. Probably wouldn't matter now anyway. The deuces'll be buried in another thirty minutes. It's already drifted up to the top of the hoods. They're pretty effective snow catchers. This motor pool's gonna be a square block of snow that's deuce-and-a-half high shortly."

I didn't bother to respond. It was a marvelous example of that infamous term originating in the Second World War, "Snafu" (situation normal, all fouled up—a sanitized version). Willy and I blasted around the post for another hour or so trying to see if anyone was stranded. Then we struggled back to regimental HQ. Willy backed the Jeep under the eaves of a long extended roof about a half block away in the hope he'd be able to get it out in the morning. We fought our way to the HQ building, made some coffee and waited it out. People had stopped calling.

About 5:30 a.m. I was jolted awake in my chair by the phone ringing. Instinctively, I knew it was going to be the commanding general, and he wouldn't be happy.

"Lieutenant, why is there snow on the streets?"

"The snow plows are snowed in, sir."

"How did that happen?"

"The drivers were snowed in, sir."

"You're the 'bank lieutenant' aren't you?"

"Yes, sir."

"You did the Manpower thing too, didn't you?"

"Yes, sir."

"From what your colonel's told me about you, I'm betting there's nothing else pertinent to say, right?

"The colonel is always correct, sir."

General Reba hung up. He didn't slam the phone down. He never had. He just quietly hung it up.

That post Motor Pool OD owed me.

6:00 a.m. arrived, the weather had calmed down, the sky was clearing and my post OD duty was over. Willy and I trudged around to the small parking area at the side of regimental HQ. My Austin-Healy Sprite was nowhere to be seen, but it was somewhere inside that ten foot snow bank. It didn't matter. The wind had blown so hard that the streets alternated between clear stretches and being blocked by huge snow drifts. I looked at Willy.

"I'll drive you home, sir."

"You can make it?"

"Grew up in this area, sir. You get used to it."

We trudged down to where he'd parked the Jeep under the roof overhang. He knew what he was doing. It had been sheltered from the wind, and about 60 feet in front of it was clear enough to get a head start at the six-foot snow drift blocking access to the street. He got the engine started and we sat there while it warmed up.

"No sense snapping a rod before we hit the road."

"Hit the road" was prescient. Willy was in four-wheel-drive and floored it. It was going as fast as the four-banger in it would spin by the time we hit the snow drift. I had my feet against the dashboard and a death grip on something. Snow went everywhere including all over the windshield and we were whited-out. I sensed the Jeep went up. It slammed down on the road right side up with all four tires hitting at once and the snow was jolted off the windshield. It stopped close to where it hit. Willy's foot had been on the brake since some point in midair. I looked over at him. He was smiling.

"Works every time, sir."

After doing that five or six more times on the way home, he deposited me in front of my Capehart housing unit and took off, pedal to the metal (the Jeeps didn't come with floor mats). I fought my way through thigh deep snow in the yard and went in through the kitchen door. My wife was feeding the kids breakfast.

She looked up, idly commenting, "Must have been a quiet night with all the snow shutting everything down."

Not long after the snow storm, my captain, the regimental adjutant, called me in.

"Congratulations, you've got an additional duty."

"What is it, sir?"

"You're going to command the mobile field units of the post Chemical, Biological and Radiological (CBR) Warfare Team."

I wondered if it had something to do with choosing to put down the Chemical Corps as a branch choice when I was in ROTC, thinking I'd never be involved in that because, except for Mrs. Hames' high school instruction concerning what happens when potassium hits water, my knowledge of chemistry was zero.

"What does that mean?"

"Well, there are five Jeeps and eleven soldiers including you. Each Jeep has a driver and a passenger, radios and a lot of measuring equipment like Geiger counters and things. There are three personnel in your Jeep because of the Officer in Charge, you."

"What do we do?"

"Focus on the word, 'radiological.' If there's a nuclear attack within a three state radius of the post, it's your team's job to measure and chart the amount of radiation as thoroughly and extensively as possible over as broad an area as the Jeeps can reach. Don't worry. They'll give you a lot of training."

"How soon do we do that after the attack?"

"As soon as you can get there."

Something wasn't quite connecting, "Well … what kind of protection do we have?"

"Oh, they'll give each of you a dosimeter. It's a tube about the size of a pen. You can hold it up to the light, look through it and there's a scale printed on the lens inside. It'll tell you how much cumulative radiation you've absorbed."

"At what point on the scale do we turn into a fried egg?"

"I'm not sure. They'll tell you. This is pretty important duty. It must be. The post commanding general handpicked you."

* * * *

56

There's No Place Like Home

Somewhere over the rainbow. . . . the dreams that you dare to dream really do come true . . .

Judy Garland
The Wizard of Oz

WELL, DURING MY TWO YEARS of active duty, Alan Shepard was the first American rocketed into space, John Glenn was the first American to orbit Earth, and I achieved a personal first by not attracting the general's attention after my appointment as the mobile CBR officer. I did find out that at a very low non-lethal dosage, we'd be pulled out of the Jeeps and someone else would go in. So, I think the general liked me after all.

My Sprite was pretty much history after those two winters and also totally impractical since my daughter was almost three and my new son was almost a year old, but Willy had a relative at a new car dealership by the post. So, we drove back to our city in the desert in a brand new 1962 Chevy II purchased at a mighty fine price.

I had a job waiting for me as a speech therapist in the public schools and loved it for the two years I did it, but teachers' salaries, at least in my town, were even lower in those days than, comparatively, they are now. I had more disposable income when I was in the army. I wanted to be able to send my kids to college and, projecting my earnings, it didn't look promising.

I expressed my dismay to my sister. You remember Shirley. She'd been busy all this time and she and her husband were both practicing lawyers. They started pressing me to go to law school, something I'd never considered even though in the army I was a defense counsel for several months and then a prosecutor for several months in our regimental Special Courts-Martial. That happened as an additional duty while I was Company B's XO.

I never won a case as defense counsel, even though I had one of my Ivy League privates as an assistant, but I won every case as a prosecutor no matter who was my assistant. When I got to regimental HQ, they appointed me Chief of the Regimental Courts and Boards Section, again as an additional duty of course. That was okay. I enjoyed my prior prosecuting and defending experience and, notwithstanding my defense record, I was good at it.

A special court-martial could give a soldier a maximum sentence of six months in the stockade in those days (one year now), and the only qualification necessary to be prosecuting or defense counsel was to be an officer. Since almost all the violations were for soldiers going AWOL, as defense counsel it was essentially impossible to win such a case no matter what the reason because the soldier had absented himself without getting permission. He was Absent Without Official Leave. Can't have that in the army.

That, of course, explains the reason for my courtroom record. The best an accused could hope for was a spirited defense that would result in a sentence of less than six months. But, the ones we vigorously defended got the max. A lot of those that didn't get the all-out defense for one appropriate reason or another, got half the max.

I think the "jury," a panel of three officers, a captain, a major and a lieutenant colonel, who were assigned to hear the cases for the same amount of time the prosecuting and defending officers were assigned their duties, were trying to send a message. Namely, as soon as a company officer, always the first witness for the prosecution, testifies no permission was given, there is no defense no matter how heart-wrenching one could make the story. So *stop wasting everybody's time*. It seems to be a principle that could be put to good use in courts these days. However, just like in today's courts, we didn't pay much attention to it either.

The regimental courtroom was in an unremarkable wood frame army building typical of most on the post, the siding painted cream with a splash of coffee in it and the trim painted a weird cucumber-seafoam green. It was a little bigger than my classroom and located on one side of the same grassy regimental quadrangle that contained the tree with the sucker. There was a side door that opened right onto the quadrangle, and windows facing it also. All in all, a pleasant setting. Of course, the ambiance was ruffled a little by the facts that it was a courtroom and there were two guards, enlisted RA corporals, positioned inside it with M1 rifles, but, just like the other guards, they didn't have any ammunition either (shooting an AWOL runner would be a little over the top, even then), although the accused didn't know that.

In the last case I prosecuted before going up to regimental HQ, the defense had rested, the panel of officers had deliberated, and the young private accused of going AWOL was standing in front of them to hear his sentence. His was far and away the most common excuse, "I wanted to see my girlfriend," and he got the max. It was a hot day and, typical of those buildings, the room had no cooling, so most of the doors and windows were open.

Upon hearing the words "sentenced to six months in the post stockade," he suddenly bolted past my table through the open side door and started cheeking it across the quadrangle. I ran out the door with the two guards right behind me. He had a pretty good head start. I stopped and motioned the guards to stop with me as I yelled, "Stop or be shot!" He started running faster. We'd never catch him at that rate. The guards were standing beside me with their rifles at port arms. In an abundance of caution, I grabbed the barrels of their rifles with either hand, pointed them up in the air and yelled as loud as I could, "Shoot to kill!" The kid stopped on a dime and his hands flew up over his head.

Again I digress. Thinking about my army courtroom experience and considering my sister's and her husband's advice, I struggled with the decision for quite some time, but in the end my gut feeling was that I should go for it, and I'd learned a lot about gut feelings after high school when I chose a college. So, I quit my job, borrowed some money and enrolled in law school; however, the rest of my life is a story for another book or two. Suffice to say that one law-related observation I've made since then is that some people are so preoccupied with their legal rights, they often overlook the right thing to do.

Right now, I think it's important to tell you this. During the time I was wrestling with that decision, I had the most vivid dream I've ever had. You know, like the ones people have who report near death experiences. While it seems like a dream because your body is just lying there, deep down inside you're actually certain it really isn't a dream because it seems as real as anything that's ever happened to you.

Here's what happened in my "dream." I was in a place I'd been in before, but it wasn't here, and people I recognized from there were all around me, Ian, Saba, Mayan, Cronen, Crena, and a bunch of others, but I didn't recognize a single soul I had known from here, except, now that I think about it, there were some people in the background that could have been my grandparents. It was a very peaceful, loving, accepting place and I was astonished because I *knew* it was where I was *from* before I got here, and why I sat straight up in bed when I was three and had the feeling of wonderment that I came from someplace else.

Saba came toward me and took my hands in hers, "C'mon, Chip. We know you haven't really forgotten all of us who love you and help you from here." Of course! As soon as she touched me, it came back in a flash. My Universal Forces!

She continued, "Believe me, Chip, every once in awhile you've been quite a challenge, but you know we're quite happy to do it. You have many things left to experience and attend to, so when you're in need of guidance, keep on following your intuitive gut feeling about the right course to take. You know it's us whispering into the corners of your mind and we'll always be arranging events for your benefit, even though it may not be immediately apparent. Just keep thinking right and doing right—the best you know how."

She kissed me on the forehead, "Know that no matter what seems to be happening, we always love you." All of them whispered, "So long, see you when you get back home." Then I couldn't see them anymore and I woke up back here. Funny thing though, even now, I can still feel them.

As I look back, a couple of important things are clear to me. First, I've learned something positive from every single thing I've done and every single thing that's happened in my life, even though it may not have seemed like it at the time. I've ultimately grown in every good way from those events, and it continues. Second, just as my Uncle Sam was *really somebody* to me, *every one of us is really somebody* to someone, and that embodies significant obligations for each of us to determine and to fulfill.

Well, I've lots left to do and learn here still. See you when we're all back "home." One of the first things I'm going to do when I get back is look up Gene Krupa.

Epilogue

Our Service Men and Women

A veteran–
whether active duty, retired, national guard, reserve
or anyone who has honorably served–
is someone who, at one point in his or her life,
wrote a blank check made payable to
'The United States of America'
for an amount of 'up to and including my life.'

Anon

While exercising a little humor in connection with our military in this book, I want to be clear that I have unlimited respect for those honorable men and women who currently serve and who have served our Country. In the words of Gene Scheer's tribute, "American Anthem," performed by Nora Jones in Ken Burn's Public Broadcasting System film, *The War*, we must never forget their courage, sacrifices and, "All we've been given by those who came before."

So, say a prayer for peace.

We in the Singular

≡

Everybody is Somebody

so

Somebody is Everybody

and

We are all Connected

thus

Everybody is Onebody

so

Love One Another

and

You Will Love Yourself

Breinigsville, PA USA
01 November 2009

226839BV00002B/2/P

9 780972 898911